Angela Thirkell

Angela Thirkell, granddaughter of Edward Burne-Jones, was born in London in 1890. At the age of twenty-eight she moved to Melbourne, Australia where she became involved in broadcasting and was a frequent contributor to the British periodicals. Mrs. Thirkell did not begin writing novels until her return to Britain in 1930; then, for the rest of her life, she produced a new book almost every year. Her stylish prose and deft portrayal of the human comedy in the imaginary county of Barsetshire have amused readers for decades. She died in 1961, just before her seventy-first birthday.

"[Thirkell's] satire is always just, apt, kindly, and pleasantly rambly. Blended in with the satire, too, are all the pleasures of an escapist romance."

—*New York Herald Tribune*

"The happy outcome of her tale is secondary to the crisp, often quaint amusement one derives from discovering how deftly Angela Thirkell makes the most unexciting incident appear important ."

—*Saturday Review of Literature*

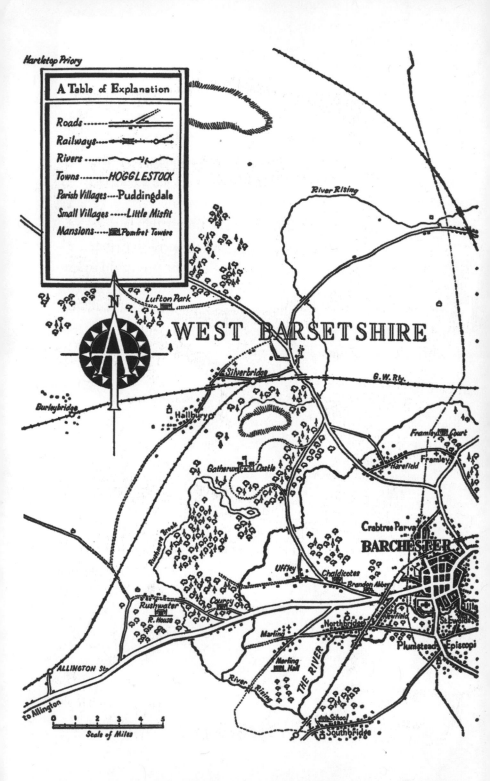

A Map of the County of

BARSETSHIRE

Shewing the Situations of the
various great Estates and Seats

HOGGLE END

HOGGLESTOCK

Rising Castle

WINTER OVERCOTES

Pomfret Madrigal

River Rising

High Rising

SHEARING JUNCT.

Low Rising

Little Misfit

Bolder's Knob

Hatch End

Scannington

Greshamsbury Hall

Winter Underclose

Pomfret Towers

Obelisk

Boxall Hill

EAST BARSETSHIRE

Buddingdale

Lambton

Boltere Priory

THE RIVER

Stogpingum

thorne

Eiderdown

Fleece

Worsted

Crabtree Canonicorum

Staple Park

Skyper

Laverings Fm.

Pooker's Piece

Great Hump

NEVER TOO LATE

A Novel by

Angela Thirkell

MOYER BELL
Wakefield, Rhode Island & London

Published by Moyer Bell
This Edition 2000

Copyright © 1956 by Angela Thirkell
Published by arrangement with Hamish Hamilton, Ltd.

LIBRARY OF CONGRESS
CATALOGING-IN-PUBLICATION DATA

Thirkell, Angela Mackail, 1890–1961.
    Never Too Late : a novel by
    Angela Thirkell. — 1st ed.
       p.   cm.
    ISBN 1-55921-235-7
    I. Title.
    PR6039.H43043   1997
    823'.912—dc21   97-3797
                             CIP

Cover illustration:
Family Group by William Glackens

Printed in the United States of America
Distributed in North America by Publishers Group West, P.O. Box 8843,
Emeryville CA 94662, 800-788-3123 (in California 510-658-3453).

NEVER TOO LATE

CHAPTER I

"There are too many Friends of Everything about."

These words were spoken by the well-known novelist Mrs. Morland, in her comfortable but quite uninteresting house at High Rising, to Dr. Ford and the George Knoxes, the avant-garde as it were of a tea-party. Since we first met Mrs. Morland some twenty-odd years ago, that gifted creature had changed very little except that she was more vague and perhaps a little more uninterested in her clothes though with occasional spurts of buying a new suit or dress, then having to get a new pair of stays (as she firmly continued to call them, disdaining such words as corset, or belt) and so being led on to what she still called a petticoat (saying darkly that slips were *not* what respectable elderly widows had) and what she now rather dashingly called a brassière, having been lately weaned by her old friend Mrs. George Knox, wife of the well-known writer of historical biographies, from saying petticoat-bodice.

Mrs. Morland's friends, who were accustomed to her gnomic or prophetic remarks, waited to hear what she meant.

"Tony says—" began Mrs. Morland, who was far too apt to quote the obiter dicta of her grown-up sons, all married and happy fathers made; though most often of her youngest.

"My dear Laura," said George Knox, "forgive a friend, a very old friend I may say, though the oldness is far more on my side than on yours who are the spirit of eternal youth—"

"No, George, I am *not*," said Mrs. Morland indignantly. "You can't call a woman who has four sons and ten grandchildren whose ages she can never remember young. Old Granny Morland, if you like."

"Look here, Laura," said Mrs. George Knox, formerly Mrs. Morland's secretary, Anne Todd, "you are overdoing it, and so is George. What *does* Tony say—if it is worth hearing," she added, having a lively though not unloving recollection of the small Tony's gift of an uninteresting and often conceited flow of speech.

Mrs. Morland looked wildly about her and pushed some hairpins further into her hair by the simple method of hitting her head with the palms of her hands.

"I have completely forgotten. I can remember Nothing now," she said proudly.

> "'Je ne sais plus rien
> J'ai perdu mémoire
> Du mal et du bien;
> O la triste histoire.'"

said George Knox, whose knowledge of French was wide, deep and loving, though the accents were those of a confirmed Anglophile.

"Stop showing off, George," said Mrs. Knox with wifely firmness. "And now, Laura, why are there too many friends about? I like friends myself."

"So do I," said Mrs. Morland. "I mean real friends. Friends that *are* friends, I mean."

> "'Mere friends are we—well friends the merest
> Keep much that I resign'"

said George Knox in a respectful quoting voice.

Dr. Ford, beloved and trusted physician to most of West

Barsetshire who cringed happily before his tongue and trusted him, literally, to the death, remarked "Browning," but no one paid any attention to him.

"And now, Laura dear," said Mrs. Knox, who still looked upon her ex-employer as a well-meaning, kindly imbecile who, in the great words of the butcher to Tom Pinch about the beefsteak, must be humoured, not drove, "what were you going to say about there being too many friends of everything?"

Mrs. Morland featured, very convincingly, complete ignorance being gradually illumined by the dawn of reason.

"There are fifteen Friends of, or Friendships of, in the London Telephone Book," said Mrs. Knox, "because I had to look up the Quakers to ask them something George wanted to know and they were under Friends, Religious Society of."

"How seldom, my dear Anne," George Knox burst in, "not excluding the rest of the party who are in their different ways— aye, many different ways though all perhaps leading towards the same end—how seldom—" and he stopped.

"Carry on, Knox," said Dr. Ford. "We are all married people here."

"But *you* aren't, Dr. Ford," said Mrs. Morland, "unless being a doctor makes you count as married—like clergymen."

"What *are* you talking about, Laura?" said George Knox, annoyed at this interruption to his flow of speech.

"It is perfectly clear, George," said Mrs. Morland, bravely concealing under these crushing words her total inability to pick up the thread of her very discursive thoughts. "Friends. There are *far* too many of them."

"If by Friends you mean the Quakers," said George Knox, "I have but little acquaintance with them, though deeply admiring all they stand for. Nor can I think that there are too many of so admirable, so inoffensive a body."

"My old great-aunt, who was a kind of Wedgwood," said Dr. Ford, thus raising in the minds of some of his hearers a picture of an aunt like a pale blue teapot with white raised designs of a classical nature on it, "never used You and Your. Always Thou and Thy."

"Ha! I have you there, Ford!" said George Knox. "It was Thee, not Thou. *I* know them."

"I know their tricks and their manners," said Mrs. Morland aloud to herself, experiencing the Schadenfreude of the Dickens addict when other and less favoured human beings do not recognize his immortal word: or again, with Miss Fanny Squeers, pitying their ignorance and despising them. "But what I mean is, there are so many Friends Of in Barsetshire that it is quite muddling and also rather expensive. I mean a guinea a year or sometimes two."

"But let me remind you, Laura," said George Knox, "not as advocatus diaboli, for heaven forbid that I should so stigmatize what are doubtless a very worthy set of men—"

"Women too, I must regretfully remind you, Knox," said Dr. Ford, who stuck firmly to the conditions before 1914 as a kind of Utopia. "Half the Civil Service are women now if it comes to that."

"Like that *most* unpleasant Miss Harvey," said Mrs. Knox, who but rarely expressed a dislike for her fellow women, or even men.

"Do you mean the sister of that impossible fellow, Harvey, of the Tape and Sealing Wax Office?" said Dr. Ford.

"The same," said Mrs. Knox, who because Dr. Ford had once cared for her quite deeply and she might have cared for him had not George Knox swiftly wooed and won her, liked occasionally to snub him in a kind way. Dr. Ford, whose love had long since evaporated into a not uncritical friendship, remarked aloud to himself: "Perhaps it was right to dissemble your love, but why did you kick me downstairs?"

"Bear with me," said George Knox in his most Johnsonian manner, "if for one moment I interrupt. What is the reference?"

Mrs. Morland said To what? thus earning the lively gratitude of the rest of her party, who were already floundering about, well out of their depth.

"Isaac Bickerstaffe," said Dr. Ford. "And the reason I know it is that it was in the Times Cross-Word Puzzle last Friday and the clue was Not Dean, nor Drapier, nor Gulliver."

"I take you, Ford, I take you," said George Knox, eager as always to know best just before anyone else could catch up with him.

"No you don't, Knox," said Dr. Ford, unmoved by his friend's enthusiasm. "One has an 'e' at the end and the other hasn't. Mine has," he added, with an air of physicianly command that almost cowed his hearers. There were several seconds' silence, broken by Mrs. Morland.

"And that reminds me," said that worthy creature, adding in a burst of confidence, "I really don't know why—that Edith Graham is coming to stay with me for the week-end."

"Nice girl," said Dr. Ford. "Good stock, well brought up. She had measles and chicken-pox and a nasty go of flu that year we all had it. But not mumps. Most of her brothers had it, but she didn't."

"Mumps are, so I believe, *far* worse for males than for females," said Mrs. Morland in her most Mrs. Siddons voice. "Not that I ever found it made any difference to my boys," at which most of her hearers had to restrain themselves from a giggle or a guffaw. "But be that as it may, Edith is coming to me and I know why I remembered it," and she gazed at nothing with fine Sibylline abstraction.

Mrs. George Knox asked why.

"Oh, it was because of Friends of Everything," said Mrs. Morland with a frankness which, her friends well knew, only meant that she had probably already forgotten what she meant to say. "We have a Friends of Rising Castle society now, which seems a little unnecessary to me as we all go there for nothing to see Lord Stoke, but now if we go as Friends we pay half-a-crown at the gate, only when Albert is on the gate he won't let Lord

Stoke's private friends pay," which left her hearers convinced, if confused.

"The name Albert, my dear Laura," said George Knox, "does not rouse any echo in my mind—that strange unexplored region or hinterland of the human consciousness—any echo, I repeat, but that of a German minor royalty known once as Albert the Good and now—by the younger members of this nation who frequent the sadly depleted groves and pastures of Kensington Gardens—as The Albert Memorial."

"Groves I grant you, Knox," said Dr. Ford. "But pastures, no."

"Oh! but there *were* pastures," said Mrs. Morland fervently. "Lots of sheep used to come to Kensington Gardens every summer to eat the grass down instead of mowing it and their fleeces were frightfully dirty. But that was when there were proper railings."

"Probably all their stomachs were black too," said Mrs. Knox. "Then one could make them into black puddings." This very logical remark brought the company back to a reasonable frame of mind and when Stoker, Mrs. Morland's faithful and tyrannical maid, came to say should she wait tea for the young lady that was coming, she found them all comfortably talking about the best way to keep the croquet or tennis lawn from growing tufts of that peculiar grass that throws one spiky leg into the air, which leg bends gracefully to the mowing-machine and rises as gracefully to its former position. And, as Mrs. Knox so truly observed, one cannot go over a whole lawn with one's scissors, because it spoils the blades.

"I feel," said Mrs. Morland, "that one could deal better with that kind of grass if one knew what its name was. Do you think it is called bent? Bent is a word, because it comes in poetry."

Dr. Ford said there was such a thing as poetic licence and what about couch-grass.

"That is what I meant," said Mrs. Morland gratefully.

"Now Laura, you really couldn't confuse bent and couch," said Mrs. Knox.

"I could," said Mrs. Morland. "Because I do. Partly," she added with an air of primitive wisdom, "because I never know if you really pronounce it cowch or cooch."

George Knox and Dr. Ford said, the one cooch, the other cowch, simultaneously. Mrs. Knox confused the issue and darkened counsel by saying suddenly Cooch Behar.

"That's all very well, Anne," said Mrs. Morland, "but it is one of those places that you know its name but haven't the faintest idea where it is, like all the names in the Far East where they are always fighting each other."

"I am now going to make the first sensible remark that anyone has made this afternoon," said Dr. Ford. "Look it up in your atlas."

"No, you look it up, Dr. Ford," said Mrs. Morland. "I can't ever find things in an atlas because when you look them up in the index it says Page Forty-One, Fifty North and Forty West."

"Plagiarist," said Dr. Ford. "You will be sued for royalties if you say things like that in public."

"Here it is," said Mrs. Knox, who had with her old quiet efficiency been consulting the atlas. "Right up on top of Bengal." But her audience had by now lost interest, though Mrs. Morland, feeling that as hostess it was incumbent upon her to say the right thing, did thank Mrs. George Knox warmly and said she had really been thinking of Poona all the time.

"You shall, if you like, Laura," said Mrs. Knox. " Poona is only right over at the other side of India, in Bombay."

"Oh, a *suburb* then," said Mrs. Morland in a disappointed voice.

"No, Laura," said her ex-secretary, suddenly resuming the competent patience with which she had been used to treat her former employer. "Not in the *town* of Bombay. In the *Presidency* of Bombay."

Mrs. Morland said she didn't know India had a President and was it Gandhi.

At this point it seemed probable, even possible, that one of

her guests would suffocate her with a sofa cushion, had not her
maid Stoker, throwing open the door, blocked the doorway with
her massive figure and said "It's Miss Graham. I thought you'd
like to know," and standing aside she let Miss Graham, better
known to us and to the county as Edith Graham, come in.

"It is all right about being today, I hope, Mrs. Morland," said
Edith, advancing with a rather charming kind of shyness which
meant nothing at all. "Even if I look a thing up twenty times I
am never quite sure if I am right, but mother was away and I
couldn't find her engagement book."

Mrs. Morland, kissing her affectionately, said it was perfectly
right and even if it hadn't been, it was, which appeared to
reassure Edith entirely. The George Knoxes had never met her
and were both, as they later confessed to each other, delighted
and surprised by the elegance and the pretty manners of Mrs.
Morland's guest. Dr. Ford greeted her as a kind of favourite
niece by courtesy who had dutifully obliged by having chicken-
pox and jaundice at the right age.

We have not seen Edith since the wet and dismal summer of
a year ago when she was very much a young lady, but still under
her mother's wing: though not without promise for the future.
Since that summer she had spent two or three months in New
York with her uncle David Leslie and his well-bred handsome
wife, she who had been Rose Bingham, daughter of the re-
doubtable Lady Dorothy Bingham before whom every fox in
her division of the county had quailed up till the day of her
death. Rose Leslie had taken her husband's young niece in hand
as competently as she had done every job all through the war and
afterwards. We think that the real Edith remained at heart the
youngest child of the large Graham family, but she had acquired
a most finished social veneer and had lapped up, like a cat with
cream, all that our translantic cousins have to teach us of the
elegances of life that two wars have almost destroyed in us,
together with a pretty self-assurance that she had not previously
possessed. She was wearing country clothes, most suitable to the

cold, wet summer, a nylon shirt, or blouse as one prefers, of a cut and crispness foreign to these shores, sheerer nylons than most of us, shoes which though perfectly suitable to the country shrieked Italy at the tops of their voices and to crown all had an impertinent and very becoming hair-do—a horrid expression but it says what we mean.

"Welcome, my dear," said Mrs. Morland, kissing her in a very friendly way. "All these people know you—at least they all know *about* you and now they know you. This is Mrs. Knox and this is George Knox who is her husband—"

"Not *the* George Knox," said Edith. "I thought he was dead. I mean because of being so famous."

"He is not dead, he is here alive," said George Knox, anxious to exculpate himself from the accusation of being a corpse, though flattered by Edith's praise.

"But not ready for me to be thy bride," said Edith.

George Knox said he failed to take her meaning.

"I thought you knew English poetry, George," said Mrs. Morland severely.

"Nor were you mistaken," said George Knox. "Few—and I say this not hastily nor in mere vanity—few, I repeat—"

"He always does," said his wife dispassionately. "But what he tells us three times is usually as true as what he says the first time. It was from The Bailiff's Daughter you were quoting, wasn't it, my dear?"

"Yes," said Edith. "And I hope you didn't mind. It wasn't meant to be impertinent; only a kind of capping verses."

"I couldn't possibly suspect you of being impertinent," said Mrs. Knox kindly. "How did you come over from Little Misfit?"

"Oh, John brought me and James in his car because Robert had taken James's," said Edith Graham. "My brothers, you know. Oh, and Ludo came too, to make four. And George Halliday and John-Arthur, that's Mr. Crosse, came in George's car."

This statement, much the same (allowing for difference of

Christian names) that was going on all over England in the summer, would probably have been accepted with placid indifference by most of the company, who had a rough idea who everyone was; but George Knox, who for all his bombast had a scholarly mind, was determined to get things clear.

"Then you have brought two brothers," he said. "And two non-brothers."

"That is quite right," said Edith approvingly. "At least not *quite* right, because there's Ludo and he is my cousin more than my brother. I mean," she added kindly, seeing George Knox's eyes slowly glazing with the effort to disentangle her relations—an effect which the Leslie family en masse often had on outsiders—"he is my cousin, but we always look on him as one of us," which speech, delivered with a prunes and prism precision of speech, made all the grown-ups laugh.

"And John-Arthur is that nice young Mr. Crosse whom I met at your mother's house, I suppose," said Mrs. Morland. "I have met him again once or twice at the Deanery. His father is some kind of cousin of Mrs. Crawley's I think."

"I think it is his mother, only she's dead," said Edith. "Because John-Arthur did say she was good West Barsetshire and his father is East Barsetshire."

Mrs. Morland, who had been vastly enjoying this county cross-talk, now took pity on George Knox and asked Edith if she would bring all her party in to tea.

"That is exactly what they hoped," said Edith. "How *very* kind of you, Mrs. Morland. You see, they all frightfully wanted to see you, so I thought you wouldn't mind if they came. They brought a rabbit pie and six bottles of beer with them, just in case."

"But of course I don't mind," said Mrs. Morland. "My own boys are just as silly when they come here. Do ask them to come in to tea, Edith. Only not to bring the rabbit pie and the beer, because Stoker might be insulted. Her teas are rather special and there will be plenty."

Edith went out to collect her escort. Stoker, who had of course been listening to most of the conversation at the half-open door, came in, her large arms folded on her capacious bosom, and surveyed the company.

"Tea for ten," she said. "Four in here and six outside makes ten, same as what my tea-leaves said this morning. Nice young lady and young gentlemen. Lucky I made some of my special cakes. I didn't mean to, seeing as there was only you, but when I saw the tea-leaves I knew it was Meant. You'll find tea in the dining-room when I ring the bell."

She turned to go, but was caught in the doorway by all the other guests with whom she exchanged some lively repartee in which she got distinctly the best of it and so went away into the kitchen.

As Edith introduced George Halliday, young Mr. Crosse, her brothers, and her cousin Lord Mellings, otherwise Ludo, to Mrs. Morland, that lady's professional eye, always at work consciously or unconsciously, saw in Lord Pomfret's heir the makings of what one could have wanted for one's own daughter. Life at Sandhurst had certainly improved the lanky shy boy of a year or two ago out of all knowledge. He had managed to get more flesh on his bony frame. He no longer felt apologetic for his height and indeed rather enjoyed being able to look over people's heads. With discipline he had also attained an air of competence, if not of absolute self-confidence. His hands were completely under control and if he took the largest size in boots among all his contemporaries, the boots were well made.

"You would really do just as well for a private as for an officer," said Mrs. Morland, speaking her thoughts aloud more to herself than to anyone else; a habit which is sadly apt to grow on one as one lives alone. "I mean being so tall. Why do they grow their officers small and other ranks tall in the Brigade?"

"I sometimes think," said Edith, eyeing her cousin Ludo dispassionately, "that Ludo is a bit like the hero of Under Two Flags."

"Oh, shut up, Edith," said Lord Mellings.

"Good God!" said George Knox. "Do you read Ouida?"

"Of course, Mr. Knox!" said Edith indignantly. "One does, you know," at which the grown-ups couldn't help laughing. "You ought to, Mr. Knox. What do you think, Dr. Ford?"

"That you are an impertinent Miss," said Dr. Ford. "Come and have tea."

Edith, at once fawning on the hand that chastised her, clung to Dr. Ford's arm in a flattering way and so accompanied him into the dining-room where Stoker had laid a magnificent tea. A faint effort was made by their hostess to mix the younger visitors with the grown-ups, but their strong tendency to coalesce like blobs of quicksilver got the upper hand. All the guests exerted themselves to pass the cakes and harmony reigned.

"It is so nice to see you again," said Mrs. Morland to Mr. Crosse. "Last time was at Lady Graham's in that dreadful cold summer last year. Not that this one is any better."

"It is nice to see you again too," said Mr. Crosse. "I remember that day very well. Lord Stoke brought you over in his brougham. I hadn't seen a proper brougham since I was a boy. And he bought a pig from Sir Robert Graham's bailiff. My father asked me to give you his very special love—or regards—I forget which. And he wants you to come over to lunch one day, if you will."

"I should love to," said Mrs. Morland. "I hardly know East Barsetshire at all, except of course Mr. Gresham, the M.P., because he comes to address our Conservative Association sometimes. One can't hear what he says very well since he had his new teeth, but the village simply adore him. Your father was extraordinarily kind to me, Mr. Crosse. He told me that your mother liked some of my books. I was so touched that I couldn't thank him properly."

"Oh, but he didn't want to be thanked," said Mr. Crosse. "It was only speaking the truth. I say, Mrs. Morland, don't laugh at me. It's true."

"I won't laugh *ever*, at *any*thing you tell me," said Mrs. Morland, "if it is about your father. When he told me about your mother, I made an oath to myself that I would *never* put it into a book."

"Do you often have to make oaths like that?" said Mr. Crosse, half curious, half amused.

"Oh no," said Mrs. Morland. "Certainly not. I use quite frightful language about things like breaking one of a set of cups, or when my pencil rolls right under my writing-table where all the dust and fluff and flue are—though why flue I shall never know. But that is simply my way of looking at things. Do you think your father would mind if I gave him a copy of my last book? It is exactly the same as all the others, but it couldn't possibly do him any harm."

"I am sure it couldn't," said Mr. Crosse, secretly amused by the suggestion that his father, an omnivorous reader of novels in English, French, and American, was capable of being shocked. "I know he has read it, because he has a standing order with his bookseller for all your books the day they are published. But he would really like a signed copy from you quite extraordinarily."

"Then I shall give you a copy to take with you, if you will be so kind," said Mrs. Morland.

"And write your name in it—and his—if you feel like it?" said Mr. Crosse, who was not much acquainted with Authors and did not wish to make a mistake in etiquette.

"Oh—of course, if your father would *really* like it," said Mrs. Morland, with a diffidence that touched and amused Mr. Crosse. And then Mrs. Morland turned to Lord Mellings.

A year or two earlier that young gentleman would have gone through agonies of dumb shyness at being addressed by a famous female writer, but ever since the Coronation Year, when the gifted actor-manager Aubrey Clover and his equally gifted wife Jessica Dean had taken him up, young Lord Mellings had come on like a house on fire, managing to combine a genuine love of his future profession as a soldier with an almost equal passion for what he liked to call the coulisses. A young man who has sufficient good looks, can act quite passably, sing quite pleasantly, and is heir to an earldom of respectable age, is bound to be welcome, even if he has not much money. Perhaps because he had known adversity in his earlier years as only a very tall, gangling, ugly duckling can know it, Lord Mellings was now enjoying his life to the full, whether at Sandhurst or in Barsetshire, and had every intention of enjoying it later in the Brigade of Guards, in and about the Palace of St. James.

"You must have put on at least a stone since I last saw you," said Mrs. Morland, which might have embarrassed some young men. But Lord Mellings appeared to take it as a compliment.

"I'm awfully glad you notice it," he said. "I shall tell my father. He always thinks it's his fault that I am so tall, but Uncle Giles—that's the old Lord Pomfret who was father's cousin—was very tall too, only he was a big man all over. Father is all length and no breadth and so was I. It's the Army that's done it," and then he wondered if he had boasted too much, for Sandhurst might be where one made a false step, or got spinal disease or something. Not that he for a moment thought this could happen to him—but in a strange country (and High Rising was strange to Lord Mellings) one might as well propitiate the god of the place, whoever he may be. Mrs. Morland had a son in the Royal Navy, so she knew something of the gods of Luck and we think she understood him.

"The real trouble," said Lord Mellings, "is growing out of one's clothes. I'm supposed to be on an allowance for clothes—I mean the ones I wear at home—and it's going to be a bit awkward. I can't borrow father's things because he is thinner than I am."

"Do you mind second-hand clothes?" said Mrs. Morland. "I mean nice ones, because my second son is as tall as you are I think, only he has got rather bigger and they don't meet and he has had to get some new ones. Luckily he can afford it because he has quite a good job in oil, and he left all his old suits here. If you would care to try them on? Not if you'd rather not, of course, but they will probably get the moth if they stay here and I wouldn't get anything if I sold them. I mean only if you would like it."

Various emotions were mirrored or shadowed in young Lord Mellings's countenance as his hostess spoke. A little pride—not much, for he had good common-sense and not too much sentiment—and to outweigh it a strong sense (which all true Fosters had) of the point up to which principle and practice were compatible. Of this mixture the late Lord Pomfret had been a shining example. The present Lord Pomfret envied but could not compass this state of mind, while his son was bidding fair to combine both qualities in equilibrium. His mind was made up in less time than it has taken to write these words and Mrs. Morland, saying they could look at the suits together after tea, turned to Dr. Ford.

"Well?" she said.

"Very well, thank you," said Dr. Ford. "As nice a set of youngsters as you'd wish to see."

"I'm over a quarter of a century old, sir," said Captain James Graham indignantly.

"I'm of age, sir," said John Graham.

"I'm of marriageable age," said Edith Graham, rather conceitedly. "The age of consent."

"That's only the age of conceit, my girl," said her eldest brother James. "You try getting married and see what father will say. Precocious, my girl, that's what you are."

"And more precocious than ever since you went to America," said her second brother John.

"Well, Aunt Agnes that was Gran's sister got engaged to a clergyman when she was seventeen," said Edith.

"Yes, and look what happened to her," said John. "She died an old maid. That'll learn you, my girl. And she did water-colour drawings—jolly bad ones too."

"Oh, I say, John, not so bad as all that," said James. "That one of the tortoiseshell cat in a lace bonnet called "Sweet Mistress Purr" is a small gem. I bet it would fetch a lot in Bond Street if it was properly written up. Period piece and all that. Or our ghastly cousin Julian could show it at his gallery."

Mrs. Morland asked if that was Julian Rivers, the one whose mother wrote novels.

"Those are the ones," said James. "I mean that's him and she's the one too."

"Grammar, grammar, my boy," said his sister Edith.

By this time such a noise was being made that even George Knox could not make himself heard, which annoyed him dreadfully, as he always had to unpack his heart (or mind) with words and had mental suffocation if he couldn't. Stoker, coming in with more hot scones, stood entranced by the spectacle of so many healthy young people eating her cakes and sandwiches. Second Lieutenant John Graham, overcome by the general row and his own wit (though no one could hear what he was saying) dropped the plate of scones on the floor by mistake, thus producing an awed silence.

"Oh, I say, I *am* sorry, Mrs. Morland," he said, though not very distinctly as he was in a position rather like the Quangle-Wangle when he had to sleep with his head in his slipper. "I think I've got them all," he added as he sat up again, very red in the face, with the mangled remains of the scones.

"You give them to me," said Stoker. "It's Master John, isn't it? That Odeena of your mother's at Holdings, she's niece to Mrs. Knox's cook, that's how I knew. One of those as get taken advantage of if she isn't careful if all her aunt says is true," she added, fixing Lieutenant Graham with a basilisk glance, as if she had discovered him in an intrigue with his mother's highly unattractive so-called parlour-maid.

"She breaks an awful lot of china," said John Graham. "A dreadful girl. She cleaned my best brown shoes with ox-blood polish instead of light tan. Ruined them."

"Takes after her aunt," said Stoker. "What was it you said her aunt did to the liver, Mrs. Knox?"

"Toasted it black at the kitchen range," said Mrs. Knox. "That was in the winter when we always have a proper fire going in the kitchen range. Which reminds me, Stoker, when will the sweep be round next?"

"He's doing the chimneys at Lord Stoke's," said Stoker. "Nasty some of them are. There's one with a turn in it and when his lordship had it repaired they found Bones there. Someone been murdered I dessay."

"Or perhaps a chimney-sweep like Tom in the Water-Babies," said Edith. "He might have got stuck there and died of hunger. Is there a ghost, Stoker?"

"Not at Stoke Castle," said Stoker scornfully. "His lordship wouldn't allow it. Do you want some more tea?"

As this question appeared to be addressed to her employer, Mrs. Morland tipped the teapot up. A few very pale yellow drops fell.

"I knew you'd need some more," said Stoker, less with pride in her prophetic gifts than pity for the gentry who, according to her view, would be entirely helpless without her and her fellows. She took the teapot and went away.

"I say, Mrs. Morland, your cook is *splendid*," said Mr. Crosse, who had not spoken much, finding it a little difficult to make head against George Knox's booming and the uninhibited noise of the younger guests. "I wish she and our butler, Peters, could meet. He used to be at the Towers," he added to Lord Mellings, "in your uncle Giles's time," at which Lord Mellings started and said he supposed so, but his uncle Giles had died when he was too small to remember. "You couldn't bring her over to our place one day, could you, Mrs. Morland? Father would simply love her."

Mrs. Morland did not appear to think this request at all out of the ordinary and said she didn't see why not, only not on a Sunday, because Stoker went to chapel and one never knew if it was going to be morning or afternoon because there was only a visiting minister or whatever they were called.

"Any day," said Mr. Crosse cheerfully. "Only name it."

"I can't name a day unless I have my engagement book," said Mrs. Morland. "I can't remember a *thing* now. Do you know who you are when you wake up in the morning?"

Mr. Crosse, feeling that there was a catch somewhere, said he thought he did.

"I don't even think," said Mrs. Morland. "The older I get the less I know where I am. And if I go away it is even worse, because I wake up there and think I am at home and I'm not, and then when I get home and wake up I expect to find myself where I was before I came home, and I'm not. I'm at home."

Mr. Crosse said it all sounded rather confusing, but he was glad she really did find herself at home when she *was* at home, and could he get her engagement book for her.

"Well, you *could*, and it is most kind of you," said Mrs. Morland, "but I don't know where it is. It is one of those days when it gets lost. Sometimes I look at it in bed before I go to sleep, to see what I am doing next day, and it becomes lost either in the bedclothes, or right down between the bed and the wall. I do keep a large engagement book on my writing-table too, the sort that has a month on a page, but I never remember to put the things I am doing down in both. So, you see, I might put down 'Lunch George'—that's George Knox—in my small engagements book and 'Lunch Lord Crosse' on the big one on my desk. I think it's the war."

"The war?" said Mr. Crosse. "I mean there isn't one just at the moment is there?"

"I mean the *effects* of the war. Delayed action," said Mrs. Morland. "I was really quite brave all through the war, even though there were never any bombs near here, but one got a sort of horrid feeling all the same. Partly wondering which of my sons was killed."

"Oh—I didn't know—I hope—" Mr. Crosse began.

"It's *quite* all right," said Mrs. Morland soothingly. "None of them were killed, or even wounded. Not that they didn't try," she added, not wishing to denigrate her offspring.

"I think we were all like that," said Mr. Crosse. "I know George Halliday was, because we've often talked about it. He's an awfully nice sort of chap. Things get him down a bit sometimes. His father is very shaky and his mother spends a good deal of time looking after him. But George is as good as they make them," and he looked across at George Halliday who was getting on very well with Mrs. Knox.

Mrs. Morland noted, with a hostess's eye, that Edith, next to George Halliday, was being—and looking—rather neglected, as Dr. Ford on her other side was deep in county talk with young Lord Mellings.

"I sometimes wish," she said, "one could just press a button and everyone would turn to the other partner."

While she was speaking, Dr. Ford had turned to Edith, whom he admired greatly, so that Mrs. Morland was able to have Lord Mellings to herself again. Owing to her long acquaintance with boys, including her own four and the whole of Southbridge School during the war, young men presented no difficulties at all to her and before Lord Mellings knew what he was doing he was telling her all about life at Sandhurst and how grateful he was to his father for making him learn to ride.

"Of course Giles, that's my young brother, is the rider," he said, with pride rather than envy. "He can ride anything bareback. Even a he-donkey—I don't know their proper name."

Mrs. Morland, summoning vague remembrances of Talk in Country Places said Would it be a Whole donkey.

"It sounds a bit coarse, but I daresay it might," said Lord Mellings, treating Mrs. Morland so much as an equal that she was secretly flattered.

"I never know the right names for all the animal sexes either, if sexes you can call them," said Mrs. Morland in a very learned way. "Except capons. And I suppose a gelding—or is that pigs?"

"Gilt," said Mr. Crosse, who had caught this fragment across the table. "I *think* it's a young female pig."

"Oh, *thank* you, John-Arthur," said Edith.

"Do you always call him both his names?" said Lord Mellings deserting Mrs. Morland, who bore up very well.

"Oh, everyone does," said Edith. "I'd call you yours, only I never remember them all."

Mrs. Morland begged to hear them.

"Ludovic Neville Eustace Guido Foster, Viscount Mellings," said the owner of the name. "Ludovic after Lord Lufton because Lady Lufton, I mean his mother, is my god-mother and Neville after some kind of ancestor and Eustace after the one that turned Catholic under James the Second and went to Italy— we've got quite a lot of relations there and Guido Strelsa that I'm called Guido after is a thoroughly bad egg. And Foster is the family name, I really don't know why. I suppose there was a reason once. Probably an heiress. Is that clear? You really ought to know these things, my girl," he added, addressing Edith. "Doesn't your mother tell you? She is Agnes after her aunt Agnes, who didn't marry."

"Gran used to talk about her sometimes," said Edith. "She was old Aunt Agnes's sister. I wonder if I'll know all about everyone when I'm as old as they are—I can't explain, but you know what I mean. When I was in America with Uncle David and Aunt Rose people used to ask me about the family and I got *awfully* mixed."

"Next time you are at the Towers I'll show you the family tree," said Lord Mellings. "It's disgraceful that you don't know more about it. What *is* my aunt Agnes about?"

"Oh, mother knows," said Edith with some pride. "She knows families like anything, only she has *seen* most of them and I haven't. Seeing makes it easier."

"Well, next time you come to the Towers, if I'm there I'll rub your nose in family trees," said Lord Mellings kindly.

"The funny thing about family trees," said James Graham,

who had not previously given tongue, except to eat large quantities of cake and jam, "is that they grow both ways up."

Everyone listened for some elucidation, but Captain Graham went on eating in a very self-satisfied way.

"How?" said Mrs. Knox.

As she was not one of his relations James Graham was willing to humour her.

"Oh, it all depends which way you go," he said. "I mean if you started with Neville de Pomfret it would spread downwards like an open umbrella. But if you started with anyone now—say with me—the tree would go up and out from me till I had about a hundred greats or great-greats, like an umbrella that's blown inside out. One might make a theory about it. There's a fellow in the regiment who says if you go by the old way you would need a piece of paper as big as Hyde Park to hold it all. But I said you'd need just as much paper if you do it the other way. It would be much simpler if everyone only had one child."

"Then there wouldn't be anyone at all soon, even if they all did get married," said Mrs. Knox. "Or am I wrong? I can't do it in my head."

"I was an only child," said Mrs. Morland in the tragic voice of a Siddons. "And my husband was an only child. Not that it was his fault," she added kindly.

"I also was an only child," said George Knox, who felt that his old friend was unfairly monopolizing the attention of the party.

"Then that makes three," said Edith, perhaps a little impertinently, but she was tired of sitting at the tea-table and secretly longing for the wonderful moment when she would be alone with Mrs. Morland, for whose books she had the almost superstitious awe and reverence that the savage feels for the arts of the white man.

"Any more?" said Stoker from the door. "Young stomachs need filling. I've just taken some brandy-snaps out of the oven."

"Oh, bless you Stoker," said Dr. Ford, "but I can't eat any more. Give them to the children."

"How many of us do you count as children, sir?" said Lord Mellings, with a formal courtesy exactly like his father's, only we fear that his tongue was where Lord Pomfret's never was, in his cheek. Dr. Ford only laughed his short laugh.

"I don't know if any of you care for boats," said Mrs. Knox. "We have a bit of river and a punt and a canoe. If anyone would like to come over—" but there was no need for her to finish the sentence. So swiftly and eagerly did the Graham boys, who happened to be on the same side of the table, rise to their feet that the table moved an appreciable number of inches towards the opposite wall. Dr. Ford, who was sitting on that side, told them what he thought of mannerless embryo soldiers in no uncertain terms and perfect cordiality reigned.

"May I stay with you, Mrs. Morland?" said Edith, which flattered her hostess vastly.

"Oh, come with us, Edith," said Mr. Crosse, but Edith said No thank you, which somehow gave pleasure to George Halliday. So all the young men went off in their own or each other's cars and the Knoxes in their own car. Dr. Ford said he must go as there would be patients at the surgery and it wouldn't do to keep them waiting. So they went into the drawing-room where Stoker had very sensibly lighted a fire.

Like a good many people who live in and by what their minds imagine, Mrs. Morland was on the whole indifferent to her surroundings. Her house had been furnished when she married— now a very long time ago—mostly with cast-offs from various older members of the family. Everything was comfortable even if not beautiful or what is called period, especially the large family sofa on which a tall man could sleep and in the case of Mrs. Morland's sons on leave often had slept. The only object of elegance was a work-table of walnut with gilded metal work on it, secret drawers which no one could possibly pretend not to see, and a mirror inside the lid, so that a lady could look at herself as she sat sewing. This had been a wedding present from George

Knox's mother, dead now many years ago, and was much valued by Mrs. Morland.

"Oh! Mrs. Morland, are those *all* your books?" said Edith, who was looking at the shelves dedicated to her hostess's works.

"Well, they are and they aren't," said Mrs. Morland, at which Edith begged her, most flatteringly, to explain, adding that it was so difficult ever to say exactly what one meant. "You see" she said "it might sound as if I wanted to know if they were all your books because I wasn't sure if some of them might be other people's, but I really meant an exclamation of being so much impressed by so many books all written by one person."

Some writers—and the name of Mrs. George Rivers at once leaps to the mind and the pencil—might have taken offence at these words, which indeed did need a considerable amount of disentangling, but Mrs. Morland, who had never had a daughter, took to young girls very kindly and found Edith's laborious explanation quite reasonable.

"I see *exactly* what you mean," she said, with a good deal of truth and also a good deal of willingness to oblige. "All those three top shelves are my books that I have written in the first editions. The next shelves are the American editions."

"Are *all* your books in American?" said Edith.

"Not quite all," said Mrs. Morland, passing over Edith's peculiar way of putting it. "You see my first novels weren't published in America, because I wasn't much known. And then one or two were published in America by different publishers and gradually they all went to one publisher, Mr. Purchase, whose name you see on them all."

"Do you have to go to America to publish them?" said Edith.

"Not a bit," said Mrs. Morland. "I have been several times and simply loved it, but my journey is not really necessary."

"Then if you go to America you have your American money," said Edith. "How lovely. I hadn't any, but Rose—that's Uncle David's wife—said I wasn't to bother because there were always plenty of dollars for me."

"Bless your heart, my dear," said Mrs. Morland. "All my American royalties have to come straight to England to pay for the National Health Service which nothing would induce me to join, or the National Debt or something. It sounds silly, but there it is."

"Anyway I don't suppose you need money much there," said Edith, "because everyone is so kind. When I was there it was just like the war."

Mrs. Morland, amused by her young friend's artless prattle, asked how it was like the war.

"Oh, I don't mean really like the war," said Edith. "I mean the way people did things for other people in the war and nearly everyone got so nice except people like Old Lady Norton."

"And some awful people from London who were war refugees at Southbridge," said Mrs. Morland, thinking of the autumn term she had spent as a kind of general help at Southbridge School in that happy first war year of an England united at home. "I can't remember their name. And that reminds me—I really cannot say why—that I promised your cousin that I'd see if some of my second son's suits would fit him. My boy put on so much weight in Germany that he couldn't get into his English civvies. Come up and see your room and I can put some of his suits out for your cousin."

So Mrs. Morland took Edith upstairs, showed her the quite pleasant and uninteresting bedroom she was to have and left her to unpack, which did not take long, for Edith, after the enviable way of our young, was unconscious of cold and almost unconscious of heat. How they do it we often wonder as we pack the woollies and tweeds that we know we shall need for a summer visit. And then Mrs. Morland called Edith into another bedroom and opened a cupboard where men's suits, both town and country, were hanging.

"But, Mrs. Morland, you can't *give* those to Ludo," said Edith. "He would feel horrid. Oh *do* let him pay something."

"It may be good for him to feel horrid," said Mrs. Morland.

"But I don't understand," said Edith, suddenly wishing she were at home again. "I mean Ludo could afford it, if that is what you mean. Or at least he could afford something."

"I am sure he could," said Mrs. Morland. "But it is very good for all of us to learn to take, as well as to give. It's more difficult sometimes, I admit. Nearly everybody is born a Giver or a Taker."

"Which are you?" said Edith.

"A giver as far as my own children go," said Mrs. Morland, "but quite a good taker otherwise. And just as well, because I was quite poor for a long time with all my boys to educate and all growing out of their clothes and not always being able to wear each other's because of a different height or shape."

Edith said she could understand taking for one's children, but not for oneself.

"You had better get over that," said Mrs. Morland, who found her young guest's philosophy amusing. "*You* mayn't mind going about in an old sack, but your boys won't like it if you do. I can't say about girls, because I never had any."

"Then I'll be your daughter-in-law," said Edith.

"I'm afraid all my boys are married," said Mrs. Morland, more touched than she would have liked to show by Edith's offer. "If you will be an honorary daughter-in-law I shall be delighted. I can't give you any good advice, but if you are in a jumble of feelings, you can tell me. I daresay I shan't understand, but that doesn't matter. And let me know when you get engaged and I will give you all my books specially bound—if you would like them."

All Edith said, after a pause in which she went pink in the face, was "Oh, Mrs. Morland," which seemed perfectly adequate.

"And I'm so glad you didn't say I could call you Laura," she went on. "You can't think how awful it is when grown-up people—I mean *very* grown-up ones—suddenly ask you to use their Christian name. You can't do it because it feels so rude, and then it feels rude to go on Mrs.-ing them when they've asked you not to, so one just says nothing. And that is rude too."

"Some day we must write a book of Etiquette for sensible people," said Mrs. Morland, "though apart from a few rules it really boils down to an educated mind and a kind heart."

"What Conque, that's my grandmother's old French maid who comes to Holdings every year, calls bonté de cœur," said Edith, and then they went downstairs again, not unwillingly, for in that horrible early summer there had to be at least one fire kept going if people were to live. The fire in the drawing-room was burning nicely and they talked about books and life in general very comfortably till the telephone rang.

"I hope it isn't mother telling me to come back," said Edith.

"Of course not," said Mrs. Morland in a sensible kind of voice as she took up the receiver. Edith had been well trained by elder brothers never to ask about telephone calls, so she quietly took an early book of Mrs. Morland's from the shelf and began to read about the beginnings of Madame Koska's fashionable dressmaking establishment where lovely mannequins were always getting abducted or locked in a cupboard by international crooks (if that term really means anything), but always saved in the nick of time. Through her reading a few disjointed words from the telephone reached her ear, among which she distinguished Southbridge and match, but Madame Koska was far too interesting for her attention to be distracted. At last Mrs. Morland put the receiver up. "It was Everard Carter, the Headmaster at Southbridge School," she said. "There is a half-term cricket match tomorrow, Old Boys v. The Rest, and he wants me to come. Would you like it?"

"To come too?" said Edith. "Oh, I'd love to, thank you. My Leslie cousins were all there and I expect one of them will be an Old Boy."

"You know," said Mrs. Morland apologetically, "I'm not really Barsetshire. I only came to live here. Are those the same cousins as the Leslies at Rushwater?"

"Oh, that's Martin, he's Uncle David's nephew, his father was killed in the first war so he had Rushwater when grandfather died," said Edith. "These ones are Uncle John's boys at Greshamsbury," which account appeared perfectly clear to her because she was talking about people she knew, but did not altogether enlighten Mrs. Morland. "Minor, that's the middle one, is a frightfully good climber. He has been up the spire of the School Chapel and over most of the cathedral roof."

"Presently I shall tell you all about my sons and their wives and children," said Mrs. Morland, with no animus, only as a reasonable statement of fact. "That sounds like your party coming back," and indeed it could not have been anything else, and in a few minutes they all came tumbling in like Mrs. Cat and her kittens in The Frog that would a-wooing go.

"Did you have a nice time?" said Mrs. Morland. "I expect you are hungry after going on the river."

"That's right," said Stoker who, as usual, had accompanied the party into the room. "Young blood, that's what it is. There's some beer in the fridge and plenty of cake."

On hearing this several members of the party offered their help.

"Get in the way, that's all the help *you*'ll give," said Stoker, whose opinion of the male sex was on the whole low. "You can all wash your hands. And then you can open your mouth and shut your eyes. *You* can come," she added to Lord Mellings. He did not particularly want to, but his natural politeness made it difficult for him to refuse a lady, so he followed her, making a face expressive of resigned despair for the benefit of his relations.

"I suppose we'd better wash our hands," said James Graham. "I got simply filthy when we got stuck in the mud."

"So you did," said Mrs. Morland, who had been looking with a mother's eye at her guests. "There is a basin in the cloakroom outside and another basin in the bathroom upstairs."

Amid scufflings and mutterings of "Bags I the bathroom" most of the river party left the room.

"I'm not really dirty," said Mr. Crosse as the noise died away. "I was only a passenger. Will you really come over to Crosse Hall, Mrs. Morland? Father would love it."

"I should like it of all things," said Mrs. Morland. "Shall we arrange a day now? I mean if it suits your father. I'm not going away this summer—if summer you can call it. What kind of day? I expect your father is in Town during the week."

Mr. Crosse said not very much now, but he himself was kept pretty busy during the week, so if Saturday, or even better a Sunday suited Mrs. Morland, how nice. And what, he added, about Edith Graham who, he gathered, was staying with her. Mrs. Morland thought this an excellent plan, so the following Sunday was fixed, subject to Lord Crosse being disengaged and the weather not being too awful.

By this time the Graham boys with George Halliday were moderately clean. All the young men said good-bye to Mrs. Morland and thanked her with rather unnecessary chivalry of speech, but were totally put out of countenance by her replying in the same vein only much better. Edith kissed her brothers in a perfunctory and sisterly way, also George Halliday with equal want of interest.

"And what to me, my love, and what to me?" said Mr. Crosse.

"Love's Labours Lost," said Edith swiftly.

"Stap my vitals, I did not know Miss was so well read," said Mr. Crosse gallantly.

"Oh, one does read, you know," said Edith in an affected voice which caused her brothers to hoot at her.

"Well, good-bye Edith," said George Halliday. "Have a nice time."

"Oh, I know I shall," said Edith. "I wish I could stay for ever, except for not seeing mother and father and all the boys and—" when she paused.

"And whom? or what?" said George Halliday and Mr. Crosse together.

"Oh, anyone," said Edith, at the same time quite disgracefully making eyes at Mr. Crosse and George Halliday.

But instead of going green and yellow with jealousy George only laughed and went home, driving his car too fast all the way, along the bad hilly road on the other side of the river. When he got home he found his father in the little summer-house where he often spent the afternoon not reading the Times. For if all the papers now have names in them that you don't know—very different from the old Morning Post where you could see everyone you knew being born and christened, married and buried and send them letters of congratulation or condolence—you might as well not bother about them. And the cross-word puzzles were so difficult now, not like the good old days when "eme" and "orlop" were in every cross-word at least twice a week. So Mr. Halliday took the Times with him as an old king might take the crown he could no longer wear, with a certain enjoyment in keeping it from his descendants.

George went gently past the summer-house resolved not to hear his father's voice, but if a voice will speak up so that one cannot pretend one does not hear it, what is one to do?

"That you, my boy?" said Mr. Halliday.

George, choking down an unfilial impulse to say "If you didn't know it was me why did you say my boy?" stopped and turned.

"I think so, father," he said. "But there was such a noise at Mrs. Morland's that I might have been anybody. Edith was there and her brothers and young Crosse and Dr. Ford and some other locals—" which relegation of himself to limbo would not at all have pleased George Knox.

"Sit down, boy," said his father, "I can't hear you very well."

George, though at heart inclined to shout in his father's ear as the Johnny Cake did to the Fox, came into the summer-house and sat down on one of the rickety cane chairs.

"I only said Edith and two of the Graham boys were there," he said. "She sent you her love," which was a pious lie, but appeared to give Mr. Halliday pleasure.

"A very nice girl," he said. "It's time she came to stay here again."

"She is staying at High Rising with Mrs. Morland, father," said George.

"Do I know anyone at High Rising?" said his father.

"Mrs. Morland lives there," said George, manfully doing his best to keep irritation out of his voice. "Edith is staying with her."

"Who?" said Mr. Halliday.

"Edith Graham, father," said George, in a kind voice for which his recording angel must have dropped several tears on his charge-sheet. "She. Is. Staying. With. Mrs. Morland."

Instead of answering, as most deaf people would have done, "Don't talk so loud as if I were an idiot," Mr. Halliday most meanly spiked George's guns by apologizing for being so deaf and a nuisance.

"Oh, rot, father," said George and sat quietly till his father dozed off again, when he got up and went away to the farm, certain that things had gone wrong just because he went out to tea. But nothing had gone wrong and what was more he found when he came in a little later his sister Sylvia Leslie in the drawing-room with his mother, which cheered him up immensely, for Sylvia's life was going well and she looked more happy and handsome every year.

"You simply must come over to Rushwater soon," she said to George. "Martin's leg has been better since they found a splinter somewhere and hoicked it out. It won't stop him limping but he has much less pain and the children are all very well and longing to see you."

"That they are not" said George. "Last time I was at Rushwater your Eleanor, who is after all the eldest, said I was Mr. Miacca. What she meant I don't know, but I didn't like it."

"Oh George!" said his sister in mild reproof. "You *must*

remember Mr. Miacca. If little boys came to his house he always ate them. A *lovely* story."

"Of course I remember it now," said George. "And I think Tommy Grimes hid under the sofa and poked a bit of wood out when Mr. Miacca wanted to feel his leg, like Hansel and Gretel. We had it again and again when we were small. Sometimes when I think of the terrifying stories mother read to us and how we didn't care in the least, I wonder if Horror-Comics really do any harm."

"Of course they do," said Sylvia. "Martin says so and he must know because of being on the Bench."

"Good Lord," said George and then apologized, saying he had mixed it up with going before the Beak.

"Did you see your father?" said Mrs. Halliday, rather over-anxiously George thought. He said he had found him in the summer-house and they had had a little talk.

"You know he thinks there is a mortgage on this house and we shall all be ruined like the Sowerbys' grandfather over Chaldicotes way" said Mrs. Halliday, but this was very old history even in her youth, so her children paid no attention.

"And how was Edith?" said Mrs. Halliday, who had become very fond of her during the past year.

"Edith? Oh she was all right" said George and even his sister Sylvia, who had had suspicions for the past year, could not tell whether he really didn't care or was pretending not to care. "Lord! how George Knox does talk—the one who writes the biographies. But his wife is awfully nice and we all went on the river in their boats, except Edith. Mrs. Morland is awfully kind. She didn't mind a bit when we all came without being invited and she's giving Mellings two very nice suits that one of her sons has grown out of."

Sylvia said, thoughtfully, that Ludo's wrists and ankles seemed to be getting not quite so long and bony at last, and then their talk drifted, as it mostly did, to the care of their various properties and the prospects of the Bath and West.

"We are sending Rushwater Ratcatcher," said Sylvia, adding rather apologetically that they were getting short of R names and some of them were too silly, like Rantipole or Ruskin.

"And I'll tell you what as Mrs. Sam Adams says," said George. "We can't do cows or bulls here. But we are sending some young pigs to the Barsetshire Agricultural. My hat! they are pigs. Sir Robert Graham's bailiff let me have one of his White Pork-minsters for breeding last year."

"How on earth did you manage?" said Sylvia, for the bailiff Goble was notoriously chary of letting any of his boars out of his sight.

"I let him talk to me," said George simply. "It always pays."

Sylvia looked at her brother admiringly and then she had to go home in the chill air of that odious early summer.

"There is only one thing that comforts me a little about your father" said Mrs. Halliday, who had decided to speak freely of her husband's health with her son, because it was but too evident how poorly he was. "He does love a fire in the evening, so I can have one without feeling guilty."

"But why guilty, mother?" said George.

"Oh, I don't know," said Mrs. Halliday. "An old habit I suppose. In the war one always felt guilty if one was comfortable."

"And you passed it on to me, mother," said George. "Never mind, we will both grumble and laugh at one another's grumbles."

CHAPTER 2

W e need hardly say that the following Saturday, the day of
the cricket match at Southbridge School, was as nasty as
it could be. Not raining yet, it is true, but grey and chill with a
wind that came from all quarters at once—or so Mrs. Morland
said.

"If you would rather not go, we needn't," said Mrs. Morland
to Edith after breakfast, hoping privately that her guest would
agree, but Edith said of course she would love it unless Mrs.
Morland didn't want to, so that Mr. Morland had to say of
course she wanted to and had only wondered. So they got into
Mrs. Morland's rather disgraceful car, which she drove far better
than anyone would have expected from her, and went away to
Southbridge, though not by Barchester which was the better
road, for on a Saturday one never knew if one would meet several
distracted bullocks in Barley Street, or a flock of sheep trying to
walk over each other's backs in the High Street. Mrs. Morland
took the other way, over the downs, across the river above Boxall
Hill, by Stogpingum and the outskirts of Ullathorne (now
entirely swallowed by Barchester), past Plumstead Episcopi,
and so down to the school. To Edith's joy the first person she
saw were her Leslie cousins who made an uncommonly handsome trio in their white flannels. Though they all had Christian
names they had always been Major, Minor, and Minimus at
school and appeared likely to remain so for the rest of their lives.

"How lucky it is that you all have white flannels," said Mrs. Morland, who usually said the first thing that came into her head.

"Well, it's rather bogus," said Minor. "I have to wear Major's old bags, but Minimus is broader than I am, so he can't wear mine, but Major can, so Minimus wears his own. They are all about the same vintage, so it doesn't really matter. If only the match could have waited for the Sales, we could have got some bargains."

"The Sales are over now," said Mrs. Morland, who knew boys inside out and felt that a little deflation would do Minor no harm at all.

"And who gets a new pair first?" said Edith.

"Intelligent girl," said her cousin Major, who was silent by nature.

"It rather depends on birthdays," said Minor. "A man sometimes gets quite good tips on his birthday. Anyway I'm still growing so I'll have to have a new pair. It's like the fox and the goose and the bag of corn. Look here, chaps, we'd better look after the parents."

Mrs. Morland said she could only see the goose, which temporarily silenced the too ebullient Minor and with courtly bows the three boys withdrew to find seats for their father and mother in the pavilion. At this moment Matron came up, quite ravishing in a flowered silk dress, rather short according to the fashion of the moment, a fresh hair-do, and one of those little straw hats that grip the head with what look like crooked lobsters' claws.

"*Well,* if it isn't Mrs. Morland," said Matron. "Now this *is* a day of joyful surprises. Only last night after supper I was pressing my nylon slip and panties, for really we are all nylon-minded now, Mrs. Morland, and there was a tiny run in one of the legs and as you know though nylons don't run the way some materials do, still a stitch in time saves nine as they say. So as I was saying, I thought I'd better just darn over it, just in case, and it made me think of that time your son, Mrs. Morland, and that nice boy Swan only really we must say Mr. Swan now since he married the Honourable Miss Lufton, helped to clear up the mess. The night that was that Hacker—but really I must remember to call him Professor Hacker now—let the bath run over because he had mislaid his spectacles and really as I was saying to Jessie—you remember our head housemaid Jessie, an excellent worker but say what I will I *cannot* get her to wear her spectacles—well now, what was it I said and really Mrs. Morland I sometimes feel I am quite a mental case and I had ought, perhaps, to retire and live with my married sister—you know Mrs. Morland, the one who has the son who is head wireless operator in one of our biggest liners."

To Edith's great admiration Mrs. Morland, who had listened with apparent interest (though it would not have deceived those who knew her best) to Matron's excursion into what her old friends called Jessie-land, said she must find a seat in the stand before it was full, as the sky looked rather threatening.

Mrs. Morland was then greeted by various other old friends, including Miss Hampton and Miss Bent, the inhabitants of Adelina Cottage down in the village, who pressed her warmly to come in for a drink after the match.

"It rather depends on the weather," said Mrs. Morland, looking at the sky which was beginning to present a drooping rather than an auspicious eye. "I have Edith Graham with me—Lady Graham's youngest daughter."

"Verb. sap." said Miss Hampton, shaking hands warmly with Edith. "Maxime debetur and so on, Mrs. Morland. *We* know. Don't give it another thought. Bring her along."

"Little did I think to see you at a cricket match mamma," said a voice from behind Edith. "My wife and all four children are at the sea—dreadful place—so I am en disponibilité. Mamma," and he gravely kissed his mother's hand, "present me."

"This is my youngest son, Tony," said Mrs. Morland, no whit

taken aback. "This is Edith Graham, Tony. She is staying with me. And Miss Hampton and Miss Bent of course you know."

"All come and put one down after the match," said Miss Hampton.

"Unfortunately I have to get back to Town," said Tony. "My troublesome employers at the Ministry of Interference have asked me to do some homework for them. I only escaped for the Honour of the School. Thank heaven there is a river here, so I never had to play cricket, dreadful game. I must go and say the right things to the Carters, mamma, before I leave."

"Conceited child," said his mother, without animus, as he went away. "But an excellent husband and father" she added for the benefit of Edith and the Adelina Cottage ladies. "Would you like to go to Miss Hampton's party?" she asked Edith, as the Adelina Cottage ladies were talking to someone else.

"Oh—I don't know," said Edith, suddenly feeling shy, a feeling which seldom came her way.

"Well, we'll see," said Mrs. Morland comfortably. "And now we had better get seats in the pavilion because there isn't much room and it looks like rain. *What* a summer."

The pavilion, by courtesy, was a rather shabby affair, mostly used by boys who wished to cultivate a reputation for eccentricity, the rest preferring to sit on the ground, or on a few benches with rickety legs. And there is something to be said for the open air where at least you know the worst at once, as against a kind of wooden steps with no backs so that you sit on the toes of the people behind you, with draughts that come sideways or down the back of your neck, not to speak of a corrugated zinc roof which is not altogether water-tight. Here they found Edith's uncle and aunt, the John Leslies, who had come to see their boys play. Not that either of them was particularly interested in cricket, but among the many sacrifices one makes for one's young, looking on at their childish sports is one. They were pleased to see Edith who was able to present them to her distinguished hostess.

"This *is* nice," said Mrs. Leslie. "I have bought every one of your books, Mrs. Morland, ever since the first one—that was Dressmakers in Danger, wasn't it?"

Mrs. Morland, who was perennially surprised and flattered that real people (in her own words, though we doubt if she knew exactly what she meant) should like her highly respect-worthy pot-boilers, responded suitably and at once fell into talk with the Leslies about various county matters and how Lord Stoke had been so rude (though in a way suitable to the representative of one of the oldest baronies in the West of England) to Lord Aberfordbury (he who was Sir Ogilvy Hibberd) about the footpath under Bolder's Knob. Edith, rather out of it, was however quite happy watching the scene on the cricket field where the white flannels were gradually congregating.

We shall not attempt to describe the cricket match, our knowledge of that great game being almost as limited as that of the young lady in the du Maurier drawing who asks what happens if the bowler is out before the batsman. Suffice it to say that Old Boys surprised in themselves, as Count Smorltork so well put it, pretty well every variety of age and status, including an Air Vice-Marshal, an ex-Solicitor-General, an Admiral of the Fleet and a financial genius who had served two years in prison for fraud on an unprecedented scale and was now out again and on the up and up; not to speak of a stiffening of younger Old Boys, of whom Leslie Major was the youngest. Faced with such a side, the stoutest team might have quailed, except that no single one of the elder gentlemen had played for at least ten years and in some cases not since their joyous Schoolboy or University Days.

"If you come to look at it," said John Leslie to Mrs. Morland, "some of the other side are a pretty rum lot. And I don't think the Vicar—Colonel Crofts—has played since he was in India about fifteen years ago and his excellent batman, Bateman—confusing, but it's his name—has only taken it up within the last few weeks, to oblige. Those two assistant masters aren't bad. I

expect you remember them, Mrs. Morland. Traill played for his
University and I think Feeder for his college. Matron's nephew—
he is a wireless operator in one of the big liners—is very good at
deck tennis, I understand, but that is hardly the same. Both sides
have a pretty poor tail. In fact our own Greshamsbury team
could give them fifty runs any day." But people are notoriously
untruthful about their own side.

By now the pavilion was housing a quite reasonable-sized
audience. The numbers for the score board had been sorted and
stacked in readiness and the white-clad figures—though we
must regretfully say that many of the flannels were rather yellow
by now and some, on closer inspection, bore distinct marks of
where the moth had got at them—were assembling. Matron,
who had been hopefully preparing a kind of small first aid
station under the pavilion, suddenly emerged halfway up the
steps which led from the underworld to the sloping seats and
looked round, rather like that depressing Erda in Rheingold.

"I wonder what Matron wants," said Minimus. "I bet she's
hoping someone will have a black eye or a broken nose. I say,
who's umpiring?"

"Edward, of course, you fool," said Minor, pointing to the
Headmaster's perfect manservant dressed in a white coat like
the gentlemen on the posters who used to paint RIPOLIN on
one another's backs.

"Fool yourself, it takes two to make an umpire," said Minimus. "Who's the other?" and he pointed to a white-coated figure
talking with Edward.

"I don't know," said Minor. "Look out, she's coming at us,"
which was a disrespectful and quite unnecessary way to speak of
Matron.

"Well, Mrs. Leslie, this is indeed a pleasant surprise," said
Matron.

Mary Leslie very nearly said it would be more surprising if she
weren't there, as her eldest son was playing.

"Indeed a Day of Surprises," said Matron, "for, do you know,

Mrs. Leslie, we were really quite in a turmoil this morning because Mr. Brown at the Red Lion was going to umpire and his sciatica came on suddenly. He rang up to tell me, so I popped down to the Red Lion to see if I could do anything, but he had *most* sensibly gone to bed with some Thermogene round him, so I just ran up to have a word with him and you will hardly credit it, but the room had quite a little smell of brandy. *Well*, I thought to myself, brandy may be the best thing for sciatica, but I wouldn't give it myself with no Doctor's Advice, so I said could I do anything to make him comfy, but he was just a wee bit peeved which one can *quite* understand with the pain. 'Nothing I can get for you, Mr. Brown?' I said, just in case there was something he wanted and I could have fetched it. 'No thank you, Matron,' he said. 'I've got some Thermogene round my leg and I'm just moistening it with a little brandy to get a bit more pep out of it,' which of course explained the smell, for it is extraordinary, you know Mrs. Leslie, how the smell does cling. Well, to make a short story of it, poor Mr. Brown had used the last of the brandy for the Thermogene, so I said 'Well, Mr. Brown,' I said, '*you* can't go downstairs, but I can,' so I went down to the bar to ask Eileen for some brandy for Mr. Brown and there was a young man sitting there and he looked at me—not a *nasty* look if you know what I mean, but just a LOOK, and he said: 'Don't you remember me, Matron, and the Christmas party here, the first year of the war?,' and then it all came back to me, quite a flash-back as the saying is."

By this time most of her audience, the younger members of which had not the faintest idea what she was talking about, were too stunned to make any comment; nor were the elder ones in much better plight.

"So I brought him back to the School with me at once," said Matron, "to see the match and I found Edward in quite a state because Haig Brown, the policeman here you know, who was to have umpired, had been called off on special duty and Edward didn't know where to turn at such short notice so I said 'Well,

Edward,' I said, 'here is the answer to prayer.' Not that any one had been praying if you see what I mean; I mean things weren't as bad as *that*, but they say prayer is answered though not always in the way you expect, and luckily the other white coat was there, so we popped it on and there we are" and she pointed dramatically towards a pleasant-faced man who might have been any age between twenty-five and thirty-five and was talking in a friendly way with Edward. But not one of them had the faintest idea who the stranger might be, when most luckily Snow, the old school carpenter, came up to talk with the Leslies and John was able to ask him who the other umpire was.

"Well, sir, you wouldn't remember him," said Snow. "It was in the beginning of the war before your young gentlemen come along here, and we had a London School evacuated, as they say, on us. We *did* have a time, sir. But some of them weren't bad when you come to know them. There was one boy, ah, *he* had the makings of a carpenter in him, sir, and I let him come in my shop and learn a bit, but his people they left London and went to Wales for the duration. But he wrote me off and on and said he was getting on fine with his schooling and I spoke to Mr. Carter about him and Mr. Carter said to invite him to come here in his holidays whenever I liked."

"Never mind about that boy," said John Leslie, quite kindly, but with the authority of a Churchwarden and a J.P. "Who *is* this umpire?"

"That's him, sir, I was telling you about," said Snow. "And as nice a lad as you'd wish to see."

"Do you mean Manners," said Matron, "that nice boy that helped us with the Christmas treat for the evacuees?"

Snow, suppressing a strong desire to put Matron between two boards and saw her in half, said coldly that Manners was the name.

"And that young fellow, sir," he added, very pointedly not addressing Matron, "he got a good scholarship to Oxford or Cambridge or one of them colleges and now he's teaching Replied

Physic or some such nonsense at Redbrick University. Same place where Professor Hacker is. Perhaps you remember him too, sir. He was the one as kept a tame chameleon. He's learning the young gentlemen Latin and Greek at Redbrick University. He's another boy as might have made a good tradesman. Well, well." And shaking his head over the vanity of human wishes, he went away.

Matron then said she must hie her away to her little field hospital, for though it was under the pavilion stand it was quite light and a basin and a little Ascot heater in case. With which last words she descended the stairs backwards on account of the steepness and disappeared.

By now the match was due to begin. The Rest won the toss, rather to Edith's disappointment, and sent their two first men in, Colonel Crofts and Matron's nephew. But though the Rest put up a gallant show, nine wickets had soon fallen for so small a score that we hesitate to invent it. The last hope of the side was now Mr. Traill and Mr. Feeder.

For those who do not particularly enjoy watching other people play games, there is always conversation, and as none of the party were going to be really interested till the next innings, when the Leslie boys would be batting, they were able to bring one another up to date with family news, while Mrs. Morland was able to tell Mrs. John Leslie exactly what had happened at Stoke Castle when the Barsetshire Archæological found a hitherto undiscovered exit from Stokey Hole, an opening in the bank below the castle on the river side, popularly supposed to communicate by subterranean passages with Capes Castle ten miles off, a disused windmill on the hills beyond Southbridge and the Tower of London.

"And what was there at the other end?" said Mrs. John Leslie.

"Exactly what any sensible person would have expected," said Mrs. Morland. "It went right under the castle and was really the

old main drain. Of course that accounts for the smell in the
butler's pantry that no one could account for."

"How fascinating," said Mrs. John Leslie. "John's father
always said there was a drain from the Pyramid—that monument on the top of the hill behind the house at Rushwater—to
the Rushmere Brook, but as there was nothing to drain, no one
ever knew. What's that?"

The That was a sound of clapping. Edith looked at the field
and saw her cousin Major, looking rather like a Dalmatian on its
hind legs so bemired were his white flannels, his right arm in the
air and the ball clutched in it, while Mr. Traill and Mr. Feeder
stood disconsolate. Which was the more disconsolate, we cannot say. True, it was Mr. Feeder who had sent that nice easy ball
straight into Leslie Major's hands, but Mr. Traill had the agony
of watching him hitting the ball exactly as he should not and in
the most dangerous direction and had stood paralysed, for
which he afterwards generously blamed himself; not that he
could have altered the course of the ball nor of Mr. Feeder's
destiny in any case, paralysis or no.

"Good Lord!" said John Leslie, looking at the score board.
"They're all out for fifty-three. It ought to be a walk-over for the
Old Boys—unless it rains which it obviously will. Come along
or we shan't get a seat," and they all went over to the Squash
Court where tea was prepared.

Of all the places for tea and talk a squash court is perhaps the
least suited, for it is apt to be taller than it is square (if our reader
sees what we mean), is usually to a high degree unventilated and
is hard on the feet. Luckily the spectators though enthusiastic
were not very numerous on account of the horrible weather, so it
might have been worse.

The table with the tea-urn and the cups and saucers was
presided over by Eileen of the Red Lion, now in private life Mrs.
Bateman, the wife of Colonel Crofts's ex-batman, gardener, and
general utility. Her slightly overpowering charm had not been
dimmed by time, nor had her brilliantly peroxided hair, and she

remained as kind and capable as ever, enjoying nothing more than to dispense refreshment to a quantity of friends.

"Nice to see you, Mrs. Leslie," said Eileen, extending the hand of friendship to Mary. "And well, if it isn't Mrs. Morland. It's quite like old times to see you again, Mrs. Morland. Me and Matron we often say we wish the war was on again. Those were the days. It was your young gentleman won the match, Mrs. Leslie, wasn't it? Ever so nice he looks in his flannels, but isn't it shocking the mud he got on them. Don't you try to wash them, Mrs. Leslie. Let them dry off nicely and then give them a good brush out in the garden. You'll be surprised the way it comes off. Then you can wash them if it's a nice day with a bit of a breeze."

Mary Leslie thanked her for the advice and asked if she could get tea for her party at one of the tables.

"I kept two tables special, Mrs. Leslie," said Eileen, "you'll find them over there. You tell your young gentlemen to put them together and you'll do nicely" and Mary thanked her, feeling with some amusement that she had practically been dismissed from the presence.

What with the crowd and the reverberations of the squash court, talk was not easy. However most of Mary's party had very hearty appetites and the boys argued in a brotherly way about the game, Leslie Minimus not omitting to tell Leslie Major that it was only a fluke.

"Anyway," said Edith, zealous in defence of her favourite cousin, "it was a whale's fluke," and she looked round with a little of the smugness she used to have when, as a small girl, she produced her impromptu poems to astonish visitors; who usually concealed their boredom very nicely.

"I say, Edith," said Minor, "you ought to make a poem about Major's catch. And next year when I'm an Old Boy you can make one about me."

Edith, a young lady in the older phraseology, not a schoolgirl now, was less self-important than she used to be. She looked imploringly at Minor, but the look was entirely lost on him.

"Fire away, Edith," said her uncle John kindly though, as she was quick enough to realize, with an entire want of interest. But the blood of the Pomfrets did not run in her veins for nothing.

"This is it," she said.

> "Old Feeder hit the ball afar,
> It rose to heaven like a star
> And when at last it came to land,
> It was in Major's mighty hand.

That's all," she added.

Mrs. Morland, who was amused by her guest's success and delighted to be free of responsibility for the present, gave her a friendly smile.

Her cousins applauded loudly. Her uncle and aunt laughed, but in a very kind way. Suddenly Edith wondered whether she had been rather babyish. It was fun to make poems, but her poems weren't as good as they had been. Her poem about the fishes' bell in the Palace pond for instance. Three verses of eight lines each, ending with the fine line, "And now the Bishop is in hell." Perhaps she was too old now. People didn't clap what one said, unless they thought one was rather a baby. For twopence she would have gone straight back to Holdings—to the safe, safe fold where the little lambs are, she thought, as a line from a song of her nursery days suddenly came into her mind—and for twopence she would have allowed the tears that were pricking her eyes to have their way. But just at that moment a kind of hubbub drew everyone's attention away, which hubbub was caused by the arrival of Captain Fairweather, R.N., a near neighbour of the Leslies at Greshamsbury, and his lovely wife, she who had been Rose Birkett. There was a great surge of people to welcome her, under cover of which Edith was able to dry her eyes—not that she was crying, oh no—and resume her ordinary face.

Rose was indeed an entrancing apparition in a dress of dusty-pink silk, a small hat of dusty-pink straw perched with a modest rakishness upon her beautifully set fair hair, her perfect legs sheathed in sheer nylons and her feet in the newest form of sandal whose price every woman in the place at once guessed and envied.

"Oh, hullo Mrs. Morland. I remember when you were here in the war," she said. "Oh, hullo Mrs. Leslie. What a marvellous catch Henry made. *Too* devastating for poor Mr. Feeder. Isn't the rain too foully dispiriting for words. Hallo John and Clive," which words made no sense to most of her hearers, for the Leslie boys had been Major, Minor, and Minimus ever since their prep. school and most people hardly knew that they had what our transatlantic cousins so prettily call given names.

"Come and have tea at our table," said Mary Leslie kindly. Major pulled up the other table, Minor offered his brother's chair to Captain Fairweather and his own chair—with the air of laying a cloak before her sandalled feet—to Rose, while Minimus with great presence of mind went to Eileen and asked if they could have more tea and *lots* of cake.

"I'm so sorry we missed the beginning of the game, Mrs. Leslie," said Captain Fairweather. "I had an Admiralty call and had to write some letters to go to London before we could start. And now, I gather, that's the end. Bad luck."

"Do you mean they aren't going to play any more?" said Mrs. Morland.

"Couldn't," said Captain Fairweather. "The pitch is practically flooded already. Listen to it," and indeed, though in the noise of so many people eating and drinking and talking in a resonant place she had not noticed it, there was a steady drumming on the glass roof. "And what's more, we'll all be asphyxiated soon. Wouldn't hurt some of us," he added, cheerfully, with an expressive glance at some of the Old Boys, more particularly the financial genius who had done time and the Admiral of the Fleet; though what he knew against this last we cannot say, for our knowledge of the Senior Service is, alas, practically non-existent.

"Excuse me, Miss Rose," said a voice at Mrs. Fairweather's elbow.

"Hullo, Edward," said Rose, looking up at the Headmaster's butler whom she had known since he was the odd man and did the boots and knives at the Southbridge Prep. School and she was the small elder daughter of the Prep. School Headmaster, now,—so does time pass—the retired Headmaster of Southbridge School.

"Excuse me, Miss Rose," said Edward, "but there's someone here as would like to see you if convenient."

Most of us on hearing such words would at once expect the worst—a creditor with a bailiff at his side, a hysterical message from next door to say Pussy had disappeared ever since last night and had we seen him, or even the daily (if we are lucky enough to have her) in whose hands the last of our grandmother's real china tea-service has come to pieces. But Rose merely asked, with a serene countenance, what it was.

"Well, miss," said Edward, "I don't know as you'd remember, but that first winter of the war when we had those schools here from London, there was a nice boy called Manners. In Mr. Bissell's school he was and he helped to decorate the tree for the children's tea-party in the gymnasium."

"I wasn't at the party, because I was at Las Palombas where John was stationed," said Rose. "But Geraldine wrote to me about it and she said it was marvellous and all the children were sick that evening or next day and there were London refugees who were awfully rich and came to the party all covered with silver foxes," to which Edward, who did not quite follow what she was saying, said Yes, miss and Manners was here and would like to see her if convenient.

"But of course," said Rose, whose social memory was, in spite of her apparent silliness, extraordinarily accurate and had been of the greatest help to her husband when he was a Naval

Attaché. "Mummy said his father was a greengrocer wasn't he, and did furniture removing in the East End. Of course I'd love to see him. Why is he here?"

"Well, miss," said Edward, "I couldn't rightly say. Matron found him in the Red Lion bar when she was getting the brandy for Mr. Brown's Thermogene so she said Why not come up to the cricket match. And we was an umpire short, miss, seeing Haig Brown had been called off on special duty, so I said Why not umpire with me, Manners, like old Times. Not that he did umpire then—nor me neither if it comes to that because the groundsman wouldn't have allowed neither of us on his cricket pitch. I'll bring him along, miss," so he went away and soon returned with Professor Manners.

"How too marvellous to see you" said Rose, looking at Manners with an intensity which puzzled him, but was only caused by her struggles to correlate his face with that of an evacuated London schoolboy nearly fifteen years ago whom she had never seen. "Now I know who you are because Geraldine, that's my sister, wrote to me about it. You helped with the tea-party for the evacuated children and you carried down a frightfully heavy roll of green baize that Matron wanted for the Christmas tree and you'd just got a scholarship for Cambridge. Is it nice?" and she turned her beautiful eyes on him and took out her lip-stick again.

"No, my girl," said her husband. "Put it away and give me your bag."

"All right, darling, but you *are* a bit damp-making," said Rose and cheerfully did as she was told.

Manners (or as it will be more polite to call him, Professor Manners), quite unperturbed by this domestic interlude, said it was extremely nice (for to choose a more suitable adjective would be wasted on Rose) and he had delightful rooms at Upping, which, he added hastily, seeing Rose's face quite devoid of understanding, was the name of his college, and he taught history to undergraduates.

"But that must be *very* nice for them," said Rose earnestly, "because of course you *saw* it."

By this time Mrs. Morland, all three Leslie boys, and their parents were listening with acute interest to the conversation. Edith was also of the listeners, but did not hear, having too many thoughts in her head.

"I wish I had noticed it more at the time," said Manners, "but I was a bit young then. It would be so much easier to write about history if one had lived in it *and* remembered it. Otherwise it's like seeing things in a looking-glass—probably all the wrong way round."

"But actually," said Rose (and Professor Manners noted with approval that she did not say ackcherly, as did practically all his women students), "they are the *right* way round. It's only because you are outside the looking-glass that they look wrong. If you got inside it—"

"Your wife," said Professor Manners to Captain Fairweather, "is a philosopher. I am going to think about what she said. I might manage to write something about it."

"A real book?" said Rose, with the simplicity of a savage.

"Certainly," said Professor Manners. "And if I may, rather unfairly perhaps, presume upon an old acquaintance with your parents—though one should not use the word old when you are in question—I would like to dedicate the book to you; if it ever gets written."

"A *real* book?" said Rose.

"Yes, my girl," said her husband. "*Not* a historical novel about the Venerable Bede's love-life. A book for educated people to read."

"Oh, *thank* you, Manners," said Rose, carried back by her enthusiasm to the Christmas of 1939, and then she blushed and her lovely eyes became misty. "Oh, dear, I *am* so sorry."

"But I like it, Mrs. Fairweather," said Professor Manners, quite truthfully, but also with the very laudable object of relieving Rose's too tender conscience. "Pray continue to call me

Manners, especially when you come to lunch with me in my rooms at Upping, as I hope you and your husband will do some day," and he bowed slightly to Captain Fairweather, who smiled back and sketched a kind of salute. "And now I must say good-bye, as I am due in Barchester for a lecture."

Captain Fairweather asked if they could drive him, but he had his own car and went away.

The rain had now ceased drumming upon the roof and was merely coming down steadily upon the already flooded cricket ground. Most of the guests had given up hope and gone home, while Everard Carter had asked some of the rest to come over to the Headmaster's house for a glass of sherry.

"I think we had better be going on to Miss Hampton's now," said Mrs. Morland. "She lives in the village. What did you think of her?"

Edith, rather cautiously, said she looked very kind and she thought she had seen her at a prizegiving once and didn't she wear rather manly clothes. "Uncle David and Aunt Rose knew one or two of that sort in New York," she continued, "only their clothes were *beautifully* cut. I didn't much care for them. And I don't think they much cared for me either," she added, by which words Mrs. Morland was on the whole relieved, for to have had to explain those worthy ladies Miss Hampton and Miss Bent to a young girl was rather beyond her. Not that she need have been troubled, for Edith, with her mother's excellent worldly sense and a winter in New York with cousins who knew everyone, was tolerably well prepared for most aspects of life.

So they got into Mrs. Morland's car and drove out of the School Yard, then to the left, straight on across the bridge over the Rising and to the left again, past the Red Lion. A little further on they came to a strip of grass on the right, beyond which stood a row of four two-storied cottages of mellow red brick surmounted by a stucco pediment on which the words "Wiple Terrace 1820" were still visible. They had been erected, as all friends of Southbridge know (though not Friends in the shape of being a society with subscriptions) by Mr. Wiple, a small master builder, as a permanent memorial to his four daughters and now belonged to Paul's College at Oxford, who also owned the Vicarage and the presentation to the living.

As we have more than once noted in earlier volumes of this meandering Chronicle, Wiple Terrace has been famed for its hospitality ever since Miss Hampton, the well-known author of Chariots of Desire, A Gentle Girl and Boy and many other powerful novels on kindred subjects, came to live in Adelina Cottage with her friend Miss Bent. Of the three other cottages Maria and Louisa were at present occupied by Mr. Traill and Mr. Feeder, assistant masters at Southbridge School, and Editha by Mrs. Feeder, the widowed mother of Mr. Feeder. Great harmony reigned in the terrace, its inhabitants seeing eye to eye on the subject of drink in all its aspects, and the only occasions when any slight cloud arose were when Mr. Traill objected to Mr. Feeder's wireless which could pick up far too many stations and foreign ones at that and far too loud, or when Mr. Feeder said if Mr. Traill put on that blinking record once more he would shoot at sight. As for Mrs. Feeder, she accepted Miss Hampton and Miss Bent as equals and women who knew what was what, exercised towards Mr. Traill a kind of motherly bullying against which he was far too afraid to expostulate, and treated her son as a well-meaning child of arrested development.

The yellow door of Adelina Cottage was ajar and from inside came a noise of talk. Since we were last within its hospitable walls the owners had made a slight change in the architecture. The wall of the narrow passage from which the sitting-room opened had been removed, so that the room occupied the full width of the house, except for the staircase whose banisters had been screened by matchboarding which went up to the ceiling, with one archway in it so that anyone going upstairs could look through at the people below, rather as Punch looks out of his house at the crowd. About three feet of what had been the partition wall had been left by the front door and a door with a glass top put across the passage, so that with care the visitor could enter, as it were, into a lock; and when the outer door had been shut could be admitted to the drawing-room. Much the same had been done in Editha Cottage at the other end of the terrace and it certainly gave a little more space for guests and bottles.

Within there was a fire, highly suitable to the season, as seasons seem to have forgotten what is expected of them. Miss Hampton, in a gentlemanly black suit with a white silk shirt and a stock, black silk stockings, and very neat black shoes with silver buckles, came forward to welcome Mrs. Morland and then Edith, whom she had seen occasionally when the Leslie boys were showing their young cousin the sights of Southbridge.

Edith then went to say how do you do to her other hostess, Miss Bent, for Lady Graham, whatever her more involuntary shortcomings as a parent may have been where her dearly loved youngest daughter was concerned, had brought her up with very good manners—as indeed she had done with all her offspring. We may add that her three sons, all of whom were following their father in the army, had each separately told her that her insistence on behaviour had been of the greatest help to him in his career. And we think that these same good manners are going to continue to help them all through their careers whether purely military, military-administrative, or military-political; or even on Boards of Directors when they retire.

"We are pleased to see you," said Miss Bent, who was looking quite her worst in a sage-green djibbah. And as few of our young readers will know what a djibbah is (or was when we were stout but comely, in our far off youth when King Edward the Seventh was on the Throne) it is a dress with no shape at all, usually made from a kind of loosely woven material in art shades, with pieces of flowered art silk in similar or contrasting tones (both of which are equally horrid) as a kind of yoke in front and behind, with extensions down each arm. The sleeves are short. The whole dress—in the beautiful words of the poet Rossetti unclasped

from neck to hem—is calculated to show off even the slimmest
and most elegant figure to great disadvantage, especially when
worn, as Miss Bent was wearing it this evening, with a kind of
undershirt of yellow butter muslin with long baggy sleeves. She
was also strung with some half dozen of her collection of bead
necklaces, some of wood, some of glass, which clanked majestically as she moved. And then in came Louisa and Maria in the
shape of Messrs. Traill and Feeder, both gentlemen with a
bottle at each side like John Gilpin, followed closely by Mr.
Feeder's mother, whose glittering eyes, bony figure, and claw-
like hands covered with rings, interested Edith very much.

"Spanish dry sherry," said Mrs. Feeder, setting a bottle down
on the window sill. "Dry isn't the word. Lifts the skin off your
teeth. Who is your charming friend, Miss Hampton?"

Edith looked round to see who the charming friend was and
found it was herself, which surprised her very much and she
smiled at Mrs. Feeder who seemed to be very kind in spite of her
witch-like aspect.

"Gin, It., French, Whisky, Sherry,—name it," said Miss
Bent to Mrs. Feeder.

"Vermouth for me," said Mrs. Feeder. "One third French, two
thirds It. I never mix my drinks."

An expression of shame and anguish passed over Miss Bent's
face.

"Hampton," she called across the room. "Have we any French
vermouth? I am sure there was a bottle yesterday."

"I finished it with Mr. Wickham," said Miss Hampton,
"when he came in to say he couldn't come today. My fault, Bent;
my fault."

"No, Hampton," said Miss Bent, not to be outdone in generosity. "The fault was mine," which Mrs. Robin Dale, had she
been present, would at once have recognized as a quotation from
her favourite poet, Lord Tennyson. "You asked me to order
some at the Red Lion. I forgot," with which noble words she

metaphorically bared her bosom for the sword of outraged friendship to be sheathed in it.

"And you write perhaps?" said Miss Hampton to Edith. "All the Young write."

Edith said only poetry and on being pressed she recited her juvenile poem about the Bishop and the fish in the Palace pond that used to come for bread when a bell rang, but this Bishop had been so stingy that he took away the bell; and how Edith's brothers had found it and put it in its place and the Bishop was ashamed to take it away again. Mrs. Morland sat and wondered a little at her guest, but then she remembered that Edith had had a season in New York which seemed to her to explain everything, though she could not have said why. And in any case the child was being perfectly natural and not in the least conceited, so let her go on.

But Edith, though very willing to do what her hostesses wished, was beginning to feel tired and would gladly have gone back to High Rising but it would not be polite to say so. The talk went on and on, largely about people and things she did not know about and there were plenty of odds and ends to eat, but nothing really satisfying. Even what Nurse used to call, rather threateningly, A nice bowl of bread and milk would have been welcome. But there was not so much noise as there would have been at a party of the same size in New York, so she decided to try to keep awake and listen to other people talking.

"I tried to ring you up just after tea," said Mrs. Feeder to Miss Hampton, "but they said the line was engaged. I tried again, but no luck."

"It was My Doing," said Miss Bent, suddenly taking the stage like the villainess who was Misled in youth by a Deceiver but really has a heart of gold and foils his latest wicked design by sacrificing her life to save the honour of a pure girl. "I know Hampton cannot bear the telephone when we have a party. She is too sensitive. So I cut it off."

Mr. Traill, much interested, said he had always wondered

how people cut a telephone off, because he understood that if you cut the line with a pair of scissors you got a frightful shock unless you wore rubber gloves.

"Quite simple, my dear man," said Miss Bent. "I took the receiver off in the bedroom. You know we have one there. Hampton might want to ring her publisher up."

It did occur to several of those present not only that one's publisher might find it inconvenient to be rung up at night when he was not at the office, though inconvenient was not quite the word as you could not miss what you did not know you had lost, but that if you left the receiver off for a matter of several hours the exchange might begin to take an interest in you and even feel annoyed; but no one liked to disillusion Miss Bent.

Mrs. Morland said she gave the girl at the exchange an advance copy of her latest book every year and it worked wonders.

"Hampton could not do that," said Miss Bent in a reverent way. "Never has she Paltered," which impressive words left her hearers speechless, all except Mrs. Morland, who said in a rebellious undertone that you could only palter with something; not palter just by itself. As it was obvious that Miss Bent thought palter to be the equivalent of bribe, a general effort was made to change the subject.

"Do tell me," said Mrs. Morland to Miss Hampton, "do you work out your books beforehand or do they come to you in a flash?"

Miss Bent, casting a look of reverent admiration at her friend, said it was a privilege to see genius at work and to be privileged to guard and shelter it, and then wished she had not used the word privilege twice; for the extra "d" the second time could not really be counted.

"Dear woman," said Miss Hampton to Mrs. Morland, paying not the slightest attention to her friend's tribute, "you and I are Makers; in the beautiful old sense of the word which is applied to those who create by the living word; or in these times by the written word."

"I have heard Hampton repeat a sentence aloud as often as ten times," said Miss Bent, "before she put it on paper, the better to get the exact sense, the feeling, the emotion of the written word."

"I wish I could do that," said Mrs. Morland to Miss Hampton with a kind of frank good-natured envy. "Now I could not possibly say one single word aloud. I get an exercise book and a pencil and sit down in great rage and annoyance and *make* the pencil write something. It doesn't matter what, just something."

"'A sunset touch,
A fancy from a flower-bell, some one's death,
A chorus-ending from Euripides'"

said Mr. Traill. And as the whole company were struck silent, he added "Browning."

"A great thinker," said Miss Hampton, "but not much knowledge of human nature. Now Shelley, in the Cenci—"

"And then what do you do next," said Mrs. Feeder with great presence of mind, at the same time casting a basilisk eye on Mr. Traill.

"Well, I don't really *know*," said Mrs. Morland. "But really it is Miss Hampton's turn because she was going to tell us about how she works."

"I find," said Miss Hampton graciously, "that Mr. Traill's quotation is not inapt. One thing leads to another. For instance, it was reading Keats's beautiful and moving lyric, In a drear-nighted December, that gave me the title of one of my best-selling books, 'A Gentle Girl and Boy.'"

"Hampton does not say," said Miss Bent reverently, "that it was Blake who inspired what I still think her finest book. You tell them, Hampton."

"As I can never follow the tune to which 'Jerusalem' is now

sung," said Miss Hampton, "on account of its not beginning at the beginning, it is difficult to explain exactly."

Her audience, not at all sure of her meaning, were silent.

"Oh, I know *exactly* what you mean," said Mrs. Morland. "Most tunes begin with the beginning, but in Jerusalem it doesn't seem to. I mean, when the preface, or introduction, or whatever you call it is over I can never get in quickly enough with 'And,' which seems a silly word to begin a song with. But it does wander a good deal in the middle too. What was the book, Miss Hampton?" But Miss Bent, shocked by such ignorance, leapt into the breach and said it was the book which got the Prix d'Immondices in Paris, Chariots of Desire, about the sex life of lorry-drivers.

"I altered the words slightly of course," said Miss Hampton. "Blake wrote 'chariot of fire.' I altered this, substituting 'desire' which occurs two lines earlier, for 'fire.'"

A kind of hum of approval rose from her audience, chiefly, we think, because no one had the faintest idea what to say. Mrs. Morland, looking at Edith, suddenly realized that the child was tired, and no wonder. So she thanked Miss Hampton and Miss Bent very much for the party. Edith, almost stumbling with boredom, said good-bye as politely as she could and Mrs. Morland took her away.

"I am so sorry, my dear," she said as they drove back. "I am always amused by those women and I forgot you must be tired."

"Not really tired," said Edith. "Please, Mrs. Morland, don't think I wasn't enjoying myself, because I was. But I did feel so sleepy" at which Mrs. Morland laughed, very kindly, and sped on through the evening to High Rising. Here Stoker was waiting for them with all the fresh village news.

"Not now, Stoker," said Mrs. Morland. "Put some hot milk in Miss Graham's room. She is going to bed at once."

"Oh, good night and thank you for a lovely day, Mrs. Morland," said Edith, almost tottering as she spoke. And what was more, she meant it. When Mrs. Morland went up, half an hour later, Edith was fast asleep.

"Nice girl," said Mrs. Morland aloud to herself. "Very nice girl," and then she settled herself to her writing.

CHAPTER 3

On Sunday morning Edith was woken at nine o'clock by Stoker with breakfast on a tray.

"Oh!" said Edith, sitting up as quickly as possible. "Have I overslept myself?"

"Now, don't you commence to worry," said Stoker, setting down the tray on a chair. "Young heads need plenty of sleep. Take it while you can get it, because you never know what's coming. That's what my mother always said to me and I didn't pay no attention, but when father took to coming home at three in the morning the worse for drink then I knew what mother meant. And *she* knew," Stoker added darkly. "Now you put that woolly round your shoulders and sit up. Here's another pillow. Still there's much to be thankful for in this life and we may as well be thankful for it here as only the Lord knows what the next life will be. Same thing all over again, I dessay, but if I meet father there I'll tell him a thing or two. Last time I saw him was when the police fetched me and mother, the day after Easter Monday it was, to see him at the mortuary. 'Yes, that's him all right,' I said, 'and a good riddance of bad rubbish.' The Benefit Society buried him and it was a lovely funeral. Mrs. Morland says don't you hurry to get up. She's writing some of her books, poor thing, and church is at eleven."

She then laid the tray across Edith's legs and went away.

Edith, who in spite of her New York season was still younger inside than she appeared from outside, ate her breakfast with a good appetite, reflecting upon the events of the previous day and the peculiar but not unattractive party she had been to. It then occurred to her that while everyone had been very nice the men had paid no attention at all to her. Not that she was in the least mortified by this, but her American experiences had conditioned her (dreadful word, but useful and probably passing into English Usage) to attention from men, and she had been distinctly gratified by the number of her beaux and the flowers they so richly sent on every occasion or even on none at all. But on reflection she had to confess that Mr. Feeder and Mr. Traill, though very nice, were not exactly beaux. More like uncles, though this comparison would have been indignantly rebutted by both gentlemen. And then she put the tray on a chair and presently was surprised to wake up again and find Mrs. Morland in the room.

"Oh, good morning, Mrs. Morland," she said sitting up. "I'm awfully sorry. I must have gone to sleep again."

"Quite right too, at your age," said Mrs. Morland. "It's ten o'clock now. I thought we would go to church at eleven and then go on to Lord Crosse. He doesn't lunch till half past one, so we shall have plenty of time. The Vicar is rather dull, but he does read the morning service properly."

"So does our Vicar, Mr. Choyce," said Edith, "which is a good thing, because father will be at home now that he has more or less retired and he is going to read the lessons and he is really annoyed if the clergyman leaves out a lot of the first prayer and he reads it aloud to himself so that everyone can hear him. He did that when we were staying at Pomfret Towers and mother and I thought people might think it was interfering, but Cousin Gillie said 'And a good thing too—I've always wanted to do it myself.'"

"That is Lord Pomfret, isn't it?" said Mrs. Morland.

"Yes. I'm sorry," said Edith. "Mother is always telling me to call people by their real names unless it's just in the family, because they mightn't know who they were" which rather muddled bit of reasoning Mrs. Morland appeared to understand and telling Edith not to hurry, but they would be starting at about a quarter to eleven, she went away.

As the weather looked nastier and nastier, Edith decided to go in the tweeds which her mother, much against Edith's wishes, had caused her to pack. She found Mrs. Morland waiting for her and they walked down towards the church, rather to Edith's surprise who, in common with her generation, thought that if one had a car one used it even to post a letter in the pillar-box round the corner, an attitude which her American experiences had not done anything to change. The service— apart from the everlasting beauty of the words—was excessively dull and as there were four hymns, not one of which Edith knew, she derived but little benefit from it, and indeed found herself thinking about the party the night before during the sermon and only got to her feet just in time. The Vicar was standing in the porch as they went out, greeting his parishioners.

"This is Edith Graham, Mr. Gould, who is staying with me," said Mrs. Morland. The Vicar pressed Edith's hand and said Graham was a fine Scottish name.

"Not this one," said Mrs. Morland. "Her father is Sir Robert Graham over at Little Misfit. He has just retired and is quite English."

Mr. Gould said Ha!

"Besides," said Mrs. Morland, looking at him severely, "her mother was Agnes Leslie, old Mr. Leslie's daughter."

Mr. Gould said Indeed, though in quite a friendly way.

"And our Vicar is Mr. Choyce," said Edith, feeling that she ought to contribute to this rather halting conversation.

"Choyce," said Mr. Gould. "Ah yes. A bachelor, I believe."

"Well," said Mrs. Morland, "there isn't any law about clergy-men getting married or not, though I believe the Bishop has a preference for celibate clergy but really, considering what life at the Palace must be, one cannot blame him."

"My dear Mrs. Morland," said Mr. Gould, suddenly emerging from his official manner, "far from blaming I am ready to make every allowance for his lordship. A veritable Socrates."

"Oh, not as bad as *that!*" said Mrs. Morland, though exactly what she meant the Vicar did not know and nor, we think, did she, unless it was an expression of general contempt for people who let themselves be henpecked.

"One does not of course *know* what goes on behind the Iron Curtain," said Mr. Gould laughing slightly to show that this was a joke, "but from what one hears, his lordship is, shall we say, slightly under female domination."

"Oh, Xantippe you mean," said Mrs. Morland. "I thought you meant he had a kind of satyr's face with a broken nose," at which Edith couldn't help laughing. "Had you heard about the black-out curtains?"

The Vicar said he thought those were, thank heaven, a thing of the past.

"Well, we don't have to use them at present," said Mrs. Morland, "though of course one never knows with space rockets or whatever they are, but these were the old black-out curtains they had at the Palace in the war and my maid Stoker says the Palace head housemaid told her that the old cat—she meant the Bishopess—was having them made into extra aprons for his lordship."

Mr. Gould very properly said he could not believe it, even of That Woman, but it was obvious that he not only could but did and would spread the glad tidings as far as possible.

Mrs. Morland then enquired after the Vicar's garden, and took Edith away.

"Are they *really* so awful at the Palace?" said Edith as they walked back to the house. "Father and mother dine there once a year and they have to ask the Palace back of course, but I wasn't old enough for dinner parties till last year and then I was in America when they did come to dinner."

"Well, my dear, I feel I oughtn't to try to influence you in any way," said Mrs. Morland. "You know, people who write books often begin to look at real people as if *they* were people in books, and the Palace to me is an example of this. I mean I only know them *very* slightly and I must say that the Bishop's wife has been quite extraordinarily rude to me once or twice, though I feel perfectly sure she didn't mean to be, but is simply so ill bred and stupid that she can't help it. But certainly I have the impression that she is a very unsuitable woman and makes a good deal of ill-feeling in the diocese."

"Perhaps she will have a stroke and die, like that Bishop's wife that darling Gran used to talk about," said Edith hopefully.

"Would that be Lady Emily Leslie?" said Mrs. Morland, which question might, to an ignorant outsider, have seemed applicable to the Bishop's wife, but Mrs. Morland knew her county, though not of county rank.

"I wish you had known Gran," said Edith. "I was almost too young then."

"And what are you now?" said Mrs. Morland, kindly.

Edith was silent as they walked. Then she said: "Really, Mrs. Morland, I don't quite know. Actually"—and though Mrs. Morland was quite sick of hearing that word from the young she gave Edith a good mark for pronouncing it distinctly and correctly—"I am a grown-up daughter at home. Emmy—that's my eldest sister—got married when she was quite young and anyway she was always cow-minded and Clarissa did go to college but she got married too," which rider amused Mrs. Morland. "But I'm not really *anything*-minded. And I think mother forgets a little that I am grown-up. Perhaps it always has to be like that with the youngest."

"I really don't know," said Mrs. Morland. "All mine are sons."

"'Your son's your son till he gets him a wife'" said Edith.

"So far so good," said Mrs. Morland. "But the second line ought to be: 'But he'll go on expecting you to help him and his family all your life.' Still, there it is."

When they got back to the house Stoker had nice cups of tea

for them which neither of them wanted in the least, but there it is, as Mrs. Morland so truly said.

"And there is one thing about the summer—if summer one can call this," she said, looking vengefully at the grey sky, the depressed flowers outside bending (or in some cases breaking or already broken) before the nasty wind, and noting with no approval that it was beginning to rain,—"it can't last for ever. Come and drink your tea while it is hot and then we will start."

The way to Crosse Hall as we know already was past the horrible new Housing Estate, over the downs and so past Boxall Hill, between which and Mr. Gresham's seat Crosse Hall was situated. As they passed the turning to Little Misfit Edith had a very short attack of homesickness, but reflecting that her parents were spending the weekend at Pomfret Towers she quickly got over it and began to look forward to lunch.

"By the way," said Mrs. Morland as she turned into the short drive that led to Lord Crosse's house, "their butler here used to be at The Towers."

"Yes, Peters," said Edith. "I saw him here last year when I came with mother. He used to make skipjacks for us when we were small. I kept mine under my pillow till nurse found out because the cobbler's wax had made the sheet so dirty," and then they stopped at the front door.

"Will you ring, dear," said Mrs. Morland, "while I put the car a little further away" and she turned the car on the gravel sweep and parked it by a clump of nasty variegated laurels. The large front door was open as at Holdings, and as at Holdings and so many other country houses, there was an inner door with glass panels in the upper part through which the hall could be seen. Edith pulled the shining brass knob to the right of the outer door and waited. A very satisfactory jangle could be heard inside the house. A boy in a neat blue suit appeared in the hall, gave an alarmed look at Edith and opened the inner door.

"I'm Miss Graham," said Edith to the boy, "and Mrs. Morland is parking the car. We have come to lunch."

"Mr. Peters only said to answer the door," said the boy, who having faithfully obeyed his superior's instructions now showed every symptom of being as silly as Casabianca. At that moment Mrs. Morland joined Edith, and Peters appeared. Ignoring the boy he bowed the guests into the house.

"His lordship is in the library, madam," he said to Mrs. Morland, "if you will come this way" and with stately tread he took them across the hall, opened the library door, announced "Mrs. Morland and Miss Graham, my lord" and went back to his pantry, where he gave the boy a cold look and told him to do those spoons all over again.

"Mr. Peters," said the boy, "can I spit on them? Dad always spits on his boots when he's polishing them for Sunday."

"Boots is one thing and his lordship's silver another," said Peters, and quite rightly we think. "You keep on rubbing till that spit comes right off. And don't look like that."

"I didn't mean to look, Mr. Peters," said the boy, "but I don't see no spit, not now."

"Now, you pay attention, my lad, or you'll never get a job in a good place, not even as boot and knife boy," said Peters. "And when you do your military service the sergeant'll tell you off good and proper if you can't clean brass. Not that his lordship's silver is brass, but it's all the same thing. Spit and polish in the army; plate powder and polish in the Pantry. And a drop of methylated with the plate powder, but don't go drowning it."

"Can I breathe on it, Mr. Peters?" said the boy.

"Certainly not," said Peters. "*You* don't breathe on the silver till you're a second footman and not even then if you don't listen to what I tell you. Carry on," with which impressive command, relic of his war experience in the Home Guard, Peters took a tray of silver away to the dining-room, thinking regretfully of the days when he had three under him, or even four in the shooting season, at Pomfret Towers what time the present earl's predecessor ruled as an autocrat before the last war. Relieved from his superior officer's presence the boy spat on the spoon, rubbed the spit off with his cuff and gave his mind to polishing.

"That's better," said Peters, who had come back for a trayful of glasses. "You do as I tell you and you'll be a mess sergeant yet, even if you don't get into good service later. You can give those glasses an extra polish while I see about the wine."

When he had gone the boy breathed into all the glasses and rubbed them with a clean corner of his apron.

"Let me see those glasses," said Peters coming back with his empty tray. "What did you polish them with?" he added, casting a suspicious eye on the polishing cloth which lay neatly folded and spotless on its shelf.

"Please, Mr. Peters, mother always does the glasses on her apron," said the boy. "She says it's the elbow grease as counts."

"Never mind what your mother does," said Peters, which pronouncement appeared to uproot the whole fabric of society in the boy's mind. "When you're in My Pantry, you pay attention to ME. Now put all those glasses under the tap and polish them again with the glass cloth. In some places you might have a glass cloth as had been used for the silver," at which words the pantry boy tried to look as if the very suggestion of such an enormity had eaten into his soul. "I suppose they learned you to read at school."

"Yes, Mr. Peters," said the boy.

"Then you see what's on this cloth," said Peters, holding a clean glass cloth as Barbara Frietchie (dreadful old bore) might have held the Union Flag.

"Yes, Mr. Peters," said the boy.

"Well, what does it say?" said Peters.

"I don't rightly know," said the boy. "It's like Htolc Ssalg or something. Ow, it's the wrong way round, Mr. Peters."

"What do you mean Wrong way round?" said the outraged Peters. "None of your sauce, my boy. Now, tumble to it," which further reminiscence of his superior's war service further confused the boy. "'Glass Cloth,' that's what it says and don't you forget it. Glass Cloths for glass and My Shammy for silver. It isn't every house where the butler would let you use His shammy, but I want you to learn proper, my lad, and then you'll get a good place. Another year or two here and you might get a place as second footman to Lord Aberfordbury, him as was Sir Ogilvy Hibberd. Not quite a gentleman's establishment, but I know Sir Ogilvy's butler and he's doing his best to learn his lordship proper behaviour. Now don't sit there chattering because there's lunch to serve. And if you do those glasses and silver properly now, next time his lordship has company I might—I say I *might*—let you sound the gong."

To this magnificent offer the pantry boy could only respond by the words "OW, Mr. Peters," but the butler felt that he had that day kindled a light which would not be put out.

"And now you've made me two minutes late with My Gong," said Peters, lest his slave should have been unduly uplifted, "and what his lordship will say, I don't know."

But in the library Lord Crosse and Mrs. Morland, with some of his lordship's excellent sherry, were perfectly happy discussing Mrs. Morland's new book, for though that worthy creature had no illusions about the literary value of her books she was grateful to them for having over the last twenty years and more earned enough money for her to finish educating her four sons and now to live comfortably though simply by herself. The fact that she had—sometimes under stress of family worries or bad health—written them all by hand herself and now commanded a faithful audience for what she freely admitted to be second-class literature, did not appear to be present to her mind. Edith, feeling rather young with two such grown-up people, had taken herself and her sherry into the far corner where there was a complete set of Punch with one volume missing (a very common form of complete sets in country houses) and was happily lost in the year of the Du Maurier French Limericks, written and illustrated by that gifted being.

"You know that book of mine you said Lady Crosse enjoyed

having read to her while she was so ill, at the end," said Mrs. Morland to her host, "the one where the Indian Ranee asks if she can come as a mannequin for a few weeks and turns out to be a Russian agent in disguise, and you said you had lost her copy. I found I had a spare one, so I brought it for you. The cover is rather dirty but one could put some brown paper over it."

"How *very* kind of you," said Lord Crosse, with real feeling. "My wife did so enjoy it, and specially the part where Gandhi's agent disguises himself as a Russian agent and tries to kidnap the Russian agent who is disguised as the Indian Ranee and Madame Koska locks them both in the stock-room and they try to set fire to it but your wonderful detective knew they were going to do it so he had sprayed everything in the stock-room with a secret preparation that stops things getting burnt and luckily they both shoot each other."

"I *am* so glad your wife liked it," said Mrs. Morland, who felt that "Lady Crosse" was perhaps a little formal now that she had got to talk to Lord Crosse so easily. "I do wish I had known her."

"So do I," said Lord Crosse, "at least I mean I wish she had had the great pleasure of knowing you. And now that you are here, will you be so kind as to write your name in your books? She always wanted to write to you about them, but felt shy," at which flattering words Mr. Morland felt rather shy herself, but said she would love to.

"Then after lunch, if you will really be so kind," said Lord Crosse, at which moment the booming of the gong, an instrument on which Peters performed as a past-master, filled their ears and indeed most of the house. Such indeed was its booming that young Mr. Crosse came into the library not only unseen, as his father and Mrs. Morland were looking out at the garden, but also unheard. Amused by their conversation he slipped further into the room with intent to listen and saw Edith sitting on a footstool with her Punch, so he went over to her.

Edith looked up, but the gong made speech impossible, so she smiled and shook her head.

"Aren't these heavenly, John-Arthur," she said as the dying fall of the gong at last made speech possible. "Look at this one, about the Nightmare."

"Is that the one that begins 'Jument de la nuit, ombre sombre'?" said Mr. Crosse. "I used to write them out for French impositions and it made M. Dupont furious. He was frightfully particular about punctuality and we used to call him Dupont de l'Heure."

"After that boring deputy one had to learn about in history?" said Edith.

"Goodness, my girl! what a lot you know," said Mr. Crosse. "That's the one, Dupont de l'Eure, and why his name stuck in our boyish minds, I don't know, or in your girlish mind either. But it's funny that we both know."

"I think rather nice," said Edith primly, and she got up and handed the Punch to Mr. Crosse who bowed and put it back in its place and went over to say how do you do to Mrs. Morland, with apologies for being a little late. Then, after giving her and Edith a questioning look which in modern English meant "Shall I top up your glass?" and getting a shake of the head in reply, he filled his own glass.

"Bring it in, boy," said his father kindly. "You know what Peters is" and he led the way with Mrs. Morland. Mr. Crosse winked at Peters, who was steadily observing a point just above Mr. Crosse's left eyebrow, and followed the grown-ups into the dining-room where lunch was at a round table in the large bay window, much more comfortable for four than the big mahogany table, even without its extra leaves.

"I say, John-Arthur," said Edith as they sat down. "How grown-up do you feel?"

Mr. Crosse said he hadn't the faintest idea and what did she mean.

"Well," said Edith, having first given an ear to what she still secretly called The Grown-Ups and found them well away on the subject of the newly discovered sewer at Rising Castle, "I mean I really feel *quite* grown-up now mostly, anyway at the Towers, or when I was with Uncle David and Aunt Rose in New York, but somehow the minute I get home I am un-grown-up again."

"Quite normal," said Mr. Crosse. "Home is the last place where one is grown-up. I'm really pretty independent—I mean I could quite well afford not to live at home and sometimes I wish I did—or do I mean didn't. But while mother was ill I couldn't suddenly move out for good and then she died and father was alone. I did have a kind of bachelor lodgings last year at the bank's temporary offices in Hatch End—"

"I remember, of course," said Edith, "and how mother wanted to re-arrange the whole house for nurseries which was rather a work of supererogation as you were a bachelor."

"Indeed I remember that," said Mr. Crosse. "I do adore Lady Graham."

"Everyone does," says Edith, simply as one stating a fact.

"Everyone meaning Everyone?" said Mr. Crosse.

"Don't try to muddle me, John-Arthur," said Edith, with a kind of appeal in her voice which Mr. Crosse couldn't quite understand.

"Far be it from me to be the last man in the world to do so," said Mr. Crosse sententiously, giving a quick look at Edith who remarked with the primness which it amused Mr. Crosse to provoke: "Fallacy of the Undistributed Middle and that's Logic because Mr. Carton at Harefield told me so. Or if it wasn't that it was something else," she added, beginning to laugh. So Mr. Crosse laughed too and their talk went back to the Old Manor House in Hatch End which belonged to Squire Halliday and had lately been for a short time the home of a branch of the Barchester bank of which Lord Crosse was a director.

"You know my father has got a long lease of the house from the Hallidays now," said Mr. Crosse, "and my elder married sister is just moving in. She has some children—I never quite know how many—which I find very expensive."

Edith asked why.

"Being an uncle," said Mr. Crosse. "Two married sisters with families are extremely expensive. Birthdays and Christmases. But some people are born to be uncles."

"And some to be aunts," said Edith. "I've got all Emmy's children—that's my eldest sister who married Tom Grantly and knows all about cows at Rushwater—and one of Clarissa's that married Charles Belton at Harefield. But she's sure to have more. We are highly prolific on the female side."

"Ridiculous girl," said Mr. Crosse, though very kindly. "And how many are *you* going to have?"

"Two of each anyway," said Edith, "but I haven't decided if I'll get married or not," and she looked quickly at Mr. Crosse and away again; rather deliberately, we fear.

"Nor have I," said Mr. Crosse calmly, at which Edith had to laugh.

Meanwhile Mrs. Morland and Lord Crosse were having a delightful talk about books and the wonderful moment when Sherlock Holmes had burst upon their young lives.

"My parents," said Lord Crosse, "had the original editions with pictures by Sydney Paget."

"I and my brother used to buy The Hound of the Baskervilles as it came out in the Strand Magazine every month," said Mrs. Morland. "The Strand was a reasonable size then and you could get it for fourpence halfpenny instead of sixpence at some shops, I can't think why. And now it is dead."

"Not quite, is it?" said Lord Crosse. "I have an impression that I saw it at my dentist's not long ago."

"Worse than death," said Mrs. Morland in her deepest and most impressive voice. "It looks like a Digest now. And why Digest I have never known."

Mr. Crosse, on hearing these words rather meanly deserted Edith and plunged into the conversation to ask what Mrs. Morland meant.

"Exactly what those words always connote," said Mrs. Morland, thus impressing all her hearers, "though I daresay I am not saying what I mean because I find one mostly doesn't. I believe," she added in a very learned way, "that what I mean is lucus a non lucendo. Though exactly what that means," she added, to the further confusion of the Crosses, "I do not know either."

"I wish more than ever that you had known my wife," said Lord Crosse when he had finished laughing—not but that his laughter was very kind. "That was just the kind of way she liked to talk. Her mind worked so quickly that I was nearly always a yard behind."

"I think *your* mind is a bit like that, John-Arthur," said Edith, eyeing Mr. Crosse in an impersonal way, and then the talk changed to the extreme horribleness of Lord Aberfordbury—he who was Sir Ogilvy Hibberd and had been so signally routed by old Lord Pomfret over the matter of Pooker's Piece.

"One wouldn't mind the fellow so much if he would stick to his own business," said Lord Crosse. "I'm a business man myself and find his various speculations interesting if not always sound. But now he is trying to get onto the West Barsetshire County Council there will be no holding him."

"Away with such a fellow from the earth" said Mrs. Morland thereby impressing her hearers, who much to their discredit did not recognize the reference.

Edith said it would be very nice if Lord Aberfordbury would marry the Dreadful Dowager, by which name Victoria, Lady Norton, was known to most of the county. This was followed by a very pleasant discussion as to which people they didn't like should be married, whether they wished it or not, to other people equally disagreeable, Mr. Crosse being judged the winner by his proposed union of the Bishop's wife—supposing his lordship to be dead and buried—to Mr. Harvey of the Ministry of Interference, with the rider that Mr. Harvey's sister, a determined civil service careerist, should marry the more disagreeable of the two Barchester cobblers in Barley Street.

As lunch drew to an end Edith, who had answered Mr. Crosse's last remarks rather vaguely, addressed her host with the words, "Oh, Lord Crosse, could I ask you something?"

Lord Crosse said he was sure she could.

"It is just about your butler," said Edith. "You see he was at the Towers for ages and I think it would be Tact if I called on him in his pantry. Of course I don't really remember old Uncle Giles, but I know mother had a talk with Peters when she was here last year, so if I had one today I could say she sent him her kind regards."

Mr. Crosse remarked aloud to himself "Little Liar."

"No, John-Arthur, diplomatist," said Edith primly. "Peters will like me to come because it's The Family, and *then* he will like it if you invite me again."

Lord Crosse said gravely that it was an excellent idea and would doubtless improve his own status with Peters. Mrs. Morland began to laugh, though very kindly, and Edith felt her cheeks peony-red, though to the unbiased eye of young Mr. Crosse they wore a very becoming pink flush.

"Look here," he said, seeing her slight embarrassment, "this would be quite a good moment. He will be putting the silver away. Come along and I'll present you. May I leave you with my Papa, Mrs. Morland?" to which Mrs. Morland, amused, said By all means and the two went off together.

"As our young people have deserted us, Mrs. Morland, shall we go to my wife's sitting-room?" said Lord Crosse. "I keep it much as it was and I should like you to see your own books which gave her so much pleasure," which suggestion pleased Mrs. Morland greatly and her host took her upstairs to a large pleasant room on the first floor overlooking the garden.

"This used to be a bedroom," said Lord Crosse, "but when my wife was an invalid I had it made into a sitting-room for her, as it opens into her bedroom. She was able to spend a good deal of time here till the last few weeks. I had that book-case specially made for her" and he showed Mrs. Morland a book-case near the window, almost entirely filled with her own works.

"OH! Lord Crosse" was all she could say.

"I think she had all your books," said Lord Crosse with some pride. "She bought them as they came out. In fact she had a standing order with her bookseller for two copies every time."

"Not *two!*" said Mrs. Morland.

"Yes, always two," said Lord Crosse. "Will you have a cigarette?"

"Oh thank you so much, but I don't know how to smoke," said Mrs. Morland.

"Nor did my wife," said Lord Crosse, "so I rather got out of the habit myself, except of course for a pipe when I was about the place. Yes, she always bought two copies, one for her bedroom and one for her sitting-room, but she wouldn't lend them to anyone."

"Quite right," said Mrs. Morland in a firm tone.

"Oh, really?" said Lord Crosse. "I thought it was a help to authors if one lent one of their books to a friend. I mean it would encourage people to read them."

"Now, my dear Lord Crosse," said Mrs. Morland, though to Lord Crosse's not insensitive ear the word dear sounded slightly ominous, "does it ever occur to you why people write books?"

"Well, I hadn't much thought about it," said Lord Crosse. "I had a sort of idea they wanted to express themselves. Not all, of course, so charmingly as you do."

"My dear good man," said Mrs. Morland with a patience far more alarming than any kind of umbrage, "practically all of us write to educate our children, or help our grandchildren, or supplement our small incomes, or to be able to travel. Not for the sake of Literature."

"I'm afraid I'm rather unliterary," said Lord Crosse meekly and obviously surprised.

"I don't think the word literary means anything at all, except names—like the Times Literary Supplement," said Mrs. Morland firmly. "Of course I don't know what other people feel like, but when my husband—who was quite nice but really very uninteresting—died, I had to do something so I wrote books."

"But you must always have had it in you," said Lord Crosse.

"I daresay I had," said Mrs. Morland, "but you can have things in you for ages only they don't come out, so you don't know they are there. I wrote a story about a dressmaker's shop, in a kind of desperation, and then Adrian Coates saw it and said it was so bad that it was worth publishing. So after that I wrote a book every year till it got into a kind of habit. About twenty-five there are now, not counting one or two extras that weren't about Madame Koska."

"Now, what were those extra books—those off the record books if you prefer it—I wonder," said Lord Crosse. "Not of course if you would prefer to remain anonymous, like Lady Silverbridge who goes on writing as Lisa Bedale. What about that Life of Molly Bangs?"

Mrs. Morland, a middle-aged woman with four grown-up sons and a considerable reputation as someone who could be relied on to produce a Nice Book regularly every year, sat and stared at her host, going gently red in the face.

"Not if you would rather not talk about it," said Lord Crosse. "Personally I think it is charming. Just enough solid fact—and your own delightful brand of humour. It was my wife who spotted it as yours. She bought three copies, because she said it would be a Rare Book one day. I mean in a *nice* way," he added hastily.

"It was really because I hadn't much to do that year," said Mrs. Morland. "I had done my Madame Koska book. Then I came across Molly Bangs in some old Memoirs and thought she was worth following up. She lived at hack and manger with half the aristocracy. So then I thought I'd find out some more. So I went to London for a bit—I used to have a small flat there—and researched like anything, really just for fun."

"But why did you write it under another name?" said Lord Crosse.

"It all came of the circulating libraries," said Mrs. Morland.

"You don't mean they would have *banned* it?" said Lord Crosse.

"Oh no, no such luck," said Mrs. Morland. "But if you write the same book over and over again as I do, people go on wanting the same book, so I didn't think it would be safe to write about someone who wasn't Madame Koska. So I thought Molly Bangs had better be by someone else and I invented Esme Porlock. He was quite a nice man, but a one-book man. He could never do it again."

"But could *you*?" said Lord Crosse.

"No," said Mrs. Morland. "But I really enjoyed going to places like the British Museum and the newspaper library at Hendon—that was before the war of course—and just reading and reading and then making notes in an exercise book which I always lost, or I couldn't read the notes."

" 'Philip. Ogygia. What did?' " said Lord Crosse, half aloud.

"OH! do you know 'Happy Thoughts'?" said Mrs. Morland. "I thought no one read it now."

"Both parts. Original editions," said Lord Crosse. "My wife had one too. That was partly why we got married. Here are hers," and he took from a shelf two small well-worn books, their red covers and general appearance bearing the marks of much reading. "Haven't you got them?"

"I did," said Mrs. Morland. "I suppose they got lost in some move. I *couldn't* have given them away. And anyway I am the only one of the family who would care for them now. Out of date," at which Lord Crosse made an indignant protest, saying that apart from motors and electric light and a few other slight differences, human nature was exactly the same.

"*It* may be. But ours isn't," said Mrs. Morland. "When you have grown-up children—who are just as trying as small children and much more expensive—you do change."

"I shall not contradict you," said Lord Crosse. "In fact I was pretty sure before I met you that you would be a person who changed—by which I don't mean a changeable person," he added. "You move with the times without effort. I thought my business—a kind of superior banking with which I won't bother you—kept one abreast of the times. But I feel an old stick-in-the-mud when I think of your versatility."

"I don't think it is very versatile to write the same book every year" said Mrs. Morland, determined not only to face the less agreeable facts of life but to invent them if necessary.

"I shall not argue," said Lord Crosse. "I shall merely stick to my own opinion. Thank you for coming up here. I always come and sit in this room with a sense of companionship, though she has left it. There will also now be your companionship," at which words Mrs. Morland felt a little of that delicious stinging behind the eyes which means that pleasant tears, idle tears, luxury tears are not far away and that one is going to have that heavenly and too rare feeling of the rapture of grief when it has really become nostalgia and will not leave a scar. "Let us go down and see what our young people are doing," said Lord Crosse. So they went down.

Meanwhile Edith had managed to have a very pleasant time, beginning with a visit to the pantry where Peters, in his apron, was putting the silver away, giving each spoon, fork, or salt-cellar a caressing massage with the shammy.

"I'm so glad Lord Crosse has proper silver, Peters," said Edith, taking the chair that Peters had dusted for her with one of his own Pantry Dusters. "It would be awful to have to do cheap silver."

"I believe you, miss," said Peters. "Like a good coachman having to learn to drive a cheap car when he's been used to horses. His lordship has quite a good show of plate. Not that I would compare it with what we had at the Towers, miss, but times do change and a baron is not the same as an earl, though a nicer gentleman than his lordship I would not wish to work for."

"Do you ever go to the Towers, Peters?" said Edith.

"I thought it better, miss, to make a Complete Break," said Peters. "It would be very painful to me, miss, to see his present lordship living in what were the Housekeeper's Rooms. I understand that his lordship—and of course her ladyship—are carrying on as one would wish in other ways. His young lordship was over here the other day. I understand that he and Mr. Crosse are trying to improve the flow of water in the Grotto. It is all done by Gravity, miss."

"Oh, I see," said Edith, rather wanting to know how, but feeling that Peters might be embarrassed if he had to try to explain.

"And when you are next at the Towers, miss," said Peters, "will you be so kind as to remember me in a suitable way to Miss Merriman. A lady I respect, miss. I've never seen anyone, man or woman, as could handle his lordship—I mean the late earl— the way she did, miss. Now, his late lordship, he *had* a temper, miss. I've heard him in the old days curse the coachman up hill and down dale because the carriage was a minute too early. 'When I say half-past two, I *mean* half-past two,' his lordship said. 'Not twenty-nine minutes past two, nor twenty-nine minutes to three. Why do you think I have the stable clock wound and set every week with all the house clocks? And if you can't bring the horses up punctually you can get another job,' his lordship said. Now, with his lordship you knew where you were," and he sighed at the thought of general degeneracy.

"I had a lovely time in New York this winter with Aunt Rose and Uncle David," said Edith. "They have a marvellous apartment in New York. A flat, you know."

"I did oblige young Lord Norton in his flat for two months in the Season before I came here, miss," said Peters. "But you cannot be expected to do justice to yourself in a flat, especially with a pantry as looked into a well. Why, the other servants there, if servants you could call them which they weren't worthy of the name, they joked across the well with the Honourable Miss Starter's maid."

"How *dreadful*," said Edith. "But Aunt Rose's apartment didn't have a well. It was a duplex—like a flat two stories high you know—and beautifully light everywhere."

Peters said darkly that wherever there was stairs there was trouble, whether it was the coals or the girls.

"And the houseman mixed lovely cocktails and wore a white coat," said Edith.

Peters said nothing at all, with considerable effect, and it became abundantly clear to Edith that she was not giving satisfaction.

"Of course here," she said lightly, "all that sort of thing would seem rather ridiculous, but in America with the time always being much later than ours one feels anything might happen."

"That's about it, miss," said Peters, ready in the cause of intellectual discussion to consider anyone's views provided that he had the last word. "But as I said to the boy, things may happen outside the pantry, I said, and that is their own affair, but what happens *in* the pantry happens *in* the pantry and the same applies, miss, to what the pantry sees. There was that time, miss, at the Towers when young Mr. Rivers—the one whose mother married the Honourable George Rivers and writes books though I have never read them—he made really what you would call a Scene on the front door steps and him and Mr. Wicklow—that is his present lordship's estate agent—had what you might call a frackass because Mr. Rivers wished to go to Nutfield to have his hair cut when there was not room in the car for another passenger when Mr. Rivers tried to get in. Mr. Wicklow pushed him off the running board. There was a young footman on approval at the time miss, and when he saw Mr. Wicklow push Mr. Rivers off the car, he so far forgot himself as to Look At Me."

"How dreadful!" said Edith, hoping that this was the right thing to say.

"You may well say that, miss," said Peters. "Of course I could not demean myself to look back at him, for I could see that he would have winked at me."

"Not at *you*, Peters," said Edith.

"Yes, indeed, miss," said Peters. "I looked straight through him miss, but conveying to him at the same time, if I make myself clear, that what he had done was only human nature and, I may say, human nature at its best, miss. Mr. Rivers was never asked to the Towers again."

"And was it really your fault—I mean was it because of you that he wasn't asked again?" said Edith.

"Well, miss, it is not for me to speak," said Peters who had been doing so with much enjoyment, "about what goes on in my employer's house, whether he is an earl or a baron, or even an honourable, but Mr. Rivers was never invited again miss, so one can draw one's own allusions."

"Mother says he is dreadful—I mean Julian Rivers," said Edith, "and she won't go to see his picture exhibitions. I say, Peters, I *have* enjoyed seeing you, and mother will simply love to hear about you. I'm staying with Mrs. Morland, but I'll tell mother as soon as I get home. Do you know where they all are?"

"His lordship has, I believe, taken Mrs. Morland to see her late ladyship's sitting-room upstairs, miss," said Peters. "Mr. Crosse is in the library, I think."

"Then I'll go and find him," said Edith. "Good-bye Peters and I'll tell mother all about our talk," and she held out her hand.

Peters wiped the plate polish off his hand and shook hers, with more warmth, we think, than he would have shown to anyone else; perhaps with a feeling that she had the root of the matter in her where a proper manner of living was concerned and would carry the torch whose scared flame he, Peters, had so long and faithfully tended. Then he put away his silver, gave a last look round to see that all was well and went to his own sitting-room where it was his habit on Sundays to put on a disgracefully shabby old shooting-jacket, formerly the property of the old earl, its leather patches almost falling off the elbows and cuffs, and in an old basket-work chair, brought by him from Pomfret Towers, to read all the more revolting of the Sunday papers from cover to cover till tea-time.

After the friendly and almost cosy atmosphere of Peters's room the house felt to Edith rather large and echoing and chill, for some large houses have a way of keeping their insides in cold storage, as it were, through the hottest weather. She had hoped to find Mrs. Morland, but if Mrs. Morland was with Lord Crosse, she felt rather shy about going upstairs to find her. Had it been her own mother, she would have pursued her cheerfully, but Mrs. Morland wrote books, which to Edith seemed something almost magical, and though she was very happy with her hostess she did not wish to appear pushing. As she crossed the hall a tall figure came in from the garden.

"Hullo, Ludo," she said. "I didn't know you were here."

"Well, I didn't know you were here either," said Lord Mellings. "I've got some leave today so I came over to the Towers and they had all gone to Gatherum for the weekend, so I rang up your mother and she said you were with Mrs. Morland at High Rising, so I rang her up and whoever answered it said you were here. So I came along. I was looking for John-Arthur. Is he anywhere about?"

No whit disturbed by her cousin's openly expressed preference for Mr. Crosse's company as against her own, Edith said she had been talking with Peters in his pantry and was looking for John-Arthur herself.

"Oh, good old Peters," said Lord Mellings. "I adore it when he talks about My Room and My Silver. I'll look him up before I go. Come on and we'll find John-Arthur," who was found with no difficulty as he was sitting in the library trying to do the cross-word puzzle in a Sunday paper.

"Hullo, Ludo," he said. "Are you any good at cross-words?

This is one of those ghastly ones where you have to black in the black squares yourself and there aren't any clues," but Lord Mellings said he only knew that if you got one black square in one place you had to get three other black squares in three other places that were in exactly the same place as the first one only in the other corners. And even then, he added, you weren't any forrader.

"Oh, confound the whole thing," said Mr. Crosse, crumpling the newspaper and throwing it at the waste-paper basket. "Oh, sorry, did anyone want it?" but no one did, or had, or wanted to, so they all went into the garden where Mr. Crosse showed them—though not at all in a boring way—various improvements that his father had made, or was thinking of making. And then they went by winding paths up the hill to the clearing in the wood where the Grotto stood, as it, or something very like it, still stands in many country estates. He went outside, turned a tap in the long grass and then unlocked the door and stood aside to let his guests pass. It was all as Edith remembered it; the light tempered (or as our formerly lively neighbours the Gauls say, sieved) by the thick green glass in the Gothic windows, the basin on a pedestal, and in the basin a small lead figure of a child holding a jar on its shoulder. But from the jar there was not a delicate arch of water. Only a little green damp in the basin spoke of its past glory.

"It's a question of the water-supply," said Mr. Crosse. "Something's happened to the pressure. I'll try turning it on again.

"There!" said Mr. Crosse. "The water used to spout out like anything. Old Admiral Palliser at Hallbury said I could clean the pipe with a spang-rod. I'd never heard of the thing nor had anyone else, but I met Mrs. Adams the other day—remarkable woman she is—and she said she could get me one from her husband. I wish she would. I'll try ringing her up again."

Lord Mellings said it might be worth having a look at the pipe from the top end to see if any of it was above ground.

"Good idea," said Mr. Crosse. "Come up to the spring," and

he led the way along a path half covered by a tangle of grass and weeds to where a little spring bubbled out of the ground some fifty yards higher up the hill.

"Rum things, these springs," said Mr. Crosse. "You'd think water lived underground. How on earth does it get up here?"

"There's one right up near the top of Coniston Old Man, or Wetherlam. I forget which," said Edith. "I saw it when mother took us to stay with our cousins up there. And the high ground between Watendlath and Thirlmere is much boggier than the low ground."

Mr. Crosse said, not very hopefully, perhaps it got syphoned up, but as he didn't know exactly what he meant, it was just as well that Edith and Lord Mellings were arguing about the water supply at Pomfret Towers.

"Well, I don't know how it got upstairs when old Uncle Giles was alive," said Lord Mellings, alluding to his father's predecessor, "but it's all done by an electric pump now. Mr. Adams had it put in when Amalgamated Vedge took over."

Mr. Crosse said if there were a mountain in the neighbourhood one might be able to get water from the top of it by gravity, but was unequal to explaining what he meant, though he assured his hearers that it was perfectly clear. Lord Mellings, who had inherited his father's slow and patient way of dealing with problems as they came, suggested that they should, if possible, follow the pipe downwards, even if it did mean going through the nettles. Accordingly they did so and as the pipe was mostly above ground it was not difficult. About twenty yards above the Grotto it vanished into a thick bed of nettles.

Without any further words Lord Mellings took a pair of bicycle trouser clips out of his jacket pocket, clipped them round his ankles and walked into the nettles. Presently he stopped.

"Hi, Edith! chuck me a stick," he called. "A strong one if you can find one. One never ought to come out without a stick."

By great good luck Edith found a fairly straight branch which she threw towards her cousin. After beating about in the tangle of long grass and weeds he stood up and stretched his long legs.

"Here you are, John-Arthur," he said. "Water spouting out of the pipe nicely. No wonder the fountain-thing didn't work. I'll leave the stick here for a mark. Do you think you could find it again?"

Mr. Crosse, who though pleased that the leak had been detected was rather ashamed that a guest, and one who, though this was nothing at all of course to do with the matter, was Edith's cousin, should have solved the mystery, said he would easily find the place now that he knew where it was, and what a fool he was not to have noticed it before.

"Are you hungry now, Ludo?" said Edith, who with three elder brothers was used to young men being perpetually ready for meals.

"I really don't know," said Lord Mellings. "I suppose I am. I didn't have any breakfast because I wanted to see the Keeper about that vixen," which to Edith sounded so grown-up that her whole view of her cousin Ludo suddenly changed. Ludo, always so much taller than she was; so slow in the uptake though he was awfully nice; never really loving horses as his brother Giles did; this Ludo talking about vixens as if he had lived with game-keeprs all his life.

"Lord!" said Mr. Crosse, "you don't mean to say she's been over your way?"

"As far as Boxall Hill, anyway," said Lord Mellings. "You can't mistake her. There must be a trail of feathers all over the county. But that's the East Barsetshire's business, my boy, so I thought I'd let you know, as Mr. Gresham is your Master over this way."

Loyal as Edith was to the tradition of preserving and hunting foxes, this was really too much. Was she to be ignored by John-Arthur whom she had thought she liked, and by Ludo, who, although the exact degree of cousinship was too tangled to follow, was kin through Gran, she who was Lady Emily Foster before she was Lady Emily Leslie and for all her long, happy married life continued to think of Pomfret Towers as Home? It was intolerable. Ludo was a dear and nice cousin, but there *were* chords in the human breast—limits to what one could put up with even from a nice cousin. So she deliberately lagged behind the young men, nursing her grievance and wondering why she minded anything so stupid, and finding with an uncomfortable kind of pleasure that they had gone on to the stables without even asking her if she would like to come too. Full of such thoughts—black and of course eternal when one is barely eighteen—she went crossly to the house and looked in at the library window. Inside the library Mrs. Morland and Lord Crosse could plainly be seen, seated at a small table. Tea-things were on the table, and what looked like particularly nice cakes, so Edith swallowed her grievances and tapped at the French window.

Lord Crosse looked round, saw her, got up and opened the window.

"Come and have tea," he said. "It has only just been made. And where have you been?"

Edith, already ashamed of her spurt of temper, said she had been to look at the Temple with John-Arthur and Ludo, and they had found where the leak was and John-Arthur was going to get it mended and then he and Ludo had gone round to the stables and she had come back; which was all fairly true but did not, to Mrs. Morland, adequately account for Edith's ruffled manner, so very unusual in her. However this was not the moment to enquire into Edith's girlish troubles, so she went on with the talk which Edith's arrival had interrupted.

"But, Lord Crosse, you don't mean to say that Mr. Gresham is really not going to stand for Parliament again?" said Mrs. Morland, evidently taking up a conversation that Edith's arrival had interrupted.

"He is as obstinate as a White Porkminster," said Lord Crosse, half annoyed with Mr. Gresham, half amused by his own annoyance. "He says he has represented East Barsetshire for nearly half a century and it's time some new blood came in. That's all very well, but where's the new blood to come from? And it isn't everyone who can afford Parliament now. All very well for men like Adams who has the health of a bull and all his business interests behind him, but our younger men here are working hard to keep their wives and families and haven't leisure for politics."

"But couldn't John-Arthur stand?" said Edith. "He doesn't have to work for his wives and families."

"Quite true," said Lord Crosse. "He is not really interested in politics, but apart from the bank, where I believe he is giving satisfaction, he likes county work. In fact I hope to see him on the East Barsetshire County Council before long. And of course at any moment he might have a wife, probably followed by a family."

"Do you mean he is engaged to someone?" said Edith, slightly piqued by the idea, though in a perfectly Platonic way.

"Not so far as I know," said Lord Crosse, amused by the child's practical way of considering the question. "But they tell one nothing now. Excellent friends but they keep one in one's place. Do you find that, Mrs. Morland?" which was kindly said to bring that lady back into the conversation. "About one's children, I mean."

"Oh, one's children," said Mrs. Morland, who had not been listening very closely. Not that she found the talk uninteresting, but an idea had suddenly come into her head—apropos of nothing at all and formed by the strange other self that lives inside us and goes quietly about its own business till it suddenly erupts without warning—for a slight improvement in the female villain of her new book and she wanted to fix it in her memory. Sometimes she had thought it would be a good idea to keep a small notebook in her bag and jot down any useful thoughts that occurred to her, but when, after a few weeks, she came to look at the book she found that she had only made three notes of which two were by now perfectly unintelligible to her and the third illegible, with a large question mark after it.

"One's children," she repeated, to gain time. "Well, all mine are sons, so I don't know about daughters. I can't exactly say that they keep me in my place, because I always *am* in my place. I mean I am very fond of them and of my grandchildren, but it is very nice not having them to stay. I expect with a house of this size they are less exhausting," and she looked round the library, evidently hoping to see some tangible and recognizable sign of grandchildren kept at bay.

"I really couldn't say," said Lord Crosse. "Luckily we have the old nurseries upstairs for grandchildren when required, but mine are still very small and not very many and now that my elder daughter has taken Mr. Halliday's charming house at Hatch End—the one that John-Arthur lived in for a few months when the bank had it—I am less likely to have grand-children here than when they lived in London. They used to come to stay."

"It seems rather waste of the nurseries," said Mrs. Morland, though more in sorrow than in anger, but at that moment the young men came in from the stables, very ready for tea and cake, and rather boring about the Grotto and its water supply—or so Edith thought. After all, one did not come to lunch at Crosse Hall simply to watch John-Arthur and Ludo looking for a hole in a pipe. But Lord Crosse and Mrs. Morland made such ample amends for her aloofness by the genuine interest they both took in the water supply to the Grotto that Edith, deciding to get over her pique, joined the talk and enjoyed herself, also making both the young men laugh by her way of puttings things— though one could hardly call John-Arthur young because he was as old as George Halliday and they had both been in the end of the war and must be quite thirty. And yet Ludo who was much younger than they were and not even a real soldier yet, seemed almost as grown-up. It was all very confusing and perhaps for the first time in her life Edith, the slightly spoilt youngest child, began to realize that life was not all beer and skittles, nor was its way always the way one meant to go. But these thoughts passed through her mind more swiftly and if possible even less intelligently than they have passed through our pen and melted like a cloud—though not in the silent summer heaven, for the sky was grey and there was now quite a nasty wind.

Mrs. Morland, who had also observed these natural phenomena, said she must take Edith back to High Rising, or they would find the roads too horribly crowded with cars going back to London. Edith, who had inherited from her mother a good sense of social obligations, asked Mr. Crosse if she could say good-bye to Peters and took her cousin Ludo with her, a visit which gave Peters great satisfaction, and Edith could not sufficiently admire the way in which Ludo quite kindly cut short Peters's flow of talk. Then Lord Mellings got into his little car and Edith got into Mrs. Morland's and they all drove to their homes.

CHAPTER 4

When Edith came down on Monday morning, having begged on the previous evening not to have breakfast in bed so that she could see more of her hostess, she found her dealing with a pile of letters and getting a good deal of butter on them not to speak of honey.

"Oh! Mrs. Morland, is that Fan-Mail?" said Edith. "Could I see some?"

"Certainly," said Mrs. Morland. "You can answer them for me, if you like, on my typewriter."

"Is it a Valiant?" said Edith, but it was a Greatheart and she wondered if she could pick up its methods easily. For although English-speaking typewriters have English-speaking type every one of them has tricks and arrangements peculiar to itself.

"I can't explain the way this one works because I only do it by heart," said Mrs. Morland. "I mean once I have mastered what things to move I can do it as long as I don't stop to think. But the moment I begin *thinking* what I'm doing I don't know what to do next. It is all extremely mortifying. Did you sleep well?"

"Oh, yes," said Edith, very nearly adding "of course" because so far in her life she had never—unless one counted toothache or the time she had chicken-pox—known anything beyond getting into bed at one end and waking up at the other, as it were.

"I rang your mother up after you had gone to bed last night," said Mrs. Morland "and she is going to call on Lord Crosse's married daughter at the Old Manor House this afternoon and asked if I would come too and bring you with me and then you can go home with her. I've never seen it, so that would be very pleasant. So this morning we will do whatever you like. Shall we go to lunch with Lord Stoke?"

"Oh, I'd love that," said Edith. "I know him a little, because he comes to see mother sometimes and he shocked Cook dreadfully because he came in by the kitchen door, but she was very proud about it really. He came to a Bring and Buy Sale once when I was quite young and he took some tickets in a raffle and won a hideous vase and he gave it to Leslie Major—that's one of my cousins that was in the cricket match on Saturday—but he had a fight with Leslie Minor and it got broken."

"It sounds *exactly* like a Bring and Buy Sale," said Mrs. Morland. "I think I was there too that day."

"I know you were there," said Edith, "because my sister Clarissa, the one that's Mrs. Charles Belton now, was there and you said you would send her a copy of your next book."

"Oh dear, and I didn't, did I?" said Mrs. Morland.

"Of *course* you did," said Edith, almost indignant with her hostess for such mistrust of herself. "And Clarissa boasted about it to everyone. She took it with her when she was married and went to live at Harefield," by which news Mrs. Morland appeared almost unreasonably flattered. For somehow to be liked by someone very young is flattering, but to have one of one's books (which one had thought to be only readable by grownups) liked by one of the young is extremely upsetting and makes one feel one is perhaps of some value after all.

"And I met Miss Merriman, Lady Pomfret's secretary," said Mrs. Morland. "I liked her so much and I want to have her to lunch one day, but she is always busy."

"She always will be," said Edith. "I don't mean," she added, going pleasantly pink in the face, "that she is busy because she doesn't want to see you. She is just busy. She is rather like those

water-flowers with very long stalks and they seem to move about
a good deal but they are always tied by one leg. She does come to
see mother because she lived at Holdings when Gran was there
in the war. But I don't think she visits anyone else unless she
goes with Sally when Sally asks her to. It is what one would call
a Dedicated Life" she added primly, on which Mrs. Morland's
comment was "Affected puss," which shows how well she and
her guest were getting on.

Accordingly Mrs. Morland rang up Rising Castle, the residence of Lord Stoke, thirteenth baron of that name. The castle
itself had a Norman keep in fair condition from outside,
though inside there was little except traces of the old stairway
which wound up between the outer wall and an inner wall of
which most had crumbled or was crumbling to pieces. The rest
of the building had been thriftfully used by the present owner's
great-grandfather who with material from the old building had
erected a comfortable mansion for himself. The remains of the
castle were now scheduled as a National Monument which
the public were allowed to visit at sixpence a head during the
summer months. This they did in quite large numbers, though
there was very little to see and most of the fabric bore notices
which said "Danger. Do not go any further," or "Private," or
"The Public are asked NOT to throw anything down the
outside shafts." But as the Public in general either cannot
read, or does not wish to, or takes all notices to be directed
against other people and not Itself, it went everywhere and
threw newspapers and cigarette ends and unwanted sandwiches
down the shafts like anything, of which rude and repulsive habit
Dr. Ford had said that the slope or glacis outside the castle on
the river side was probably now nearer its primitive condition
than it had ever been since interior plumbing was introduced.

The present residence of his lordship is only a stone's throw
(though this would depend upon what sort of stone and who
threw it) from the Castle and is quite hideous, though comfortable. Lord Stoke, who had never married and disliked change,

had kept everything more or less as it had been in his mother's lifetime, a lady of strong character who always went out in buttoned boots and for the whole of her life had them buttoned by her personal maid. His only remaining near relative was his half-sister Lucasta, Lady Bond—a form of address upon which her ladyship had insisted since her husband's death when her son and his very capable wife, niece of Mr. Middleton over at Skeynes, had come into the title. But she would have done better to let herself be known as the Dowager Lady Bond (even as old Lady Lufton had gladly done when her son married Lucy Robarts the sister of the parson) for the consequence was that the village, with the fine English gift for getting rank and titles wrong, mostly addressed her ladyship as Lady Lucasta, some of the more modern and subversive members even going so far as to call her—though never to her face—Lady Luke, in a very dashing way. But as she had never been called Lady Luke, neither she nor the county would have known what people were talking about.

Mrs. Morland was looked upon with favour by Lord Stoke's servants because she always asked after their wife, their husband, their children, or their bad leg, as the case might be and stood no nonsense from his lordship. With his lordship's present butler she was on particularly friendly terms, as his elder sister Annie had been for many years the faithful and very trying housemaid to George Knox. When George Knox married Anne Todd, she who was Mrs. Morland's secretary, he had secretly hoped that Annie would give notice, as faithful servants of a bachelor mostly do when another female is introduced into the establishment. But nothing was further from Annie's thoughts and after one or two stand-up fights with her mistress she had settled down nicely, recognizing in the new Mrs. Knox one of the ruling class.

"How are you, Albert?" said Mrs. Morland. "Miss Graham hasn't been here before. Her father is Sir Robert Graham over at Hatch End."

"Oh, how do you do, Albert," said Edith who, luckily for her, had no fears or inhibitions about servants, treating them as friends though with an invisible line drawn over which no well-trained servant ever stepped, realizing as that vanishing class did and still does, that nearly every human being is of value in his own sphere and that for a butler to take any liberty with even the youngest of his employer's guests would be almost as bad—though of course not quite—as if a guest took a liberty with his host's staff. "I think Mrs. Panter at Hatch End is a cousin of yours."

"That's right, miss," said Albert, "and I'm much obliged to you, I'm sure. She's a wonderful one at getting up shirts she is. I take his lordship's best dress shirts over to her and she gets them up lovely. It's a treat the way she does the fronts, miss."

"Does his lordship still dress for dinner then?" said Mrs. Morland.

"Oh *yes*, madam," said Albert, almost shocked by such ignorance in one who, although she wrote books, was an old friend of his lordship's and didn't pay no attention to his lordship when he was a bit waxy. "Every evening I put out his lordship's dinner jacket suit. His lordship has the two pairs of trousers for it, madam, with braid down the seam which I understand was quite the thing in his lordship's younger days, and I keep them nicely pressed, turn and turn about as they say, and I put the studs in his shirts, and lay out two black ties."

Mrs. Morland asked why two.

"Well, madam," said Albert, "his lordship doesn't hold with ready made up ties—and really, madam, one doesn't hardly know what to think things is coming to if gentlemen have made-up ties—and his lordship sometimes finds a little difficulty in tying the tie just the way he likes it tied, and I've seen his lordship throw three white ties—that was when we used to have proper dinner parties, madam, and his lordship was wearing his tails—on the floor because they didn't go the way he liked. But with the black ties we find the two are enough."

Though Edith could have listened with fascination to this conversation for ever, it was obvious that they could not spend the day in the hall. Her admiration for Mrs. Morland rose when that lady said two black ties were certainly enough and where was Lord Stoke.

"His lordship," said Albert, in a quite different voice, recalled by Mrs. Morland to his status as butler-valet, "was in the gun-room, madam, when I last seen him. If you and Miss Graham will come into the morning-room, madam, I will find his lordship."

Mrs. Morland said she would take Miss Graham to the morning-room, so Albert went to look for his employer.

"It's a very nice room," said Edith, "but not so grand as Lord Crosse's. And look, Mrs. Morland, the books are all in the wrong order here."

Anything to do with books, even their outsides, was a magnet to Mrs. Morland, who would sooner have read Bradshaw, or even one of Mrs. Rivers's novels, than not have a book to her hand.

"Oh dear," she said, "indeed they are. What a lovely set of Gibbon in that binding. It always makes me think of the Bible."

Edith said was that because the Bible ought to have very beautiful bindings because it was a Great Book.

"Oh dear me, no," said Mrs. Morland. "Not of course," she added quickly, lest she should be disturbing Edith's belief, "that I don't think it *oughtn't* to have a beautiful binding, because it ought. Only they will put it into that rather scrunchy, floppy, black binding and a cross on the front which is of course quite religious but so unnecessary because people who like to read it wouldn't mind what it was like outside, and often the edges of the pages all gilded which makes them stick together and you can't get them undone properly without blowing rather hard, which annoys people."

Edith said there was a really old Bible at Holdings and it was so heavy that no one ever used it, which made Mrs. Morland embark upon one of her snipe-flights and wonder if it would be better to have it on a lectern in the drawing-room.

"Well, not really," said Edith, "because it has become all crumbling with old age and the cover falls off if you open it. I mean the front cover does, but if you did open it at the wrong end then the end cover would come off. Mother keeps it on a table that Gran used to do her drawing and painting at and no one opens it, so it is quite safe."

"What's that?" said Lord Stoke who had come in while Edith was speaking. "How are you. Mrs. Morland? Well, young lady," he continued, addressing Edith, "what's all this about a safe, eh? You can't do better than Bubb's safes. Rum name Bubb. There was a feller called Bubb Dodington—queer thing, Mrs. Morland, the way things come back to you—and blest if you can remember anything about them. Haven't the ghost of an idea who the feller was."

Edith rather rashly said they couldn't really have come back to you if you couldn't remember anything about them. His lordship, taking these words for some form of acquiescence in what he had previously said, appeared pleased with her support and asked Mrs. Morland who she was.

"I. Told. You. Lord. Stoke," said Mrs. Morland, managing by a miracle of tact to keep all trace of impatience out of her voice. "Lady Graham's youngest girl. Her name is Edith. After old Lady Pomfret."

"She was old Pomfret's wife, the seventh earl," said Lord Stoke, who was Burke and Debrett rolled into one as far as Barsetshire families were concerned. "Handsome woman, she was. This girl of yours is going to be a good-looker, Mrs. Morland. Nice-stepping little filly."

"Not. My. Girl. Lord. Stoke," said Mrs. Morland, who saw that Edith, far from being annoyed at being called a filly, was slightly preening herself. "She is Lady Graham's youngest girl. She was in America this winter with the David Leslies."

"Bone lazy, that David Leslie," said Lord Stoke. "Living in

America. I never lived in America. Never went there in my life. My old mother never went there either. When she wanted to go abroad she went to Cannes, or to Florence. Dull place Florence, all full of people talking about art. So's Cannes; full of people you don't know. If I want a change I go up to London to my club. Lot of fellers there I've never seen—all the change I want. Well, what's the matter?" These last words were not directed against either of his guests, though Edith had almost jumped with the suddenness of his question, but to Albert who looked straight into space and said Lunch Was Served My Lord.

"Come along, come along," said Lord Stoke. "It's only the three of us, Mrs. Morland. I'm sorry, my dear," he added to Edith as they went to the dining-room, "that there isn't anyone young for you. But I'll tell you one thing, Mrs. Morland. My sister is *not* coming. She was up here two days ago hinting that she would like to come, but I couldn't hear her. She's gone to Bournemouth for the weekend. She ought to live there. Much better for everyone. And what do you like to drink, my dear?" he went on to Edith having by now quite accepted her as one of the small circle of his friends, which was lessening in the older ranks far too rapidly. "The claret isn't bad, and there is a nice hock. Don't care for it myself, but some people do. The port's all right," and he mentioned a name and year which meant nothing at all to Edith, so we shall not invent them.

Edith hesitated. She did not want wine, which she did not really like, and was wondering if it would be rude to say so when Albert, approaching Lord Stoke, said in a voice modelled on that of Mr. Simnet, butler to Canon and Mrs. Joram:

"I have orange juice here, my lord. Also lemonade. And there is iced water if the young lady would like it, or soda water, my lord."

Mrs. Morland knew that Albert was an excellent butler, but never before had she so fully realized his gifts. A voice which while perfectly clear did not at the same time imply—as our voice when speaking to the deaf so often does—that our hearer is not only deaf by nature, but also deliberately deaf and broadly speaking a congenital idiot.

"What? orange juice?" said his lordship, "and lemonade? All right, all right, you needn't shout. I'm not deaf. Which will you have, my dear?" he added with a kind of courtliness to Edith that surprised and pleased Mrs. Morland.

Edith said lemonade please.

"All right. Miss Graham will have lemonade," said Lord Stoke, assuming quite unnecessarily the part of intermediary between his guest and his butler. "And some ice, if you've got it."

"I am glad to say, my lord, that the fridge is in excellent order," said Albert who felt, not unreasonably, that his lordship was doing him out of his proper position as butler—even if he were single-handed and also his lordship's valet.

"You won't mind, my dear, if I call you Edith, I hope," said Lord Stoke to his young guest. "I have known your people off and on in the country for a very long time. I had great respect and affection for Lady Pomfret—Edith—who was your grand-mother's sister-in-law. I'm well over eighty, you know."

"Are you really?" said Edith. "When is your birthday?"

"First of October," said Lord Stoke. "My father was a very good shot, used to be asked to all the Gatherum shoots, so he told his man to call him early and went off in the dog-cart with his groom about six o'clock and had breakfast at Framley on the way with Lord Lufton. They had one of the best days they've ever had at Gatherum. I forget how many brace. So what with one thing and another he spent the night at Gatherum and sent the groom back to tell my mother to expect him next morning about twelve. So when he got home he told the butler to tell her ladyship he was back and the butler said: 'I'm sorry, my lord, but your lordship has a son and her ladyship and the young Honour-able are doing very well,' 'Are they, by God?' said my father, 'then get me some lunch and bring the '64 port and you can open a bottle of the '63 for the servants' hall.' Now, *was* it the '63? I forget everything now, but I know it was a poor vintage, so the butler gave the servants' hall a bottle of the poor port and drank the rest of my father's port himself. My father spotted it though, when he was going through the wine with the butler and the cellar book."

"So what did he do?" said Edith.

"Said he'd never heard such a good story against himself before," said Lord Stoke, "and old Lord Pomfret—I don't mean this man's uncle but *his* father—said it was the best story he had ever heard."

Mrs. Morland said aloud to herself that the sixth earl must have been a relation of Mr. Peter Magnus's friends, but as neither Lord Stoke nor Edith heard her, and we doubt whether either of them would have picked up the allusion, she kept it to herself.

Having disposed of the Pomfrets, Lord Stoke went on, via the story he had already told about his own birth, to the Omniums. Mrs. Morland, though not Barsetshire by birth, had so well assimilated the county during her life at High Rising that she could hold her own pretty well, but she had to confess to herself that before Lord Stoke she was but as a child picking up pebbles on the beach. Edith also was listening, fascinated, with all her ears, and trying swiftly to memorize stories that she knew her mother would like. Stories some of which her mother would be able to cap, or supplement, some of which she would add to her hereditary knowledge of families and relationships.

"Rum thing how blood does tell," said Lord Stoke. "I was talking to Sir Edmund Pridham and he must be a good ten years older than I am now. I've forgotten what we were talking about. Probably about one thing and another as one does. What the dickens was it I was going to say?" he added crossly. "*You* ought to know, Mrs. Morland. You write books. Have to remember a lot of things to write books. Can't think how you do it. And get them published too. Old Lord Pomfret got his book published. How do people get books published, Mrs. Morland?"

"Are you writing one then?" said Edith, rather pertly her hostess thought.

"No, no. Not in my line," said Lord Stoke. "I was thinking of old Lord Pomfret—this man's cousin but of a much older generation—Pomfret speaks of him and his wife as uncle and aunt, but that's not the real relationship. Never mind. Do you remember Lady Pomfret—I mean the seventh earl's wife— Mrs. Morland?"

But Mrs. Morland, though she had seen her at various functions, had never met her.

"She was a countess, every inch of her," said Lord Stoke. "Port for you, Mrs. Morland? No? And not for Miss Edith I presume. All right, Albert. You can leave the port in front of me. You ladies will not think it uncivil if I drink alone?"

Mrs. Morland said she would willingly pay sixpence *not* to drink port on any day of the year. Edith added, rather primly, that it was not a wine for ladies.

"So that is what you think, young lady?" said his lordship, much amused. "Let me tell you that my dear mother had a glass of port wine and a sweet biscuit at eleven o'clock in the morning every day of her life. Said it was medicinal. So did all her women friends. And how they enjoyed their medicinal drink."

"Did Lady Pomfret—I mean the one you were talking about, Lord Stoke, have port at eleven too?" said Edith.

"Probably," said Lord Stoke. "But in those days the men didn't see much of the women till the afternoon in the big houses, especially in the shooting seasons."

"Like Disraeli," said Edith, full of excited interest.

"Dizzy? Before my time," said Lord Stoke. "None of our people knew him. Queer bird, but by Gad! he made England respected," which expletive gave intense pleasure to both his guests.

"I only wondered," said Edith, "because I've been reading his political novels and it all sounds just like what you were saying.

I mean the women not seeing the men till after lunch, or whatever they called it. Time is *very* mixing."

"Much better plan not to see the women till after lunch," said Lord Stoke unchivalrously.

"And much more fun for the women too," said Edith, "because they could have lovely talks to one another about the men, and laugh at them."

"I daresay you are right, my dear," said Lord Stoke. "You are nearly a woman yourself now. She was Edith too."

"Who was?" said Edith, rather perplexed. Mrs. Morland, informed by the novelist's unaccountable sixth sense that more was going on than she could at the moment grasp, waited for enlightenment to come.

"Lady Pomfret. The wife of the seventh earl. She was Edith Thorne. The Thornes were one of our very old Barsetshire families, as good blood as any in the county, or outside it for that matter," said Lord Stoke, fingering his glass of port and speaking rather to himself than to Edith. "She and Pomfret didn't get on too well. They lost their only son, Mellings, in some Indian border skirmish, when he was only a subaltern. People said it would bring them together, but it didn't," said his lordship with a kind of triumph over people who said things.

"You don't mean they quarreled, Lord Stoke?" said Edith.

"Quarreled? Nothing to quarrel about," said Lord Stoke. "She hadn't any money of her own—the Thornes never had much, but they had blood—and Pomfret settled something very handsome on her. She used to go to Italy every winter to the Casa Strelsa. Guido Strelsa, that cousin of Pomfret's, lent it to her. Now he *was* a scoundrel, if you like. Turned out of pretty well every gambling hall in Europe. He and Pomfret couldn't get on at all, but he admired Lady Pomfret and lent her the villa whenever she wanted it. Edith Thorne—yes indeed," and his lordship was silent.

Edith did not understand and we doubt whether even Mrs. Morland quite understood, so they also were silent. Then Edith remembered that her mother said one oughtn't to let the conversation come to a complete stop, even if one said something silly. So she summoned up her courage and said: "Lord Stoke, if I had some port—I mean really a *very* little—could we drink Lady Pomfret's health—I mean the Lady Pomfret that was Edith?"

Lord Stoke, coming out of the depths of his silence, listened courteously to his young guest. There was a silence and Edith wished she had not spoken. Mrs. Morland, suddenly faced by a side of her old friend quite strange to her, found nothing to say either.

"Here!" said Lord Stoke, at which word of power Albert immediately appeared. "The special port and clean glasses."

Albert, already in his mind improving his lordship's words for repetition in the servants' hall, went to get the wine. Edith, feeling something she could not understand, looked to Mrs. Morland for guidance, but Mrs. Morland, though she thought she could guess what was happening, also thought it wiser not to try to explain. So she smiled at Edith in a way that to Edith's quick eye and mind evidently conveyed what she wished to convey and both guests sat silent. Albert came back bearing a bottle as an acolyte might have borne the Grail and set it before Lord Stoke. His lordship poured out a little for himself, ceremoniously went through the ritual of tasting and told Albert he could go, which Albert did with a mixture of willingness to get to the servants' hall and tell the company what was happening and unwillingness to leave a scene which—or so he afterwards said—was nearly as good as Glamora Tudor's new film "They Loved too Well" where someone called Treestarn drank wine out of an empty goblet and gave the rest to the heroine whose name was Essolda, just like the Essoldo cinema in Barley Street.

"I should like to give you some of this port, Mrs. Morland," said Lord Stoke. "You will never taste anything like it again" for which Mrs. Morland felt truly grateful, for like many good women she found all ports exactly alike and the good ones just as nasty as the bad ones.

"And you too, young lady," he added, kindly pouring only half a glass for Edith. "I should like you both to drink the health of a very great lady: Edith Thorne." He raised his glass and drank. Mrs. Morland, who of course was by now almost in tears with emotion, repeated the name and drank and Edith followed her example, perplexed, vaguely feeling that something rather solemn and special was happening and at the same time forming a determination not to tell her mother about it if she could avoid the question, because it seemed rather private.

Then there was a short silence which somehow reminded Edith of the silence on Armistice Day, broken by Lord Stoke who said in quite an ordinary voice: "And now, young woman, we'll drink your health and you must come again to Rising Castle. Get Mrs. Morland to bring you."

Mrs. Morland, relieved that Lord Stoke had returned to normal life, drank Edith's health willingly and then Edith said she thought they ought to drink to Lord Stoke's health, which appeared to give his lordship considerable pleasure.

"We must go now," said Mrs. Morland. "I have to take Edith over to Hatch End. We are going to meet Lady Graham there and call on Lord Crosse's married daughter who has taken the Old Manor House."

"Good house," said Lord Stoke, who knew more about the dwellings of Barsetshire inside and out than any other man alive. "Belongs to the Hallidays. They're good stock too. Always stuck to the farm. How are your father's pigs, young lady?"

This question brought everything back comfortably to earth, and Mrs. Morland said again that she and Edith must really go.

"Well, my dear, it was good of you to come and see an old man," said Lord Stoke to Edith. "Enjoyed my talk with you. Pity Edith—Lady Pomfret—couldn't have seen her name sake. She would have got on with you. We used to think she was too good for Pomfret. Artistic and all that sort of thing. But it's queer as you get older," said his lordship, who could not but remember such things, "you forget so much and then you remember more than you thought you knew. Wait a moment. There's something I'd like to show you. Come this way," and he took them back to the morning-room, went to a small ma-hogany cabinet, fished a long chain with a bunch of keys at the end of it out of his trouser pocket and unlocked a drawer. In it were several rather shabby little red leather boxes. He took out one and opened it. Inside lay a necklace of small baroque pearls in which many colours were faintly adumbrated. He took it out and undid the little clasp, set with rose diamonds.

"It belonged to someone called Edith," he said. "I gave it to her, a great many years ago, but she gave it back to me. Pearls need wearing, you know, Miss Edith. So you wear them and tell your mother they belonged to her uncle's wife who was Edith Thorne. She'll know what I mean."

By this time Mrs. Morland, whose sympathetic mind felt the scene deeply, was quite ready to cry if encouraged. But as Lord Stoke appeared to be genuinely pleased by Edith's pleasure, and Edith herself, though slightly bewildered, was in the seventh heaven of delight, Mrs. Morland suppressed her wish for a delightful cry and said how the pearls were just right for Edith.

"Oh, THANK you, Lord Stoke," said Edith. "But I hope," she added rather anxiously, "that the Edith who wore them wouldn't mind. I shall tell mother all about it. Thank you again most *awfully*" and almost unconsciously she took Lord Stoke's hands and put up her face to be kissed, which his lordship immediately did with great good humour.

"Now, wait a moment," said Lord Stoke, as Mrs. Morland showed signs of wishing to get away. "Tell your mother, my dear, that these pearls are insured. I'll get my lawyer to have them insured in your name and send you the papers. Then if you lose them you'll be able to buy something else."

"But I don't *want* to lose them," said Edith. "I shall wear them *always*. Clarissa has some diamonds that mother gave her, but I don't like diamonds. I simply *love* the pearls, Lord Stoke."

"You would be very silly if you didn't, young lady," said Lord Stoke. "Come again, my dear. And mind you don't get married without my permission. Bring the young man here when he turns up. Perhaps he has turned up?"

"Oh *no*," said Edith. "I am excessively heart-free," which remark, primly made and—we may add—perfectly truthful, made Lord Stoke laugh in a loud though very kind way.

"And now you've got the pearls out of the old man, off you go" he said, in high good humour. "Good-bye, Mrs. Morland. Come and see me again before long and if you have anymore guests like Miss Edith, bring them too. But let me know a day or two beforehand and I'll make sure that Lucasta doesn't come. Tiresome woman. Can't think why Bond married her, but he always was a bit of a fool. Young Bond isn't a fool, nor's his wife. Now I'm going to read the Times," and without waiting for more good-byes he went back to the gun-room, sat down in a large, shabby leather arm chair and began to read the deaths, for like most of us as we get older he took a deep and even malicious pleasure in seeing that old Hoskins, or Lord Lundy, who were several years his junior, had been weak-minded enough to hop the twig.

"Oh, *thank* you, Mrs. Morland, for taking me to see Lord Stoke," said Edith. "Now when he comes to Holdings I shall feel he is a little bit mine."

"Wasn't he at all yours before?" said Mrs. Morland, mildly puzzled.

"Oh no, he was mother's," said Edith. "They all are," but these words were spoken, as far as Mrs. Morland could tell, in perfect affection and simplicity. All the same, she felt, it would not do the child any harm to spread her wings. Lord Stoke had shown her bits of a new world; perhaps she would explore some more by herself.

"And now I really must attend to the traffic," said Mrs. Morland as they turned into the main road, so Edith sat silent for a time, partly thinking what a nice time it had been and partly how nice it was to be going home again.

The present tenant of the Old Manor House was, as we know, Lord Crosse's elder daughter, but so far she has been nameless; partly because there are already far too many people in Barsetshire and partly, we think, because we have not yet invented it. But as it became known at Hatch End that real gentry were going to live in the house once more, after its period of neglect, it also became known that her name was the Honourable Mrs. Carter but her husband owing to not being, as his wife was, the offspring of a peer, was not an honourable and only Richard A. Carter Esq., this last being contributed by the postman who prided himself on knowing how people did ought to be spoke to or addressed on an envelope and if there was a man as saw as many envelopes as he did in the year, he'd give sixpence to that man. So short a time had Mrs. Carter been in the village that people had not yet begun calling and Lady Graham was the first to welcome the new-comer. To this end she had driven herself to the village where she proposed to do a little shopping and then meet Edith with Mrs. Morland at the Old Manor House and take her daughter home.

When she got to the Old Manor House she put her car into the little gravel semi-circle which lay back from the road, opposite the house, went up the stone steps and rang the bell. The door was opened by a girl in a very neat print dress which reminded Lady Graham in a nostalgic flash of the proper servants that she remembered in her girlhood.

"Pliss?" said the girl.

"No, Lady Graham," said that lady. Then light suddenly burst upon her.

"Was it the Mixo-Lydian Ambassador, Madame Gradka, who sent you here?" she asked.

"Pliss, yes," said the girl. "Her mother which is dead is cousin to my father's sister which is dead too, God be thanked."

"Was she not a nice person then?" said Lady Graham.

"Bog! if it is nice you are sayink you misconstruct yourself," said the girl. "It was the upside-down of nice which she was. Schwenk I call her, which is a peeg which is becomm dead and eaten of fat flies. They are so fat because of all the meat they have eaten weech is becomm bad and so is thrown out to the little river."

"Gutter, I think you mean," said Lady Graham kindly. "Not a river like the Rising."

"So, I thank you," said the girl. "Now shall I know that a large river is a river and a little stream is a gutter. Pliss, which name do you have?"

Lady Graham, finding her well meant efforts at education not very successful, gave her name to the girl and followed her along the black and white marble flagged hall to the long drawing-room which ran from the front to the back of the house and was now full of the afternoon light. With real pleasure she saw that both understanding and money were being given to the house. The paint was fresh, the mahogany doors well polished and their ornate brass handles newly rebrassed (or whatever one does with brass). The window curtains at the turn of the shallow stairs were warm apricot velveteen or plush or whatever that material is now; the handsome brass lantern hanging from the hall roof had been renovated and looked like gold; an oriental rug in the hall was not too wide to hide the beauty of the flags, nor so narrow as to look stingy and of just the right amount of fadedness, for one not to feel one oughtn't to walk on it. The words "a haunt of ancient peace" floated into her ladyship's mind and as gently floated away before she could pin them down.

"Lady Graham is comm," said the girl, opening the drawing-room door. "You will be house-mistress to her, yes? I shall prepare tea."

"Thank you, Dumka," said her mistress. "How kind of you to come, Lady Graham. Father said you were coming sometime and your husband knows Dick, I think. At least Dick was under him at the War Office for a bit. I do hope you will like the house."

"Indeed I do," said Lady Graham, looking round the drawing-room which was blooming under the hands of people who loved it and could pay for its caprices. "What lovely curtains. They are the same as the curtains on the stairs, aren't they?"

"Aren't they divine?" said Mrs. Carter. "They are really quite old. My husband's great-uncle I think it was, who was an archdeacon, married a Lady Sibyl Somebody, and they had lots of money and went to Italy a lot and brought back lots of things and the stuff for these curtains. I say, would you like to see the house? I adore seeing people's houses."

"If it wouldn't tire you I should love it," said Lady Graham. "I did go over the house when your brother was looking after that branch of the bank here, but he only used it in the week and it was really more like camping."

"Good old John-Arthur. I never knew anyone who took less care of himself," said Mrs. Carter. "I'm always telling him he ought to marry, but he hasn't. Never mind; better late than never. Do come upstairs," and she led the way, stopping at every few steps to point out some beauty of the house, or some beauty she and her husband had added to it, or were just going to add. To Lady Graham's fastidious eye, which was also the eye of a sensible woman of the world, all was good. Money had been spent in the right way, on the right things. Nothing looked too new, everything looked fresh and clean.

"When I think what it was like when I saw it last year—" said Lady Graham, leaving her sentence unfinished. But her hostess understood and said it certainly had been a bit of a headache, still it had been fun to do.

"And I'll tell you who has been awfully helpful," she said.

"That nice Mr. Halliday, our landlord. His daughter—Sylvia Leslie at Rushwater—is rather a friend of ours and she put in a word for us. Her brother was nice but he's a bit stuffy, isn't he? I mean he's not awfully keen on parties and things."

"Poor George Halliday. I expect he is too tired by the end of the day," said Lady Graham. "He is running the whole farm now his father is so ill, and the cows and the pigs. Of course he's got one or two labourers, but he has to do the thinking as well as the work."

"We did go over to Hatch House one day," said Mrs. Carter, "and I liked Mrs. Halliday awfully. But it was a bit of a depresser to see old Mr. Halliday sitting in his chair and not always quite knowing what one said. If daddy got like that I really don't know what I'd do."

"You would do what you felt you ought to do," said Lady Graham, without the least affectation. "My mother was an invalid for the last year or two of her life and her mind was often rather remote, but she became more and more sweet and loving," and Lady Graham turned her head aside for a moment to look at a Morland print, but she could not see it very well. "I am sure," she went on, after gently patting her eyes with her soft handkerchief, "that Mr. Halliday will quietly go, just as darling mamma went, when he is too tired to live here any longer. And now, my dear, *may* I see the nurseries?"

Mrs. Carter, pleased to be deared, flattered by Lady Graham's interest in her children, took her guest to the top floor and opened a door into a large room at the back of the house, looking across the garden to where the downs began to heave their green sides from the valley, flooded with afternoon light. The walls were white and all that was not white in the room was pink, all very shiny.

"*Exactly* what I meant!" said Lady Graham.

"But how?" said her hostess. "Oh, I *do* hope you weren't thinking of taking it. I couldn't bear to have ousted you."

"Oh, not that at all, my dear," said Lady Graham. "It is only that I *am* so pleased because this is *exactly* what these rooms should be. I saw it in my mind's eye, but you have done it."

"I am terribly pleased," said Mrs. Carter. "And there is something else I want to show you. I do hope you will approve," and she took Lady Graham into the room next door which was a small nursery kitchen where a light meal could be prepared and there was a refrigerator for the nursery milk and butter.

"Perfect," said Lady Graham with a kind of sigh of joy. "There was just one other thing—" and even as she said the words she heard Mrs. Carter saying "And there is just one other thing—"

"Don't tell me," said Lady Graham. "I know. It's a lift."

"How on earth did you know that?" said Mrs. Carter, almost sitting down flat on the floor in her surprise.

"My dear child," said Lady Graham, "when your brother let us see this house, I saw at *once* what was wanted to make the nursery floor perfect. I hope the lift door is fool-proof," and Mrs. Carter showed her how the lift locked itself when up and could only be opened by nurse by a handle far above the children's heads, and the same—only the other way up—when it was down. There was also a house-telephone from nursery to kitchen.

"Of course the telephone is going to lead to all sorts of offence being taken between the nursery and the kitchen," said Mrs. Carter cheerfully, "but I shall keep nurse whatever happens and I know she won't go because Mrs. Panter is her sister."

"You mean Mrs. Panter whose husband is Mr. Halliday's carter?" said Lady Graham. "I didn't know she had a sister."

"Well, her sister is much younger than she is and went as under-nurse to Mrs. Francis Brandon at Pomfret Madrigal for a time," said Mrs. Carter, "and she is very well trained. Oh, here you are, nurse. This is Lady Graham."

Lady Graham said How do you do very pleasantly in what nurse at once felt to be the right kind of voice, and further met with nurse's approval by not offering to shake hands. That, in nurse's opinion, was how a lady that *was* a lady should behave and not go making herself cheap like some people—by whom she meant, we think, Mr. Grant who was Mrs. Francis Brandon's aunt by marriage and lived mostly in Calabria, importing on her happily rare visits to Barsetshire Calabrian customs which met with no approval from anyone. Lady Graham then further pleased nurse by asking to see the night nursery, which was a pleasant airy room and if she felt that one could have too much of pink, that after all was Mrs. Carter's business and nothing to do with herself. As the visit then threatened to become rather boring, she said she was sure nurse had lots of things to do and shook hands with her as a farewell. This nurse highly approved as it showed according to Nanny-etiquette that the visitor, having been duly impressed by nurse and Her Nursery, was now asking a boon rather than conferring one.

"They *are* delightful nurseries," said Lady Graham as they went downstairs, with such untruthful sincerity in her voice that Mrs. Carter asked her to stop and look at the bedrooms on the first floor which also had been done up very charmingly and quite conventionally with pale greens and soft whites and plenty of shiny chintz covers and curtains and so they came back to the drawing-room.

"Quite, quite lovely," said Lady Graham, "and I hope you and your husband will come to dinner soon. Now that my husband is not so much in London I want to have some parties," and Mrs. Carter said how nice it would be.

"And what is your husband's part of the country?" said Lady Graham, only just stopping herself in time from saying county, for though Barsetshire is of course the loveliest, the most diverse, the most friendly county in the South (for of the North we know alas little or nothing), there are other counties and there is even London, where Aubrey Clover the brilliant playwright-actor-manager and his wife who keeps her maiden name of Jessica Dean for theatre purposes have their home, though owing to tours in America they are not always there.

"Well, it's London really," said Mrs. Carter half apologetically. "His people were rather Anglo-Indian and lived in South Kensington. His great-uncle—or great-great, I can never remember—was an archdeacon and married a Lady Sibyl somebody and they hadn't any children, but there was another great-uncle who married and had a family. Everard Carter, the headmaster of Southbridge School, is a kind of cousin of ours. Do you know him?"

"My brother John Leslie's boys were all at Southbridge School," said Lady Graham delighted, as we always are, to find a link with people we have liked. "How very nice. I must ask them to dinner and perhaps you and your husband will come and meet them. His wife is a sister of Lady Merton, I expect you know her; her husband is Sir Noel Merton the Q. C.," and then it turned out that Mrs. Carter had met the Mertons in London so everything became very comfortable.

"Of course our people aren't very real Barsetshire yet," said Mrs. Carter. "I mean the Crosses, father's people. They've only been here for two generations, but father seems to have settled and John-Arthur is quite Barsetshire now. At least he will be if he gets married. My sister and I did our best for him when he was in London, but it somehow didn't click."

"Never mind," said Lady Graham soothingly. "I must tell my married daughters to ask him to dinner," after which words her ladyship sat back with the face of an angel who was busying itself (for we cannot think of angels as either he's or she's, owing to their all wearing the same kind of clothes) with mundane affairs. So then young Mrs. Carter had to ask who her married daughters were and nearly went mad in trying to disentangle Leslies and Beltons. "And of course your brother has been to Holdings," her ladyship went on, "and we love having him, but Edith—my youngest girl—was in America all this winter so I went to London with my husband for several weeks and really we have seen no one. But I hope you and your husband will come soon."

Mrs. Carter said they would love to and then Lady Graham wondered when Edith would come and seemed a little anxious, so Mrs. Carter asked her to look at the kitchens which she was delighted to do, for with every year she grew more like her mother, Lady Emily Leslie, in an all-embracing desire to poke into other people's houses.

We need hardly say that Mrs. Carter's cook, a foreigner from Barchester (and when we say foreigner we do not mean Mixo-Lydian, but merely born outside Hatch End) was graciously pleased to receive her ladyship and not only showed her the new patent practically-non-coal-consuming Begum cooker, but also the gas installation for central heating and the new scullery sink of stainless steel. And of course Lady Graham was enchanted to poke about and ask piercing questions, just as her mother would have done, but when she asked about the scullery sink cook pursed up her lips and said there was some said one thing and some said another, but it didn't seem right-like to have a sink as wasn't white.

"Yes, I do so see what you mean, cook," said Lady Graham. "You can't ever make steel look as *white* as a nice porcelain sink. Of course a steel sink doesn't chip, which is something—though I am sure you would never let a sink be chipped."

"Of course not, my lady," said cook, whose face had darkened at the word chip, but after Lady Graham's rider was again composed. "And I'm not saying, my lady," cook continued, "as these stainless steel sinks are *wrong*. After all we do use stainless steel saucepans, my lady, but when you come to clean them with that wire-wool it fair takes the skin off your finger-tips, and I don't fancy doing out the sink with wool-wire, but Mrs. Carter says she'll have a nice white one put in if I don't get on with this one."

"Now that *would* be nice," said Lady Graham, rather basely truckling to cook, Mrs. Carter thought. "But I suppose it would be rather old-fashioned now. The Duke of Omnium has stainless steel sinks at Gatherum Castle and so does Lady Pomfret at the Towers," which statements were noble lies, or at the least statements made with the express desire of helping Mrs. Carter not to have to install new and expensive sinks, and in the hope, almost amounting to a certainty, that what she had said would never reach Gatherum or the Towers.

"Well, of course, your ladyship," said cook, visibly shaken, "I'm sure I've nothing *against* stainless steel sinks if madam wants them, but I always say with a sink you want one as you can *see* the dirt on."

Lady Graham said that was what she always thought herself and so departed with her hostess to the upper regions. Even as they came into the hall the front door-bell began to ring loudly. Mrs. Carter said she thought the maid was out and opened the door herself to Mrs. Morland and Edith Graham.

"May we come in?" said Mrs. Morland. "I have brought Edith back to her mother."

Mrs. Carter welcomed her and Edith and took them into the drawing-room where Agnes was now sitting in a large comfortable arm-chair, looking at her lovely hands and thinking peacefully of all her children and their various perfections. When she saw Mrs. Morland and Edith she got up and came forward with a charming smile—so like her mother Lady Emily Leslie's smile, only Lady Emily's smile and her keen eyes were like a hawk's (if hawks can smile) while Lady Graham's were like a dove's (if doves had large dark eyes and not small round ones).

"How kind of you to bring Edith back, Mrs. Morland," she said, shaking hands with that lady. "And of course you know Mrs. Carter."

It did occur both to Mrs. Morland and to Mrs. Carter that if any introductions were necessary they should be made rather by the hostess than by one of her guests, and they exchanged smiles, but both ladies were intelligent enough to realize that Lady Graham, far from presuming, was merely being herself. Edith said how do you do to Mrs. Carter very nicely, though she could hardly wait to tell her mother about the lunch at Rising Castle.

"And do look what Lord Stoke gave me, mother," she said, lifting the little string of pearls from where they lay on her neck. "He said he gave them to someone else called Edith, a very long time ago, and she gave it back to him. Edith Thorne I think he said. Isn't it lovely, mother. I always frightfully wanted some pearls. Aunt Rose did give me some lovely pretence ones in New York, much bigger than these, but these are really pearls."

"How lovely, darling," said Lady Graham, who was quickly putting together in her mind half-forgotten stories about the late Lady Pomfret. "You must tell me all about it presently."

Edith, a little ashamed of having made a social gaffe, said she was sorry she had talked so much, but it was so exciting to have some real pearls, and she had always frightfully wanted some.

"And it is so delightful that you have come to live here," she continued to Mrs. Carter, with a kind of unconscious parody of what grown-up people said. "I mean this house wants to be lived in and the Hallidays wanted the right people to live here. They are extremely nice, and George is quite a good farmer and has bought some of father's pigs," at which point Lady Graham looked at her daughter and Edith subsided, suddenly realizing that she was putting herself forward too much.

"Edith was in New York all last winter with my brother David Leslie and his wife," said Lady Graham to her hostess, with an air of explaining everything. "I hope she was a good guest with you, Mrs. Morland."

"As good as gold," said Mrs. Morland. "We went over to Crosse Hall and saw Lord Crosse and your brother, Mrs. Carter, and Edith's cousin Ludovic was there, so it was very pleasant. And today we lunched with Lord Stoke. He is older than he was. Of course we are all older than we were every moment of our lives, but sometimes one suddenly notices oldness in a person. I expect our children see it in us long before we know it is there."

As usual Mrs. Morland had hit the nail, in her own rambling way, on the head, but we doubt whether her hostess quite understood her, for a young mother of two agreeable babies still thinks of the present as all and the future as something which may never happen and in any case is not worth bothering about. Lady Graham did understand, for she had begun to see age in her own delightful, incalculable mother, Lady Emily Leslie, and try to guard her against its ills, long before Lady Emily herself recognized her adversary. Though when she did recognize him, she had returned his salute with her own peculiar loving mockery and had not kicked against the pricks.

The Mixo-Lydian maid then irrupted into the room and stood gazing at the company.

"Yes, Dumka?" said Mrs. Carter, who apparently found this apparition quite in order.

"The tea is placed on the table, Prodska Carter," said Dumka. "Also have I made a Prjoskoffen, because there is a young maiden here."

Mrs. Carter, apparently quite unmoved by these remarks, said they were having tea in the dining-room because tea was much more comfortable on a table and shepherded her guests across the hall into another delightful room looking over the garden to the downs. Here a round table was spread and everyone sat down.

"Thank you, Dumka, that is all," said Mrs. Carter.

"You are not yet seeink the Prjoskoffen, Prodska Carter," said Dumka, pointing to a large, flat, round cake. "I shall be tellink that he is made with butter—Bog! which butter you have here, from cows, not like our butter in Mixo-Lydia which is from the milk of a donkey-woman."

"She means a she-ass," said Mrs. Carter, calmly. "Please sit down. Do come here, Mrs. Morland. You get a lovely view up the garden to the downs," and indeed it was most lovely, but to a student of human nature like Mrs. Morland not so attractive at the moment as her hostess's maid.

"What good English you speak," she said. "Did you learn it here?"

"I kiss your feet, Prodska Morland, that you flatten me so," said Dumka.

"Flatter, not flatten," said Mrs. Morland kindly.

"So, I thank you," said Dumka. "Already I had with all correctness learned English at Bunting College which is the University of Mixo-Lydia, and I am Letter-maiden, which you say in English Bachelor of Letters, but for us it is Letter-maiden, which is more correct. It is our Ambassador here, Excellence Gradka, which is foundling this college."

"Thank you, Dumka. It is founding, not foundling. You can go now," said Mrs. Carter.

"So, I thank you," said Dumka, "Now do I go to clean that sink which is a robbish. In Mixo-Lydia we would laugh ourselves of a sink. In Mixo-Lydia we have a stream in the middle of the street where all the Sczarhzy, what you call housemistress, wash all the clothes two times in the year and ollso the dirty plates one time in the year. In Slavo-Lydia, which is inhabited of pigs and devils, they wash the dirty plates in a hole where the pigs—"

"Thank you, Dumka, that will do," said Mrs. Carter, thus earning the respect of her guests for her way of dealing with her maid and also their eternal annoyance at not being able to hear exactly how the Slavo-Lydian plates were washed, and with a kind of curtsey Dumka went away.

Lady Graham and Mrs. Morland, both mothers of grown-up families, began to compare notes about grandchildren. Mrs. Carter would rather have liked to listen, but as a hostess she felt she should entertain Edith in case she felt out of it and asked her what she was doing.

"Well, really nothing at present," said Edith. "My brothers are all in the army and both my sisters are married and what I would like to be is a grown-up daughter at home for a bit. You see I was in New York with Uncle David and it was lovely and exciting but rather same-ish, if you see what I mean. I mean I had a marvellous time but it was always the same thing. At home such a lot of things are always happening and there are the cows and the pigs. Do you have pigs, Mrs. Carter?"

Mrs. Carter said the garden wasn't large enough for a pig-stye, though she liked pigs very much.

"You have been to my father's house, haven't you?" she said.

"Oh yes; twice," said Edith. "I would like to go again because Lord Crosse's butler used to be the butler at the Towers when old Uncle Giles was alive. I'm Edith after old Aunt Edith," at which point Mrs. Carter had to say that she felt quite giddy with all Edith's relations.

"You see I haven't very many," she said. "There's my brother, my elder sister who lives in London with her husband and family and some Carters at Southbridge. Mother had some distant cousins but we never see them. You know my brother, don't you?"

"John-Arthur? Oh, of course," said Edith. "First he was in this house when the bank still had it and then mother took me to lunch at Crosse Hall and John-Arthur showed me the Grotto and then John-Arthur came to tea with us and then Mrs. Morland took me to lunch yesterday at Crosse Hall again but the boys were highly uncivil."

Mrs. Carter, amused by Edith's way of speech, asked her how they were uncivil. "If John-Arthur was uncivil I will scold him," she added.

"Oh, it was just as much Ludo's fault," said Edith.

Mrs. Carter asked who Ludo was.

"Oh, he is really Ludovic," said Edith. "His father is mother's cousin in a sort of way, only he's Lord Pomfret, and Ludo is at Sandhurst and then he will be in the Brigade of Guards and I shall go to lunch with him at St. James's Palace."

"All by yourself?" said Mrs. Carter, amused by her guest's mixture of worldliness and ingenuousness.

"Oh no, one *couldn't*," said Edith with a kind of grown-up

shockedness that made her hostess want to laugh. "Mother will take me, or perhaps Emmy or Clarissa because they are married," at which point Mrs. Carter gave it up and said she could never do families and would Edith like to see the nursery after tea, which Edith said she would; not that she cared particularly for children unless it were her own nephews and nieces or her cousin Martin Leslie's children; but if your hostess offers you a treat, it is polite to accept it.

"I sometimes wish I were like Gran," said Edith, who felt that Mrs. Carter was well-disposed to her and wondered if she herself were being a truly good guest. "She got on with everybody and everybody loved her," to which Mrs. Carter found no immediate answer, for though she found this youngest Graham girl most agreeable and amusing company, she was confused by the number of relations that came into her talk and was not sure who Gran was. And even had she been told it is possible that it would not have meant very much to her, for she had not known much of West Barsetshire and among new-comers the name of Lady Emily Leslie was unknown, or but an old far-off echo.

Then as a good hostess Mrs. Carter turned to her older guests and asked Lady Graham's advice very prettily about people in the neighbourhood and what the clergyman was like. Luckily Lady Graham was able to give Mr. Choyce, the Vicar, an excellent character, though when Mrs. Carter came to think it over she could remember nothing very definite except that he read the lessons well and Lady Graham's husband was Vicar's Churchwarden, and there was a monkey-puzzle in front of the Vicarage that everyone wanted to cut down but they were afraid of the spikes.

At this moment the rather loud but pleasant sound of the front door-bell was heard, followed by Dumka's heavy footstep across the hall and a man's voice. The dining-room door was flung open and Dumka announced Prodshk Hoggleby. As no one came in, Mrs. Carter asked her who it was.

"Since it is housewives which carouse," said Dumka, "I do not bring in the stranger, which is a young man. In Mixo-Lydia if it is the woman-meal, it is the costom that the yong man stays outside till the Prodshka, which is the housemother, ask him to comm. Then must he spit on the door and comm in."

Mrs. Morland knew she would have the giggles in a moment. Lady Graham looked on with a wholly charming want of interest and Edith stared. But Mrs. Carter, quite unmoved by her maid's exposition of correct etiquette, told her to bring the guest in at once, and in came George Halliday, giving Dumka a kind of token chuck under the chin as he passed her, we regret to say.

"Oh, it is you, Mr. Halliday," said Mrs. Carter. "How nice of you to come. You all know each other I expect."

Lady Graham and Edith of course did and Mrs. Morland said hadn't he been somewhere near Vache-en-Étable during the war as she was sure her youngest son who was a temporary gunner had met him.

"I'm sure we did," said George, sliding himself in beside Edith. "What was his name?"

"Morland; Tony, Second Lieutenant, guns," said Mrs. Morland in what her hearers (and indeed she herself) felt to be a most dashing and military way.

"Oh, *rather*," said George. "Sometimes talks nineteen to the dozen and then is as mum as a sphinx? Good fellow. Last time I saw him his O.P.—sorry, observation post—was on top of a factory chimney about seventy feet high, with a sway of anything up to twelve or eighteen inches at the top. He looked as green as—as—well, as anything—when he came down, but we got a spot of medical comforts off the M.O. and he was as fit as a fiddle. Nice chap. Oh, I do hope I'm not saying the wrong thing—I mean one doesn't hear about fellows and you mostly don't see them again—I mean I hope I've not said anything—I mean—"

"No, he wasn't killed," said Mrs. Morland calmly. "He is married and has hundreds of children which is *most* expensive."

"I'm sure it's worth it," said George Halliday. "I mean, well after all your children *are* your children."

"And so are your grandchildren," said Mrs. Morland in her most impressive voice and fixing George Halliday with an Ancient Mariner's eye as she spoke. "Your son's your son till he gets him a wife, But he goes on expecting you to help him to support all his children all your life," which words, spoken in the kind of voice which the Sibyl doubtless used to Tarquin, quite silenced George Halliday, when suddenly Edith began to laugh, in a very friendly way but quite unrestrainedly, and everyone else laughed too.

"I do hope I'm not butting in, Mrs. Carter," said George Halliday, "but mother wants to know if you need a broody hen as one of ours has just started brooding."

"Exactly what I do want," said Mrs. Carter. "Shall I come and fetch her?"

"She's in the back of my car," said George. "She's less than no use at home at the moment and upsetting all the other girls with her talk about a lay-down strike. If you really have some eggs for her it'll give her something to think about."

Mrs. Carter entirely approved the idea and asked about George's pigs.

"Though really I ought to say your father's pigs," she added. "How is he?"

"It's awfully good of you to ask, Mrs. Carter," said George, "but there isn't much to say. He is going out quietly. Dr. Ford says it might be a week, or a month, or even a year. But Caxton doesn't."

Mrs. Carter asked who Caxton was.

"Oh, I'm sorry," said George. "You know you seem so exactly right in the Old Manor House that I forget you are father's tenant. I can't help thinking of you as the real owner. Caxton is our estate carpenter."

"And he can do anything," said Edith, who was feeling rather out of the conversation. "Carpentering and the electric light and the ram down by the spring and—oh anything."

"Isn't your house on the mains then?" said Mrs. Carter. "We are here."

George laughed and said they were on the mains now all right, but with the animals to be watered on the upper part of the farm, his father had put in a small pumping machine.

"And I'm sorry I must be off, Mrs. Carter," he said. "The cowman is having a few days off and I am stop-gap."

Everyone, we think, was sorry that he had to go. Mrs. Carter said he must come to supper and she would get her brother over. Lady Graham said he knew he was always welcome at Holdings and Mrs. Morland said when he had time he must come to High Rising for a night and meet George Knox again, as she felt sure they had lots of things to talk about.

"I should love to," said George Halliday. "I am sure he will tell me exactly how to bring up the runt of a litter and what kind of food to give a sow before the Barsetshire Agricultural Show," and Mrs. Morland felt sorely tempted to say "Oh you naughty man" to him for this impertinence, but didn't.

So he went away and though the darkness slightly dimmed the day for Edith, it by no means took the grace from all alive for her elders. Lady Graham was able to give Mrs. Carter a good deal of useful information, such as the fact that if one needed a rabbit, or some game, Geo. Panter of the Mellings Arms could always supply it at a day's notice, only a very little above market price and no questions to be asked. It was better of course only to ask for it in season, but even out of season Geo. Panter would do his best.

"Oh, there is one thing I did want to ask," said Mrs. Carter to Lady Graham. "Do you know if this house has a pew of its own in the church?"

Lady Graham said would Mrs. Carter come to the Graham pew next Sunday and then they could enquire about the Old Manor House pew, which invitation Mrs. Carter accepted with a very nice courtesy towards an older woman who was showing her a kindness.

"If you would care to meet my cousin Everard, the headmaster of Southbridge School, I'll ask him and his wife," she said. "And if her sister and brother-in-law the Noel Mertons are down here, I'll ask them too. My husband would love it. Saturday is the best day for Everard because he usually has a few senior boys to Sunday supper. Would that be all right?"

Lady Graham began to realize, but without any rancour, that this pleasant new-comer was going to be the very capable Queen of Hatch End in a very short time and determined to be on good terms with the rising sun. Not that her ladyship needed any social aspirations, for her position together with her husband's was unassailable and while the village would give lip service to the Carters as open-handed gentry living in a good house, it would be to Holdings that mothers would aspire to send their girls when they reached the floor-slopping and china-breaking age, to be trained by Lady Graham's old cook into wringing out your cloth in the suds, my girl, before you wash the kitchen floor with it and none of your slopping water about and if I catch you with the soap laying in the pail when there's water in it you won't have no chance to do it again, and mind when you do her ladyship's best china and don't go pulling the handles off the cups when you dry them the way some girls do as haven't been brought up proper.

"I'm sorry John-Arthur isn't here," said Mrs. Carter as Lady Graham began her good-byes. "He's in town all this week, but I hope he will be down at Crosse Hall for some time after that. Perhaps if I get him you will all come to dinner."

Lady Graham said they would love to and so went away with Edith.

Mrs. Morland said she must be going too. Mrs. Carter thanked her very prettily for calling and said she must come over to dinner while the evenings were long; perhaps on the same day that the Everard Carters came, which Mrs. Morland said she would like of all things and Mrs. Carter and her husband must come over to High Rising and make the acquaintance of the George Knoxes, which Mrs. Carter said would be delightful, and so Mrs. Morland drove away, having much enjoyed her excursions to Rising Castle and Hatch End, but quite glad as always to get back again to her own house and writing-table. Although she drove herself about Barsetshire a good deal, she had hardly ever been known to spend even a night away from home and perhaps she was wise. For when we stay with friends of whom we don't know very much, their bread is not usually bitter, but some of them do have extraordinarily uncomfortable beds. And whether the beds are the kind that sink to a trough in the middle that you roll into and can't get out of, or those that rise to a steep mountain from whose side you roll off all night, they are equally revolting and yet a bulwark of our English liberties. For if every man's house should be his castle we presume that the fifty-seven varieties of Procrustes' bed are also canonically admissible. But do not let us sleep in them.

CHAPTER 5

People who met Lady Graham for the first time were apt to underestimate her ladyship, judging her by her gentle manner and rather cooing voice to be what in that part of Barsetshire was known as a soft gobbin. But no soft gobbin could have managed so well a clever and rather difficult husband, three sons now all in the army, and three daughters of quite different temperaments. Lady Graham's mother, Lady Emily Leslie, had said, in one of her flashes of inspired insight, that she *knew* Agnes's children each had a different father and she thought they each had a different mother as well. Which really seemed to cover the matter pretty thoroughly.

"Now, you have had so much experience of young people in your Liverpool parish, Mr. Choyce," said her ladyship to the Vicar who had come to see her about some small parish matter, "that I am sure you can help me."

Mr. Choyce, feeling that his ministry in a Merseyside parish where most of the young were ignorant of the laws both of God and Man (which was perhaps just as well as they would then have broken them deliberately instead of in cheerful ignorance) was hardly a helpful preparation, begged to know in what way he could assist, either by counsel or by works; though he had very little confidence of being able to help her with either.

"It is simply about Mrs. Carter," said her ladyship.

"But I thought you said young people," said the Vicar.

"Young compared with us, I mean," said Lady Graham. "After all her two children are only babies and mine are quite old. Even Edith. Mrs. Carter seems *very* young to me, but perhaps that is only because her children are so small. I could easily be their grandmother but of course having sons before daughters does set one back though Clarissa and Emmy have done very well. Dear James, I do hope he will marry. A wife is *so* useful in the Brigade of Guards if she is the right kind. John isn't married either nor is Robert, but of course they are too young to consider it seriously."

"If" said Mr. Choyce, who had not liked to interrupt Lady Graham but felt he really must get her to draw to a point if possible, "I can be of any assistance, you know you may command me."

"Of course I know your kindness, Mr. Choyce," said Lady Graham, who was unpicking a little bit of petit point that had gone wrong and not paying much attention to her guest's answer. "Do you see a pair of scissors with gold handles anywhere?"

Mr. Choyce looked on the floor, saw the scissors half under a small footstool, retrieved them and gave them to their mistress.

"Oh *thank* you, Mr. Choyce," said Lady Graham, "but I never think the woman who lost a piece of silver need have swept the *whole* house in the middle of the night and made all the servants get up and asked everyone to rejoice with her, but I expect it was easier to get servants then. If you had not found my scissors so kindly I should have waited till tomorrow and told Odeena or Aggie to look for them. But I daresay that is rather different."

"There is something to be said for doing nothing and waiting," said Mr. Choyce, but he was thinking of a Bach cantata beginning Sei nur still und harr auf Gott and though his feelings for Lady Graham were of a deeply admiring kind he was pretty sure that her ladyship would not take the allusion, and to explain Bach and German and their relation to a small pair of gold-handled scissors was for the moment beyond him. It then occurred to him that Milton had said something of the same sort in much the same words, which annoyed him, till he reflected that Milton's words had not been set most movingly to music, which cheered him considerably, and such is the speed of thought that all this happened while Lady Graham was putting the gold-handled scissors back into their red morocco case and did not notice his silence.

"I will tell you what it is, Mr. Choyce," she said. "Mrs. Carter doesn't know if the Old Manor House has a pew and I don't know either, so we thought you could tell us."

"It is the third from the front on the left of the aisle," said Mr. Choyce, "and Caxton can tell you all about it. It is such a comfort to have a sexton who knows everything. Of course the Old Manor House has not been lived in since that last old Miss Halliday died, and she never went to church because she was bed-ridden, or so Caxton tells me. I will ask him. It was in my predecessor's time."

"How good are you, Mr. Choyce," said Lady Graham. "If there is a Manor House pew of course the Manor House must use it. I daresay the hassocks will want looking at, because there was a lot of moth in the church just before you came and we had to get some new ones. It might be a good idea to have plastic covers for the mothy ones."

Mr. Choyce said that was indeed an idea.

"Unless of course it is Forbidden," said Lady Graham.

The Vicar asked how.

"Well, I mean there are all sorts of extraordinary things in the Bible one mustn't do though one would never dream of doing them," said Lady Graham. "I mean like not seething the kid in its mother's milk which is really quite unreasonable. But I daresay it all meant something quite different originally, and of course plastic wasn't invented then."

Mr. Choyce, though deeply moved by these words, did not quite know what to say, so far had her ladyship's divagations taken them from the subject under discussion, namely Had the

Old Manor House a pew and whether the Carters would wish to use it.

"But I will tell you what I *will* do, Mr. Choyce," said Lady Graham, her lovely eyes shining even as her mother's used to shine when Lady Emily had thought of some particularly good piece of meddling. "I will ask Mrs. Carter to come into our pew and after the service we can speak to Caxton about it. And perhaps then you will come back to lunch here."

The Vicar thought these suggestions admirable, though the last came highest in his estimation, and then Edith who had been to lunch with Mrs. Halliday came in, full of information about the home farm and how George Halliday was going to plough up that nasty bit of land and try potatoes in it and if that succeeded he might do some market gardening as well as farming. Mr. Choyce, who knew nothing whatever about potatoes, tried to look wise but gave it up as a bad job and only wondered, for human nature was his great interest, whether Edith was becoming as masterful as her eldest sister Emmy who bade fair to rival Mrs. Samuel Adams in telling people what. But Mrs. Adams was much more gentle now and even apt to be a little boring about her children upon whom she looked with the adoring surprise of a hen who has hatched a brood of particoloured ducklings.

Odeena, who we may add for the benefit of such readers as do not know, was called after the Barchester Odeon by her film-sodden mother, then brought in tea which was always very good at Holdings and both Agnes and her daughter waited on Mr. Choyce till he felt almost embarrassed; but by reflecting that it was the Office that commanded respect rather than the Man he managed to make a very good meal.

"We were talking, darling," said Lady Graham to her daughter, "about the Old Manor House pew."

Edith asked which one it was.

"It is that pew where we usually put some of the Harvest

Festival offerings when there are too many of them," said Mr. Choyce.

"I cannot quite see it," said Lady Graham, who had closed her eyes as if communing with some inner vision of the church.

"Yes, mother," said Edith. "The one that has the Mothers' Union banner in the corner."

"Then that is why I had forgotten," said Lady Graham, who by this time had as usual reduced her audience to a state where faith was better than understanding. "But we can't leave it there if Mrs. Carter and her family are going to use it, Mr. Choyce."

The Vicar did not quite see why a banner leaning against a wall in the far corner of a pew should be a serious inconvenience to a family of whom only two were of church-going age, but such was his reverence for Lady Graham's feelings that he did not like to say so.

"Oh, mother!" said Edith, "don't you remember the time that clamp-thing that holds it up came out of the wall and the banner fell down while the Bishop was preaching? You weren't here then, Mr. Choyce. It was a locum."

The fact of Mr. Choyce having been away would not seem decisive in itself, but it appeared to satisfy Lady Graham who said of course the Mothers' Union banner could be left there and how stupid of her not to remember.

"I'll tell you how we can arrange it, Mr. Choyce," said Lady Graham. "When I have Mrs. Carter in our pew on Sunday I will show her which the Old Manor House pew used to be and then afterwards we could have a word with you and Caxton."

"Of course!" said Mr. Choyce. "You think of everything for us, Lady Graham. But—if I may suggest it—could we not have the word at the vicarage? One of my Liverpool helpers, a well-to-do man in the shipping line, has just sent me a case of sherry and one of Marsala. I did not know Marsala, but I have opened a bottle and found it excellent. Rather softer than sherry, but not heavy."

"Of *course* not," said Lady Graham.

"Do you know it then?" said Mr. Choyce. "So few people do. I think they confuse it with Madeira."

At this Lady Graham laughed in a most charming way, without at all disturbing her still lovely face where the only signs of middle age were some faint lines at the outer corners of her dove's eyes.

"How young you look when you laugh" said the Vicar and then felt confused, but Lady Graham appeared pleased with his tribute.

"So did darling mamma," she said. "Sometimes one gets like one's parents as one gets older."

"Then I'm glad you're my mother," said Edith. "How awful it would be to get like old Mrs. Panter," but as Mrs. Panter, mother of Geo. Panter of the Mellings Arms, had a hooky nose and within the memory of all the oldest and most untruthful inhabitants had had a grey rather curly beard, it did not seem likely that Lady Graham would pass on any of these characteristics to her youngest daughter.

"We mustn't keep you, Mr. Choyce," said Lady Graham, and though there was no particular reason for the Vicar to go home he felt that Lady Graham was somehow being—as when was she not—particularly kind and thoughtful, and so took his leave.

After dinner Lady Graham rang up Mrs. Carter and explained the plan. Mrs. Carter said Might she just ask her husband, which Lady Graham felt to be a very suitable attitude. In a short time Mrs. Carter was back at the telephone to say that her husband thanked Lady Graham very much and ought he to wear a dark suit or should he come just as he was.

"Oh, just as he likes," said Lady Graham. "Robert usually wears a dark blue suit for church but he is so seldom here, I am sorry to say, that it hardly counts. When he retired last year I thought we should see more of him, but he has collected so many boards that he is always travelling. He is in Bristol this weekend, I really do not know why. He will be so disappointed to miss you, but you will come to dinner soon, I hope."

"So that is all right," she said to Edith. "And, darling," she added, "do you think you ought to be taking up something?"

"What sort of something, mother?" said Edith.

"Well, I don't quite know," said Lady Graham. "Of course I married quite young—older than you are but not so very much. It was near the end of my first season and I had kept a dance for your father, he was only a Colonel then, of course, and—"

"Look here, mother," said Edith lovingly but firmly. "You simply *mustn't* tell me that one again. The boys and I all think so. I mean we adore it, but after all we *do* know it. Do you mind?"

Lady Graham was quite silent.

"I haven't been horrid, have I mother?" said Edith, already repenting her protest. "I didn't *ever* mean to."

"Not a bit horrid," said Lady Graham. "You couldn't be. I hope I have never been horrid to you."

"Of *course* you haven't," said Edith. "Did you think you had?"

"Oh no, not in the least," said Lady Graham. "But one ought to know. At least perhaps one oughtn't. Some people believe in telling other people about all the things they think the other people have done that were stupid, but it is extremely stupid of them to think it. Of course darling mamma did it so sweetly that one couldn't possibly mind. And I don't think she thought one would either. And I think you were quite right about that story of my engagement, darling, but you see you don't know about being engaged and how it was heaven and still is in a sort of way. We will have a plan and if I tell my story more than once to the same person, you can make a special face at me. We will plan a face. But if it is the first time you mustn't make a face," and her ladyship looked at her youngest daughter with a smile almost as lovely and touching as her mother's had been.

"Oh, mother!" said Edith, her eyes brimming. "I'm *sorry*."

"But why, darling?" said her mother. "Someone would have

said it to me soon. One of your friends, I expect. George Halliday or young Mr. Crosse."

"Oh mother! George and John-Arthur *couldn't* be so impertinent," said Edith. "Oh mother! was *I* impertinent?"

"I don't think so," said Lady Graham. "If I had said it to darling mamma, who had her own ways and words in everything, I think she would have smiled. But it would have been her lovely sad, wistful smile, not the gay mischievous one and it would have broken my heart."

"Oh, mother!" said Edith, perhaps for the first time in her happy sheltered life as the youngest of a large affectionate family, feeling that she was outside in a chill wind and the rain beginning to fall. "Have I broken your heart?"

"Not a bit, darling," said her mother cheerfully. "Someone would have told me that someday and far less nicely. And if you *could* remember to look at your stockings before you put them on sometimes?" and Edith looked down at her very presentable legs which were both wearing very sheer American brown nylons, with a slight but distinct difference in the browns.

"Oh mother, how awful!" said Edith, her attention now distracted from her penitence to more important objects. "I know why it was, because one's nylons always ladder in one half of the pair and not the other half and one always keeps the good halves in case they happen to match anything else, but they never do and then they get all mixed up."

"Then it would be a good plan always to buy the same sort and the same shade if you can," said Lady Graham.

"There are some shops where you can buy three at a time for when one ladders," said Edith, "but even then the other one would ladder sometime. I think your plan of buying millions of pairs exactly the same is the best."

"I was once told—though by whom I cannot think—" said Lady Graham, "that nylon stockings Perish if you keep them too long before you wear them and you ought to keep them in an air-tight tin canister. I wonder if we have one?" and her ladyship looked hopefully about the room. But canister there was none, air-tight or otherwise, and then Edith was sleepy and said she would go to bed and kissed her mother.

"Oh, mother," she said, "do you remember when I was *very* young and always making poetry?"

Lady Graham thought her daughter was still very young, in spite of her New York winter, and said she hoped Edith would go on making poetry, which was a much nicer word than writing poetry which sounded like a person at a desk trying to do a thousand lines.

"I wish I could make real poetry," said Edith. "I don't mean the sort that people make thin little books of and you can't understand it, but the sort people might like to read, or to say to each other. But it was a silly poem that I made when I was so very young. It was Darling Mummy, I love you with my whole tummy. And I still do," she added, perhaps slightly ashamed of this precocious piece of rhyme.

"Of course you do, darling," said Lady Graham, whose gift for accepting and rationalizing—horrible word but as it seems to have come to stay we might as well use it—facts and words was not one of the least remarkable things about her. "And now you really must go to bed." So Edith went to bed and very quickly to sleep.

All we can say about the various arrangements for meeting the Carters on their own front doorstep, or outside the church-yard, or inside the church, is that after a good deal of discussion, complicated first by Mr. Carter not being in and then by his having gone out again because there wasn't enough beer in the house and the Mellings Arms would always oblige, in and out of hours, it was decided that just inside the lych-gate was the best place, because one could park one's car under the church-yard wall in the lane if it wasn't too full. So at about a quarter to eleven on Sunday morning Lady Graham with Edith was at the lych-gate and almost at once Mr. and Mrs. Carter drove up

and parked their car among the nettles up against the churchyard wall.

"I hope we aren't late," said Mrs. Carter as she got ungrace-
fully out of the car, for to get out of modern cars gracefully would
be impossible even to Taglioni were she alive, except that the
shortness and fullness of her gauze skirts would have been easier
than Mrs. Carter's pencil-slim grey skirt. But in both cases all
onlookers would have had an almost full-length view of the legs
concerned—and very nice legs too in Mrs. Carter's case.

Mrs. Carter shook hands with Lady Graham and said this
was Dick, only everyone called him Paterson, which Agnes
accepted without question but Edith asked why.

"Carter Paterson," said Mrs. Carter, to which Edith said Why
not Seeds, or Little Liver Pills. Her mother looked at her.

"It was so kind of you to meet us here," said Mrs. Carter,
ignoring (though not unkindly) Edith's silly joke and addressing
herself to Lady Graham. "The whole pew question is beyond us
and we are only new-comers. I don't even know how you begin
to acquire one."

"Oh, nor do I," said Lady Graham sympathetically, "because
of course at home, at Rushwater—do you know Rushwater,
Mrs. Carter?"

Mrs. Carter said she was sorry but she didn't.

"It is where darling mamma used to live only now it is my
nephew Martin's and he breeds prize bulls because he still has a
very painful leg owing to the Italians," said Lady Graham,
which did not really elucidate the question.

Mrs. Carter said she had heard that Italian doctors were very
clever but had never met one.

"It wasn't the doctors, Mrs. Carter," said Edith, "it was the
war."

"I know," said Mr. Carter, who apart from lifting his hat and
looking amiable had not yet had a chance to make himself felt.
"I was in the last year of it and got some sort of bug in Italy. I
daresay their doctors were very clever but my bug beat them,"

which words he uttered with a kind of fine insular pride in not being cured by foreigners. "And it beat our doctors too," he added, more with pride in his own peculiar bug than in denigration of the English Medical School.

"I am so glad you will come to the Holdings pew," said Lady Graham, "and then afterwards we can have a really quiet talk with the Vicar and with Caxton who really knows everything."

"Do we know Caxton?" said Mrs. Carter to her husband.

"You don't, but I do," said Mr. Carter. "He is Mr. Halliday's estate carpenter. I've talked to him in the Mellings Arms once or twice. He's the sort of man that can always produce a screwdriver or sixpennyworth of two inch nails from one of his pockets, or knock you up something eight by three by one and a half," which light-hearted outline of Caxton's capabilities made his wife and Edith laugh. And if Lady Graham did not laugh it was partly because with all her social gifts and her charm she did not see jokes very quickly and partly because she had not paid much attention to what Mr. Carter was saying, being occupied by planning how everyone was to sit in the Holdings pew.

The bell began to give those last single strokes which warn late-comers that they had better hurry up.

"Come in," said Lady Graham encouragingly to Mr. and Mrs. Carter, and she led her guests up the aisle to the Holdings pew, where she stood aside. "Will you go to the end, Mrs. Carter" she said, "and then I will come. Edith darling, you come next and will you sit near the door, Mr. Carter. At least one can hardly call it a door when there isn't one" said Lady Graham, bestowing a kind of religious smile on her guest, "but some pews still do have doors though here they haven't" and then, rather to Mr. Carter's relief, her ladyship put herself into what one can only call a token kneeling position, sitting well forward on the hard seat with her head bowed onto her hands. The rest of the party did much the same and what thoughts passed through their minds one would very much like to know. For to very few of us is it given to be able

to empty our minds of mundane thoughts even in the very act of
kneeling, which also includes having to rake a hassock towards
us with one leg or, if the hassock is one of those miserable, thin
squabs which are undignifiedly hung by a ring onto a hook when
not in use, to ignore it and, sitting well forward on the extreme
edge of the hard seat, bend our body reverently over the back of
the pew in front, while wondering if we have half a crown in our
bag because a ten-shilling note would look like showing-off and
a florin wouldn't be enough, while to put in a half crown made
up of smaller silver and base metal coins would feel irreligious.

The service began. The Vicar read well and spoke well and
used the noble words set down for us just as they are in the prayer
book. Under a former Vicar there had been considerable back-
sliding in the way of reading only the first and the last sentence
of certain prayers or exhortations; this manner of reading being
considered by many (and they, alas, the most ready to be up and
doing anything so long as it is something) to make the service
not only shorter, which it does, but better understood of the
people, which it doesn't. For as a large number of the congregation had never quite known what all the prayers meant, loving
them none the less through long association, so did another part
of the congregation love them through a quiet search into their
meaning and a decision that the Morning and Evening Service
were on the whole part of the Bible. And if one did find things
that were beyond comprehension it was probably because one
could not yet comprehend; but one could love very comfortably
without comprehending and perhaps gradually begin to understand without knowing it.

Those members of the congregation, mostly humble folk,
who remembered Lady Graham's mother, Lady Emily Leslie,
were apt to think of her in church more than elsewhere, as her
ladyship's arrival with her invaluable secretary Miss Merriman
in attendance was one of the weekly festivals of the village, so
did she trail and drop her belongings and fuss with the hymn
book; lose, find, and lose again her large bag; converse aloud

with herself about the amount of money she should give for the offertory; drop whatever sum she had chosen and have to get someone else to pick it up for her because of her stiffness; suddenly remember that the book she had wanted to bring to church so that she could lend it to the Vicar who did not particularly wish to read it had been left on the garden seat the day before; all these she turned to favour and to prettiness. But already, so kindly do our minds and hearts unite in healing sore wounds, Lady Emily was remembered as a lovely echo of past days and the stories that grew round her were being in part transferred to Lady Graham. And so it is with each generation. The wavelet laps the shore, a larger wave comes from the sea and carries both forward; in the backward pull of the sea both wave and wavelet return to their home, while other waves large and small in their turn advance and retreat. Now it was to Lady Graham that the village looked; later it would be some one of her sons or daughters and so the endless chain of life will go on, though we can hardly believe in it for we shall not be there— and how can anything, how can the world itself go on if ourselves are not there to see?

The service went on. Lady Graham, to whom the words and the feeling meant more than most people knew, became lost in the old, ever-new orderly sequence and had almost forgotten her pew-guests till the little bustle of settling down to the sermon came, at which moment her ladyship began to apply her mind to what she would say afterwards to Caxton. Time passed. Hymn six hundred and sixty-six was announced and Edith made a cross face to herself because it was not what she called a real hymn. Coins clinked and paper rustled (though in most cases it didn't, being of very bad quality and not often enough renewed). The two sidesmen tried to look as if they did not know what each member of the congregation was putting into the plate, which in both cases was a very handsome silver-gilt one, the gift of Sir Robert Graham's grandfather. Lady Graham put in a ten-shilling note. She usually gave a pound but she felt this

might be ostentatious before her new acquaintances, and was
gently ruffled to see that Mr. and Mrs. Carter each put in a
pound; but reflecting that this was perhaps their entrance fee as
it were, upon their first visit, she forgot about it almost at once.
The little congregation was silent. Mr. Choyce lifted the plate as
an offering before the altar, the final words of blessing and
dismissal were spoken and the little congregation dispersed.

There must sometimes rise in the minds of people as they
come out of church the proverb, kept in our memory by Shakespeare: "Out of God's blessing into the warm sun." There are
few country churches in which one does not feel an air combined
of cold, damp, and mustiness, wish one had brought a warmer
coat, and find that Brother Ass, that beloved and too sensitive
tenant of our mortal frames, is kicking against the pricks like
anything. Some churches it is true have hot water pipes under
the floor, where hot air comes up through gratings, thus giving
to bad little boys an opportunity to drop bits of tissue paper on
them and see how far up the draught will carry them. Others
have one immense cylinder which dries and scorches all within
its immediate neighbourhood, requiring unlimited quantities of
coke and breeding much ill-feeling between the sexton and any
other church hangers-on as to whose duty it is (a) to keep it
burning, (b) to see that it doesn't get red hot, and (c) to rake it
out with a piece of iron turned up at the end and re-fill it with
coke. Not to speak of the cleaning of the large pipe that carries
away most of the hot air through a hole in the wall. But Mr.
Choyce, whose experiences among the Liverpool docks district
had given him a working acquaintance with many ships' engi-
neers, had learnt the ways of this stove and stood no nonsense
from it; neither did Caxton, who as a master carpenter despised
metal and gloried in getting the better of it. So the church was
usually kept pretty warm and in a cold summer Caxton would
get the stove going for a weekend just as a great violinist might
take out his fiddle for his own private delight. On this particular

weekend he had got the stove going on Saturday night and let it die down during the morning, so the cold was not unbearable.

Mr. Choyce, as was his laudable custom, was waiting outside the church to greet his parishioners and to him Lady Graham introduced Mr. and Mrs. Carter in form. Just as they were getting into their cars a man, grey-flannelled in compliment to the season rather than the weather, came down the lane.

"It's John-Arthur," said Edith.

Mrs. Carter greeted her brother with the sisterly words that she and Tommy were going out to lunch and there was nothing at the Old Manor House but the nursery dinner which was probably nearly over.

"You'd better come with us," said Mr. Carter. "We're going to Lady Graham's and Miss Graham is with us."

"Oh, but I'm not invited," said Mr. Crosse. "I only came over to look you up."

"Yes, you are, John-Arthur," said Edith, looking out of the car. "Do come," upon which invitation Mr. Crosse at once got into his sister's car and began to talk to his brother-in-law about the chances that Fox, Sly and Co., would go into liquidation before the month was up. And as we have not the faintest idea what he meant we will say no more about it.

Owing to the prevalence of pigs and poultry, there was always plenty to eat at Holdings in any emergency, but Edith, since her return from New York, had been so frightfully boring about food storage and a deep freeze that her father had lost his temper and had the largest and most expensive refrigerator that money could buy installed in the old dairy so that there could never be any difficulty about feeding unexpected guests. Not that the refrigerator had to be called upon today, for cook had bullied the butcher into a very large real sirloin of real home-grown beef and to mind he left the undercut on or that would be the last time he would be asked to have tea in the kitchen. So the addition of one more guest to the party was of no consequence and was indeed a good thing, making the numbers equal as it did. And if anyone thinks we have miscounted our numbers and are a man short, such an one is in error, for Mr. Choyce had a standing invitation to Sunday lunch and shortly afterwards turned up on his bicycle which he preferred to his car for short distances, on the grounds that it cost less, could be easily parked anywhere and was good for his figure, though this last was in excellent trim and did not need taking down.

"Now don't you forget, Odeena," said cook to that young woman, "that if Mr. Choyce is here he'll say grace. So when her ladyship and the rest have sat down, don't you go making a noise with the plates till Mr. Choyce has finished."

After a slight difficulty in arranging the table because of the Carters and Mr. Crosse all being related, her ladyship got them placed to her satisfaction with Mr. Choyce in virtue of his office on one side of her and Mr. Carter as a guest for the first time at Holdings on her other side, while Mr. Crosse was between Mrs. Carter and Edith. Lady Graham was not entirely satisfied with this arrangement, which put Mr. Crosse and his sister next to one another, but reflecting that the ties of consanguinity would prevent their marrying and that at any rate Mrs. Carter even though she was John-Arthur's sister, was married already, thought it wisest to leave things as they were. And as everyone could easily talk across the round table to everyone else, no one had any fault to find.

The sirloin of beef was in superb condition. Mr. Choyce, a fine amateur carver, volunteered to deal with it which he did with exquisite skill and taste so that no one could grumble and those who liked fat also had a delicious piece, its outside slightly browned and crackly. The gravy, made by cook's own hands from proper stock as had set nicely and done in the baking tin the way you get all the richness and no need for browning nor any of them meat cubes made of goodness knows what, was rich and superb. The potatoes were done to a turn under the joint, the sauce was made from cook's own store of garden horseradish, the French beans were almost too young to be killed though well worth it, the salad picked early that morning and coolly fresh from the fridge.

"I say, Lady Graham, this is Prime," said Mr. Carter with his mouth rather too full, but so much heart in his words that Lady Graham overlooked it and said she was sure his father-in-law had very good beef.

"I wish we had," said young Mr. Crosse. "Our butcher doesn't really understand beef. But," he added, zealous for the honour of his father's house, "we do get some Southdown mutton that is superb. It eats like sweetbread," which remark caused his sister to say that whenever she went to stay at Crosse Hall she put on at least half a stone. Not to be beaten in his own parish, Mr. Choyce said that he had partaken of a sucking pig at the Hallidays' and had been quite unable to eat anything for the next twenty-four hours, partly owing to feeling too full and partly because of the flavor which was so exquisite that he did not wish to spoil the memory of it.

"What about you, Edith?" said Mr. Crosse. "Did you have something wonderful in New York? A barbecue, or clams, or corn on the cob, or gumbo?"

Edith, considering these remarks as foolish and on the whole disrespectful to her dignity as a traveller, said coldly that she had not been in the South.

"I say, you *have* missed something," said Mr. Crosse. "When I was in Charleston—" but his sister very lovingly said that no one could care less what he ate in Charleston or anywhere else and could he tell her if father would be in that afternoon, as she had rung up twice and got no answer.

"I expect no one was in," said Mr. Crosse. "It's Peter's day off and father has gone over to High Rising."

"High Rising?" said Mrs. Carter. "Who on earth lives there?"

"Oh, Mrs. Morland who writes the thrillers," said Mr. Crosse. "She and father have made quite a friendship lately. You know mother loved her books."

"So do I," said Mrs. Carter. "Father *is* a beast not to take me too."

"Perhaps you weren't asked," said her husband, though quite kindly; "and anyway you wouldn't have got such a good lunch. Would it be grossly rude, Lady Graham, to ask for a third helping? It's a thing I've not done since I was a schoolboy back for the holidays," and far from thinking her guest rude, Lady Graham was delighted and said it reminded her of when her three boys were all at home for the holidays and James ate twelve sausages at breakfast for a bet with his brother John and then ate a thirteenth just to show.

"I think it is such a good plan for him to go to lunch with Mrs. Morland, because then he can meet George Knox who writes all those historical books and call on Lord Stoke at Rising Castle," said Lady Graham, who looked upon any expedition as a jumping-off point for visiting as many friends as possible, whether convenient to them or not—just as her mother Lady Emily would have done.

"I don't think he knows Lord Stoke properly," said Mr. Crosse. "Only at the Barsetshire Archaeological and things of that sort. Besides Mrs. Morland is going to show him a book she once published under another name and perhaps give him an autographed copy," which led to a conversation about people who wrote under other names like Ouida and that man who writes thrillers under six different names only I've forgotten what they are, which last contribution was from Mrs. Carter.

"And that gifted woman who wrote the thriller about Richard the Third," said Mr. Carter, "only I don't remember *her* name. She had three, I think," and so the talk drifted on in a highly intellectual way, each talker knowing perfectly well what book by which author he or she meant, but never being able to remember the author's name or pseudonym and rarely able to describe the plot clearly.

"Do you know, Mr. Choyce," said Lady Graham, drawing the Vicar aside as it were from the conversation, "we never asked

Caxton about the Old Manor House pew. But we were so much interested in your sermon that we quite forgot."

"I thought you might forget, Lady Graham," said the Vicar, without rancour or disappointment, as one stating an ineluctable fact. "So I had a talk with Caxton myself and as far as I can make out the pew really belongs to Squire Halliday because he is the Lord of the Manor here. I didn't like to bother Halliday because he gets tired so easily, but I asked George to find out."

"He *is* a good boy," said Lady Graham. "When I say boy he is as old as John-Arthur there," and she looked across the table to where young Mr. Crosse was racing Edith with cherries, when you put the tip of the stalk between your teeth and eat the stalk and the cherry up into your mouth as quickly as you can, which is as a rule not very quickly. "Somehow," she went on "those young men who were in the end of the war are younger than their age as well as being, alas, much older than their age," and if anyone thinks it was affected to say alas, let us tell such an one that it can be done without affectation and is splendidly disconcerting to the person one is talking to and gives one a chance to go on talking oneself.

"I know, Lady Graham, I know," said Mr. Choyce. "I sometimes think that they have missed a part of their youth and are trying to recapture lost time without knowing it. I will go up and see Halliday soon, on one of his good days. When he isn't in pain he remembers very well."

"So did darling mamma," said Lady Graham, "except at the very end when she wanted to see papa—she meant the Lord Pomfret who was her father—and then she thought Martin was his own father, my eldest brother who was killed in the first war. Perhaps it is like that in heaven, which I am sure will be a *most* confusing place, though of course perfectly delightful, rather like going abroad only worse. How we are to know who anyone is I don't know, but I am sure it will all be arranged quite perfectly," and her ladyship sank into a kind of glorious vision of The Hotel Paradise and Jerusalem with carpets of rainbows and plenty of celestial servants and all one's nicest friends and relations.

Mr. Choyce, feeling that heaven might perhaps be different for different people, did not like to correct Lady Graham, nor indeed could he have corrected her on any very definite grounds as after all what do the wisest of us know about what comes next. He was roused from these thoughts by his hostess adding, in what for her was almost an unkind voice: "But if Victoria Norton or that odious little Mr. Holt are there, I shall have to go somewhere else."

"If you mean the Dreadful Dowager," said Mr. Choyce, for by that name was Victoria, Lady Norton, known all through Barsetshire, "I am all with you. But who is—or was—Mr. Holt?"

"Oh, a *dreadful* little man who used to come to Rushwater and be a selfish bore," said Lady Graham, who hardly ever said an unkind word about people she knew. "And he was odious to people who could not answer back, like Merry. You remember Miss Merriman who was mamma's secretary?"

Mr. Choyce said of course he did and had admired her more than he could say when she was with Lady Emily at Holdings, but now alas he saw her but too rarely.

"That is because she is always at the Towers," said Lady Graham, "but I must get her over here when Sally is in London. We will make a plan," and Mr. Choyce felt, as he had often felt before, that there was in Lady Graham something approaching the angelic, by which no one would have been more surprised than Lady Graham herself.

At this point Lady Graham felt as a hostess that Mr. Choyce was having too long an innings and turning to Mr. Carter asked him earnestly what he thought of the Holdings pew.

"Do you know, I didn't really think very much," he began.

"Oh, I *am* so sorry," said Lady Graham. "Was it the cushion on the seat? I do so know those long cushions, so full of knots. No one has ever unripped them and picked over the inside since the war."

Mr. Carter said he didn't quite get her, by which he meant understand.

"Well, in the chapel at the Towers," said Lady Graham, "all the long cushions were stuffed with horsehair and every two years they were all taken into the vestry and unripped and all the horsehair taken out of them and teased."

"I'm afraid I don't quite understand," said Mr. Carter. "Teased?"

"I am too old-fashioned," said Lady Graham, looking at Mr. Carter with a kind of reproachful yet loving forgiveness. "What I should have said was that they were unripped and then all the horsehair taken out of them and—"

"I am so sorry," said Mr. Carter. "What a fool I am. Of course. The horsehair was taken out and *teased*."

"I knew you would understand," said Lady Graham, gratified. "Before the war the village women did it here and they all had to tie handkerchiefs over their mouths and noses because of the dust from the horsehair, but now they borrow our big vacuum-cleaner and do the cushions in the pews."

"I see," said Mr. Carter. "The dirt comes out but the horsehair stays knobbly. As soon as I get a free weekend I'll have the cushions out of the Old Manor House pew and teased within an inch of their life. Seldom have I had such an uncomfortable morning. Not since my prep. school when Bullard Major put some nice prickly horse-chestnuts into my knickerbockers just before prayers and first they gave me hell—sorry, Lady Graham—and then they fell out and I got a whacking and two hundred lines for brawling in chapel."

"If you don't mind a little gossip," said Lady Graham, "Hetty Scatcherd who lives with her brother who is an artist at the end of the village is very good at anything of that sort."

Mr. Carter said he loved gossip and wanted to learn all he could about Hatch End as he had come to live there.

"Don't worry, Carter," said Mr. Choyce who had overheard the end of this talk. "You will hear about everything from Hetty

Scatcherd till you wish you were at Jericho, or even further. She can mend and darn quite beautifully, so your wife might find her useful. But don't let her iron anything. She scorched my surplice quite dreadfully and though the patch she put in was a work of art, it is not what is used to be. I keep it for when the Bishop comes—which luckily is but seldom," he added, which made even the Carters laugh, for though they were not up in Hatch End gossip they heard a good deal of talk from the Close in one way and another and were anti-Palace to the core.

"I *am* so much relieved to hear you say that," said Lady Graham. "Of course one should not judge people lightly—"

Mr. Choyce said he had never yet heard Lady Graham say anything kind about the Bishop, and if that was judging people lightly he was all for it. He then begged her ladyship's forgiveness.

With raspberry fool and cream and cook's special sponge-fingers and coffee the meal came gently to an end. The Carters thanked Lady Graham in a heartfelt way for the lunch and the talk and before they knew where they were Mr. Carter had promised to speak for the Boy Scouts and Mrs. Carter for the Women's Institute and both had pledged themselves to join the local Conservative Association and mentioned, in a very modest way, the gratifyingly large subscription they would like to give, after which they went home, slightly exhausted, but having enjoyed their visit very much.

Edith invited Mr. Crosse to go up the river in the canoe and see if the young swans were about, so that Lady Graham and the Vicar were left peacefully alone. The Vicar said he ought to be going.

"Do stay a little," said Lady Graham. "I found some of darling mamma's lovely drawings that I want to show you. I thought I had gone through everything of hers, but you remember how she used to put things away like a squirrel and I found these at the bottom of a pile of old photograph albums from Rushwater that Martin and Sylvia gave me."

The Vicar, who like most men had a respectful adoration for her ladyship, said he would like it of all things, so they went to the large drawing-room, known as the Saloon, which was now in an almost permanent state of shut-up-ness in the winter on account of the difficulty of heating it, but during the summer was kept open and aired.

"Now, I ought to know where I put those drawings of mamma's" said Lady Graham, "because I put them there specially so that I could find them, but I can't. This is an old Visitors' Book from Rushwater," she added. "I really ought to give it back to Martin, but as I know a lot of the people in it, I won't. Will you make a little room at that table, Mr. Choyce. Oh, *thank* you," for with quick skilful movements the Vicar had folded back the faded green velvet cloth that lay over the table, shifted a pile of books, boxes, pieces of material, and other non-disposable odds and ends to one end, dusted the cleared part with the end of a dust sheet off a neighbouring chair, and was standing to attention, ready for the next job.

"Chairs, I think," he said and brought them forward.

"Oh, thank you, Mr. Choyce," said her ladyship sitting down, "and now we can have a really comfortable time. These are after the first war when we still thought everything would be all right for ever. This is a shooting party. Darling mamma always had a photographer over from Barchester when there was a shooting party and everyone had to be photographed whether they liked it or not. That is partly why they all look so cross, especially darling papa because he hated being photographed. Here he is, Mr. Choyce."

The Vicar followed her pointing finger to where Mr. Leslie in full country-gentleman panoply of check suiting, with knicker-bockers, a cap to match, and gaiters, was seated in the front row not enjoying himself. A number of gentlemen and ladies wearing what, after being first fashionable, then grossly out of date, were now fine period clothes, were some seated, some standing behind them and some sitting cross-legged upon the ground, flanked by two keepers. Mr. Choyce expressed his admiration and asked who they all were.

"Lady Emily of course I could recognize anywhere," he said, "but I confess I cannot do the others."

"I thought you wouldn't know me," said Lady Graham, not without an air of proud satisfaction. "I was still in the schoolroom but allowed out for parties or if they were a man too many at dinner. How dreadful I was," and indeed the plump girl with her hair obviously backcombed to frizz it out in front and a large bow tying it behind was more like Miss Hoyden than anything else. "But darling mamma had me properly groomed when I came out. I must see if there are some photographs of me in my first season," and she turned over several pages. "Yes, there I am, looking *too* dreadful. That was the year I met my husband. We danced together a great deal. Did I ever tell you how he proposed to me, Mr. Choyce?"

Mr. Choyce had heard more than once the enthralling story of how Colonel Graham, as he was then, had offered his hand to Miss Leslie, and indeed was rather tired of it, but from his hostess he was willing to hear it again if it gave her pleasure, in which he differed from Lady Graham's sons and her brother John Leslie's sons who shrieked, hooted, and whistled to express their disapproval. But not unkindly, and the scene always ended with laughter and a good deal of embracing.

Mr. Choyce, torn between his total want of desire to hear the story again and his reverent affection for his Church-warden's wife, was trying to formulate words which while expressing both points of view would not very distinctly express either when a shadow passed over the photograph album. Lady Graham looked up.

"Merry! how lovely!" she said. "Come and sit down. Mr. Choyce and I are looking at old photographs."

Miss Merriman, who had got to know Mr. Choyce very well when living with her beloved and trying employer Lady Emily

Leslie at Holdings, during the war years, shook hands with a smile and sat down.

"You know *everything*, Merry," said Lady Graham. "Who is this extraordinary woman in the tailor made? I can't place her. She looks as if she were saying 'Ha, dirt! I will speak to thee this once.'"

"I expect she was," said Miss Merriman calmly. "It is Mrs. George Rivers."

"That *dreadful* Hermione Rivers?" said Lady Graham. "So it is. I can never think how cousin George came to marry her."

"They do, you know," said Mr. Choyce, as one who while recognizing follies of this world was far above them.

"I must say for Hermione," said Lady Graham, "that though she writes those *most* improbable books about women of her age being fallen in love with by quite young men, I am sure she is excessively virtuous which," said her ladyship with a learned air as of one who knew Jung and Krafft-Ebing inside out, "makes it all the more peculiar."

"I only read one of hers," said Mr. Choyce, "an early one, I think, about a French nobleman who never travelled without his Steinway Upright Grand and met the heroine whose husband was a baronet and cold in manner at Angkor Wat."

"Was that all?" said Lady Graham.

"Well, really it was," said Mr. Choyce apologetically. "She did weaken a little when the Marquis dei Franchi—a deliberate crib from Dumas' Corsican Brothers by the way—played the slow movements of Beethoven's sonatas to her in the moonlight on the Steinway Upright Grand but Nothing Happened."

"So what happened then?" said Lady Graham, which was a more sensible question than it sounds.

"Oh, she went back to Singapore and met her husband at his hotel. They had separate rooms, both opening onto the same balcony, and all lived happily ever after," said Mr. Choyce. "I believe the marquis is still playing the slow movements aloud to himself somewhere" at which both ladies had to laugh, their laughter being considerably helped by their dislike of the gifted writer.

"I wish I had met Mrs. George Rivers," said Mr. Choyce, rather touchingly for so worthy and hardworking a priest.

"I do not think you would have liked her, Mr. Choyce," said Miss Merriman.

"I have the greatest respect for your judgment, Miss Merriman," said Mr. Choyce, "but I should like to try for myself," which made everyone laugh and indeed, had they all been a little younger, one might have called it having the giggles. Then Lady Graham enquired after her Pomfret cousins.

"Ludo is going on some special course later, something to do with Sandhurst," said Miss Merriman, "but I am so afraid of saying the wrong thing that I shan't try to say what it is. He will be alone at the Towers for some time, but I think he wants to work. I shall be there too, but I am hardly a companion for him."

"Dear boy," said his cousin Agnes. "Couldn't you both come over here for a week, Merry?"

Miss Merriman, who had hardly ever spoken without thinking, was silent.

"And don't say, 'If you really want me,'" said Lady Graham, which made Miss Merriman laugh and say that she would like it very much and would give Ludo Lady Graham's message and was sure he would like it too.

"I can't tell you what Sandhurst has done for him," she said. "When he first went he was so tall and thin and nervous that I think we all wondered if it was the sensible thing. I know Lord and Lady Pomfret were not at all happy about it. But evidently it suits him. Of course Giles will romp through. In fact no one would be surprised if he were expelled for high spirits. But we were all anxious about Ludo."

"So we all were about Gillie when he first came to the Towers" said Agnes. "I remember how dreadfully shy and quiet he was and then he somehow took command. I think you helped him a great deal, Merry."

"Yes, I did my best," said Miss Merriman, in a rather absent voice, thinking perhaps of the day when the present Lord Pomfret who was then plain young Mr. Foster had proposed marriage to the estate agent's sister, the present countess, and how sincerely she had congratulated him on what had been the best match from almost every point of view that his friends could wish for him. How she had passed the night after the announcement was, and always would be, like the rest of her private life, only her own affair.

"You know," said Lady Graham to Miss Merriman, "we have people in the Old Manor House now. Lord Crosse's elder daughter and her husband, a Mr. Carter who turns out to be a cousin of the Headmaster of Southbridge School where my brother John's boys were, so it is all in the family so to speak. I must take you over to Crosse Hall, Merry. Lord Crosse is most pleasant and a widower," at which Mr. Choyce nearly laughed and then felt slightly displeased, but both feelings vanished as a nightmare vanishes once we really know we are awake and not merely mad.

"Well now, that is really all settled," said Lady Graham to Miss Merriman. "Thank goodness Conque is not coming here this summer," for Lady Emily Leslie's rude and graceless French maid had become almost a yearly institution at Holdings. "She is going to France to quarrel with all her relations about a field of beetroot that someone left to somebody. I am sure she will have a delightful time," and to this day neither of her hearers have decided whether this was her own charming idiocy or a sudden outburst of sarcasm from a dove.

"Miss Merriman," said Mr. Choyce, "may I ask a great favour?"

"Certainly," said Miss Merriman, with her usual indefinable quiet aloofness and a kind of politeness which, as the Noel Mertons' agent Mr. Wickham had once said, made one wonder what the hell she really thought about things, to which tribute he had added that he would dearly like to see her down two or three stiff ones and wait for what would come out. But we think that Miss Merriman even in her cups—if anyone could possibly have imagined her in that condition—would have still been the picture of perfect discretion.

"It is our Mothers' Union Annual Meeting," said Mr. Choyce. "You may remember how kind Lady Emily was to them and came and gave a talk once," which Miss Merriman said, with her usual composure, she very well remembered, as Lady Emily had wanted to paint one of her free arabesques of flowers and fishes on the wall where the Mothers' Union Flag was hung and had with difficulty been headed off.

"If you could, in a way, continue her kindness by speaking to them while you are at Holdings," said Mr. Choyce, "it would give them the greatest pleasure."

Miss Merriman said she would be delighted to be of help.

"Have you any particular subject on which you would like to speak?" said Mr. Choyce. "I don't mean Biblical, though of course if you wished to say anything of that kind we should all appreciate it," and then his sentence tailed away and he felt he had got everything as wrong as he possibly could.

"How would it do," said Miss Merriman, who with her mind and eye trained to watchfulness for those she cared for had noticed Mr. Choyce's nervousness, "if I talked about the way the Towers was run in old Lord Pomfret's time? I know some of the women here worked in good houses when they were young."

"Splendid, splendid," said Mr. Choyce.

"As it will presumably be in the afternoon and there cannot be lantern slides," said Miss Merriman, "I could bring some large photographs of Pomfret Towers as it was in the late Lord Pomfret's time, with the dining-room table laid for twenty-four and all the plate out. And if Lady Pomfret will allow me, I could bring one of the old Lady Pomfret's dinner gowns. It is purple velvet embroidered with black sequins and some very fine real lace at the neck and sleeves."

Mr. Choyce nearly said God bless you, Miss Merriman, but

refrained. Not that he was afraid of testifying, but he felt that the words would somehow be unsuitable in the present surroundings, which is understandable if unreasonable.

"And I *think* I could find a pair of purple velvet evening shoes and a purple ostrich-feather boa," said Miss Merriman.

"If only someone could wear them," said Mr. Choyce wistfully, looking at the ladies as he spoke, but neither of them was as tall as the old Countess of Pomfret, nor did he think either of them would care to be mannequins.

"Perhaps," said Lady Graham who had been thinking—an act of which she was much more capable than most people would have believed—"we could get Mrs. Carter to dress up. She is tall and has a good figure."

"Admirable!" said Mr. Choyce. "That is," he added, turning to Miss Merriman and speaking with a kind of apologetic courtesy to one who had made the suggestion, "if you feel it would be fitting."

"Darling mamma, how *she* would have loved to dress up," said Lady Graham. "I remember when I was quite little she went to some big ball in London where everyone had to be their grandmother and looked superb in a crinoline that had belonged to a Countess of Pomfret. She had such a lovely neck and shoulders. So has Edith," which words her ladyship spoke in a kind of reverie, almost forgetting the generations.

"Then may I really count upon your help, Miss Merriman," said Mr. Choyce. "I shall have to send the notices out and I am sure all our members will come."

Miss Merriman said yes very pleasantly and was we think glad to have the chance of making one of her former employer's dresses useful, for her Lady Pomfret had the welfare of the people on the estate very much at heart and though her kindness was rather impersonal it was well organized and could be absolutely relied upon, as the agent and the clergyman of her day could have testified.

Then Miss Merriman returned to her task of helping Lady

Graham, who had embarked upon writing the names of the people in the old family albums beneath their photographs while the Vicar, who for once did not happen to have any pressing business and greatly enjoyed the society of two such delightful women, sat and watched them. Lady Graham had the advantage of remembering personally a good many of the originals but Miss Merriman, partly from her many family talks with her late employer Lady Emily Leslie, partly from other long talks with Mrs. Siddon the ex-housekeeper at Rushwater and partly from her own neat and almost scholarly mind where people were concerned, could fill in a good many gaps, though—as almost always happens with old family photograph albums—there were one or two people who appeared regularly in almost every group to whom neither lady had the faintest clue. One particularly plain woman who always wore a feather boa was provisionally identified by Lady Graham as a young version of Victoria Lady Norton, but a man in a check shooting suit with bicycle-handle moustaches remains unidentified to this day unless he was that man whose name no one could remember who wanted to sell someone an option on a sapphire mine in Burma and had been at Cambridge with the Honourable George Rivers's uncle.

Then with the Vicar's help the ladies put all the books neatly back in their places and went back to the drawing-room where Lady Graham said they would not wait tea for the young people, but almost at once Edith and Mr. Crosse came in. Edith hugged Miss Merriman who took the hug sedately, though with an inner warmth of heart that the namesake of old Lady Pomfret and beloved grand-daughter of Lady Emily Leslie should still feel and show affection for her.

"We went up as far as the hatches," said Edith, "and saw two kingfishers. John-Arthur sculled up and I sculled down. I'm getting some splendid blisters" and she exhibited, not without legitimate pride, several quite unpleasant examples.

"Run a needle and thread through each of them," said Miss Merriman. "Then they will empty themselves."

"And don't try to pick the scabs off, however tempting," said Mr. Choyce. "I've done it myself and wished I hadn't. Much better to get callouses if you really want to scull."

"But they will look horrid," said Edith, examining her hands which were not so elegant as were her sister Clarissa Belton's whose elegant tip-tilted fingers were the joy of all connoisseurs, but nice fingers all the same.

"No one is going to look at the palms of your hands, my girl," said Mr. Crosse with almost brotherly frankness and then both the scullers applied themselves to a hearty tea.

Presently a knock was heard at the door, so unusual a sound in these days that everyone looked up, almost expecting a masked emissary from the Vehmgericht or the Camorra.

"Come in," said Lady Graham with a smile of apology to Mr. Crosse and in came Odeena with the words "It's the lord my lady." She then plunged back towards the kitchen, feeling she had done her duty by the visitor who was Lord Crosse.

"May I come in?" said Lord Crosse, standing in the doorway, slightly though amusedly embarrassed. "I am on my way back from High Rising. Mrs. Morland sent you her love, Edith, and says come again soon," which pleased that young lady very much.

"I cannot tell you, Lord Crosse," said Lady Graham, "how pleased we are to have your young people here. They came to lunch today after church. I asked them to come to our pew as it was their first visit and then they are going to use the Old Manor House pew. It is a very nice one and only needs the cushions making over as they are full of knobs and it will seat the whole family," and if any of her audience felt that it would be a long time, if ever, before Mrs. Carter's two small children developed into the half dozen or more that the pew could easily take as well as the grown-ups, no one mentioned it.

Lord Crosse looked gratified.

"And now," said Lady Graham, knowing that men would rather talk about what they have been doing, however dull, than hear what other people have been doing, however interesting, "do tell us all about Mrs. Morland."

"Not very much to tell," said Lord Crosse, "but extraordinarily pleasant. I have never met a woman who seemed so entirely unconscious of herself. After all, she is a very famous writer, but no one would guess it."

Edith, rather impertinently her mother and Miss Merriman thought, said all Mrs. Morland's books were exactly the same because she had read them nearly all.

"You need a course in logic, my girl," said Mr. Crosse unchivalrously. "Lucas a non lucendo or something of the sort. I can tell you that my mother, bless her, said that the reason she loved Mrs. Morland's books was that although they were all the same they were all different. And she," he added, "had read every one of them. Even the two Mrs. Morland wrote under another name. Hadn't she, father?"

"She was particularly proud of having those two," said Lord Crosse, "because hardly anybody else knew about them. How she found out I don't know. But she was so clever at everything," and for a moment his face clouded and there was the slightest hold up, as it were, in the conversation.

"I never knew that Mrs. Morland had written anonymous books" said Miss Merriman. "How *very* clever of her," a remark with which we somehow agree, though at the same time fully perceiving its non-sequiturishness.

"What were the books?" said Edith, who having stayed with Mrs. Morland felt that she was peculiarly constituted to be an authority on that lady and ought to know all about her.

"I don't think you would have heard of them," said Lord Crosse, not unkindly. "One was a quite frivolous book about three Ladies of the Town in the early nineteenth century who were called Mrs. Bangs, Mrs. Patten, and Mrs. Pancras and lived in Covent Garden. It was all quite true and the ladies richly deserved their ultimate fates. The other was an experience of her own when she got mixed up during the war with an Anglo-Mixo-Lydian association. Of course she couldn't write it under her own name because of libel, but it was extremely funny. She has the makings of an excellent reporter in her if only she could keep to the point."

"And what were the ultimate fates of those women, poor things?" said Lady Graham who, as often occurred when she was not much interested in the conversation, was by now well behind-hand.

Lord Crosse said gravely that he thought it was Bridewell and three paupers' graves, but as Lady Graham looked distressed (though Edith and Mr. Crosse were having to suppress their giggles) he changed the subject and said he and Mrs. Morland had been over to see Lord Stoke who had sent Edith his love and said she must come again some day.

"Oh, *dear* Lord Stoke," said Edith. "You know he gave me a darling pearl necklace when Mrs. Morland took me to lunch with him, because he liked the name Edith, he said. Mother is taking care of it for me and I shall wear it on Occasions. I wish I'd had it in New York though."

"You can get much better looking costume jewellery—dreadful expression—in New York than you can ever afford in real jewellery here," said Mr. Crosse.

"Oh, but NO, John-Arthur," said Edith with a prim earnestness that made Lord Crosse laugh. "When I am presented I can't possibly go in sham pearls, can I mother?"

Lady Graham said, with a kind of adumbration of a shudder, that some people had gone in false pearls, but they were not the right sort.

"If you have pearls you wear them. If you haven't, you do not," said her ladyship, with the air of reciting one of Euclid's Axioms.

"But I can wear Lord Stoke's," said Edith, "because he gave them to me because he knew the other Edith he was very fond of," and had she not been a well-brought up girl she might—so Mr. Crosse felt—easily have said, "So there!"

Miss Merriman sat silent as she so often had and so often still did. A few words that old Lady Pomfret had sometimes let fall; some letters with a baron's coronet on the envelope which she had quietly burnt towards the end of her life, not greatly caring, after the manner of those of her rank brought up in pre-war days, what her secretary saw or did not see; a wreath of violets at the funeral whose sender was not identified except that a footman said he thought the groom that brought it was from Rising Castle but couldn't be sure and thought perhaps he wasn't; even all these put together did not prove anything. But that Lord Stoke had given to the young Edith a pearl necklace because she was Edith—also an Edith—well, whatever had once happened was gone and that was that.

"Tired, Merry?" said Lady Graham kindly.

"No. Just thinking," said Miss Merriman.

"Of darling mother?" said Lady Graham. "I do think of her so often, Merry, but I don't think she is thinking of us. She is asking cherubs and seraphs for their feathers to make pens so that she can write in red ink and blue ink," which unwonted flight of fancy from her ladyship surprised Miss Merriman and made her think of a song she had heard on the wireless about Laughing with Tears in my Eyes.

"I must get Blundells to look at Edith's necklace and see that the string and the clasp are in good order," said Lady Graham, at once becoming practical. "Robert's family have always dealt with them and he got my engagement ring there" and her ladyship looked with becoming sentiment at the very lovely diamond in an open setting which she always wore except when Messrs. Blundells' man came down once a year to clean and revalue her jewellery. Though it must in fairness be said that last time Mr. Hooker had come he had said that if her ladyship gave any more of her good pieces to her daughters when they married it would hardly be worth while for him to come. But we need not say that he didn't mean it and Lady Graham still possessed the diamond tiara and necklace that her husband had given her after the birth of their eldest son and very handsome she looked in them, though the occasions for wearing them were now sadly few.

"And I often wonder," Lady Graham continued, so did one thing lead to another in her fertile mind, "which of you ought to have the tiara."

"From my long knowledge of families, Lady Graham," said Mr. Choyce, "I should suggest giving it to whoever marries the richest wife or husband, because they are more likely to take care of it," a novel point of view but one upon which Miss Merriman at once brought her strong common-sense to bear, and silently agree.

"Then I shall have to wait quite a long time," said Lady Graham, "because the boys won't be able to afford to marry for ages, and if Emmy had it, she would probably wear it all the time and take it off when it got heavy and hang it on a hook in the cowsheds. Clarissa could carry it off beautifully, but for a school-master's wife it would look outré," at which point Edith and Mr. Crosse began to have the giggles and even the Vicar and Lord Crosse were hard put to it to look grown-up.

"Then I'll have it, mother," said Edith, "and throw it over the windmill—only there isn't one. But there's the thing up behind Hatch House on the downs that George put up that pumps the water up to the cattle tank. I'll throw it over that. George can pick it up for me."

"And now we will talk about something else," said Lady Graham whose sixth or social sense told her that Edith's non-sense had gone on quite long enough and that a joke of that sort would probably hurt George Halliday if it came to his ears— which she hoped it wouldn't. Miss Merriman who saw more than she said, at once spoke of the Old Manor House and said Lady Graham had told her how charming Lord Crosse's daugh-ter and her husband had made it and what excellent babies they had, while Lady Graham asked the Vicar when Septuagesima Sunday was and why it had that extraordinary name, though when he had kindly and fully explained she did not in the least understand; but we think this was really because she was still too much disturbed by her youngest daughter's silliness to listen, or even to pretend to listen; and probably Mr. Choyce realized this too. Edith got up and walked away to the window, Mr. Crosse following her.

"Don't," said Edith in a cross voice. "If a person can't be alone when they are cross, what's the use?"

"If," said Mr. Crosse calmly, "one person is they, what a lot of people must be in the room. But you oughtn't to, Edith."

"Oughtn't to what?" said Edith in a sulky voice.

"To cheek your mamma," said Mr. Crosse. "Extremely bad form. Most embarrassing for me, who am the person who really matters," which statement so puzzled Edith that she forgot to be cross.

"But why do *you* matter, John-Arthur?" she said, rather hoping to catch him and somehow take him down a peg.

"Because, as I said, you have made me extremely uncomfortable," said Mr. Crosse. "You have been impertinent to your mother. If I—or George Halliday for that matter—heard anyone being rude to his mother—I can't say my mother because she is dead—we should be livid."

"And you are livid now?" said Edith in a very small voice which also had a very slight mocking inflection in it, but to this Mr. Crosse was adamant.

"No," said Mr. Crosse, half amused, half sorry for Edith who was such good company but had behaved really badly, "just thoroughly disappointed. You need something to do, you know. I shall speak to your mother about it. No I shan't, I shall speak to Miss Merriman. I say, father, if we are to look in at the Old Manor House we must go, or the children will be in bed— incommunicado."

So Lord Crosse and his son went away, and then Miss

Merriman said she would drive Mr. Choyce back to the Rectory as there was some talk of his exchanging pulpits one Sunday with the clergyman at Nutfield only the difficulty was that Lady Pomfret wanted it to be when she and all her family were at home, but the Vicar at Nutfield must not know this or he would be jealous. Mr. Choyce obligingly offered to come disguised as a very High Church Archdeacon, and then was serious and said how much he would like to come.

"Your man was in the army, I think," he said.

"Yes he was a Captain in the Barsetshire Yeomanry," said Miss Merriman, "and he likes to be Captain The Reverend on his letters."

"I suppose I oughtn't to say this," said Mr. Choyce, "because I wasn't in the army myself, but I do so envy people who are two things at once, like that very nice man over at Southbridge who is Colonel the Reverend something—Edward Crofts—that's his name."

"I like it too," said Miss Merriman. "It seems to me very fine and English that His Majesty's—I mean Her Majesty's—Commission comes first. Of course when you get marquises—or dukes' sons—it is more complicated. But it must be rather fun to be The Reverend Lord Henry Somebody. Is that right?" she said anxiously.

"Yes. I think you are correct," said Mr. Choyce, "though I have never had to face that particular question. Will you come in for a few moments?"

Miss Merriman was not in a hurry and said she would like to and had Mr. Choyce invented any new gadgets; for his ingenious anti-burglar devices and cat-doors were much admired not only in Hatch End but as far afield as Barchester, where the Dean had been heard to say, warmly, that a man like Choyce ought to be in the Close, evidently feeling that a priest of Mr. Choyce's ingenuity would be a valuable weapon against the Palace.

"Nothing very particular," said Mr. Choyce modestly, "but I

did think of something for my spare room—I can't bear the expression guest-room, I don't know why."

Miss Merriman said she thought it was because it somehow sounded like an iron bedstead, a very thin and rather lumpy mattress with not enough blankets, and transparent window curtains that didn't meet, which point of view, put with her usual air of calm decision, struck Mr. Choyce very much.

"If you don't mind coming upstairs?" he said, rather—or so Miss Merriman thought amusedly—as if he were assuring her that his intentions were honourable. Miss Merriman said she would be delighted, so Mr. Choyce led the way to the first floor and opened a door, showing a pleasant bedroom of good size looking over the front garden and away towards the church and the village. His guest's skilled eye, trained by many years of looking after other people and their comfort, at once saw that the bed was a really good one, snugly set in a corner away from draughts, but near enough to a window to make reading in bed easy and—almost as important—with the light coming from the left hand so that one could write letters in bed.

"A delightful room," she said.

"Praise from you, Miss Merriman, with your experience," said Mr. Choyce, much gratified, "and now I must show you what I have got for this room. It is one of those things like a padded arm-chair without any legs to sit up in bed in. It lives in this cupboard, so that any guest who wants breakfast in bed can have it comfortably. Of course I have a proper tray as well, with legs that go up or flat with a spring."

Miss Merriman said it was so comfortable that any guest of his would want to be ill for a day, just for the fun of it.

"And washing-things in this cupboard," Mr. Choyce went on, opening a door. "A basin, you see, with hot and cold, and it tips up to empty it. And a house-telephone by the bed so that my guests can talk to me if they wish and a real telephone as well. When the Archdeacon was here he said he had half a mind to get me unfrocked and take the living himself. And now may I show you my other spare room? It will not tire you?"

Miss Merriman, amused, interested and rather touched by the Vicar's thought for his guests' comfort, said she would be delighted. He took her along the passage and down a few steps into a large, light room with six camp beds, their blankets neatly folded, stacked, and dust-sheeted on them.

"I must explain this," he said, not without pride. "You know I had a large rather poor parish in Liverpool, near the docks, before I came here. I got very fond of my parishioners after I had knocked one or two of the liveliest out—fair fighting of course—and I think they liked me and I didn't want to lose touch with them. They gave me some very handsome silver when I left the parish. I never liked to ask where it came from, but there were a good many varieties of crest on it. Most of the young men are dock workers or seamen and some come south, so I keep this room as a kind of dormitory for them. If they are at Southampton they can easily lorry-hop to Barchester. But I am boring you?"

Miss Merriman did not answer for a moment.

"It doesn't bore me," she said. "It interests me very much, Mr. Choyce. I know a good deal about boys and young men. From a different class it is true, but they are all the same when they are young. I think our work has been rather the same—looking after people. You know what my work was during the war when Lady Emily Leslie was living with Lady Graham at Holdings and I was more or less in charge of her."

Mr. Choyce said no one could ever forget her and how distracting she was to the congregation and how entirely unconscious of it and always so kind and so lovely.

"And now I am doing what I can for Lady Pomfret," Miss Merriman said. "But that cannot go on for ever and she will need a younger woman to help her. Forgive me, Mr. Choyce. I didn't mean to talk about myself."

"I may say, and quite truly, that I have never known you speak of yourself before," said Mr. Choyce. "I feel it is an honour. I shall remember it and keep it to myself. Shall we go downstairs?" so they went down and when Miss Merriman had thanked Mr. Choyce for letting her see the Vicarage and he had sent friendly messages for the Pomfrets she got into her car and drove away to the Towers.

CHAPTER 6

A t the Old Manor House the front door was not locked by day, so father and son went in and found their respective daughter and sister, otherwise Mrs. Carter, at home and to her they suggested a dinner party to be given by her for Lady Graham; the guests, as far as she could make out, having also been chosen by them in advance. Some married daughters might quite reasonably have been slightly put out by a party so arranged over their head as it were, but good-natured Mrs. Carter said it would be absolutely marvellous and how clever of father to think of it and she would invite them next week.

Lord Crosse said not Monday as he was dining at the Deanery and not Friday because that was a dinner of the Barchester Club. So Mrs. Carter said Wednesday then and why not ask her husband's cousins the Everard Carters from Southbridge School as Lady Graham's nephews had been there; which was no reason at all, but quite a good one if one liked it.

"That's us, two," said Mrs. Carter. "Everard and Kate four; you five, father, Lady Graham six, and we'd better have four more. The table takes ten easily. Oh, George Halliday. He never seems to get treats."

"I feel sorry for that boy," said Lord Crosse, though George's boyhood had gone a good many years ago, just as young Mr. Crosse's had, when the last years of the war took them both. "His mother is a delightful woman, but his father isn't much good now. If I begin to get invalidish and slow and don't sleep and feel sorry for myself, and grumble, you must buy a poison pill for me," which his dutiful daughter at once promised to do—for one's own father would of course never be really old and certainly not like poor Mr. Halliday. "Yes, do have him," Lord Crosse went on. "And what about John-Arthur? You might ask Edith for him. She is rather spoilt, but it isn't her fault. I can't think why Lady Graham doesn't get her into a job."

"Oh, he must come of course, father," said Mrs. Carter. "That's five men and we want one more woman. It's funny to be a woman short. Why not Mrs. Morland? She's awfully nice."

Lord Crosse made a little noise as though he were beginning to speak, checked himself, and then said it wasn't a bad idea.

"Of course it isn't," said Mrs. Carter rather indignantly, "and if it had been your own idea, father, you would have been awfully pleased. I'll ring her up. There's a bit of the road up this side of Low Rising and I'll remind her about it."

"I could send for her, easily," said Lord Crosse, upon which his undutiful daughter called him an old fusspot and then repented and kissed him very lovingly and invited him to come and see the children in their bath.

Nurse had got them both in the large bath together, very pink and clean and splashing each other, though not very fiercely for both were still of the age when their arms and legs are almost boneless. Nurse said Not to wet poor grandfather, but this was evidently only a token remark, for the children splashed more wildly and aimlessly than ever till nurse took the younger out, wrapped it in a towel and gave it to its grandfather, taking the older one herself to dry its hair.

"Gib," said the younger child with a divine toothless smile, poking vaguely with one fat finger at where it thought its grandpapa kept his eye and making a very bad shot at it.

"She nearly said Grandfather," said Lord Crosse proudly.

"It wasn't grandfather," said nurse. "She meant your watch, my lord. When you made it strike for her last time you saw them in their bath, your lordship said 'Tick-tick,' and she never forgets anything," said nurse proudly. "You take our big boy, my lord, and I'll dry baby's hair," which she then did by rubbing it with a soft towel and twisting it into neat damp light brown ringlets, when it looked so silly and divine that its besotted grandfather had to bend over and kiss the nape of its soft neck which made it give a kind of crow of joy, considered by all present to be extremely brilliant and accomplished. Then nurse took the boy and gave the girl back to Lord Crosse, who held her in exactly the right way, so earning nurse's approval.

Mrs. Carter, who was now quite used to having two babies about the place, was not as besotted about them as her father, but approved the whole scene and then nurse graciously gave them their congé on the grounds that Some People wanted a nice drink of milk and beddy-byes.

"That woman does make me feel small," said Lord Crosse to his daughter. "I've not felt so put down since I went to my prep. school. Your nurse was much the same, and your mother and I sometimes wondered what belonged to whom. She obviously owned you and the nursery maid and most of the staff—except the cook. She and cook didn't speak which was rather restful as then your mother and I didn't have to listen to what nurse had said or what cook said nurse had said."

"Oh, I won't stand for anything of that sort, father," said Mrs. Carter. "I just happen to be the mistress of the house and nurse jolly well knows it. And I've got my eye on a village girl, Cissie Panter. Her father is Mr. Halliday's carter and her mother washes all the children's things and irons them beautifully and Mr. Panter at the Mellings Arms is her uncle. It's just as well to be in with the village. One would never get a Barchester girl to come here. Come down and have some sherry."

So they had their sherry and talked and Lord Crosse was amused—and also pleased—to see how his rather masterful daughter was getting the village under her thumb. And being older and possibly wiser than his daughter he thought that presently the village would have her under its thumb, but she probably would not know it, for it would come as gently as a large snake slowly engulfing a small animal, though less painfully. A line from a great singer came to his mind, "But now England hath taken me" and he thought that with the slight alteration of Hatch End for England it would apply very well to his elder daughter, which made him laugh.

"What is it, father?" said Mrs. Carter, but he could not explain so he asked if she had heard from her sister lately as he hadn't.

"Oh, they've gone on a cruise somewhere, and left the children with his mother" said Mrs. Carter, "and she says it's awfully cold and there's an Archdeacon on board who will have prayers on Sunday—not a proper service like on a liner when the Captain does it, but in the card room at half-past nine. She says it's a bit of a bore to be up so early but after all it's a shame to keep the card-fiends out of their room. I want her to bring the family here for Christmas. Will you come too, father? There's heaps of room if we squash up a bit."

"Much as I love you, I will *not* squash up," said Lord Crosse. "Suppose you all come to me for a week—both families?"

"Well—" Mrs. Carter began.

"That means no, I suppose," said her father, with perfect good-humour.

"Oh, not like that," said Mrs. Carter, "of course I'd adore to come, father, but I'm going to make the Vicar let me decorate the church and there's a Carol Service and I want to try to teach some of the women to sing in parts, and arrange a party for the over-sixties who seem to be half the village, but I'm sure some of them are cheating. Could we come for the New Year, father, and you come to us for Christmas?"

Lord Crosse thought for a very few seconds.

"I would love to have you all for the New Year," he said, "but I won't come to you for Christmas. I am going to be quite truthful and say that though I love my grandchildren like anything I would find a Christmas with them and nurse, not to speak of the over-sixties and everything else, too exhausting. If you all come for the New Year I shall love it. I wish your mother could be there and see those babies of yours—but she can't."

"I know, father darling," said Mrs. Carter, getting up and rubbing her cheek on the top of his head. "I *do* know and I'm sure mother would. We'll come to you for the New Year of course. But don't get into a habit of never going anywhere, father. We do want to see you," which kind words touched Lord Crosse more than he would or perhaps could show.

"There is a book by Mrs. Gatty, called Parables from Nature," he said, speaking half to his daughter, half to himself. "My mother used to read it me when I was small and one story was called 'Purring When You're Pleased.' It was about a little girl who had to live with relations—very kind loving ones—because her parents were dead, and she was always shy and even rather rude. And the house cat had kittens and one was given to her for her own and she loved it, but it wouldn't purr for milk or being stroked, and its brothers and sisters did purr. So she cried and cried till her aunt asked what it was and then of course there was a tiny sermon about showing your happiness and gratitude because only feeling it wasn't enough."

"And of course everything came right and she purred when she was pleased for ever and ever," said his daughter. "All right, father, I do understand. Only you've *got* to purr sometimes. Mother purred like anything when she was pleased, didn't she?"

"She did; she did," said Lord Crosse. "You are quite right, my dear, as you always are. I don't know what John-Arthur is doing. Tell him I've gone home."

Then his lordship drove himself back to his large house and had his usual solitary dinner and dealt with a number of dull official and business letters and so to bed.

Mrs. Carter was one of the happy people for whom life has been, is, and probably will be as smooth as is possible for human life under present conditions. One does not for a moment grudge them their happiness, for they give it away in lumps to other people, but one cannot help wishing, a little, that one could have say a fortnight of it once a year for oneself. She adored her husband, intended to have and adore at least two more children and was able to deal with Hatch End as its superiors had always dealt with it: fairly but firmly, a little bullying for their good, as little favouritism as possible. And what is more she had from the first kept nurse in her place, much to the surprise of that worthy woman who looked upon young mothers with a baby from the month as half-wits, to be bullied and kept in their place, and seldom had she been more surprised than when Mrs. Carter not only came into what nurse had always called My Nursery as often as she liked, but even altered the children's hours and food as she thought fit. Mr. Carter, for the male of the species is usually more timid than the female, had once or twice expostulated, fearing an explosion in the nursery and Notice from nurse, but his wife only told him not to be silly and if he did it again she would come to the office and disgrace him in public. And as she was very truthful and always kept her word, he very sensibly stopped discussing nurse and left everything to his wife. But, as all the village said, Mrs. Carter was a lady as *was* a lady. By which we think they meant that she would allow them to think they were getting the better of her once and would pounce if they tried it on a second time. Only once had Mr. Carter asserted his authority, when the Mixo-Lydian maid Dumka, whom Mrs. Carter had engaged before she knew the potentialities of the village, had a kind of Central European Rising all by herself, occasioned by a request from cook to keep that nasty garlic out of her kitchen, which Dumka countered with loud Mixo-Lydian patriotic songs and letting the milk boil over. On that horrid day, when Mrs. Carter was over at Crosse Hall, Mr. Carter had taken immediate action, rung up Mixo-Lydian House, the hostel supported (most unnecessarily) by Her Britannic Majesty's Government, and said they must remove her at once or he would get the matter brought up in Parliament. Within a few hours a large car with three large Mixo-Lydian officials had arrived, collected Dumka and her luggage and the wages owing to her (which with mistaken generosity her employers had paid a month in advance) and take her away. Nature abhors a vacuum and her place had been filled at once from the village, but rather in what we are given to understand is the Chinese method, namely that so long as you have a servant his or her provenance is not your business, nor are you to be surprised if he, or she, is a different one sometimes.

"You are lucky," said George Halliday when Mr. Carter told him this interesting story at the Mellings Arms where both gentlemen were fetching some beer and strictly obeying the Scriptural injunction about not muzzling oxen that tread the corn by standing one another two pints each. "It takes an outsider to do that, or an old inhabitant. Father could. I'm not sure if I could," but this was false modesty, for though Mr. Halliday was rarely seen in the village now, or indeed on his own farm, his name still commanded attention and we believe that George Halliday was quietly, though quite unconsciously, slipping into the Squire's place which his father would not hold much longer.

And not for nothing had Mrs. Carter come from a line of respectable landowners who were now hereditary peers and though not Barsetshire by ancestry were proving themselves to be worthy of the county. As a girl at Crosse Hall she had watched her mother and learnt much, among other things just how far you should let the people on your place go and where it would be a good thing to be generous and where it would be better to be just; and even on occasions to bully. On the few occasions when she and George Halliday had talked together she had learnt a good deal of his inherited and acquired knowledge of the place, had used it well, and intended to learn more.

All the invitations were accepted. Cook spread the good news of a dinner for ten in the village and for a short time the kitchen yard was like Mafeking Day with crowds clamouring to be allowed to help, till cook—who most luckily was a Barsetshire woman herself though from over Hartletop way which is terra incognita—came majestically out of the kitchen, picked a couple of tried helpers out of the crowd and sent the rest away. Peters, hearing at Crosse Hall via the girl at the telephone exchange that Mrs. Carter was having a dinner party, wrote to his employer's daughter to offer his services for the evening, an offer which Mrs. Carter gratefully accepted and then had a delightful sense of security, like floating in a padded boat on a very calm sea or, even better, being in an extremely comfortable bed with a string quartet playing softly in the next room. Lord Crosse being informed, after the deed, of what Peters had done, said he supposed Peters would have to go and he had better take half a dozen of that good champagne with him.

"Thank you, my lord. The one that her ladyship used to fancy, if I remember," said Peters.

Lord Crosse did not answer.

"Is that all, my lord?" said Peters.

"Yes, yes," said Lord Crosse. "Her ladyship would have liked them to have it. You can take the little car, Peters. I will have the Bentley. You had better go over early and see what you can do for Mrs. Carter. How many will there be, do you know?"

"Ten, I believe, my lord," said Peters," and black ties. I will leave your lordship's things ready before I go," and he went back to his pantry and told the pantry boy that if the silver was well done he might come and look at him—Mr. Peters—in his black evening suit before he went over to help the Honourable Mrs. Carter with her dinner party.

"Oh, *thank* you, Mr. Peters," said the boy. "I'll tell mum to press my suit so as I'll be smart when I come to look at you."

"You'll *ask* your mum, my boy," said Peters, "not *tell* her. If I'd have told my mother to do anything I'd have had the stick. Time you learnt to press your own suit. You'll never get into good service if you can't press a gentleman's suits, and brush them and sponge them too. *I* don't know how you boys expect to get into good places."

"Please, Mr. Peters," said the boy, "mum says I'm not to be a servant, Mr. Peters. She says I ought to look higher."

"Now, one more word like that, young fellow, and back home you go for good," said the justly outraged Peters. "Where would I be, do you think, if I hadn't learnt my work proper, the same as you're learning it now under ME. Why, I might be behind a counter selling bacon, or stockings. Or I might be a clurk sitting in an office adding up figures all day."

"Oh, you couldn't do *that*, Mr. Peters," said the boy, not so much in doubt of Mr. Peters' capacity to add any number of figures or sell any quantities of stockings or groceries, as in recognition of his great personality, intended by Providence for high places.

"Now, you listen, my lad," said Peters. "If you see your Sunday suit's clean and your boots properly shined and your hair brushed and clean hands and don't you forget behind your ears and your nails, I might take you to help at the Honourable Mrs. Carter's dinner party. I say I *might*."

"OW!" said the boy in a whisper. "You *are* good, Mr. Peters."

"Good's nothing to do with it," said Peters. "I know my place, the same as his lordship knows his, and if you learn to know yours you might be butler in a Good House some day, or a Gentleman's Gentleman. There's still houses where they have them. And mind you don't eat nothing as comes out of the dining-room, it doesn't look well. There'll be supper afterwards and I'll let you taste the champagne. But don't you tell your mother all that. Just say Mr. Peters wants you to come and help."

He began to re-arrange the silver in the drawers, dreaming of a day when perhaps Crosse Hall would have a mistress again and entertain properly. But that wouldn't be in his lordship's time, no nor in his neither. Still, it wouldn't do the silver any harm to give it another rub.

*   *   *

News of a dinner-party for ten at the Old Manor House spread quickly through the village and gave considerable satisfaction, for it stood to reason, said Mrs. Panter, who did all her ironing just inside her kitchen door the better to see what was going on down the street, that the Old Manor House was the right kind of house for the gentry and Mrs. Carter was a very nice lady and most of her smalls went real silk except her nylons that were washed at home. And the children had nice things and there was some lovely table-linen. Not that sort with lace all round it and bits let in and try how you will you're almost bound to get just a tiny crease here and there if the lace isn't quite on the square, but Reel Linen, as good as Mrs. Halliday's; that heavy the tablecloths were it was all she could do to get them on the line and came up beautiful with hardly any starch. This joyful rumour ran up and down the village and the Mellings Arms counted on a profitable evening.

The first guests to come were Mr. Carter's cousins, the Headmaster of Southbridge School, Everard Carter, and his wife who was Lady Merton's elder sister. Everard was the fair type which does not appreciably age till one day you look at it in strong sunlight and see that it has gently withered, as it were. His wife except for being slightly on the buxom side had altered very little since Everard had fallen in love with her at sight during the summer holidays nearly twenty years ago and both were much liked by the boys (who are pretty fair judges), most of the masters and parents and—perhaps most important of all— the school staff. Everard Carter had hardly overstated matters when he once said that if he died and no one were told except the form masters of the school could run quite nicely for another year without anyone noticing. To which his wife had replied that she would mind so dreadfully that it wouldn't be worth his dying.

"I'm glad you've come first, Everard," said Mr. Carter, "because I want to put my boy down for Southbridge. He's nearly three."

"Don't lead your aces, my boy," said Everard. "I'll probably have retired by then and the school gone down at least ten places, like Snakes and Ladders. Write to the School Registrar and put it in another envelope addressed to me, and I'll see your chap is safely down, even if it means putting Adams' boy or Lady Cora Waring's down a peg. I'm all for nepotism."

"Can I see the children?" said Kate Carter, a request which her cousin-in-law found highly reasonable and took her upstairs leaving the men to talk, which was chiefly about Carter ramifications and their common great-, or great-great uncle the Archdeacon who was an Egyptologist and married a Lady Sibyl Somebody who was distinctly peculiar.

"It's a pity they had no children," said Mr. Carter, thinking of his two upstairs and every intention of more to come.

"Well," said Everard, "I don't know. They were both pretty dotty. I wouldn't have liked my family to take after them. Not that Lady Sibyl was any relation, but old Uncle Tom was. Anyway I don't believe much in heredity. Look at Pomfret. His father, old Major Foster, was no good at all and no one knows much about his mother. He never wanted to come into the title and the place and look at him now."

Mr. Carter said he did not really know the Pomfrets and he thought Lord Pomfret didn't look very well.

"He isn't," said Everard. "But he does all he ought to do and more. That's where blood does tell in the end. And his wife is a wonder and runs half West Barsetshire, which must be nearly as difficult as running a school. Of course they have Miss Merriman. A *most* remarkable woman. She has been a kind of secretary-companion all her life and never made a false step as far as one knows. She pretty well ran the Towers when old Lady Pomfret was alive and she pretty well ran Lady Emily till her death and was on good terms with everyone. She practically runs

the Towers now, though everyone doesn't know it. Who have
you got tonight?"

Mr. Carter mentioned the names of the guests. Everard expressed the great pleasure that he would feel to see Mrs. Morland, who had been such a help to the School at the outbreak of
war, and almost immediately upon these words that lady arrived,
from which moment Mr. Carter felt that he was an un-noticed
guest in his own house. For though his guests tried to include
him in their conversation it was obvious that Mrs. Morland was
their real flame. Lady Graham and Edith arrived simultaneously
with Lord Crosse and Mr. Crosse in their various cars and the
noise, to the accompaniment of sherry, became as deafening as
only a small party of well-bred people can be.

"We're all here, aren't we?" said Mr. Carter to his wife, who
said she thought so, but would ask Peters, who knew everything.
But even as she said these words Peters, who was vastly enjoying
the ritual of opening the front door and greeting the guests,
announced Mr. George Halliday. We think that most of those
present had rather forgotten about him, which of course made
everyone greet him with more than usual friendliness, especially
Lady Graham who did not forget him and perhaps saw more of
him and his parents than anyone else in Hatch End. For when
the darkness of a long illness descends upon a house and the
sufferer often has not the strength and hardly even the wish to
see old friends, it is ten to one that friends, unless specially
invited, will gradually stop coming. Mrs. Halliday, seeing much
and saying little, sometimes wished that her son had work that
took him away from home, even if it were in China, or Mngangaland where at least Canon Joram could have given him excellent introductions to the present King, who after taking a third
at Balliol (largely owing to an over-riding interest in games of
skill and chance) had gone home, ritually murdered his father,
given small government jobs to his seventy-nine brothers and
sisters, and was gently leading his countrymen back to their
primitive condition of laziness, squalor, and over-eating varied

by periods of abstinence when game was scarce or the crop of Mnganga-hoko, the staple diet of the country, failed because the inhabitants had alternatively forgotten to plant it, or were all at the cinema on the ritual night for collecting the harvest; which state of things had gotten even worse since the arrival of three-dimensional films.

But as no opening in Mngangaland had occurred, George Halliday was still adscriptus glebae as Mr. Choyce had neatly put it, and probably would remain so. He loved the place and put his whole strength and interest into it, but whether he was happy even his mother could not guess. Sometimes she blamed herself for what was not her fault; but if George did go away into the world, how would the place go on? All of which made him increasingly silent and but for Lady Graham who treated him almost as a son, he might have lost touch altogether with his neighbours. But all of those present were pleased to see him and the Babel of talk from ten quiet county gentlefolk might have been heard as far up as the hatches.

The door was opened and Peters appeared. All were now silent and held their countenances intently, the while from the drawing-room door Peters the majordomo thus spoke:

"Dinner is served, madam."

"Thank you, Peters," said Mrs. Carter. "I did try to get us into couples," she went on, addressing her guests, "because I thought it would be fun to go in properly because one is hardly ever even numbers now, but I couldn't remember who came where in order of precedence except father being a baron, only he doesn't count," by which apologia we think she meant that her father, being under her roof, had somehow abrogated his undoubted right to his title. What her guests thought, we do not know, but very probably nothing, and they all went into the dining-room where Mrs. Carter had taken the precaution of putting their names in their places, owing to which foresight on her part one or two short-sighted people, Mrs. Morland among them, had made at least one and a half tours of the table before being rescued by Peters and put into their proper seats.

To the great satisfaction of Everard Carter and Mrs. Morland they were side by side and at once plunged into reminiscences of the war and how helpful that nice Margot Phelps who kept goats had been and how nice it was that she had married the rich Mr. Macfadyen, and the changes in Wiple Terrace, and how Eileen at the Red Lion became more golden-haired every year in spite of matrimony, and how splendid Matron had been and still was and too dreadful to think that she might be retiring and there would never be anyone in his, Everard's, time who knew so much about the School, almost more than he did, so that it was with difficulty that they were separated when it was time for Everard to turn to Lady Graham and Mrs. Morland to Lord Crosse.

"I wish I could have had the pleasure of fetching you," said Lord Crosse. "My daughter tells me that the road is up over your way. I did ring up twice but couldn't get an answer."

"Oh, Stoker—you know my fat tyrant Stoker—was away" said Mrs. Morland, "and so when I was out the telephone wasn't answered. She goes to Plaistow where she was born every two years or so. I don't mean she was *born* every two years or so."

"I quite understand," said Lord Crosse. "She goes, every two years, to Plaistow, where she was born," but he said this very kindly.

"That is the worst of words," said Mrs. Morland. "Sometimes I wish there weren't any. They will *not* do what you want."

"I am sure they do what *you* want," said Lord Crosse. "My wife used to say that part of the pleasure she had from your books was the way you used your words. She said you made them do everything you wanted with no apparent effort."

"Blood, tears and sweat," said Mrs. Morland in her most Mrs. Siddons tones. "I don't believe in taking a year to write one page or loading every rift with ore—or whatever it was that whoever said it said—but there are times when words are like a roadblock. You can't move it and you can't pass and you can't go back."

Lord Crosse said he had occasionally experienced that feeling when trying to write business letters, because the business world had a quite dreadful style of its own, calculated to obscure the simplest issue and he had never mastered it. Luckily, he added, his secretary at the office could write most of them for him. "But of course," he added, "your secretary couldn't write your books."

"My good man," said Mrs. Morland, quite forgetting that she addressed a peer of the realm and a baron to boot, the oldest rank in our aristocracy, "I have never had a secretary in my life. Mrs. George Knox used to type for me before she married and looked up things for me sometimes when I couldn't remember what I meant, but that is all."

"Do you mean you write everything *yourself*, by hand?" said Lord Crosse.

"Well, how else?" said Mrs. Morland. "I mean if you have thoughts you have to be very careful. If you dictate them you are apt to become verbose, like—" and she mentioned several distinguished names among writers of fiction. "Or else you can't think of anything to dictate and your secretary sits and looks patient till you could kill her."

"But what about your fan-mail?" said Lord Crosse. "You must have a great many letters."

"A fair lot," said Mrs. Morland judicially. "But they all get answered. It's part of the job. And if people take the trouble to write to you, you like to show your gratitude. It's all in the day's work, if only one's hand didn't get tired. I am expecting Writer's Cramp at any moment," at which Lord Crosse, though slightly concerned, could not help laughing.

"I shall not try to arrange your life for you," he said kindly. "Only do go on writing for us. And if ever you *do* want a secretary, let me know. I can lend you a woman who actually understands what one is saying and puts in the commas," which Mrs. Morland thought excellent qualifications.

On the opposite side of the table George Halliday (rather tired after one of the days when everything goes wrong from a defect in the pumping engine or ram to a sow overlaying her two best piglets and a hen who was a good layer entangling herself fatally in a piece of loose wire and having to be killed, not to speak of Mr. Halliday being in a low state and convinced that George ought to dig up the garden and put it under vegetables because of the war) was gratefully eating Mrs. Carter's good dinner and drinking Mr. Carter's excellent wine, safely between his hostess and Kate, whose conversation in particular he found most soothing as it was almost entirely about her children whom he did not know. So he sat and let her gentle tide of talk flow over him and listened to her placid and, if we must say it, complacent account of her three children, including the surpassing cleverness of Bobbie who was soaring through his education on scholarships, the charm and good looks of Angela who was top of her form at school and thank goodness her second teeth which were a little crooked had been quite beautifully straightened, and the gifts of Philip, aged thirteen, who was fairly good at his books and first class at all games.

"Why don't you come over to Southbridge, Mr. Halliday?" she said. "We should love to see you and it would be a change for you."

George, who was completely captivated by her soft manner, said there was nothing he would like better, but he didn't like to leave the place much.

"You see," he said, "father is really pretty ill now and mother is with him most of the time and she does get tired, so I try to take him on in the evenings. He likes to play backgammon only he doesn't remember the moves very well and I simply *loathe* the game. I loathe all games and I never could play cards because I'm so stupid at remembering what I have and can never guess what the other people have."

"But couldn't you have someone to be with your father?" said

Kate Carter. "I don't mean so as to make him feel he was ill, but just to help your mother?"

George said he had often thought of it, but he didn't think his father would like it.

"Now, you will not mind this question," said Kate, "but could you afford a suitable person if you could find her?"

The question did seem to George a little sudden, but there was something so kind and motherly about Mrs. Everard Carter that he could not be annoyed and even blamed himself for thinking he might be annoyed when she was obviously trying to help him.

"Oh, that's fairly all right," he said. "I've been into it with father's bank and they say we can manage. I have a power of attorney or whatever it is because of the farm, so the money part is all right. But I can't spare time from the farm to take him on and mother is killing herself. If one could find the right person—but I don't think anyone could stand father for long."

"I am so very sorry," said Kate with such sincerity that George would have liked to shake hands with her. "If I could hear of someone, might I let you know?"

George said it was very kind of her, though not in a hopeful voice.

"But, good gracious, what am I thinking of?" said Kate, and then paused.

"I give it up," said George.

"But of course I know exactly the person you want," said Kate. "Did you ever know old Miss Pemberton at Northbridge who knew all about Provençal poetry?"

George said Not in his line of country, but what about her.

"Oh only that she is dead," said Kate. "I heard all about it from my sister Lydia who lives over there. She was ill for some time before she died and practically bed-ridden but quite sensible," to which George's unspoken comment was that he wished his father were like that instead of being pretty dotty and all about the place. "And," Kate went on, "a very nice Sister Heath looked after her for the last months, a retired nurse who lives in Northbridge but takes cases for the right people. She is free at present and would like another job. She got on very well with Miss Pemberton and anyone who did that can get on with anyone. She is a great friend of that nice Sister Chiffinch who was with Dr. Dale at Hallbury when he died and several other people."

George thought this sounded full of hope and first blamed himself for his thought and then laughed at himself for blaming himself. Kate Carter looked a little surprised.

"I beg your pardon, Mrs. Carter. I was just remembering how rude father was to the district nurse some years ago when he had lumbago" said George, not very truthfully.

"But he wouldn't be rude to Sister Heath," said Kate, in such a headmaster's wife's tone of calm assurance that George at once believed her. "Would you like to have her address; or shall I ask her to write to you?"

"I would be most grateful for the address," said George, "and so would mother, though she won't admit it. Father will kill her soon if I can't help her. Thank you so very much, Mrs. Carter."

Kate said she would ring up Sister Heath next morning and ask her to ring George up and what would be the best time. So George told her the hours between which Sister Heath could safely talk to Mrs. Halliday by herself and felt such relief as he had not known he could ever feel; for not till the burden begins to lift do we feel what the weight has been. With a very kind motherly smile for George, Kate turned to Mr. Crosse and of course won his heart immediately by her calm pleasant voice and ways, so that he asked if he could put all his children down for Southbridge as soon as he had any.

"Oh dear, haven't you any?" said Kate.

"Not so far as I know," said Mr. Crosse, "but you see I'm not married. I only meant that when I am married I would like my boys to be with you," but Kate, who was nothing if not practical, said that though her husband liked it when Old Boys put down their sons' names very early, she was sure he wouldn't think it quite fair to put down sons who had not yet got a mother.

"Besides," she said, "you ought to send your sons when you have any to your own old school—unless you were very unhappy there. Where were you?"

Mr. Crosse said Winchester, because his people always did, and he certainly wasn't unhappy, but he liked New College much better.

"But of course you would," said Kate earnestly. "I mean it is so much nicer for a young man to be with other young men" at which point Mr. Crosse nearly had the giggles, but not quite, and asked Kate if she and her husband would come to Crosse Hall one day in the holidays and see the house and garden, which she said would be very nice and then they talked about various county matters.

Meanwhile Edith, who was after all the only unmarried lady present and felt people ought to value her as such, was making rather heavy weather with her host, while Mr. Carter was wishing his wife had let him arrange the table so that he could talk to Mrs. Morland and not to this pretty chit. But a host must be agreeable and he did his best.

"And what are you going to do now?" he said and then felt he was behaving like an uncle, but one couldn't sit and say nothing.

"I don't know," said Edith, which she said quite truthfully, because it had never before occurred to her to ask herself that question. "I like being at home."

"Which is most unusual in people of your age," said her host kindly.

"Well, I've never really been anywhere else," said Edith. "At least I did go to New York in the winter to my uncle and aunt and it was great fun but I liked coming home. Now father has retired I would like to help him with the place. I know a lot about pigs. Of course my sister Emmy Grantly over at Rush-water is the cow one. But what I'd really like would be to learn about estate management—I mean what father's man Goble does. It would be splendid to run a place and see that the accounts are right."

"And what do you know about accounts?" said Mr. Carter, amused.

"Not much, but I'd easily learn," said Edith. "Then I could really help father, or go to the Towers and help Cousin Giles and Cousin Sally. They really have more than they can do and father has Goble and he will be here himself much more now."

"That's a very good idea," said Mr. Carter. "I believe the Barchester City Council have a first-rate School of Agricultural Economy. It's a two-year course I think for people who want to take it up professionally, but you can take a one-year course and get quite a fair knowledge of how a place should be run. I expect you know something about it already."

"Of course I'd have to ask father and mother," said Edith, adding in a lower voice, "but if they said no I could do it just the same."

Mr. Carter asked how.

"Oh, just do it," said Edith. "I like figures and arithmetic. Father is very good at them too—that's why he's on so many boards, besides common-sense. I'm not quite sure how much common-sense I've got."

Mr. Carter thought that a young woman who saw her own limitations so clearly—though he also thought that she under-estimated her abilities—would be an extremely useful person in the county, though of course she was bound to marry and throw it all away. But at this moment the talk became rather a general uproar because of a dreadful rumour, started by George Halli-day, that Lord Aberfordbury, he who had been Sir Ogilvy Hibberd and so signally defeated by old Lord Pomfret about the matter of Pooker's Piece, was going to re-open the Bishop's suggestion of erecting a chapel to the memory of the Reverend Thomas Bohun, M.A., who was a Canon of Barchester from 1657 to 1665 and the author of a number of highly erotic poems, some of which had been rescued, edited, and republished by Oliver Marling, Mrs. Samuel Adams' brother.

As several of the company did not know about Bohun the others were able to explain him to them and there was a good deal of noise. Mrs. Morland said that Oliver Marling must wish he hadn't written that book, but everyone wrote something they were ashamed of at one time or another.

"Not *you*, Mrs. Morland," said Edith.

"Yes, indeed, my dear," said Mrs. Morland. "I once wrote a story which was so bad that I can't think why Adrian Coates ever published it. It had excessively bad reviews which, I must say, were perfectly justified, and a black cover which was also rather depressing. For a long time I didn't like to think of it, but now I don't care."

"How many books have you written, Mrs. Morland?" said Lord Crosse.

"About thirty, counting the ones that aren't books," said the gifted author.

"What *do* you mean, Mrs. Morland?" said George Halliday.

"Well, some that aren't novels," said Mrs. Morland. "But they are quite good. And a book for children with the most divine stories. I cry whenever I read them because they are so beautiful. But I couldn't do it again. You do things when you are younger that you can't do when you are older."

"Gone, alas, like our youth, too soon," said Lord Crosse, quoting a lovely romantic song that still makes us cry if we hear it.

"Still, one can do things when one is older that one couldn't do when one was younger, so it all works out," said Mrs. Morland. "But one must be practical" she added. "If anybody is doing anything about stopping Lord Aberfordbury getting a chapel erected for Bohun, we must join them. I'm sorry about all the present participles" she added apologetically.

"Who has a better right to use them than you?" said Lord Crosse, which remark was gravely received by all the company (who had at once given up their own talk when the name of Aberfordbury reached their ears) except the recipient of the compliment who laughed so whole-heartedly that the rest had to follow her.

"But I don't think we need worry," said Mrs. Morland, "because the Dean simply loathes Lord Aberfordbury and luckily the Bishop can't meddle with the cathedral."

"It's Lord Aberfordbury's horrible son, Mr. Hibberd, who is ruining Mr. Scatcherd," said Edith.

Mr. Carter said he was a new-comer and would Edith explain.

"Oh, Mr. Scatcherd is an artist here," said Edith "and he paints very bad views of the river and the cathedral and sells them to tourists, but Mr. Hibberd is a director of a the National Rotochrome Polychrome Universal Picture Post Card Company and makes picture postcards of the views and Mr. Scatcherd says he is ruining Art," at which everyone laughed but quickly became serious again when Mr. Carter said he was new to Hatch End and had never heard the Horrid Truth, but he would from now onwards hate Lord Aberfordbury and his son more than ever and subscribe to anyone and anything against him.

"I will get the Dean and Mrs. Crawley to dinner," said Lord Crosse. "Perhaps you would come too, Mrs. Morland. Aberfordbury is really intolerable. These new lords!"

"Come, come, father, you're only third baron yourself," said Mr. Crosse, which Lord Crosse took very good-humouredly and said unless his son married and did his duty by the country he would be the fourth and last baron, after which remark that side of the table laughed a good deal and the other side wanted to know why, and the noise was so loud that Peters, standing in the pantry like the Turk with his doxies around (except that by no stretch of the imagination could the village helpers be considered as such), said it reminded him of the parties His Former Lordship used to have at the Towers in the hunting season while

Her Ladyship was in Italy, and if the ladies liked to finish that last bottle of champagne he was sure his lordship would have no objection, and The Boy could have just a taste, seeing as he'd never had champagne before.

"But mind you don't tell your mother, my lad," said Peters, to which words of wisdom the boy, such is the effect of the Demon Drink, said You betcher life I won't Mr. Peters, sir and all the women said There now, wasn't he a one. But we are glad to say that the boy, his soul as set on pleasing his superior and so raising himself from the ranks as was Sir Galahad's on the Holy Grail, never said a word about it to either of his parents, nor did he boast about it among his young companions; from which we confidently predict a good future for that boy whether in service or in any other walk of life.

By this time Mrs. Carter had withdrawn her ladies to go up and see her babies asleep in their cots, all the devil in them drowned in the angel, with petal-soft warm cheeks, hair slightly damp with the exertion of sleeping and small starfish hands on the coverings, or thrown up above the head—and only mothers know how long it is before a baby's ridiculous macaroni arms can meet above its ridiculously out-size head—bless them.

So the men now were able, if they wished, to se débrailler (Lord Crosse, who had for a short time been in the diplomatic service and prided himself upon his French), or Use Oaths, or Talk Lightly of Women, or lose a thousand pounds at écarté, pledge their family plate, their equipages and even their French cook and win it all back in a throw of the dice. But if we are to be truthful, they drank a glass of port each and discussed (a) Mr. Macfadyen's new vegetable marrow crossed with a pumpkin and (b) what the profits of Mr. Adams's great engineering works at Hogglestock were likely to be, and as none of them knew any definite facts about either of these subjects they got on very well.

"I say, father," said Mr. Crosse, "Edith wants to read that book of Mrs. Morland's that's out of print and she can't get a copy. I said you'd lend her yours."

"Well, you were the more deceived," said Lord Crosse. "I will give a book—if I have a duplicate—but lend: Never. Lending books breaks more old friendships than I would like to mention. There is a copy in the Barchester Free Library because I gave them one. You can get it out for Edith if she can't get it out for herself."

Mr. Crosse thought of taking offence for a moment, but he was a good son and said All Right and then the three other men took up the same tale, Everard Carter being particularly fierce about the books which—in spite of all rules—were yearly missing from the school library, though he must say if he was to be fair (which he evidently did not wish to be) that the staff were on the whole much more careless than the boys, and Matron had kept a book of Mrs. Morland's for three months before it was run to earth.

It was of course almost inevitable that the three younger men, George Halliday, Mr. Crosse, and his brother-in-law Mr. Carter should get together over war reminiscences and when it was discovered that Mr. Carter, who was artillery, had been within ten miles of Vache-en-Étable a month after the other two had left it, they became rather noisy brothers-in-arms.

"I say, George," said Mr. Crosse, "do you remember that Australian medical bloke, Major Something, when the diggers lost the A.P.M. in the canal? He was a hard case. I wonder what happened to him?"

George Halliday said he had forgotten that one, but did John-Arthur remember the English Colonel who wore his eye-glasses even when he was asleep and—at which point Mr. Carter said he didn't want to interrupt, but would anyone like to see the children in bed before going to the drawing-room.

This is an invitation which is always difficult to refuse unless one has a really lame leg and cannot easily get upstairs. The gentler sex—by which we mean women—are always ready to go up two or three pair of stairs to worship, though we doubt whether the Rest really want to. But Mr. Carter was still a young parent, his wife was delightful, the food and drink had been good, the company amusing and friendly, so up they trooped, to be received by nurse with a fine mixture of condescension as from a Worker to the Idle Classes and proper pride that Her babies should be properly appreciated by a Lord (even if Lord Crosse was but Poor Granpa in nurse's estimation), the heir to a barony (to be known henceforth as Uncle John), a Headmaster, and The Young Squire, for so the elder villagers called George Halliday. As for Daddy, by which name Mr. Carter was now doomed to be known though he much disliked that particular form of his name, he stood low in the list, being only the children's father.

For the honour of grandparents—being seven ourself so to speak—it must be said that Lord Crosse behaved magnificently, speaking with just the right mixture of lordly arrogance and servile respect to nurse and remembering both children's ages; but as he had had a rehearsal not so long ago this was perhaps not quite fair. Everard Carter as a father of three and in loco parentis to a number of older boys was graciously approved by nurse who said she was sure Our Young Gentleman would like to go to a nice school. But as O.Y.G. was fathoms deep in slumber with one flushed cheek visible and the downy curls on his head damp with the exertion of going to sleep, he could not speak for himself; not that he could have said much to the point if awake. As for Everard he disliked the idea of touting for school-fodder and parried nurse's hints with considerable skill.

"I always feel an awful fool with babies," said George Halliday to Mr. Crosse as they came downstairs. "I don't mind my sister's, that's Martin Leslie's wife, because—oh well after all they're hers. But I don't really want to see even hers when they're small. They're quite jolly later on," to which Mr. Crosse cordially agreed and so they joined the ladies who had been enjoying their segregation vastly, discussing such really interesting subjects as whether Mrs. Macfadyen, formerly Margot Phelps, daughter of the Admiral at Southbridge, was likely to have a baby or not, thus leading to an ill-informed discussion as to the ultimate age at which one could expect a baby, till Edith instanced Sarah who, to her own great surprise, had a child at a highly advanced age. But this was not received with favour by the rest of the party and in any case, said Mrs. Morland, one never knew what people's ages really were in the Old Testament and perhaps the word that was translated year was really only month, or perhaps something like three months, which would of course make it all much easier. Lady Graham then instanced Methuselah, but as no one could remember how many years old the Bible said he was, it was not much good trying to reckon how old he might have been if the years had been months.

Mrs. Morland, with a feeling that Edith was not quite at her ease, presently got her onto a large sofa with kind Kate Carter where the talk could be on the level of everyday's most quiet need by sun and candlelight and they enjoyed themselves very much while Lady Graham and Mrs. Carter talked village, a talk that like the Midgard Worm has its tail in its mouth, so that you can go on for ever.

"Mrs. Morland," said Edith, "did you ever want to have a job when you were young. I mean—"

"When I wasn't as old as I am now, you mean," said Mrs. Morland kindly. "No. I can't say that I did . Then I got married and had four boys which was quite enough job for anyone. And then my husband died so I had to write books. No, I don't think I ever wanted a job."

"I really wouldn't have had time for a job," said Kate Carter, "I did no much for mother at home. I did do some secretarying for the Dean and Mrs. Crawley, but then I got married which was much nicer."

"But you both did *do* jobs, even if you didn't *have* jobs," said Edith, sticking to her idea with all her mother's gentle tenacity of purpose. "I do want to have a job. Something about managing places. Not all cows like Emmy, or schoolboys like Clarissa—"

Mrs. Morland interrupted to ask if Clarissa Belton was teaching at Harefield House School.

"Oh no, not teaching," said Edith, "but she and Charles have a House now and Clarissa runs it all. It's twenty boys but Clarissa says she could easily do thirty if they had one more bathroom—they've only three. It sounds lovely," which words made Mrs. Morland think. Both Grahams and Leslies were managers. Lady Emily Leslie, that enchanting, wayward, loving, maddening creature, had managed everyone and everything that came within her orbit. Sir Robert Graham was a leader of men and affairs. Perhaps Edith had it in her too. She would have liked to talk with Miss Merriman about it, but this could wait. As a mother of boys only she did not know girls very well and though she was fond of Edith and found her a very agreeable companion, she did not feel that she knew what was going on inside.

Kate Carter, appealed to by their hostess for information about the Friends of Barchester Hospital, went over to sit with her and Lady Graham, leaving Mrs. Morland and Edith alone.

"Can I tell you something, Mrs. Morland?" said Edith.

"Of course you can," said Mrs. Morland, "and I can listen. But don't expect me to be able to help you much. I am not in the least practical."

"It isn't practical," said Edith. "At least perhaps it is. You know Emmy always loved the Home Farm and she went to live at Rushwater with our cousin Martin Leslie and do cows when she left school and then when she got married to Tom Grantly she went on living there and Tom says she can judge stock as well as Lord Stoke. And Clarissa wanted dreadfully to go to college, so she did, and then she got married to Charles Belton, and—" at which she stopped.

"And you dreadfully want to do something?" said Mrs. Morland kindly, feeling at the same time pretty sure that Edith would also wish to leave the nest.

"Yes. Don't think it's awfully silly," said Edith, "but I want to

do a course in Estate Management and help father. I was talking
to Mr. Carter about it," she added in a grown-up voice. "I got
that stupid thing one has to get when one leaves school, but I
don't want to go to college like Clarissa. I'd rather learn about
managing a place. I'll help father with Holdings and when I'm
married I'll know how to run my husband's place."

Mrs. Morland marvelled, as all we elders marvel, forgetting
that we too were once young and confident in our power to
tackle anything, that this spoilt baby of the Graham family
should be so sure of herself. Yet she envied it. So had not all her
own generation been sure, except that they nearly all expected to
marry and most of them did. But to tackle a professional
training in estate management and be prepared to take on one's
father's place under present conditions was an undertaking that
almost frightened her.

"I expect you will," she said. "I never learnt to do anything, so
I just had four sons and got them educated with writing books
and now I go on writing books to help to educate my grandchildren."

"But that is what is so depressing," said Edith. "You did
everything on your own and I don't see how I can ever do things
on my own. Emmy did cows on her own, but Tom does the
estate part. And Clarissa just helps Charles. But I've no one to
help me."

From some girls this might have been taken as an almost
Victorian "I'm a poor helpless little thing and you are a Great
Big Man" attitude, but Mrs. Morland felt that this was not so,
that Edith was rather blindly trying to justify her existence. As if
such a darling girl needed justifying, said Mrs. Morland indignantly to herself. But that was life now. And though Edith had
said no word about her parents, Mrs. Morland wondered if
perhaps Lady Graham was coddling this last duck of her brood,
keeping her young too long, without realizing what she was
doing. Hardly a case where an outsider could interfere.

But now with the men coming in all this was put aside and the talk became general and quite interesting about county affairs and particularly about the contemplated chapel to Canon Bohun and the necessity for a strong lay party to support the Dean and Canon Joram who were already active in the anti-Bohun party.

"If," said Mr. Carter thoughtfully, "it were possible to get the Bishopess to read those poems of Bohun's that Oliver Marling edited, I think even she would be shocked."

Lord Crosse, a loyal supporter of the anti-Palace faction, said he doubted whether the Bishopess could read. He knew, he said, from his secretary at the office, who got her books from Messrs, Gaiters, that she and the Bishopess were both served by Miss Black, who had told his secretary that really, the books the Palace had you wouldn't hardly credit. All that Russian stuff and worse, his secretary had said darkly, and that really not quite nice book of Mrs. Rivers's about the Decameron in modern life, all about people going on, well, one wouldn't like to credit such things could happen, not a bit like the home life of Our Dear Royal Family, at which words nearly everyone felt the faint mist in the eyes and slight constriction of the throat that the thought of Majesty brings to us.

Then this subject died and other matters for interest or amusement came up and presently, to everyone's surprise, it was eleven o'clock and Lady Graham began to say good-bye to her hostess, with plans to see more of her and catch her for even more village matters.

Mrs. Morland said she must be going.

"Would you think me interfering if I asked if I could drive you home, Mrs. Morland?" said Lord Crosse. "I hear that the road is up over in your direction."

"Well, that is very kind of you," said Mrs. Morland, "but I saw just where it was up when I came over and it can't be upper. I mean no one will be working on it now. Besides if you drive me home in my car you won't get home and if you drive me in your

car, how shall I get my car over from Hatch End to High
Rising?"

"Quite simple," said Lord Crosse, noticing with faint disapproval that his daughter and his son were listening. "If I may
drive you home in my car Peters can follow with your car to
High Rising and then I shall drive him back to Hatch End
where he will pick up my other car."

"But what about your boy?" said Mrs. Morland. "I saw him
through the service door drinking the dregs of the glasses."

"He can come with Peters," said Lord Crosse firmly. "But
how good of you to think of him. I only hope he hasn't been a
nuisance to my daughter's staff."

So after good-byes Lord Crosse helped Mrs. Morland into
his car and drove her home, followed by Peters with her car. And
we can only hope that the fact of driving the well-known
novelist was its own reward, for Mrs. Morland, who was not
often out late, was so sleepy that she almost needed shaking up
from time to time like Mrs. Smallweed, and could only say
Good-night in a very dazed way to her kind admirer. When the
front door had closed, and Peters had put Mrs. Morland's car
into the garage, he got into the back of Lord Crosse's car and
they went back to Hatch End. Here the Boy, who had been fast
asleep in cook's arm-chair in the servants' sitting-room, was
more or less roused and bundled into the small car by Peters who
took him home, told his mother he had been a good lad and he
could have his sleep out tomorrow, which condescension so
impressed the Boy's mother that she darned his socks before she
went to bed, it being now well on midnight. By this time Lord
Crosse was in bed, reading one of Mrs. Morland's earlier novels
and thinking of his wife and how she would have enjoyed the
evening. And we think she would, for she was very fond of him
and would have liked of all things to see him happy.

The rest of the party quickly dispersed, Lady Graham and
Edith, who was yawning like anything, to Holdings and bed;

the Carters to Southbridge, and George Halliday across the river to his home and his duties. To his relief the house was dark, so he drove round by the back entrance, left the car in the yard and went quietly upstairs, grateful for silence. He did not lie long awake with star-defeated sighs, for he was very tired. He remembered suddenly what that kind Mrs. Carter had said about a nurse who liked elderly invalids and understood the difficulties of staff and housekeeping in these days. That might be the answer if it came off. More rest and more leisure for his mother. A kind, competent hand firmly upon his father. And for himself some respite from having to tell an ill man every day about the farm, knowing that his father hardly understood now who or where he was except for his dependence on his wife; for George had realized some time ago that the time and work and patience he gave to the place meant nothing, now, to his father. But work must go on and day follow the escape of night. He went to sleep with the light still on and did not wake till late next morning—or late for him. His first thought was of Sister Heath, but he told himself to be patient and his self was fairly obedient.

CHAPTER 7

Mrs. Everard Carter was not one to let grass grow under her feet when a kindness could be done. Next morning she rang up her sister Lady Merton at Northbridge and told her about the Hallidays' plight. Lydia, who possessed the strong benevolence of soul attributed by Pope to General Oglethrope, at once flew from Pole to Pole, or in other words drove down to Punshions, an old stone cottage formerly the cold uncomfortable home of the Provençal scholar Miss Pemberton and her co-worker on the great Biographical Dictionary of Provence, Mr. Downing. Mr. Downing was now happily married to Mrs. Turner, a delightful widow with a comfortable house and some money and Punshions had been taken, after Miss Pemberton's death, by Miss Heath a very nice and capable retired nursing sister and her friend Miss Ward, also an ex-nurse with some private means. And here the two ladies led a very happy life, putting thick carpets over the stone floor of the living-room and the far too slippery shiny wooden staircase, painting the depressing original and very crooked beams and rafters a nice shade of cream, fixing draught excluders (or whatever their name is) to the bottoms of the ill-fitting old doors and installing gas-radiators all over the place. They also had the large open fireplace in the living-room safely shut up with matchboarding painted pink and a nice gas fire put in so that all their friends said it was too cosy for words. As indeed it was, but better be cosy than cold at any time. Miss Ward had quoted the words "the clartier the cosier" more than once with great satisfaction and as neither she, nor Miss Heath, nor any of their local friends were well acquainted with the Lowland Doric, the description gave great satisfaction, making one think, as Mrs. Downing had said, of a Nicht wi' Burns. Luckily her husband had not heard these words which would have troubled his accurate scholarly mind: but even if he had heard them we think he would have over-looked them as one of the many inexplicable and much-loved barbarisms of his much-loved and very loving wife. Those who knew Mr. Downing best from his academic days were wont to say with his old Oxford friend Mr. Fanshawe, now Master of Paul's College, that a man who could marry a wife called Poppy was, as M. de Voltaire so truly remarked about the prophet Habakkuk, capable de tout. But as no one in Northbridge except the Rector knew the allusion and we doubt whether any of them had ever seriously attempted to read the work in question, although one of the four shortest prophetic books, the matter had gone no further.

With the house they had taken over Effie Bunce, daughter of the wicked old ferryman up the river who though now unequal to ferrying (which was just as well for his boat was falling to pieces and he had no intention of having a new one unless They, unspecified, gave him one for nothing) was a very good hand at cadging drinks at the local. Miss Bunce and her sister Ruby, housemaid to Lady Merton, were a shining example of the wages of sin being not death, but very nice positions as daily helps with handsome salaries (for we cannot repeat the word wages so soon) a very good table kept and unlimited freedom to gossip at the backdoor, while their good-looking, healthy chil-dren of shame were getting free education and free transport to the local school from The State, which would probably support them in one way and another for the rest of their lives.

Miss Heath and Miss Ward, having long experience of ward-maids (mostly the offspring of Dark Rosaleen and doing ex-

tremely well in England under the Saxon Oppressor), had at
once taken Effie Bunce's measure and that too friendly being
found herself—for the first time in her life and to her own great
surprise—doing exactly what she was told and even giving up
bright red paint on her nails. What Miss Heath had said no one
ever knew, but she gave Effie some nail cream and a nice
washleather buffer and Effie's shining nails in their natural
colour had become the cynosure of neighbouring eyes. So much
so, indeed, that everyone was afraid she might qualify once more
for the enviable status of an unmarried mother. But everyone
was wrong, for Miss Bunce knew exactly on which side her
bread was buttered and was indeed considered by her friends to
be giving herself airs because she was doing for real trained
hospital nurses. The expression "doing for" being used in its
domestic, not its murderous sense.

It was always doubtful to visitors at Punshions which meal its
owners were having: partly because having lived so long by
routine in hospitals they were apt to have meals at extraordinary
hours as a kind of symbol of freedom, and partly because they
had not as yet decided whether lunch, tea, or supper should be
the Principal Meal; which name, hitherto unknown to them,
fascinated Mrs. Villiers and her friends, including Lydia Merton who though she did not live in Northbridge itself had many
friends there and did there such shopping as she did not do in
Barchester. But it was obvious by the crockery on the table that
they were having tea; that is to say *tea* which you have at any time
between half-past three and half-past five, not TEA which you
have at any time between half-past five and half-past seven or
later.

Miss Heath and Miss Ward, looking up as they saw Lydia's
car pass the window, both said it was that nice Lady Merton,
which lady shortly appeared from the kitchen, commonly used
as an entrance by friends of the house. She apologized—as our
old Lydia Keith would probably not have done—for coming
round by the back because she didn't know if anyone was in and

it was easier to turn the car in the yard, which explanation appeared to satisfy the hostesses, who at once asked her to join them and they would make some fresh tea, an invitation which usually leads to a lot of argle-bargling about Oh no, I really *like* it cold, and We were just saying we must make some fresh for ourselves. But Lady Merton accepted her hostesses' decision with a word of thanks and sat down, while Miss Ward picked up the now tepid teapot and went into the kitchen where a large kettle was talking aloud to itself on the expensive Sultan combined cooker and water heater which the owners had installed. Miss Heath, being the soul of honour, did not ask Lydia any questions and told her about the Nasty Finger that Effie Bunce's fourth child, a little boy popularly supposed to be the result of a day excursion to the coast in one of the Southbridge United Viator Passenger Company's fleet of motor coaches, had been having and how Dr. Ford had lanced it and The Place was doing nicely and by the time she had taken the last bandage off Master Hovis Bunce (so called from Hovis House where Effie Bunce had sometimes worked for Mrs. Dunsford and her daughter) Miss Ward came in carrying a large tea-tray heaped with crockery and food.

Lydia, full of admiration, said Miss Ward ought to be a turn in a Music Hall and get a thousand pounds a week.

"I carried some pretty heavy trays when I was a V.A.D. in the war," she said, "but Matron wouldn't let us have the teapot. We had to bring that separately. She was ghastly. Her name was Miss Mells so of course we all called her Smells."

Miss Heath and Miss Ward looked at each other.

"Well," said Miss Heath, "it never rains but it pours as the saying is and I did my training with old Smelly. She was A1 on the surgical cases but I beat her hollow on prems. In fact Matron said to me: 'I've seen plenty of abdominal cases and Mells isn't so bad, but when it comes to prems, Heath's the man every time.' Of course man was just her jocular way of passing the remark,

Lady Merton, but though it isn't for me to say it, when there's a nasty abdominal I'm—well I can't exactly express it."

"Like a guided missile," said Lydia, rather despising herself for getting so much into the spirit of the thing, but her words appeared to command the admiration of Miss Ward who laughed heartily and said she did hear that men working on guided missiles were apt to get Hopkinson's Disease, at which words Miss Heath looked very grave, so Lydia tried to look grave too. But as it was evident that both her hostesses were burning to discuss their whole careers from probationers upwards with special reference to Hopkinson's Disease, she assumed—as she had taught herself to do, the better to be able to protect her husband—rather a Lady of the Manor air and said How interesting, but she must not forget what she had come about.

"There! we've been going on about your prems, Heath," said Miss Ward. "We *do* talk," but Lydia said she liked it and sometimes she wished she were back in the hospital where she nursed in the early years of the war; which was perhaps not quite true, but had some truth in it.

"What I really came about," said Lydia, "was a friend of mine, at least we both are friends of the same people."

Miss Ward said Quite a case of Our Mutual Friend.

Stifling a strong and reasonable wish to say that (a) it wasn't and (b) that with the deepest respect and love for Charles Dickens a friend cannot be Mutual, though he (or she) may be Common, and realizing with a quickness of which our old Lydia would not have been capable that what she was saying would probably sound like rubbish to her kind hostesses, she at once began to tell them about the Hallidays and the sore need for them to be helped. It was obvious from the pursed lips, the headshakings, and the glances of her hostesses that the story was, to use a most unsuitable phrase, exactly their cup of tea.

"A sadly common case," said Miss Heath. "You remember,

Wardy, poor Lady Babs Solway. She died exactly a week after the General—absolutely worn out."

"And there was the Honourable Henry King," said Miss Ward. "You remember how he would *not* let his wife go into a nursing home when she was so mental and in the end *he* had to be certified. Such a charming man and I hear he beats all the other patients at double bézique and thinks he has broken the bank at Monte Carlo."

Entrancing though these Notes from a Casebook were, Lydia felt they were not getting her much nearer her object and time was passing.

"I will just give you a few details," she said in her Committee Voice, at which both her hostesses immediately came to heel. "Old Squire Halliday at Hatch End is a permanent invalid and I'm afraid his mind is affected,"—Miss Ward said Just like old Mrs. Banton, poor old dear,—"and his wife," Lydia continued, unmoved by Mrs. Banton, "is working herself to death to nurse him and keep him happy—" Miss Heath said You never know of course what those senile cases were *really* feeling inside even if they *looked* happy "—and their son, George Halliday, who was all through the war, is running the estate and his father's affairs and doing half the farmwork himself and trying to keep his father happy and he'll go mad quite soon," said Lydia.

"They don't," said Miss Ward, pursing up her mouth very wisely. "It's never the ones that you expect that go mad. You remember that nice R. E. Major, Heathy, at Gib. in the war," but before Miss Heath could answer Lydia—slightly despising herself for so doing but there are limits to one's patience, let alone one's time—put on her Lady of the Manor air and said she was terribly sorry she had to go on to a Red Cross meeting and would Miss Heath and Miss Ward talk it over and let her know as soon as possible if either of them would be available for an indefinite period and so took her leave, having done her best to honour her sister Kate Carter's blank cheque and pretty certain that one or other lady if not both would jump at the offer.

And so, we are glad to say, it proved. By lunch time Miss Heath had rung up Northbridge Manor and told Lydia that she found she could go as soon as it suited Mrs. Halliday and if there were any difficulties (which made Lydia suddenly think of Mrs. Gamp and her infallible methods for elderly or mentally unsound patients) she was sure she could deal with them and if any further help were necessary, or night nursing, Wardy would come at the shortest notice.

Lydia thanked her warmly and hung up the receiver with the sigh of relief that we can only spell as Ouf! Then she rang up her sister Kate, who in her turn rang up Mrs. Carter at Hatch End and asked if she would let George Halliday know, because she had to go over to Gatherum Castle for a committee meeting of the St. John and Red Cross Hospital Libraries, and so, almost with the words "Over to you," took her mind off the Hallidays' affairs and applied it to her own again.

Mrs. Carter was as good as her word and rang up Mrs. Halliday who, sincerely touched by the trouble taken for her, said she would come over and see her, but Mrs. Carter, kindly compassionate in her young energy, said that was nonsense and she would come over to Hatch End. There was a short silence which made Mrs. Carter wonder if she had ignorantly transgressed some local etiquette. Then there was a quick reply of acceptance and the telephone was dumb, but just as it died Mrs. Carter thought she heard another voice.

As there were various small household shoppings to be done, Mrs. Carter picked up her basket and went up the village street which still, we are glad to say, retained some of its immemorial village aspect, with the old country names—Vidlers, Hubbacks, Caxtons, Panters—over the little shops. And there were still, here and there, cottages of what was almost wattle and daub, and there were still one or two garden walls made of a kind of primitive clay and straw mixture, roofed with soft rounded red tiles to keep the rain from disintegrating the tops of the walls and to protect the fruit trees that were espaliered against them on the sunny side. Not to last much longer, but to be held fast in remembering that such things were.

Having dealt with The Fish (left by Vidlers' van at No. 6 Clarence Cottages with Mrs. Panter, wife of Mr. Halliday's carter, for the gentry; whereas the serfs and villeins happily collected theirs from the Mellings Arms where it was dumped by courtesy of Geo. Panter, cousin of the carter, in a corner of the stables) she was just going into The Shop, which was also the post office and sold everything in the world except the thing you particularly wanted, when she saw, seated on a camp stool, what was undoubtedly An Artist; an elderly man wearing a Norfolk jacket with a belt, knickerbockers buttoning below the knee, a battered Panama hat swathed in a green veil and a faded silk scarf passed through a kind of flat ring. In his left hand he held a sketching block, in his right a pencil and Mrs. Carter, who had not been born yesterday, observed that as she approached he began to draw with sweeping lines, sitting back after each sweep, the better to admire his own work. Having no very pressing business on hand she stopped to watch him. After a few moments of frenzied work the artist stopped, suddenly saw Mrs. Carter whom he had been seeing for at least a minute, laid down his pencil, took off his Panama hat and made as sweeping a bow as anyone sitting on a camp stool can manage.

"How do you do?" said Mrs. Carter politely. "A lovely day for sketching."

"Ah!" said the sketcher. "That's what you ladies say, but to the Reel artist there isn't no good or bad days for Art. If it was to rain like old Noah," he went on, apparently confusing the Patriarch with the Flood, "I should see in the Mind's Eye what it would be like on a nice day like this. A Nartist, ah, he's the crux. All those great old masters, Rubens and Jawjone and the rest, they didn't copy nature, they saw nature the way she *should* be and they painted what they saw."

"Le peintre qui voit d'une certaine façon et peint comme il voit," said Mrs. Carter, perhaps rather showing-off where it wasn't necessary.

"It's like a glass of champagne frappy to hear you say so, madam," said the artist. "Scatcherd is my name and it's well known in these parts."

"Oh, of *course*, Scatcherd's Stores at Northbridge," said Mrs. Carter. "Lots of my friends deal there."

"My brother, madam," said the artist. "He stuck to the shop. I did not. I have never repented it. Ars may be long, but it will be longer before I've done with it. And when I think of those Beings, which I would scorn to call men, as make coloured photos of the landscape, ruining the Artist's Profession, well, madam, I feel I could paint their faces Prussian Blue."

"We were talking about those people that make coloured photographs of places only a night or two ago at dinner," said Mrs. Carter, who had an inherited gift for talking to duke or dustman in almost exactly the same kind, interested, unemotional way. "That young Mr. Hibberd whose father is Lord Aberfordbury only it is such a silly name that I never get it right. He is a director of the National Rotochrome Polychrome Universal Picture Post Card Company. No one seems to like him."

At these apparently harmless words Mrs. Carter saw Mr. Scatcherd go so red in the face that she wondered if he was going to have a fit, but as she could not remember from a brief course of first-aid she had done as a girl what you did for fits, she thought it would be safer to do nothing.

"HIM!" said Mr. Scatcherd, his drooping moustache almost standing on end with rage. "Him and his commercial photos. If Art dies in this dear old country of ours, it will be him as done it. *He* doesn't sit sketching in all weathers the way I do and get the pewmonia. *He* doesn't know what it is to be A Nartist. *He* doesn't know the Feelings a man has when he sees Nature; no nor Architecture neether."

"I quite agree," said Mrs. Carter. "And what is worse Mr.

Hibberd's father wants to make the Bishop have a memorial chapel to a clergyman who wrote shocking immoral poetry. Really dreadful poems."

"And I'll lay a sovereign that Lord Aberfordbury as this young spark's father calls hisself, has read those poems cover to cover. Sort of books gentlemen keep under the bed, or locked up if there's housemaids. But *they* don't know Vice. Lord Whatshisname he may buy those sort of books but *he* don't know. I *do*. I was at Bulloyne once, a week I was, in a hotel and I KNOW. If Lord Whateverhisnameis had been to Bulloyne and in a certain address I could give him, though I expect the Madam is dead now as she was a fine old piece of work when I knew her, that would open his eyes. Experience is what us artists need. I've had experience. I KNOW."

Pleased by this peculiar interlude, but quite unmoved, Mrs. Carter asked if she could buy one of his lovely views, chose one of the river with a tall bulrush in the background and gave him half a crown. "And please don't bother about the change, Mr. Scatcherd," she said. "I shall ask you to do a few more views for me. Why don't you do a caricature of Lord Aberfordbury?"

Mr. Scatcherd remained silent, bouche bée as his Boulogne friend might have said though probably in less classical language.

"Or would he be too difficult?" said Mrs. Carter rather treacherously.

"AH! that as the poet says is the Question," said Mr. Scatcherd. "It all depends on the artist. Now that young chap, Hibberd, though chap's too good a name for him, he's not a Nartist. Commercial, that's what he is. All for money. Now, mind you, I'm not against Money as such, but what I say is, What does it buy?"

Mrs. Carter suggested food

"Food I grant you," said Mr. Scatcherd. "But there's other things than food. There's—"

"I know: drink. And clothes," said Mrs. Carter, and we are

sorry to say that she added in the jargon of her contemporaries, "and how right you are about food. It really stands by itself."

"And only stands by itself, madam," said Mr. Scatcherd, forgetting the artist's status and harking back to his early life in the grocery business when Politeness to Customers was still the rule in good business. "Drink hasn't a leg to stand on compared with food. But to go back to the subject under discussion—"

"What was it *exactly*?" said Mrs. Carter who was not only beginning to feel mad but, even worse, a little bored.

"Ah, that is the Crux," said Mr. Scatcherd.

"Well, I must be going on," said Mrs. Carter. "I shall show your picture to my husband. I think that tall bulrush in the background is so effective. It seems to pull the whole thing together" and if she had been in a comic strip a balloon would have been issuing from her mouth with the words: "Thinks: I have said quite the right thing."

But far from appearing gratified by her appreciation of his card, Mr. Scatcherd swelled visibly with the Wounded Pride of an Artist.

"If it is to the Spire of the Cathedral you are reluding to, madam," said he, with (in his opinion) the courtesy that is more biting than downright discourtesy, "I regret that you are in Error. It is my impression—and, mind you, I only say my *impression*—of Our Spire."

Mrs. Carter nearly had the giggles, but she was not the daughter of a very intelligent man of affairs for nothing.

"Oh, not the *Spire*," she said. "I meant the bulrush in the *foreground*. It gives that extra touch."

"That indeed alters the case," said Mr. Scatcherd, unbending. "The bulrush to which you relude, madam, was put there by Me for that very reason as you said. When I looked at the sketch— for it is only a sketch," he went on, implying that the finished picture would be about twelve feet wide by seven high, in oils and a heavily gilt frame, "I said to myself in the very same identical words as you said, I said It Needs The Extra Touch."

"Well, that is delightful," said Mrs. Carter. "*Good*-bye" and before Mr. Scatcherd could even open his mouth she was away at a quick pace to The Shop where she ordered some groceries, left her shopping basket to be called for later and walked over the long narrow bridge which carried high on stone arches spanned the water meadows and the Rising above the reach of floods: even above the level of the great flood of 1863 when a jack-ass had been carried down for seven miles and subsequently was found unhurt in a willow tree, from which four men were needed to get it down.

At the farther end, facing the river, was Hatch House, the home of Hallidays for many generations; a square red brick house with well proportioned sash windows and a small front lawn which is embanked by a high wall above the old road to Barchester. So far it had kept up its appearance of the Squire's House, though how long that would go on it was impossible to say. As so often was the case, Mrs. Halliday was on her knees by a flower bed, a hessian apron with large pockets tied round her waist and wearing an old pair of her husband's riding gloves.

"May I come in?" said Mrs. Carter from the gate.

Mrs. Halliday turned her head, recognized her caller and got up with a welcoming face.

"I thought I'd come over," said Mrs. Carter "in case the telephone disturbed your husband."

"How kind of you," said Mrs. Halliday. "He sometimes thinks he hears the telephone when it isn't really ringing so one gets rather confused when it really does. Shall we sit in the summer-house?" and she took her guest to a small shelter facing the river where three or four people could sit and talk, or watch birds through field-glasses, or take a book to read and go to sleep while the book lay open, sprawling face downwards on the floor, unable to scream for help.

"If Leonard wakes up and hears people talking in the house he always comes to see who it is," said Mrs. Halliday, "so it is easier to talk here," which she said in a quiet, tired voice, as one making a simple statement. But to Mrs. Carter there was a good deal more behind her words and her kind nature felt sorry for her hostess. "Your nice Miss Heath rang me up later," Mrs. Halliday went on, "and she is coming this afternoon. I ought to have told you, but I forget everything now."

"So do I," said Mrs. Carter, hoping to cheer her hostess. "I often go down from the nursery to telephone and when I get downstairs I can't remember who I wanted to telephone to and then I have to go up to the top of the house again to remember who it was," at which graphic description of the kind of mental woolliness to which we have been reduced by the war, the years after the war, the rising cost of everything essential (for the luxuries we have mostly relegated to the luxury class where they belong), the increasing apprehension of more troubles at home and abroad to come and the way that a Pound means about two and elevenpence three farthings, Mrs. Halliday had to laugh. And as the laugh was not only on account of Mrs. Carter's words but also a little against herself and her own worries, she felt all the better for it.

"By the way, I must explain why I rang off so quickly just now," said Mrs. Halliday. "I don't want to bore you with my troubles, but Leonard—my husband—always seems to hear the telephone in spite of being rather deaf now and he is apt to think it is someone important who wants to talk to him and comes to answer it and wants to know everything. Not that there is anything to hide, goodness knows," she went on, talking in her tired voice almost to herself, "but if he had known it was you on the telephone I should have had to explain again who you are and—oh well," and she looked away over the water-meadows to the line of the downs, unchanged in shape through centuries, ever changing in colour with the seasons, the sun, the rain, the pasture land and the cornland with cloud-shadows sailing across them. Mrs. Carter did not speak. She thought Mrs. Halliday wanted to tell her something and was finding it difficult and that the kindest thing to do would be to say nothing.

"You see his mind is going," said Mrs. Halliday and smiled.

Mrs. Carter was for a moment quite at a loss, a thing which we think had never before occurred in her happy, well-regulated life.

"And that," Mrs. Halliday went on, "is why I hope Miss Heath may be a success. She ought to be here at any moment now. Shall we go in? Leonard would like to see you," and she got up, looked once more away across the river to the village and the church and took Mrs. Carter into the house.

"I won't do much introducing or explaining," she said to Mrs. Carter. "It only confuses him. And if he thinks you are someone else you won't mind?" to which Mrs. Carter could only reply, with great truth, that she would like to be anyone that Mr. Halliday wanted her to be, and so they went into the drawing-room.

As Mrs. Carter had not yet seen Mr. Halliday she very naturally did not know what to expect. Mrs. Halliday's words had rather prepared her for a gibbering dotard so it was with distinct relief that she saw what was certainly a rather invalidish-looking person but otherwise just like a lot of other elderly men she had known. He was reading a book and did not at first notice their entrance, but when his wife said, "Leonard, I have brought a friend to see you" he looked up. For a moment he seemed perplexed and then he saw his wife and the look of worry was banished.

"It is Mrs. Carter, Leonard," said Mrs. Halliday in a most matter-of-fact ordinary voice (though how hard she had worked to make it ordinary we do not quite know). "She and her husband are living in the Old Manor House. Her father is Lord Crosse."

"Yes. I know Lord Crosse," said Mr. Halliday, "but this isn't Lord Crosse, Eleanor. He is in London."

Mrs. Carter, who had a good deal of courage, decided that one might as well do any nettle-grasping that had to be done at once. So she held out her hand and said very kindly—but not too kindly—that Lord Crosse couldn't come today but he would come soon.

"And I am his daughter," she said, "so I came to see you."

"Then you are Enid," said Mr. Halliday.

Mrs. Carter saw a look of almost despair on her hostess's face.

"He thinks you are your mother," said Mrs. Halliday quietly.

"So I am, if he likes it," said Mrs. Carter, also quietly, and then she sat down by Mr. Halliday and began to tell him how nice it was to be back in Barsetshire and how glad she was to see him.

"And we are living in that lovely Old Manor House," she said, in a very ordinary voice, at which point Mrs. Halliday went away: not in annoyance, but with a feeling that this nice daughter of Lord Crosse's was dealing very competently with a situation that had got quite beyond her control. In the hall her faithful old maid Hubback—sister, aunt, female cousin, to half the village—was waiting for her.

"Miss Heath's come," she said. "I've taken her suitcase up."

Mrs. Halliday asked where Miss Heath was, feeling that Hubback in some unexplained access of feudal loyalty might have pushed her into the larder and locked the door pending further enquiry.

"I took her up to her room," said Hubback, who in private chose to dispense with all outward forms of courtesy though none could announce a visitor more high and disposedly when she liked. "I expect she'd like to unpack and then she can come down. I'll bring tea as soon as she comes" and so went away to the kitchen and tried to smother the anxiety she felt by getting tea ready. For however well people face things there is always a chink and Hubback knew, with the sure instinct of her class, that once a trained Nurse got into the house, someone went out feet foremost, a belief very firmly held in those parts on no grounds at all.

So Mrs. Halliday went upstairs and found the bedroom door

open and a pleasant-faced, middle-aged woman in a neat suit putting her belongings into various drawers and cupboards.

"Miss Heath? I am so glad to see you," she said, shaking hands. "I do hope Hubback, that's our old maid, has been kind to you."

"Very kind indeed," said Miss Heath, "and quite a character. What a charming room and such a lovely view. I always think a view is quite an important part of a bedroom. When I was with Lady Norton—old Lady Norton it was, not her daughter-in-law—her bedroom looked out over the rose-garden to the church."

As Mrs. Halliday was uncertain whether this was to the bedroom's credit or discredit, she pretended to be straightening a picture.

"I always think," said Miss Heath, "that a churchyard is so peaceful. Some people find the church clock chiming keeps them awake. I am a splendid sleeper when I'm off duty but if I do hear a church clock strike I always say to myself, 'Well, there's someone awake as well as yourself' and then I usually go right off almost at once. I have brought my uniform in case it is wanted, Mrs. Halliday, but I thought just to start with I'd come just as an ordinary visitor if you see what I mean."

Mrs. Halliday said, rather weakly, what a kind thought and tea would be ready almost at once.

"This was my daughter's room—Mrs. Martin Leslie—before she married," said Mrs. Halliday. "The furniture is rather old, but the bed has a proper mattress—the old one was like a sack of potatoes. There is a large cupboard here and all the drawers are empty. The bathroom is just across the passage and no one else will be using it except George—my son. He runs the farm now. If you want anything, please ring," and she pointed to a rather tattered bell-pull of linen embroidered with art-nouveau tulips. "Tea will be ready as soon as you come down. And do please ring if you need anything. Hubback loves looking after our guests," and she went down again to the drawing-room where Mr. Halliday was talking to Mrs. Carter about the ball where they had first met and Mrs. Carter was most obligingly pretending to be her mother which, as Mr. Halliday wanted to talk and not to listen, was not difficult. And under his talk Mrs. Halliday told Mrs. Carter that the nurse had come, so Mrs. Carter found she had to get back to her children, said her good-byes and went away.

Meanwhile Miss Heath had unpacked her suitcase with swift proficiency, looked at herself in the glass, thought what a good thing it was she got her hair re-permed last week, and then went downstairs.

"How quick you have been," said Mrs. Halliday to her guest. "Leonard, this is Miss Heath. She is a friend of Lady Merton's and has come for a little visit."

"I am very glad to see you," said Mr. Halliday and began to make the motions of getting up but Miss Heath was so swift in her movement that she was beside him before he had levered himself up from his arm-chair, and shook hands with a kind of gentle firmness that made him sit down again in his place.

"You are a friend of Lady Merton," he said. "I don't think I know her. Do I, Ellie?"

Mrs. Halliday, much relieved at being able to speak the truth which she could rarely do now with her husband, said she didn't think he had met Lady Merton, but he would remember her people, the Keiths, who lived at Northbridge. With his usual courtesy Mr. Halliday tried to remember if he could remember them, but the effort was painful, which being observed by Miss Heath she said what a nice bedroom Mrs. Halliday had given her and such a nice bit of embroidery on the bell-pull.

"My grandmother embroidered it," said Mr. Halliday. "She did a lot of embroidery. Ellie, we must show—" and he stopped and looked confused. "Do I know you?" he said to Miss Heath, not—much to his wife's relief—with any apparent embarrassment, but a kind of trust that she would tell him the truth.

"No, it's the first time I've been here, Mr. Halliday," said Miss

Heath. "But I have met Mrs. Halliday and heard so much about your lovely house that it's quite a pleasure to see it. What a lovely garden you have in front."

"My wife does it all," said Mr. Halliday, looking at her with such affectionate admiration that Miss Heath, whom years of experienced nursing had inured to every peculiarity of invalids, suddenly felt rather like crying. "My mother loves gardening too. Ellie, did Caxton rake the gravel in front today? My mother likes it to be raked."

Mrs. Halliday, with perfect self-command, said the gravel had been raked and his mother would be delighted. There would have to be explanations and she hoped Miss Heath would understand. At this moment Hubback brought in the tea-things.

Mrs. Halliday had rather wondered how Hubback would take the arrival of what she would at once have recognized to be a nurse in disguise if she had not been warned. But Hubback was not for nothing a servant of the old school. Nurses, in her opinion, were a nuisance, whether it was for the children when they were young or for anyone in bed—except of course in the case of a monthly nurse who was a necessary evil and must be endured with resignation—but if Mr. Halliday was ill and Mrs. Halliday wearing and worrying herself to death and Mr. George working and worrying *his* self to death (which, we may say, was quite untrue of both of them, for though they were anxious they were extremely sane) then a nurse it must be. And Hubback had—we regret to say—only waited for Sister Heath to go down to the drawing-room to run up to her room and discreetly look at her belongings. Everything she saw gave satisfaction. Miss Heath's ordinary clothes were neatly hung in the large wardrobe; her underwear, with to Hubback's mind just the right amount of elegance without fuss and good material too and some nice nylons, neatly laid in a drawer; and in another drawer her professional uniform, neatly laid out ready for immediate use in any emergency. Also Miss Heath had a quite revolting nightdress case of mauve satin embroidered with pansies in purple and yellow silk with a frill of ekroo lace (better known perhaps as écru, though equally disliked) which gave Hubback great satisfaction and she went to the linen cupboard and got out two of the really big bath towels which as a rule she would not allow guests to have and two of the best real linen face towels, beautifully marked in embroidery by Mr. Halliday's mother and now almost as fine as lawn, though more comfortably absorbent, and put them in Miss Heath's room. Only one thing was wanting. Nurses, she had observed, often had to be up in the night even if the patient wasn't really ill. So she went down to the kitchen and collected an electric kettle, a tin of mixed biscuits with a very tight-fitting lid, and the general paraphernalia for tea-making in the night watches. These she carried upstairs on a tray and put in the guest's room which had a proper hole—or rather a triangle of holes—to plug the electric into, filled the kettle, and stood back to survey her handiwork. One more thing was wanting: flowers. It wasn't like Mrs. Halliday to forget flowers for the spare room but being so worried about the Squire, well it wasn't to be surprised at, so down she went again, picked a large, tight bunch of various flowers, crammed them ruthlessly into a mauve vase with a picture of a rustic cottage on it (her own private possession, much valued), and put it on the dressing-table. Then she looked at all she had done and, behold, it was very good, so she went downstairs and got the drawing-room tea.

Apart from a slight gentility which Mrs. Halliday felt she could easily get used to with anyone who was kind to her husband, tea went very well. Sister Heath, studying the ground, let Mr. Halliday do most of the talking and showed what Mrs. Halliday gratefully felt to be great tact in sheering off any subject that seemed likely to perplex or annoy her host. Presently, through the window that looked out at the back of the room, over towards the downs, came a loud clanking noise.

"That is my son coming back with the tractor," said Mrs. Halliday to her guest. "They are working up on the top field."

"I told George turnips would do no good in that field," said Mr. Halliday, who was making a very good tea for an invalid and his wife's spirits sank, for though George was very good and patient in letting his father give him instructions which, owing to their entire unsuitability he had not the faintest intention of carrying out, he was sometimes hard put to it to keep his temper under paternal questioning and criticism.

"I really must pass a remark," said Sister Heath to her host, "about that cup of yours, Mr. Halliday. It's the Eddystone Lighthouse isn't it?"

"My old nurse gave it to me when I was quite small," said Mr. Halliday, pleased by the guest's attention. "Yes, that side has the Eddystone Lighthouse. The other side has Rule Britannia," and he turned the cup so that she might the better admire it.

"Well, that *is* original," said Sister Heath; at which moment George Halliday came in, clean as to the hands and face but otherwise in well worn and much stained working clothes.

"Oh, this is my son George," said Mrs. Halliday.

George, who had previously been primed by his mother about Sister Heath's arrival, shook hands and said he hoped she wouldn't mind having the same bathroom and if she would tell him when she liked her bath, he would keep out of the way. Sister Heath, with the faintly flirtatious manner that any personable young man—even if not so young now—can provoke in our sex, said she was sure he was the one that needed the bath after all his hard work.

"Well, I must say I rather do," said George, "especially with a visitor here. If I have the bathroom before supper will that be O.K.?"

"Now isn't that funny," said Sister Heath, "because it's just what I would have suggested. I usually have mine before I go to bed as it seems to make one nice and sleepy. Some people find it has absolutely the opposite effect and wakes them up, but I think it just makes you relax nicely."

"That's splendid," said George, obviously relieved. "I have mine before supper as I'm usually in a bit of a mess after a day on the farm and then if I do want another one I have a cold shower in the morning in summer. But not in winter. Not till we can get central heating in the house—which will be never," he added in a lower voice, not wanting to hurt his father's feelings; but we much doubt whether Mr. Halliday would have noticed the words unless they were distinctly and rather loudly addressed to him personally and even then—as Mrs. Halliday was beginning to realize and to face the fact—he might look puzzled and a little afraid, like a child faced by a difficult lesson.

Just then Hubback came into the room, announced "Miss Sylvia, madam," and held the door for the Hallidays' daughter, now for nearly ten years happily married to Martin Leslie and chatelaine of Rushwater, the Leslie family home, with several very nice children. Her shining golden hair was as golden as ever, and if she was now more Juno than Diana in her looks and her walk, it suited her admirably.

"Darling, how nice to see you," said Mrs. Halliday. "This is Miss Heath, a friend of Lady Merton's. She is staying here and I hope she won't find it dull," which words she accompanied by a conspirator's look at Sister Heath, not because she thought it was necessary, but because she thought her guest would like to feel that she also was in the conspiracy: in which Mrs. Halliday was probably right.

"Hullo, Sister Heath," said Sylvia, shaking hands in a very friendly way with the visitor. "What fun to see you again. Last time was when we had that go of flu at Rushwater and you saved all our lives. Are you here—" and instead of finishing her sentence she looked at her father.

"I am so glad to meet you again, Mrs. Leslie," said Sister Heath. "I am having such a nice time here and it is so kind of

Mrs. Halliday to have me. After tea I'd like to tell you all about my new home where I am living with my friend Miss Ward."

"Oh, I know," said Sylvia. "I hear all about her from Sister Chiffinch who comes to us for a holiday sometimes. We always pretend the children are hers when she comes, as she was there for all of them."

Sister Heath said she would love it and must have a real talk with Mrs. Leslie sometime, at which point Sylvia realized the state of things and that her father probably didn't know Sister Heath was a nurse and felt very glad that her mother had so efficient a help. Any awkwardness there might have been was stopped by Hubback coming in with fresh tea and some more cakes and another outsize cup for Sylvia, only this was just a flowered one with a gilt line round the top of the cup.

"What a lovely bit of Screwby," said Sister Heath. "My friend Sister Chiffinch has a lovely collection of china cups and mugs. I collect china cats. I've got about twenty, every size from those big china ones with glass eyes and spots on them that you can sit by the fire so that they look quite natural except that they are usually yellow—or blue—to some sweetly pretty little ones I got in Sweden when I went on a cruise last year made in Japan which really made me quite uncomfortable when I saw it on them afterwards."

"Still they are English cats now" said Mr. Halliday, most unexpectedly.

His wife wondered if she had gone mad, or if the husband she knew had really returned, so long was it since he had been alive to what happened around him, but having said his say he relapsed into his usual state of withdrawal into some far place where his wife could not reach him.

Sister Heath said she liked cats, they were quite like companions, but some people felt really quite funny about them and instanced several cases of friends who always knew if a cat had been in the room and usually had hay-fever in consequence. Under this instructive though uninteresting flow of talk Mr.

Halliday gently went to sleep. Sylvia looked at her mother and got up. Mrs. Halliday went with her daughter to the back yard, where Sylvia had left her car.

"Can I do anything for you, mother?" said Sylvia, who in her capacity as head of a large house with cottages on the estate was used to running people's lives for them.

"Nothing, darling. Nothing," said her mother. "But it's worse for George. He is so alone. Of course he has the farm and the men about the place. But it isn't the same. And he hardly ever gets out to see young people."

"But look here, mother," said Sylvia. "George isn't young. I'm not young now if it comes to that. Old George is all right and he's sure to marry someone sometime. Any girl would jump at him."

"I wish she would," said Mrs. Halliday. "I had rather wondered—"

"Look here, mother," said Sylvia. "Now you've got Sister Heath, can't George come over to Rushwater now and then? I can always find some girls for tennis and things. I'm glad you've got old Heathy. She's been with lots of my friends for babies and she does know her job. But George doesn't get about enough. He is turning into an old stick-in-the-mud. What about Edith Graham?"

"Such a nice girl," said her mother, "but only a child. Now if George could find someone like Lady Graham, or that nice Mrs. Carter at the Old Manor House who is Lord Crosse's daughter—"

"—or a film star or a princess" said Sylvia, half laughing, half a little cross at her mother's want of energy. "Tell him to come over to Rushwater soon. John's boys will be there and I know Minor will break his neck on something. He wants to do the church tower and everyone knows the tower is all crumbly and the battlements fall off it as soon as look at you. Send George along and I'll do the rest," and with a very loving hug she said good-bye and drove away. Mrs. Halliday's world, which had been growing warm and alive suddenly became grey and cold, so she went back into the house. At the door she paused and looked away up the river valley to where Barchester spire used to be visible in her younger days though the growth of trees had hidden it now. Then she looked across the valley to Hatch End where the Old Manor House was now the lively home of two babies and quite likely more to come, with that kind Mrs. Carter the efficient ruler of it all. So had Hatch House been in her early married days and for many, many years. A fragment of a simple, lovely song came to her mind,

> "The smiles, the tears of boyhood's years,
>   The words of love then spoken;
>   The eyes that shone, now dimmed and gone,
>   The cheerful hearts now broken,"

and she felt the pricking behind the eyes which means, fatally, that tears are very near. For a moment she let them well up and one even got out and ran down her face. But this was too much. Angrily she banged it back with her handkerchief and went back to the drawing-room, where she found her husband playing halma with Sister Heath.

"We are having such a nice game, Mrs. Halliday," said Sister Heath. "I've won one and Mr. Halliday has won one and now we are having the Cup Final. Now, I see a lovely move you can make, Mr. Halliday, and if you do I shall be O-U-T, Out," but Mr. Halliday, as intent on the game as any champion chess player, paid no attention at all. At last he picked up a man (if halma men can be called that, but we know no other name) and moved it.

"Well, that *was* a mean trick, Mr. Halliday," said Sister Heath cheerfully and at the same time—so Mrs. Halliday observed— quietly moving one of her own men into a very dangerous position. "Your move again."

With a careful hand Mr. Halliday pushed one of his men into the hole left by Sister Heath and looked up triumphantly.

"Well! you do make some good moves, Mr. Halliday," she said.

Mr. Halliday said in a careless way that he had luck with games of chance, which was a mean thing to say of halma where skill, or at any rate concentration, is certainly needed. But as he seemed happy to have won, neither lady was disposed to criticize. Then there was the six o'clock news which was a mixture of the dull and the depressing as so much news is apt to be now that science and what calls itself democracy have got the upper hand. Among the announcements was the death of Mr. L. N. B. Porter, C.B.E., a retired member of the Civil Service, in consequence of a fractured leg sustained when endeavoring to cross the white crossing lines on a rainy day, which announcement gave Mr. Halliday lively pleasure, for he and Mr. Porter had been at Oxford together, and Mr. Porter was his junior by two years and there is something agreeable about showing those younger men that they may be weak-minded enough to die if they like, but it isn't the sort of thing *you* would do. And such was Mr. Halliday's exultation that Sister Heath wondered if she ought to get a sedative from her little box of medicines in case he didn't sleep. But his hour of glory had passed and he fell asleep in his chair.

Mrs. Halliday, with a mixture of relief and anxiety, went to find George who was, as she expected, in what was now called the Estate Office though it was once the servants' hall. But it was a nice room with two large windows looking out towards the downs and easily heated in the winter as it was over the furnace. Here, as usual, George was rounding off the farmer's day by doing some accounts and letters up to date.

"Am I disturbing you, darling?" said Mrs. Halliday, sitting down.

"Yes, darling, you are," said George. But seeing that she took this seriously he put down his papers and came and sat beside her. "But I like your Miss Heath. I've half a mind to have delayed war shock or something and have her to myself. She'll get awfully bored here though. There isn't really much to do, is there?"

"I don't know," said Mrs. Halliday. "But one has to think ahead."

"Sorry, darling," said George. "I ought to have seen what you mean; and I'm awfully glad you've got someone. You know, mother—it's perhaps rather a horrid thing to say—but—"

"Your father is getting old very quickly now," said Mrs. Halliday. "Dr. Ford isn't too hopeful. So I thought—no, I didn't even think—I'm too tired. It was Mrs. Carter who thought. She got Lady Merton to ask Sister Heath if she or her friend could come here."

"Well, it's a bit of a shock, but I'm awfully glad," said George. "And now I hope you will have breakfast in bed sometimes or lie down in the afternoon. She's a fine woman, Sister Heath, and I'll jolly her along. Look here, mother. I don't want to sound beastly, but you know the arrangement about the place."

"You mean your father making it over to you?" said his mother. "He has talked about it sometimes lately."

"Well, I've been so busy one way and another that I haven't had time to think much about it," said George, "but I had to go to Keith and Keith—you know, our solicitors in the Close— the other day about things in general and I asked them about the place. Look here, mother, you mustn't worry—you're all right—but father never did make the place over to me. Mr. Keith said he had talked about it and then the matter had never gone any further—that was ages ago. Father must have thought he did. Anyway if he had I'd probably have died first and then he would have had to pay the death duties. You can't get past them," by which term we think he meant the heavenly powers in general who have placed us on a globe that we can't get off and then pour water on our heads.

There was not any answer to what George had said. Mrs.

Halliday almost felt the rage of the lioness when her cub is in danger—and owing to the oversight of the lion. It would probably mean the end of Hatch House, the passing of Wm. Halliday's house and lands from the family; or George being tied to the land he could not afford to keep as it should be kept; a day-labourer without wages. She felt a sudden dull resentment against Keith and Keith—against the Government—against the world and even against her husband.

"Well, we're not dead yet, mother," said George, with a good attempt at cheerfulness. "And now I've told you the worst. You're all right, mother, with a settlement—never mind details now—and Sylvia had her whack when she married. Now I'll tell you something not quite so bad. When father wasn't so dot—I mean some time ago before he got old, he did tell me he had been insuring against death duties. It only came back to me today when I was up in the top field, because it was there he told me about it—oh, ages ago. He did rather like to do things on his own and he mayn't have done it through the solicitors. Anyway I'm going into it with Robert Keith next week and I'm going through every paper of father's here as well. Now let's forget it. And if he didn't—well, we'll manage somehow, mother."

Mrs. Halliday could have cried, but as one gets older that blessed relief is denied. With Sylvia happy and safe she would have been quite happy to live in a very small way—perhaps in the village—leaving George with the house for some possible wife some day. But what would he have to offer to a wife now? In a kind of hen-like frenzy her thoughts rushed about inside her head, counting the possible brides with good dowers for George that the county could provide and then she had to laugh at herself inside and think she would just try to live for the present, from day to day. All she could say to George was "Darling" and she did not kiss him, nor even touch him, for when the cup is full to the brim it needs but a touch and it overflows.

"Don't let's think about it yet, mother," said George. "God

knows we don't want father to die. But he seems so tired and mostly doesn't care much about anything—except you of course. I'll be all right. Don't worry, darling."

"No, I won't," said Mrs. Halliday. "But it's so hard for you, George, doing all you do for the place. You ought to have married."

"Listen, mother," said George, very kindly but firmly, "you've said that to me now about thirty-six times a year for the last—oh more years than I can count; ever since the war and several times during and before it. I don't particularly want to get married. And if this insurance doesn't work I'll have precious little to offer a girl, even if I knew a girl that would like me. You know, mother, we old war horses aren't as young as we were. But I'll ask Sister Heath if you like," at which his mother had to laugh. The slightly emotional moment passed and she went back to the drawing-room where Sister Heath was telling Mr. Halliday about the Clovers' new play that she had been to a matinee of when she went to London and he was simultaneously telling her about how he had seen Irving once when he was a boy and as neither of them was in the least interested in what the other was saying they were getting on splendidly.

"We had the nine o'clock news while you were out of the room, Mrs. Halliday," said Sister Heath. "Mr. Eden was speaking, but we just missed that bit, and then there was a Party Broadcast with a Labour peer speaking in a really quite disagreeable way. I don't mean bad language but just a rather nasty kind of way if you see what I mean. So I said to Mr. Halliday did he want to hear any more, and he said he didn't because he couldn't hear what the speaker was saying which really was no loss if you see what I mean. He had a most peculiar name, Aber-something, but I daresay he was Welsh which would account for it. The Welsh do really have quite peculiar names."

"Was it Aberfordbury?" said Mrs. Halliday, very cleverly seizing a moment when Sister Heath had to breathe.

"There now! I knew you'd know, Mrs. Halliday. I said to Mr.

Halliday, 'I'm sure Mrs. Halliday will know,'" but Mrs. Halliday was hardly listening. She was looking at her husband with deep love and telling herself that she must try not to grudge him anything he wanted, for a day might be near when she would give the world and if necessary her immortal soul if they would help him; but they would not.

"You have been so kind, Sister," said Mrs. Halliday, forgetting Sister Heath's rôle as visitor, only seeing her as the embodiment of authority and such help as could be given. "I'm not much help, I'm afraid."

"There's just the one thing you *could* do, Mrs. Halliday," said Sister Heath, who through practice was able to speak to her patients' friends without the patient noticing much. "Will you say I look tired and ought to go to bed?"

"Leonard, dear," said Mrs. Halliday, coming close to her husband, "I think our guest is rather tired and ought to go to bed now."

"Yes, my dear. Who is she?" said Mr. Halliday.

"Miss Heath, a friend of that nice Lady Merton," said Mrs. Halliday, wondering in a tired way how often she would have to act a part. "The stairs are rather slippery for a stranger and she might slip. Do you remember when your mother came here and slipped on the stairs and we had to keep her in bed for a couple of days?"

"Poor old mother," said Mr. Halliday in almost his old voice. "How rude she was to Dr. Ford."

"Well, I'm rather anxious about Miss Heath," said Mrs. Halliday. "It's the first time she has been here and I don't want her to have a fall like your mother. Could you give her your arm upstairs?"

Even if Mr. Halliday's mind was vague his feeling of courtesy to a guest was strong. He got up, with a little help from his wife, and offered his arm to Sister Heath who at once took it and with it his whole weight and the whole future responsibility for him. Mrs. Halliday watched them go up the dark shining staircase and disappear along the corridor and then she sat down, suddenly too tired to stand and mercifully too tired to think. Here George found her and asked where his father was.

"Sister Heath has taken him upstairs—at least he thinks he is taking her upstairs," said Mrs. Halliday.

"Good for Sister," said George and as he said the words his mother suddenly realized that everything was normal. Her husband was old and failing. A nurse was in the house—a nice woman too with good manners and pleasant speech, knowing many of their county friends—and Leonard was safe with her, which was the only thing that mattered.

"Yes, good for her indeed," she said. "And just in time," with which plain speaking George absolutely agreed and told her so.

"Because, mother," he said, realizing that the welfare of her menfolk was more important than anything to her now, "if father gets a bit more invalidish now it will be too much for you and I simply can't leave the farm till we've got through the work. Now, what you have to do is to let Sister Heath take on the job. And don't you go thinking that he will be unhappy, because he's going to have the time of his life. Heath isn't a bad looking woman and they'll be as snug as a bug in a rug," at which beautiful simile Mrs. Halliday had to laugh and so did her son and they both felt much more cheerful.

"Now, look here, mother, you go to bed," said George. "You can't do anything and old Heath is on the spot. It's lucky you and father don't have a double bed. It would be a frightful nuisance for him to be ill and not be able to call his bed his own. Do you remember the Caldecott picture books we had in the nursery, mother, and the one of the Babes in the Wood where the father and mother are both lying in nightcaps in a double bed? Sylvia and I adored it and we used to get into her bed when Nanny was out of the room and pretend we were the father and mother. Nanny was furious when she found us and we both had to stand in the corner."

"I never knew Nanny put you in the corner," said Mrs. Halliday indignantly. "What a shame."

"Of course you didn't know, mother," said George. "We thought it was rather fun and had a kind of secret society about it. We called it FOST, which were the beginning letters of Finding Out Secret Things."

"And did you find anything, darling?" said Mrs. Halliday.

"Nothing at all," said George, "except that if we only took one lump of sugar each out of the nursery sugar basin, Nanny didn't notice. Come along, mother. Bed for all and I'm as sleepy as a dormouse."

So he turned out the lights and they went upstairs. Sister Heath had heard them and was on the landing to tell Mrs. Halliday that Mr. Halliday was nice and comfy in bed and she had given him something to help him to sleep.

"And if you do hear me move in the night, Mrs. Halliday," she went on, "it will only be if Mr. Halliday wants some nice warm milk but I don't think he will. He is sleeping beautifully."

At that moment, though without words, Mrs. Halliday gave her husband entirely to Sister Heath, without any sense of loss, with gratitude to someone who could help him better than she could.

"I've put a thermos of nice hot milk by your bed, Mrs. Halliday," Sister Heath went on, "and the sugar in case you like it sweet. And now don't worry, because I'll have the door open between my room and Mr. Halliday's and I'll hear him at once if he wants anything."

"Thank you, Sister, very much," said Mrs. Halliday, almost like a child. "And have you something to read? I put some books in your room."

"Now, how kind of you, Mrs. Halliday," said Sister Heath. "I did see the books and believe it or not, there was Mrs. Morland's new book. I'm a great one for reading and I always read hers, but this is one I hadn't seen, The Mannequin Mystery. I know I

shall thoroughly enjoy it. So now I'll pop into bed with my book
and I expect we shall all sleep soundly."

"*What* a nice woman," said Mrs. Halliday, more to herself
than to George. He agreed warmly with her and said good-
night. Mrs. Halliday did not longer over her undressing, for
bed seemed to her a safe place, a view which she knew to be
unreasonable, but could not be bothered to argue with herself
about. She had given Sister Heath the new Mrs. Morland, but
for herself she had kept the new thriller by Lady Silverbridge,
better known to the great library reading public by her pen-
name of Lisa Bedale. The plot was mysterious; the detective,
Gerry Marston, as debonair and attractive as ever; the heroine of
just the right silliness and attractiveness. And what was best of
all, she did stop reading presently and turn out the light. It
needed courage, but her common-sense told her that to go to
sleep with the light on and then to wake at two or three o'clock
not knowing who or where one is, does not make for a quiet
spirit. And we are glad to say that in spite of anxiety both she and
George slept well through the night. George had to be up fairly
early and met Sister Heath, looking very dashing in a boudoir
cap of pink silk and a pink silk padded dressing-gown, over a cup
of tea. All so far was well and another day was before him.

We need hardly say that the joyful news of serious illness and
a hospital nurse was swiftly relayed through the neighbourhood.
The Milk was the first to get it and through him it percolated
rapidly to the Mellings Arms where Mr. Geo. Panter washed his
face—an operation usually postponed by him till the dead hour
of mid-afternoon—and rolled his shirt-sleeves up to the elbows, anticipating a rush of custom. Nor was he disappointed.
At eleven o'clock there was a rush of four people to the door, at
half-past eleven there were at least half a dozen and when the
barman, who was a young lady in a pullover and a kind of naval
trousers highly unbecoming to the female form, opened the
door she was obliged to get behind it for her life. Twelve pints

were served by Mr. Geo. Panter himself in the first ten minutes.
Opinions were divided, some saying it was The War as done it,
some that it was those German bastards as done it (though
another word beginning with b and of stronger pejorative quality was also much in favour); some that it was the Government,
taxing a man till that man didn't rightly know if he was on his
head or his heels; others again that they daresayed old Staylin
was at the bottom of it. The names of Old Gandhi and Old
Franco were also brought forward, but disallowed as frivolous by
a large majority, the company having now almost doubled
owing to the wives coming in to see if their husbands were there
and to hurry up if they wanted their dinner because you couldn't
expect your dinner to keep hot by itself and what was the good of
cooking dinner if a man didn't come in punctually and they
wouldn't be surprised if it wasn't the Government.

"Ah! if we'd a had old Winnie there wouldn't have been none
of this," said The Fish, represented by Mr. Vidler who had a flat
cart (all intelligent readers will understand this) and came out
from Northbridge, sometimes as himself, sometimes by proxy as
The Boy. "He knew what was what, old Winnie did," to which
fine though rather vague tribute the company responded by such
good old Wessex monosyllables as Ar and 'Sright. Young Vidler
(who was well over forty) went so far as to say that They did say,
but was at once shut up by his father. In the middle of the slight
commotion caused by the shutting-up Caxton, Mr. Halliday's
estate carpenter, came in. All were now silent and kept such of
their countenances as were not dealing with a half-pint fixed
upon him.

"Morning," said Caxton in a general way. "Usual, miss."

The trousered barmaid drew a pint of Pilward's Entire and
pushed it towards him. Even as the augurs watched the flight of
birds, so did the company assembled watch Caxton's face and
with about the same result, namely being just as wise as they
were before.

"Same again, miss," said Caxton, putting his mug down. This

time Mr. Geo. Panter filled it, leaving the barmaid to attend to
lesser customers.

"Any news, Mr. Caxton?" said Mrs. Panter, wife of Mr.
Halliday's carter.

"There *are* some," said Caxton, glancing round the assembly
and apparently not seeing any spies, "as looks for good news and
some as looks for bad."

"It isn't good news, nor yet bad news we want," said Mrs.
Panter. "It's News. How's the Squire? When I see the car go by
yesterday afternoon with Sister Heath driving—a *nice* lady she
is and I know what I'm saying because when I was in the Cottage
Hospital with My Bad Leg, ten years ago that was, she was there
and she said she'd never seed such a shocking Leg in her born
days—it gave me quite a turn. Well, what's the news?"

"There *are* some," said Caxton, observing the same lofty
abstraction from mundane affairs, "as likes to hear good news
and some as likes to hear bad. Well, it's neether."

Murmurs arose from the public of "Same as my old uncle—
laid in bed for eleven years he did with no stomach" and "Auntie
was took like that, it was a Creeping Paralysis and she couldn't
do a thing for herself," and, last, loneliest though far from
loveliest, an unsolicited testimonial from Lord Pomfret's under-
keeper who had come to see Geo. Panter about that old dog-fox
who was popularly held to have an earth in every part of West
Barsetshire and peculiar powers (probably infernal) of trans-
porting himself from one part of the county to another, just to
annoy, to the effect that Squire Halliday he was a gentleman as
was a gentleman and when the hounds met at Hatch House they
were sure of a good run. And of some good beer, he added. Beer
as was beer. But this last, we think, was more a piece of atavism
than a criticism of Pilward's Entire; a tradition from his grandfather's time when Pomfrets and Hallidays still brewed at home;
already an affectation of Old Times by then, but pleasant.

By lunch-time the whole neighbourhood, high and low,
knew that Mr. Halliday had a hospital nurse and when Dr.

Ford's rackety little car was seen going over the bridge to Hatch House, the very worst was expected and we may almost say hoped. Not that anyone wished him to die, for he had been a kind and a just Squire and done his duty in every way, but we all have a hankering for something exciting and unusual to happen and though death is inevitable, each death is a fresh surprise and makes us, as Mr. Macfadyen the rich market-gardener and man of business was wont to say, think of our latter end.

"My old mother, she remembered Old Squire's funeral" said Mr. Geo. Panter. "Squire's father that was. That *was* a funeral. They had the undertaker from Barchester and everything tip-top and the coffin was took down to the church in the big farm-waggon and black rosettes on the harness."

"It'll be one of them motor-hearses now," said Mrs. Panter. "I wouldn't go in one of them things not if you paid me."

"Ah, but you'll be Carried, Mrs. Panter," said Vidler— known, rather like a depressing Irish play, as Vidler the Fish. "*That's* the way to do it and no mistake. Though, mind you, there's always a risk with Carrying. You want the Bearers all of a height. I've seed a coffin nearly fall down in the Church Porch itself because one of the Bearers was ill and they had to get Hubback to help—him as was Miss Hubback's uncle up at Hatch House—and he was a good six inches too short. Dreadful it was. My wife said it gave her quite a turn."

This fascinating subject having been exhausted the party broke up and went back to its shop or its kitchen or other work.

Meanwhile Dr. Ford in his disgraceful old rattle-trap had arrived at Hatch House where he was always welcome not only as the doctor but as an old and trusted friend. According to his usual custom he drove into the back yard and went in by the kitchen where, as he said, one always got a good idea of what was going on, and though he was equally welcome in Lord Pomfret's hideous and imposing seat and in Gatherum's monstrous pile, he was apt to appear via the servants' quarters. With the tact—or it may be the knowledge of the more selfish side of human nature that he had brought to a fine art during a long professional life—he greeted Hubback, sat down and asked after her leg, which limb had a Pain in it deeply valued by its owner, who took a commendable pride in its having baffled the highest medical authorities for many years.

"Well, we mustn't complain, sir," said Hubback, "but sometimes it hurts me cruel. Just like a knife it is and catches me all of a sudden just as I'm taking the tray in to lay lunch. I wonder I haven't broke a dozen glasses lately with this leg."

Dr. Ford, not without a passing reflection upon the difficulties of the English language, said he would give her some more of the Embrocation.

"I knew I'd find you in trouble," he said, "so I brought a bottle with me. And what's the news here? The Squire not too well, eh?"

There had been so many cries of Wolf in the last year that Dr. Ford may be forgiven for a slight scepticism, but Hubback's really heartfelt description of the change in him during the last few days was a call to action.

"The Nurse is a very nice lady," said Hubback. "No trouble at all and Mr. Halliday took his breakfast nicely. But I don't like the look of him, sir."

"Well, what he looks like is my business," said Dr. Ford putting four lumps of sugar in the cup of tea Hubback had set in front of him. "That's a nice big cup—Mr. Halliday's isn't it?"

"Oh *no*, sir," said Hubback, shocked that he should suspect her of such treachery to her master. "That's the other big one, sir, the cup with the Eddystone Lighthouse on it. I've always washed it myself, sir. These girls—" which speech she left unfinished, knowing that Dr. Ford would fill in the gap for himself.

"Well, I'd better go up" said Dr. Ford. "Tell Mrs. Halliday I'm here. No, don't trouble. I'll just go through," and he went out of the kitchen and so into the hall where, doubtless warned by the noise of his car, Mrs. Halliday was waiting for him.

"I'm sorry about the Squire," he said. "What's up?"

Mrs. Halliday told him and added that Sister Heath, most luckily, had come yesterday and was in charge.

"A bit long in the tooth but knows her job," said Dr. Ford unchivalrously. "Are you getting some sleep?"

Mrs. Halliday said she had slept quite well last night and would take some of those sleeping things that Dr. Ford had given her last year if she felt wakeful and then Sister Heath, resplendent in her proper uniform, came out of Mr. Halliday's room.

"Good-morning, Doctor Ford," she said. "It's quite like old times to see you again," to which Dr. Ford gallantly replied that Sister Heath was looking like a two-year-old and Sister Heath bridled. Then, becoming her professional self again, she went with the doctor into her patient's room. Mrs. Halliday tried not to think, but it was too difficult, so she went downstairs into the kitchen and helped Hubback to drink several cups of very strong Indian tea (which she loathed) with a great deal of sugar (which she never took) and they talked about old days and how Mr. Halliday would ride that mare at the point to point and had to have his arm in a splint and how Master George nearly got a finger cut off in the circular saw which Caxton had told him not to touch and how Miss Sylvia had been chased by the old turkey and had nightmares for a week and so many little things from the past, soon forgotten at the time, remembered now. While they were drinking their second cups of tea George Halliday came in, as he often did, to look for the elevenses that Hubback loved to provide for Master George.

"I suppose Dr. Ford's upstairs, mother," he said. "I saw his car in the yard. Tea please Hubback, hot and strong and four lumps."

"You'll ruin your teeth, Master George," said Hubback, and gave him five.

As no one had anything special to say they very sensibly did not try to say anything till Dr. Ford came in. Hubback at once got up and began to make fresh tea but did not go out of earshot.

"Well, you've got one of the best nurses in the county, Mrs. Halliday," he said. "She has done everything as well as I could have done myself. And I have telephoned to her friend Miss Ward to come over. Your husband will be better with a night nurse and a day nurse. I shan't say Don't Worry, because nothing will stop you women worrying. I shall come in again this afternoon or this evening. He is asleep now. I can't promise anything, but I think he won't be in pain. The works are running down," and after laying a kind hand upon her shoulder for a minute, he turned to go.

"One moment, Dr. Ford," said Mrs. Halliday. "I'll come to your car with you. No George, you needn't come," and she went out into the kitchen yard with Dr. Ford.

"And now what's up?" said Dr. Ford. "Don't tell me *you* are feeling unwell. We can't have another invalid," which may sound unkind, but all Dr. Ford's old patients knew his ways and in any case Mrs. Halliday had no intention of feeling ill, or of giving way at any point.

"It's not exactly the moment to think of business," said Mrs. Halliday as they came into the kitchen yard, sheltered and sunny, "but I must tell you something. You know Leonard thinks he made the place over to George some time ago, but as far as the lawyers know he didn't and we may have to sell the place. There have been Hallidays here for nearly two hundred years. That's all."

"You needn't have told me that," said Dr. Ford, though very kindly, "and I do value your confidence. I should have done all I could, absolutely everything in my power, without knowing about it. But now I know I'll have the whole British Medical Association down here if necessary and all the quacks in the county too if you like. There's no question of medical etiquette when your husband and the place are in question. Good-bye."

After this life became a strange dream as far as Mrs. Halliday was concerned, not unpleasant, for everyone was kind, her husband seemed vaguely pleased to see her for short visits, once taking her for Lady Pomfret and once for a very nice stranger who had come to visit him. As she left him she heard him ask Sister Heath who that pleasant woman was and whether his mother had come back from Barchester, and whatever Sister Heath answered seemed to please him. Before lunch Miss Ward came, also in her own little car, had a short talk with Mrs. Halliday and went upstairs to her room to emerge as a nurse and looking distinctly more charming than she did in what she called her civvies.

"Well, here I am, all ready for the fray," said Sister Ward, coming into the drawing-room. "I've sent Heathy—well I suppose I ought to say Sister Heath now we're on duty—to have a nice little nap and I shall be with Mr. Halliday. We'll soon get our times on duty arranged. Heathy and I have worked together ever since we were at Knight's. I've just had a nice chat with your old cook, Mrs. Halliday, such a character and really quite devoted to the family and she's going to give me a recipe for Barchester Buns and now you must just relax and try not to worry. And I said to your son—George isn't it?—I said to Mr. George he'd be much better out on the farm because he's no use here at present and he's going to show me his baby pigs some- time and how the tractor works. So he's gone off really quite cheerful," and although Mrs. Halliday found it difficult in her present dazed condition to believe that George, or she herself, could ever feel cheerful again, she was grateful to Sister Ward.

The news spread fast. Many neighbours brought flowers for Mrs. Halliday but did not try to intrude. After lunch she arranged the flowers, taking particular pains to make lovely vasefuls for the two nurses and then there was nothing to do. She dared not go far in case she were needed, though Sister Ward had assured her that Mr. Halliday was having a nice little nap. George was on the farm. She rang her daughter Sylvia

Leslie up and said she mustn't racket about because of the expected baby, to which Sylvia replied that the baby was perfectly able to look after itself and she would come over that afternoon and bring butter and eggs and a couple of fowls from the home farm. Then the telephoning was over and there was the long, warm afternoon before her and she could not read, or deal with her letters, because she listened always—though to what or for what she did not quite know. So she went out into the garden to which so much of her love and care had been given and began to clip off dead roses and carnations, and then that was done and it was only half-past three. She went round by the back of the house to the workshop and found Caxton there, as he mostly was.

"Come in, mum," he said, touching the square paper cap (like the cap of Mr. Chips the Carpenter in the Happy Families of our youth, a game now forgotten or vulgarized by a kind of horror-comic cards) which he always wore at work, folding a fresh one for himself every day. Mrs. Halliday sat down on an upturned box and they talked about old times when Mrs. Halliday had first come to Hatch End as a bride.

"I have still got that lovely box with the cedar-wood lining you made for me to put my furs in" said Mrs. Halliday. "You always managed to get good wood, Caxton. You've got some fine bits over in that corner."

"Best seasoned elm as I've seen in many a year, mum," said Caxton. "I marked that tree and I kept my eye on her when I first began to work here, mum, I dunnomany years ago, over at old Lord Pomfret's place she was and his head carpenter was by way of being a friend of my father's, and a couple of years ago she had to come down because his lordship had to sell some timber, so I went to Mr. Wicklow, his lordship's agent, and I asked if I could buy some of the wood when she was felled and Mr. Wicklow is a gentleman, he is, and he said, You and Wheeler—that was his lordship's head carpenter then—you manage it between you. So when she was felled and Wheeler had cut her up nice he let me pick some good bits and I've looked after them and they're well seasoned."

"They make coffins of elm, don't they?" said Mrs. Halliday, thinking of Mrs. Gamp and her brilliant extemporization of The Woodpecker Tapping the Hollow Elm Tree, in place of Oak Tree, when she came to call on Mr. and Mrs. Mould.

"Well, mum," said Caxton, apparently embarrassed, which was unusual in him as he had an excellent opinion of himself, "they do in a manner of speaking—and a lovely wood it is," he added, carried away by professional feeling. "A pleasure to work on, mum."

"I think the Squire," said Mrs. Halliday, deliberately using her husband's territorial name, "would like to have a coffin made on the place when his time comes. And he would like you to be the man to make it, Caxton. Well, I must go back to the house," and she got up and went away with a feeling of sad pride, almost of happiness, that the old servant might do one last service for his master.

CHAPTER 8

There is, if we examine ourselves, an almost Awful Pleasure which many of us feel in a death when it does not really affect us. Perhaps this feeling is strongest among we happy many—and if a Carping Critic or Peevish Purist says among we is not good grammar, we do not think that us would be at all euphonious here, if that is the word we mean, or if it means what we think it means, who though our mother bore us in a Southern Clime are Scotch by right of a traceable though modest line of Scotch forbears. Our first glance every week-day morning at the *Thunderer* is at the Deaths to see if we have outlived a contemporary or, even more creditable, someone a good deal younger than ourself.

Mrs. Morland, who though her mental processes were confused had, as Mr. Macfadyen had once said, the root of the matter in her, always started her day by the Deaths but very rarely got as far as the obituaries. For this she had several excellent reasons, one being that they had nearly all been written before the person died, which didn't seem fair. She also had a bone to pick with the compositors in that on the front page announcements they so often arranged the lay-out (which, she said in a learned way, she took to be the way the printer arranged the lines of the front page) so that someone came just where the paper is folded in the middle when you get it, so that unless you open it right out and iron it, which is impossible unless you have

a large flat table, because your arms aren't long enough, you will
probably miss it. But at this point her old friend George Knox,
to whom she was imparting these views, said that to call a table
flat was a pleonasm as no tables were unflat. Mrs. Morland said
she had used flat simply to explain to George Knox *exactly* the
kind of table she meant, because everyone knew that if you
opened the Times right out and spread it on a table it was apt to
slide off somehow if you weren't careful, but on a really *flat* table
that wouldn't happen. If, said George Knox, by flat she meant
that it had a large plane surface, she was confusing the issue; to
which Mrs. Morland very nimbly retorted that she meant the
current issue, as if it were yesterday's she wouldn't be reading it
today and if it were tomorrow's it wouldn't be here. And then
Mrs. George Knox said tea was ready and Laura must stay for it,
which she did.

The news of Mr. Halliday's death after a steady and mercifully
short decay of every faculty, was no surprise. He had been
respected by all and loved by many. His uneventful life had been
lived on his own land, his home was happy, his children good
citizens and very good-looking. George had done his duty
through the war and later for the land. Sylvia's marriage with
Martin Leslie had been a very happy one and she was carrying
on the traditions of Rushwater just as all Leslies would have
wished.

The funeral service was at the little church in the village and
the coffin that Caxton had made was carried by the farm
servants. Mr. Choyce read the words which bade farewell and
Godspeed to the Squire and he was buried beside his ancestors,
all of whom, from Wm. Halliday, Gent. who had built Hatch
House in 1721, had in their turn been laid where they had
worshipped. Kind Sisters Heath and Ward who had places of
honour were truly moved, and luckily will never know how
much better they looked in their professional uniform than they
did in their best blacks. After a funeral there is always the

question of a party so that the old friends who have come may meet quietly and see one another. Mrs. Halliday who was county to the bone would willingly have asked her friends to Hatch House, but George, using his new authority, said it would probably be the end of her. Both Dr. Ford and the nurses agreed, so her daughter Sylvia said she would take her mother back to Rushwater directly after the service. There she could be as quiet and retired as she liked and would have delightful grandchildren to play with.

It was a warm day of late summer and as the little congregation came from the church they lingered to talk. Mrs. Halliday, who had behaved as a lady should all through the last difficult month, did not fail her own standard, but much as she valued the feelings which had brought so many old friends to the church she was not fit for any further exertion and was glad when her daughter Sylvia put her into the car, without waiting for the friends who had gathered, and took her away. Kind Sister Heath and Sister Ward also drove away to Northbridge with a pressing invitation to George to come and have tea with them one day. Friends and villagers came to take George Halliday's hand. Lady Graham, who had asked him to come to Holdings for lunch and get away from people, naturally took this opportunity—just as her mother Lady Emily Leslie would in similar circumstances have done—to issue a general invitation to the rest of the company, some of whom accepted with pleasure. These were mostly relations and the older friends. Lord Crosse, who had worked with Mr. Halliday on matters affecting Barsetshire as a whole where East and West were for the moment united, had come from Crosse Hall, as had his son. His daughter Mrs. Carter was there too with her husband, George's tenants now at the Old Manor House. Lord Stoke too, whose boast it was that he had never missed a funeral in the county yet, had brought Mrs. Morland. Not that she had known the Hallidays much, but Lord Stoke liked to have someone to talk to during the drive and she was always welcome at Holdings.

Lady Graham—again just as her mother would have done—
took charge of all arrangements as a matter of course and before
George knew where he was Lady Graham had got him into
her car with her eldest soldier son, who had leave that weekend. Lady Graham put the professional soldier and the war-
commission George in front and took Edith in the back with
her. This arrangement was the best that could have been made,
for the young officer in The Brigade of Guards was properly
impressed by having a War Veteran beside him and George
found himself telling Captain James Graham what war was
really like and forgetting his own troubles. Everyone else got
into his or her own or someone else's car.

"But there's a fellow who knows just as much as I do, or
more," said George, who had taken an immediate liking to the
young soldier. Not that the Graham boys were unknown to him,
but there were years enough between them and such different
ways of life that they rarely met of late. "Young Crosse, I mean.
We were in quite a lot of places at the same time."

"How did you manage that?" said Captain James Graham,
too innocently.

"That's what only old soldiers know," said George and they
both laughed and George told Captain James Graham how
magnificent the Brigade had been in the fighting outside Traire-
les-Vaches and how ten men had held Vache-en-Étable against
practically the whole of the German army who were occupying
Vache-en-Foin at the moment; while he, George, and his
Yeomanry were at Vachen-en-Écurie.

"I say, I wish I'd been old enough to be there," said Captain
Graham.

"Just as well you weren't, as you probably wouldn't be here
now," said George. "Toes up, that's what you would have been."

Captain Graham at once adopted George Halliday as his
model.

"My young brothers will be simply sick that I've met you,"
said Captain Graham. "I say, when they next get leave, do you

think they could see you? I mean you come to lunch or something and let them talk to you. Or when you're in London could
you possibly lunch with us at St. James's. We do our guests
pretty well there. My next brother, Robert, is a bit of a poet. John
knows all about art, but we rag him, because he's the youngest
and they're always a bit cheeky," which brief view of the Brigade
of Guards as exemplified in the younger Grahams left George a
little confused and feeling very old. But he liked the well-
mannered youngster and said he would love to come, only it was
difficult to get to London because of the farm.

"Oh, I say, you could leave it for a couple of nights," said
Captain Graham. "Father always says no one is indispensable
which" he added with an amusing pompousness "is correct,
because Holdings gets on just as well when he isn't there which
he quite often isn't because of missions and boards and things."

"But you've got Goble," said George. "We haven't got a
bailiff. But we've a very good carpenter."

"Oh, I know all about your Caxton," said Captain Graham.
"He comes over to see Goble with a bit of three-ply or an oak
beam and things of that sort and swaps them for some of Goble's
glazed drain-pipes. Pure barter."

"Perhaps it's really Bartershire," said George, who suddenly
felt much younger and rather happy, at which Captain James
Graham, of Her Majesty's Brigade of Guards, suddenly ex-
ploded into a guffaw and thought George Halliday was one of
the nicest fellows he had seen for a long time. All very well to be
a Captain in peace time, but here was a real War Captain who
had been in France and fought the Germans.

By this time they were at Holdings, quickly followed by
Lord Stoke with Mrs. Morland and Miss Merriman with Mr.
Choyce, and one or two other friends. Lady Graham had
arranged a kind of picnic lunch in the Saloon as the large
drawing-room was called, with everything on the table and no
servant, which was just as well, as Odeena would certainly

have dropped or broken something in her sympathy with the mourners.

"It was such a beautiful ceremony, Mr. Choyce, and wonderful weather. You do things so well," said Lady Graham to her Vicar, apparently under the impression that he had been entirely responsible for Mr. Halliday's dying at the right moment so that he could be buried on a fine hot summer day.

Mr. Choyce said it was very good of her.

"And so nice to have *proper* hymns," said her ladyship. "Not those dreadful ones up in the high numbers for all sorts of things one has never heard about like Zenana Missions and Trades Unions."

"I do wish, Lady Graham, that you wouldn't make me laugh," said Mr. Choyce. "I absolutely agree with you, but unfortunately the Bishop doesn't. He has found a new hymn by a religious Atheist beginning:

> 'O God, although Thou art not there,
> Men sing to Thee as if Thou were,'"

at which Captain James Graham and ex-Captain George Halliday burst into a loud and most un-funereal guffaw.

"What are you laughing at, young fellers?" said Lord Stoke, who had vastly enjoyed his outing and was making an excellent lunch in the proud consciousness of being much older than Squire Halliday and very much more alive. Several people told him it was a hymn.

"Him. Which him?" said his lordship.

"Not him, Lord Stoke, hymn," said Lady Graham. "Oh Mrs. Morland, do explain to Lord Stoke."

Mrs. Morland, always willing to oblige, leaned towards Lord Stoke and said very distinctly, "Mr. Choyce. quoted. a. silly. bit. of. a. Hymn. that . made. US. LAUGH."

Lord Stoke said she must mean one of these horror-comics

and part of the table began to describe, or invent, dreadful films or strip-drawings it had seen.

As the party was going so well Lady Graham sat back and thought about nothing in particular. Miss Merriman asked Mr. Choyce if he had done anything about the monkey-puzzle outside the Vicarage.

"Oh, it's gone," said Mr. Choyce.

"Do you mean someone has taken it?" said Miss Merriman, who had thought of that horror as a permanent part of Vicarage grounds. "What an extraordinary thing."

"Oh, I don't think anyone here would do such a thing," said Mr. Choyce. "No, I had it removed. After you had been to see my house I began to dislike that tree. Also it made the wall where my Arundel prints are so dark that I could hardly see them; trees do grow so if you don't cut them back and I was really afraid to try to cut it: it *was* so spiky. So I asked one of the men who were mending the road if they could push it over with the tractor, but we found that might break some of the windows, so they very kindly put a chain round it and pulled. It was a splendid sight. I felt like Joshua before Jericho."

"And had you a ram's horn to blow?" said Miss Merriman.

"Now, how did you guess that?" said Mr. Choyce. "I haven't got a ram's horn — besides one needs seven priests bearing seven trumpets of rams' horns to get a city wall down. But I did remember the passage to which you refer in Joshua, chapter six verse thirteen I think, and I had my speaking trumpet."

"How did you come to have one?" said Miss Merriman admiringly.

"It was left to me lately by a very deaf old aunt," said Mr. Choyce. "She also left me quite a considerable sum of money. And so, as I was saying, I shouted at the men through the speaking-trumpet, just as the two men — I never know who they are — shout at the tug-of-war teams. And they gave a great tug each time and up came its roots and down it fell. Then I didn't know what to do with it and just then that nice young Crosse came along—Lord Crosse's son you know" he added, looking towards Mr. Crosse, "and he gave them two pounds for their trouble and told them to deliver it at Lord—I can never remember his name, Sir Ogilvy Hibberb that was—Lord Aberfordbury that's it—at his house. So that was the last of it."

Miss Merriman looked towards young Mr. Crosse with amusement and admiration. This was the way to behave. So would old Lord Pomfret have behaved. So, though by different methods, would Lady Emily Leslie have behaved. So would Lady Emily Foster now in her roaring teens behave and so would the Honourable Giles Foster. But not Lord Mellings, she thought.

"And now," said Mr. Choyce, "one can see the Arundel prints quite well. You did say you wished one could see them better when you did me the honour to look over my house. I hope you will come again and see how the place is improved now. Will you?"

Miss Merriman said she did not think she could get away at the moment, but when Lord and Lady Pomfret and the younger children went to Italy as usual, she would love to come.

"I may be staying with Lady Graham for a few days" she said, "and then we can make a plan."

"I am glad you are to be at Holdings," said Mr. Choyce. "You see I don't know Pomfret Towers so I cannot visualize you there," to which Miss Merriman replied that she thought she was much the same at the Towers as she was anywhere else.

"Yes, I expect you are," said Mr. Choyce. "Varium et mutabile was not written for you," but as Miss Merriman was not acquainted with the works of P. Virgilius Maro, she merely smiled kindly, taking it for granted that Mr. Choyce's comment was meant to be agreeable, as indeed it was.

"Who's your parson fellow, Lady Graham?" said Lord Stoke to Lady Graham, in his usual loud voice. "Our man at High Rising doesn't do the service as well as your man. He's got three girls. Eldest one's getting a bit long in the tooth."

"You know quite well who the Vicar is, Lord Stoke," said Lady Graham. "Mr. Choyce. He has been here for a long time and we all like him very much. He used to be a clergyman at Liverpool."

"Liverpool, eh?" said Lord Stoke. "Never was at Liverpool in my life, but he took the service very well. Made you feel it was all right. Not like our man. He mumbles."

"Old Uncle Giles had a clergyman who mumbled," said Lady Graham. "They used to have a private service for the family and staff at the Towers in his time and Uncle Giles used to tell him to speak up."

"Good man, Pomfret," said Lord Stoke. "One was always sure of a fox when he had the hounds—in my young days that was. And he swore better than any man I've ever known. Whole field could hear him if anything went wrong. I've heard him curse old Lord Norton up hill and down dale. Norton always managed to get mixed up with the hounds. Don't think much of his son, he's a stick. So's his wife—shockin' style. No children and the title dies with him."

"What happens to your title, Lord Stoke?" said Lady Graham, who had the complete freedom from social inhibitions that often goes with good blood; though never used consciously in an unkind way.

"Ought to go to my sister's boy, young Bond," said Lord Stoke, "but it doesn't. You know Lucasta, Lady Graham. Only my half-sister though. Why my old governor married a second time if that was all he could do, I don't know. But Bond's a good lad, even if his father's people were in trade, and he's got a good wife. Bit of county blood in her too. Blood tells. Your Edith has it. Ought to. Good stock on both sides. Where's your husband, eh?"

"I did hope he would be here," said Lady Graham, "but he had to go over to Gatherum about a heifer."

"Io, eh?" said Lord Stoke, with what we can only call a lascivious chuckle, but Lady Graham was not listening, which was perhaps just as well, as if she had asked for an explanation Lord Stoke might have regretted his outburst. The reason she was not listening was that Mrs. Morland was involved in a discussion about the way one was always losing things because you put them in a safe place and then you don't know where it is. The younger members of the party with sad want of manners were beginning to shout, young Mr. Crosse being active among them though not so very young.

"I say, Mrs. Morland," said Captain James Graham, "how long do you give a thing if you lose it? I mean when do you give up?"

"Well, I used to look for things till I ran them to earth," said Mrs. Morland, "but I found that was waste of time. So now I just ignore them. Then they come back. But what I do hate is the people that make one lose the things," and she looked vengefully in the direction of the ceiling.

"You allude to supernatural powers, Mrs. Morland?" said young Mr. Crosse who was fascinated by her.

"THEY," said Mrs. Morland. "I don't mean Kipling," she added hastily, "because I'd have to pay royalties if I did. I mean Whoever They Are."

"'To The Unknown God,'" said Mr. Choyce, but no one noticed him owing to the noise except Miss Merriman, who caught his eye and smiled. An intelligent woman he felt, and then listened courteously to Mrs. Morland's disquisition on losing things and the peculiar malevolence of inanimate objects in getting themselves lost for no reason at all.

While all this noise was going on Edith Graham had been talking to her cousin Lord Pomfret, who with his usual kind, tired consideration for others, thought she was rather less lively than usual and asked what she was doing now.

"I really don't know," said Edith. "I think what I need is a job."

Her cousin asked what kind of job.

"Oh, I don't know," said Edith. "You see, Cousin Gillie," she went on in a quiet voice, "I don't know where I am."

"Explain," said Lord Pomfret.

"Well, I love being at home and the farm," said Edith, "but there's really nothing to do. Clarissa went to college because she wanted to but I'd loathe it and anyway she's married now. Emmy adores cows and married Tom Grantly, but I don't adore cows and can't marry Tom," at which they both laughed and Edith began to feel better and went on: "All the boys are soldiers and aren't here much. I do love Holdings, frightfully, but there's *nothing* to do and I don't think mother understands. I don't mean that nastily," she added.

"Of course you don't," said Lord Pomfret quietly. "I know rather what you feel like, because when I was a very young man I was really quite at a loose end—that was before Uncle Giles died and I turned into a lord. And I hadn't even got parents to consult. Mother died when I was young and father and I never got on. But it all came out all right—thanks to Sally" and he looked at his wife with the affection that had never changed since the day that the heir to the earldom had proposed to the agent's sister after tea in the estate office.

"If only I had a Sally," said Edith. "But I suppose for me it would have to be a husband and really that is impossible."

"I don't see why," said her cousin.

"Oh, I don't mean that I'll never get married," said Edith. "Of course I shall some day, but not at present. I must look about a bit. What I'd like to do would be to learn estate work properly and help father. He will be much more at home now. I know a fair amount, but only things I've picked up. There's a place Mr. Carter told me about in Barchester where you can do a good course of estate management, but I don't know if they would like it," and Lord Pomfret guessed that they meant her parents.

Lord Pomfret was silent for a moment, interested in his young cousin in whom all the landed proprietor strain was coming out so strongly: even more strongly than in her sister Emmy Grantly who was almost purely a cow specialist.

"Look here, Edith," said Lord Pomfret. "Keep your head and don't panic. I have a kind of nebulous idea that Sally and I might help. How would you like to come to the Towers for a bit in the autumn and help us? Miss Merriman could teach you a lot and so could Roddy. I often think how lucky I was to marry the agent's sister. And you could easily go to your Agrarian Economy School or whatever it is in Barchester, but I warn you that you have to be pretty good at arithmetic. Farming isn't all cows and cabbages now. It's high and complicated finance as well, and a bit of law work. Are you game?"

The rather spoilt youngest daughter of the Grahams thought for a minute.

"I'm game, Cousin Gillie," she said, "if you can square mother."

"Done" said Lord Pomfret and raised his glass. Edith also raised her glass of orangeade and they drank ceremoniously, which, being observed by some of the younger members, healths were drunk with bows across the table till nearly everyone had the giggles or choked.

"Now that's what I like to see," said Lord Stoke, who naturally did not know what the disturbance was about. "Good old custom to remember the dead. Lot of fellows dead now. More than there used to be. Well, when a man's dead he's dead. Stone dead has no fellow as Shakespeare says somewhere—clever fellow he was, knew his world. He's dead too. And here's to you as well, Mrs. Morland," and he raised his glass. Mrs. Morland responded suitably, suppressing a wish to laugh at her old friend.

"Wonderful what a lot of people die," said Lord Stoke to the table in general. "There's hardly a man of my age alive now. The women are tougher. My half-sister Lucasta will see all of us into our graves. There's old Pomfret gone and the Warings and—oh well. My old governor used to talk about people joining the majority when I was a shaver and I thought he meant they had got a commission," at which Captain James Graham let out a large guffaw and then felt ashamed of himself. "I'm about the oldest left now except Pridham."

"Sir Edmund is eighty-five, Lord Stoke," said Mrs. Morland. "I know he is, because he showed me his name in the Family Bible last time I went to see him."

"Can't get away with that," said Lord Stoke. "Might easily have put it in himself. Now I've got my old father's Bible and there's my name in the beginning, Algernon Courcy Stoke, born 1876, in my father's writing. Old Lord de Courcy—none of you would remember him—was my godfather. He gave me a silver gilt mug, but not a penny more except bad tips for races. Never let your godfather give you tips for races—can't trust 'em."

"Like the tip you gave me for the Derby, Lord Stoke," said Mrs. Morland at which there was a laugh and the talk became general and then Lady Graham got up and the party began to disperse.

"What are you doing, dear boy?" she said to George Halliday who had been very quiet during lunch. But, as his watchful hostess observed that he had made a very good meal, she did not feel disturbed about him.

"I really don't know," said George. "There's plenty to do on the farm. I told them they could have the morning off, but I'd better go back and see that they are working. If it weren't for the farm, Lady Graham, I don't know what I'd do. Things do get one down a bit, but once you get on the land it's not so bad. Will you say good-bye to everyone for me and thank them for coming and I'll slip away."

So he went into the hall and there met Edith.

"Oh, it's you," said Edith. "I thought it was Ludo. He rang up just now and said he had a spot of leave and would be here soon."

"And my leave is up and I must go back to the farm," said George. "I left my car by the church so I'll walk up."

"I thought we might have gone on the river," said Edith. "Of

course, if you must go you must, I suppose. I say, George, don't
forget us. Come again soon. And I'm really awfully sorry about
your father," and she reached up, kissed him in a friendly way
before he was aware, and with a wave of her hand went back to
the party.

Suddenly quite desperately lonely, George stood for a moment, wondering if he could face an empty Hatch House. Mr.
Choyce was talking to Miss Merriman in the drive and stopped
him.

"I don't want to gate-crash, Halliday," he said, "but if you are
going home may I walk up with you? I have to go back to the
Vicarage in any case. I promised to show Miss Merriman my
drawing-room. I had that dreadful monkey-puzzle taken away
and everything looks quite different. Miss Merriman will come
on later."

George was grateful for anything that would put off the
moment of finding himself alone at Hatch House and the two
men walked back to the village. At the churchyard gate George
slackened his pace and then turned to the Vicar.

"Do you mind if I just go in for a moment?" he said. "I think
father would like it."

Mr. Choyce cordially agreed in petto, though he did not
speak, and they turned into the churchyard where the newly
tenanted grave was heaped with flowers. He paused, waiting for
George.

"Oh, not *that*," said George, speaking as much to himself as
to Mr. Choyce. "Father isn't *there*. I mean inside," and he went
into the church, followed by the Vicar, and straight to the
Squire's pew where he knelt. Mr. Choyce went into the chancel
where stones underfoot commemorated past Hallidays and
waited there, thinking of many things, among them how extremely difficult it was to concentrate when one's thoughts were
flying in different directions. And as he did not feel very able to
consider himself, he considered George Halliday and asked that

George might be helped both to remember and to forget. Then George got up and both men went out again.

"And now," said Mr. Choyce, as if this were a treat he had been waiting for all day, "may I come back to Hatch House with you? Only if you would like it."

George's expression passed from stupefaction to a rather touching gratitude, or so Mr. Choyce felt.

"Thanks awfully, padre," he said, using the familiar army name. "I'm not really afraid, but I'm jibbing a bit. Still, I suppose I must take my fences."

Mr. Choyce said he could not at the moment think of any proper comment unless it were Trust in God and keep your powder dry, at which George laughed so loudly and flatteringly that the Vicar was pleasingly surprised.

"But first I must go and see the Vicarage without the monkey-puzzle," said George, with a consideration for the Vicar which touched him. "And you are expecting Miss Merriman, aren't you? I do like Miss Merriman."

"So do I," said Mr. Choyce, who in his kind zeal to comfort George had temporarily forgotten Miss Merriman. "I saw a great deal of her when she was at Holdings with Lady Emily Leslie during the war. A very unusual woman.

By this time they had reached the Vicarage garden. For the first time in a great many years the whole of the small but handsome red brick building, some hundred and fifty years old, could be seen. In front of one wing there was a raw, untidy place where the monkey-puzzle had been—but far better any kind of ground than one of those trees, if trees one could call them.

"*What* a jolly front" said George.

"The Palace wanted to have it secularized and put me into a nice council house with walls one brick thick and plate glass windows," said the Vicar, "but the Chancellor—Sir Robert Fielding—was extremely helpful and here I still am. It will take time to clear the lawn of course, but my predecessor left a large roller in the back yard and I shall borrow a pony and cut the grass and roll it. The only difficulty is boots."

George asked the Vicar if he meant gum-boots, as he might be able to find him a pair.

"Oh dear, no," said the Vicar. "I mean for the pony. A nice set of four leather boots."

"Lord! I'd forgotten about that," said George. "Oh! look here, Mr. Choyce. I believe we've got a pair—I mean a quartet or whatever they are called—in Caxton's shop. Come on!" and forgetting the past and the mound in the churchyard he almost dragged Mr. Choyce to his car. The Vicar, delighted to feel that he could really be of use, got in without a word and within a very few minutes they were at Hatch House. The front looked strange and the Vicar saw that all the blinds were down.

"Hell!" said George, pulling the car up short so ardently that the Vicar feared for his uppers. "I *told* Hubback to have those blinds up. She's been drinking too much tea" and he drove round to the stable yard, got out and strode towards the kitchen, the Vicar, amused and anxious at his heels.

George opened the kitchen door, disclosing Hubback, Caxton and the faithful old cook Mrs. Fothergill who felt her age and her legs and was mostly having a nice cup of tea or a quiet lay down, so that she was little use except that she never went out and so was always about the place. But for her perpetual presence Mrs. Halliday would have found it difficult to leave her husband as his health failed and everyone felt grateful to her, though as Caxton said, The Lord *He* knew Mrs. Fothergill wouldn't have woken up for no one if she was having her afternoon sleep, not if it was the Day of Judgment.

The tea-party, much to their annoyance, all felt a little guilty. Not that Hubback had anything to be ashamed of in having her tea with Mrs. Fothergill, but the fact that Caxton was present rather showed that the mice were playing when the new master was away. Caxton got up, wiped his mouth on the back of his hand and said he must be getting back to his shop.

"All right, Caxton," said George. "I'm coming out to the shop. I've something to ask you," and Caxton went away with his slow Wessex tread.

"Well, Mr. George, I'm sure it was a lovely service," said Hubback, seeking to avert the Wrath to Come. "If only the poor dear gentleman could have been there I'm sure he would have said the same."

"And if father were here," said George, "he would want to know why the blinds are still down. You know perfectly well, Hubback, that the blinds have to be pulled up as soon as the funeral is over. If mother knows she will be shocked. Please pull them all up. Now. I don't know what the Vicar will think," which final shot was obviously unfair, but George, suffering from repressed emotion, was in no state to mince matters. And we rather think that at the back of his mind was the feeling that now, if ever, he must show that he was the Squire and repre-sented authority.

"Well, Mr. George, I'm sure I'm very sorry," said Hubback, with these few words, almost unknown by any self-respecting old servant, accepting George as what he was—the new Squire.

"Then don't do it again," said George, which words kindly but firmly spoken had a strong effect on both Hubback and Mrs. Fothergill, though if they—or he—had stopped to reflect, they might have considered that the death of an elderly father was not likely to happen again for a very long time—if ever. Hub-back went away to open the rooms and Mrs. Fothergill, whose feet were a source of great pride to her owing to being very bad, got up with an effort.

"Oh, Master George," she said. "It's a sad day. And one of the best bits of veal I've ever seen waiting to be cooked and Squire isn't here. He fancied veal, poor gentleman," and she began to cry.

George gave her a kind of hug with one arm, pushed her in the direction of her bedroom and went out with the Vicar.

Caxton, who was in the yard, drew himself up as if he were still the soldier he once had been, awaiting a court-martial.

"I'm glad you are here, Caxton," said George. "Mr. Choyce wants some leather shoes for his pony to mow the lawn," which was not perhaps particularly good English, but explained itself. "Didn't we have a set once?"

"You come into my workshop, Mr. George—leastways Squire I should say—and we'll have a look," said Caxton.

"Mr. George will do very well," said George. "Come along, Vicar."

They followed Caxton to his workshop. Here he hung his cap on a hook, assumed the square paper cap which he still affected, his badge of master carpenter, and rummaged at the back of the shop among what looked like the sack of Troy, or Krook's shop in Cook's Court, Cursitor Street, but was in reality an ordered heap of useful, or possibly useful, objects hoarded by him against such an emergency as this.

"I knew they were here" he proclaimed as he straightened himself again. "As pretty a set as anyone could want. Old Propett's father over at Northbridge made those, Master George, when we used to have the old mowing machine and the pony. You used to ride on the pony while he pulled the mower and a fair young varmint you were, Master George. I've kept them nicely greased and if Mr. Choyce would like to have them he's very welcome."

Without considering whether it was Caxton who was giving the shoes or George Halliday, the Vicar took them and admired them in a way that went to Caxton's heart and head. George then offered to drive the Vicar back, but Mr. Choyce said he would like the walk and it was only ten minutes and with a hearty handshake to George and a suitable douceur to Caxton, he went away and George went back to the house.

So the young squire was left alone and did not quite know what to do. This day was over, his father laid in the earth, his mother safely at Rushwater under Sylvia's wing, with agreeable grandchildren when she wanted a change. The next thing, George supposed, would be lawyers and all the lengthy business of settling the estate. Sylvia had had her dowry when she married. His mother was also provided for and the rest would come to him when the government and the lawyers had got all they could. Luckily his lawyers, Keith and Keith, were old family friends. Robert Keith was a good fellow, brother to that nice Lady Merton who had provided Sister Heath. There would be much to be done, but George had learnt patience in the army and on the land, and knew that to do things slowly and in proper form is always the best. The professionals, the lawyers, must do the worrying; for him the first duty was to see that the work of the farm went on in its diurnal course. All these thoughts ran through his mind in the little estate room where his fore-bears had worked, where his father had worked and George had learnt from him. Now he would have to do everything for himself. He supposed his mother would live with him, as there was no Dower House and they could not afford to keep it up even if there were. Much as he loved his mother—and he did love her a great deal—he did not quite like the thought and then he blamed himself for selfishness and felt that feeling of univer-sal guilt that we all—not particularly guilty—know far too well.

A shadow fell across the table. He looked up and saw young Mr. Crosse.

"Hullo," said George.

"Hullo yourself" said Mr. Crosse. "I know what it's like when a parent goes. When mother died I didn't know which way to look—nor did father for that matter. I must say the governor came up to form magnificently. So will you. What about din-ner?"

"I don't know," said George. "I daresay Mrs. Fothergill and Hubback will do something about it. Anyway it's a long way off."

"Look here, Captain," said Mr. Crosse, "I'm going to take you off to Barchester and we'll have dinner at the White Hart. Do you good."

"It's awfully good of you, John-Arthur, but I can't," said George.

"All right, you've said it and now you needn't say it again," said Mr. Crosse cheerfully. "J'y suis, j'y reste as we used to say at Vache-en-Écurie. But you might let me see the pigs."

So they went round to the yard and scratched the pigs' backs with sticks and smelt the strong but agreeable smell of well kept pig-styes and talked about the Barsetshire Agricultural Show which was to take place at Pomfret Towers this year, as a kind of joint tribute to Lord Pomfret whose land it was and Mr. Macfadyen and Mr. Pilward whose great and allied businesses of Amalgamated Vedge and Pilward's Entire had joined with the wealthy ironmaster and self-made financier Mr. Samuel Adams to lease part of Pomfret Towers itself for clerical work and a considerable piece of the estate for experiments in fruit and vegetables growing.

"And it will be a slap-up affair, my boy," said Mr. Crosse, "I can tell you. I say, can I see your house? I don't want to take it, so don't think I do, but I've never seen upstairs."

Whether George really wanted to show his father's house to Mr. Crosse, even though they were brothers-in-arms, we do not know; but by the time they had got up to the first floor he was becoming almost boastful about its charms; and Mr. Crosse far from discouraging him was the first to suggest that they make a do of it and see the top floor and the roof. Nothing loth and already feeling much happier, George showed him the rooms at the top of the house which were pleasant if a little low in the ceiling and an interesting discussion took place as to whether servants were all undersized then, or had to stoop to get into their rooms.

"I bet you five shillings that our top-floor rooms at Crosse Hall are lower than yours," said Mr. Crosse, "*and* the windows even more difficult to open."

"Hand it over," said George. "These windows don't open at all. At least I mean there aren't any sash cords and you have to keep them open with a bit of wood or your hairbrush. And our view beats yours hollow," and indeed the landscape from the front windows was very lovely, with the water-meadows in the foreground, Hatch End with its mixture of Saxon wattle and daub with fine stone and brick houses, and the ground rising away from the river, sloping and undulating to the noble line of the downs where corn was ripe and sheep bells were tinkling, and the mellow afternoon sun was over all.

"Kamarad," said Mr. Crosse and pulling a handful of change from his pocket he counted out a florin, a shilling, two sixpences, two threepenny bits, and six pennies, which he gave to George, adding that he was sorry he couldn't make it four pennies and two halfpennies and four farthings.

Much heartened by this unexpected windfall George took Mr. Crosse up onto the roof to look for loose tiles so that he could score off Caxton who was apt to boast about the way the house was kept in repair. Happily there were no less than three, so George came down in better spirits than he could have thought possible. Mr. Crosse said he would mostly be at home for the present and would ring George up and make a plan.

"I'd ask you to ring me up and then you'd have to pay" he said chivalrously, "but I'm afraid you wouldn't. Thumbs up and all that rot, George. We'll go to the Barsetshire Agricultural together if you don't look out," and then he went away. George looked after him till the car had crossed the river and then went back to the house and began to answer the letters from friends that had been accumulating. Later Hubback brought him a good dinner after which he worked again till sheer fatigue drove him to bed and a dreamless sleep.

When Mr. Choyce left Hatch House he did so with sorrow in his compassionate heart. Perhaps the saddest thought to him was that he could do so little to help, but he reflected that at least he could always stand by. Life as a parish priest was, thank God, always full of duties and of opportunities for service and he would jolly well put salt on the tail of every opportunity of helping George that came his way. As he approached the Vicarage he saw Miss Merriman's car outside and then Miss Merriman sitting on a bench in the sun just outside the house.

"I am more sorry than I can tell you" he said. "I went back with George Halliday and time passed. He *is* a good fellow."

"I guessed you might be there," said Miss Merriman, "so I waited. Isn't it lovely not to see that horrid monkey-puzzle."

"I never knew quite how much I hated that Upas-tree till I saw it coming down," said Mr. Choyce. "I felt, if it is not presumptuous to say so, rather like Samson when he pulled down the pillars of the Philistines' temple. I have sometimes wondered about that and thought that possibly the Authorized Version has not quite reproduced the original text and the pillars were really wooden columns kept in their place with wedges. As a child and later one always thought of them as about fifty feet high of solid stone and at least ten feet in diameter—or round-about that. Of course in the opera they are only cardboard. It is extraordinary how ignorantly one thinks."

So they admired the brickwork of the house, now free to the sun and air, and then went indoors to see the Arundel prints. What value in terms of art these reproductions may have, we do not know, but they became familiar to many of us in our youth in the houses of our parents' friends and in those far-off days represented the last word in colour reproduction. Probably now, compared with the results of today's processes, they would look dull and lifeless, and where they have all gone one does not know. However the fact remains that Mr. Choyce's set, dealing with the Martyrdom of St. Ursula and her really unnecessarily large train of female attendants, are among our early memories and therefore neither good nor bad but simply themselves. Mr. Choyce's pictures hung along one wall of the study in plain unpolished oak frames, and as the rays of the late afternoon sun could now strike directly on each it was impossible to see anything but dazzle and glare. Mr. Choyce's University trophies and photographs were re-examined and admired in this new light and they talked of the war days when Lady Emily Leslie was living with her daughter Lady Graham at Holdings, and so came to Lady Graham's children.

"I am sorry you had to go so soon, Mr. Choyce," said Miss Merriman. "Lord Mellings turned up a little later and he and Edith and the other young people went on the river. I wish Mr. Halliday could have stayed."

"I am glad you mentioned that," said Mr. Choyce. "I am rather concerned about him. He is taking things very seriously. Better than too lightly perhaps, but it won't be good for him to live alone."

Miss Merriman said he had his mother.

"I know, I know," said Mr. Choyce. "But it may not be easy. He is master now and will have to make changes."

"Yes, I see," said Miss Merriman thoughtfully. "The Dowager is always a possible problem. Not my business of course. He must marry."

From some people, unconnected by any ties of blood or old friendship with the Hallidays, this might have seemed pure meddling. But Miss Merriman in her hardly acquired status of what we must—with great deference to her—call Éminence Grise to the Nobility and Landed Gentry, had a profound store of knowledge, quietly garnered and much pondered in her own heart as well as her mind.

"I quite agree with you," said Mr. Choyce. "But whom?"

"There I am at present quite helpless," said Miss Merriman quietly: and this, we think, was the first time in her long service and care of the Pomfret family that she had come near admitting defeat. "And," she added, looking away from her host towards the churchyard where Squire Halliday was sleeping his long sleep as far as this world was concerned, "I do not even begin to see light. Any more than I do at present for Edith."

"Why Edith? Isn't she rather young to be worried about?" said Mrs. Choyce.

"Not when three young men who are all on good terms are thinking about her," said Miss Merriman.

"George Halliday and young Crosse one can see with half an eye," said Mr. Choyce, "but I confess I don't see another, unless it is Lord Crosse; he's a widower," at which Miss Merriman had to laugh and said she was perfectly sure that Lord Crosse never thought of her at all except as a pretty rather spoilt chit.

"No, I meant Ludo," she said.

"Lord Mellings? But he is only a boy," said Mr. Choyce.

"Edith is barely more than a child," said Miss Merriman. "They are cousins and have been practically brought up together."

Mr. Choyce, thinking aloud, said "Propinquity, propinquity," and though Miss Merriman thought it quite a good comment we do not think she quite took the allusion.

"So what happens next?" said Mr. Choyce.

"I don't know yet," said Miss Merriman. "Edith is like Clarissa in some ways, but she feels she does not have a confidante. Clarissa used to tell Lady Emily her thoughts; Edith is self-contained. Too self-contained for happiness perhaps. And I do not see my way to helping her at present. I am a failure and I don't like it, Mr. Choyce."

"There is only one answer and I am going to make it even if you don't like it," said Mr. Choyce. "Don't be silly. The word failure has nothing to do with you, Miss Merriman."

Miss Merriman was silent and Mr. Choyce wondered if he had gone too far. Then she got up, touched his hand very lightly and said: "Thank you. You have reminded me of my duty. I shall carry on," and she went out of the house, followed by Mr. Choyce. He shut the door of her car and then laid his hand on the top of the open window.

"Duty? I don't understand," said Mr. Choyce.

"Duty to old Lady Pomfret and then to Lady Emily for many

years," said Miss Merriman. "And because of that, duty to her granddaughter Edith. And also through her my duty to Lord and Lady Pomfret and Ludovic. And love—of one kind—has gone with all the duties."

"You are rather like a pelican," said Mr. Choyce thoughtfully. Miss Merriman asked why.

"You are ready to feed all your nurselings with drops of your heart's blood," said Mr. Choyce, almost angrily. "Do you *never* think of yourself?"

"Oh yes," said Miss Merriman calmly. "Quite often. I have thought of myself several times today. I have thought how pleasant it would be to see your study now the monkey-puzzle is down and it has been even more pleasant than I thought. Now I must go or Lady Graham will make hay of the supper arrangements and we have a good many of the young people staying on, I think. Good-bye, Mr. Choyce," and she laid her hand on his.

"Good-bye, Miss Merriman, and thank you a thousand times," said Mr. Choyce, "and God bless you," which words he said so simply that they were not in the least embarrassing. We do not mean that anyone would mind being so addressed with so good a wish, but the difficulty is to know what answer to make.

"Then God bless you too," said Miss Merriman and she quietly withdrew her hand and drove away to Holdings. Mr. Choyce did a little weeding in his garden and as he weeded it occurred to him that when Miss Merriman spoke of Lady Graham making hay of the supper arrangements, it was the first time in his acquaintance with her—and that had begun some fifteen years or so ago when Lady Emily Leslie came to live with her daughter Lady Graham at Holdings—that he had ever heard one word of criticism of her employers. At least it was hardly criticism in an unkind sense, but for once she had spoken of Lady Graham just as one of Lady Graham's own friends might—quite kindly and with considerable reason—have spoken.

*   *   *

At Holdings as usual life was in full swing. Lord Mellings had
turned up in the little car which his father's generosity had
allowed him to buy. Emmy Grantly had come over from Rushwater to see her mother and father and talk to Goble the bailiff
about some pigs for her cousin Martin Leslie and boast about
the success of Rushwater Ranelagh in the local show and
how they were showing several heifers at the Barsetshire Agricultural, but not the young bulls because they had already been
bought practically before they were born by Señor Garcia a very
rich Argentine breeder who came to England every year and was
also celebrated for his wholesale purchases of any pictures of
chocolate-box English beauty. The three Leslie cousins had
come over from Greshamsbury and were having friendly battles
with their Graham male relations. Edith was being alternately
bullied and flattered to the top of her bent and Mr. Crosse had
said at least four times that he must really go, but as no one had
paid the faintest attention to him he was still there. Mrs.
Morland, enjoying the noise and the life, was perfectly happy to
sit in a sheltered sunny corner on the terrace till such time as
Lord Stoke had finished bargaining with the bailiff Goble about
a sow in farrow. So pleasurably was she thinking about nothing
that a voice saying How do you do, Mrs. Morland, made her
jump and looking up she saw Lord Crosse.

"May I sit with you?" said Lord Crosse. "I came to see Sir
Robert about the Barsetshire Agricultural's next meeting, but he
is about the farm as usual, so I will sit here, if I may, till he turns
up."

"Yes, do," said Mrs. Morland. "I was just wondering what my
next villain should be. My publisher tells me that I ought to have
an English villain for a change, but I don't *want* the English to
be Villains."

"A very proper sentiment, if I may say so," said Lord Crosse,
"though one has to remember that there are exceptions to every
rule. And after all a lot of the best novels have them. Think of

Scott's Varney and Rashleigh Osbaldistone. Think of Count Fosco. Think of all Dickens's immortal villains."

"Yes, but you can't help rather loving Dickens's villains," said Mrs. Morland, "because they do so enjoy being villainous and he enjoys making them, bless him. The only real villain I can think of at the moment is Lord Whatshisname—I mean the one that was Sir Ogilvy Hibberd."

"It is extraordinary how no one can remember that man's name," said Lord Crosse thoughtfully. "Aberfordbury is the nearest I can get."

"But it *is* Aberfordbury, isn't it?" said Mrs. Morland, "only I don't think I could use his name in a book. It would be plagiarism, wouldn't it?"

"More likely libel," said Lord Crosse. "He could be very nasty if he took offence, so do be careful. I should hate you to be involved in anything of that sort."

"Well, if he wasn't pleased I would write a letter and say I meant quite a different person with the same name," said Mrs. Morland seriously.

"Really, dear Mrs. Morland, for an intelligent woman you are the silliest woman I have ever met," said Lord Crosse, looking at her with much admiration. "I do beg you not to try to use that man in a book. He is simply bursting with spite and might make things rather unpleasant for you, which I could not bear. He is really quite capable of going to law."

"In that case I won't," said Mrs. Morland. "It would be so uncomfortable to be in a law-suit like Jarndyce v. Jarndyce, going on for several generations, and I am sure my boys wouldn't like it," at which Lord Crosse couldn't help laughing, though very kindly, and then by way of apology he asked her if she would come to the Barsetshire Agricultural show with him. Mrs. Morland asked if he was exhibiting.

"Oh no," said Lord Crosse. "I have a couple of cows for the household but I couldn't possibly be a landed gentleman. You must remember I am not county. John-Arthur's children may be; his grandchildren probably will be, if there is any county left. I am only a climber so far."

"Well, that is all very comfortable," said Mrs. Morland, "because I am just Mrs. Morland who writes those books, so there we are. After all, you are a baron and Lord Stoke says the barons are the oldest and best titles."

"Oldest certainly. I don't know about best," said Lord Crosse. "After all Aberfordbury is one. And I do hope John-Arthur will marry, because it seems waste of a title not to keep it going. There's a lot to be said for life-peerages—they are less strain on a family."

"Of course I don't know, as I have never been a life-peer— nor a peeress either for that matter," said Mrs. Morland. "Did your wife like being a peeress?"

"Yes, I think she did," said Lord Crosse. "We had always done everything together and whatever it was she tackled it."

"I do wish I had known her," said Mrs. Morland, not for the first time, for much as she liked Lord Crosse and felt safe and comfortable with him, there are times when a woman finds women very restful. "We could have talked about our children. You see there is really no one at High Rising to talk to about my children. George Knox wouldn't listen if I did and even if he listened he wouldn't hear because he would really be thinking of what he was going to say next."

"A great defect in a listener," said Lord Crosse gravely. "I hope you don't find it in me."

"Oh no," said Mrs. Morland. "You are really very fair. You do talk rather a lot about your daughters' families, and if your other daughter's family is as nice as Mrs. Carter's I don't wonder. If I talked to you about my family though, you would be bored."

Lord Crosse did not make any answer for a moment.

"I do apologize," he said after a pause. "I am a bore myself. Nearly as bad about grandchildren as Victor Hugo—though if all were known I expect his grandchildren found *him* a frightful bore and spoilsport."

"But you aren't Victor Hugo," said Mrs. Morland.

"No, thank God," said Lord Crosse. "In the first place because I would be French and in the second because I should be dead and not have the pleasure of sitting with you; of having got to know you of late; of admiring your courage and your delightful inconsequence and indeed everything about you."

"It is very nice of you to say so," said Mrs. Morland, "but men really do prefer men. You only have to be in a mixed party with a hostess who doesn't bother to make people mix and you will find all the men getting together to talk about dull things."

"And don't all the women get together too?" said Lord Crosse.

"Of course," said Mrs. Morland. "But to talk about really interesting things. I like men very much. But if I *had* to be on a desert island with one sort only, I think I'd choose women. Rather a bore at times perhaps, but I'm not sure if men wouldn't be worse. What do *you* think?"

Lord Crosse, rather taken aback by his novel view of desert islands, said he thought men. After all, he said, the three boys in Coral Island managed very well, and then rather spoilt his case by adding that boys wouldn't want a woman on an island— unless it were a mother.

"Then we will each stick to our own island," said Mrs. Morland.

Lord Crosse was silent. Then he said, "Do you really mean that?"

Mrs. Morland, looking at some distant invisible object, said she really did.

"Then I am sorry I said as much as I did," said Lord Crosse, in his turn looking away across the water-meadows. There was a silence.

"If I weren't sitting on a bench in full view of everyone, I would sit down flat on the garden path like Miss Betsey Trotwood," said Mrs. Morland. "Did you mean what you said, Lord

Crosse; or am I only imagining? I do imagine, you know. It's my profession."

"Yes, I did say it," said Lord Crosse. "I said it because I meant it. And if my wife were here I would say exactly the same— and what is more, *she* would understand" he said; almost like a schoolboy's "And sucks to you," or whatever today's equivalent is.

"I am extremely sorry, but I simply couldn't," said Mrs. Morland. "That is if you mean what I suppose you mean. To begin with, there is your wife to consider. It isn't fair to take it for granted that she would understand when she isn't here to speak for herself. Oh, *please*, Lord Crosse, go back to where we were five minutes ago. You can, you know. And I shan't ever say a word."

"That I do believe," said Lord Crosse and fell silent, looking away across the garden and the water-meadows. "Nor shall I. Nor shall anyone else as far as I am concerned. Or if they do, it won't be because I have said anything. My one wish is that no one should ever know—for your sake."

"Thank you," said Mrs. Morland and laid her hand on his knee for a moment. "And I am sure your wife must be thinking what a couple of sillies we are," at which Lord Crosse couldn't help laughing and then he said that whatever Mrs. Morland might be, *he* certainly wasn't a silly, because he knew how to take good advice. "So it is to be Farewell and Hail," he said. "I renounce my hopes of indulging in the felicity Of unbounded domesticity."

"And we will not be parsonified, Conjugally matrimonified," said Mrs. Morland. "And I shall not say a word to anyone— though I might cry just a little," she added, hitting her eyes with her handkerchief.

"And I may have an extra glass of port tonight and think of a permanent widower's future," said Lord Crosse, "but there shall *not* be a night of memories and of sighs."

"And when I get home" said Mrs. Morland, "I shall write a

beautiful scene where Madame Koska refuses to marry the nice detective who has helped her from so many villains, because she feels she is too old to be bothered with a man about the house—you see she had been married before, years ago, and her husband was really practically nothing but an expense," at which words Lord Crosse had an uneasy feeling that this was partly autobiographical. As indeed it was, but all so long ago, and now like a dream.

"In that case," said Lord Crosse, "may I ask you to have lunch with me at the County Club one day and go on to the Barsetshire Agricultural Show?" which invitation Mrs. Morland accepted with the greatest pleasure.

"If," said a quiet voice with considerable authority in it, "you can tell me where my wife is, I shall be much obliged. She has the most provoking way of not being here when I need her."

Mrs. Morland looked up, as did Lord Crosse. A middle-aged man of slight wiry build, with greying hair and moustache and dark piercing eyes, dressed in good well-worn tweeds and those rather old-fashioned short gaiters that prevent burrs and bits of grass and corn getting into one's boots, was standing before them, holding a stick which Mrs. Morland at once recognized as one which was always in the hall, waiting obediently for its master.

"How do you do, Sir Robert," she said, and got up and shook hands with him. "How very nice that you are at Holdings for good. When I last saw Lady Graham she was in the Saloon. You know Lord Crosse?"

"By name of course," said Sir Robert, holding out his hand which Lord Crosse was glad to take. "Pomfret says you are a great acquisition to the East Barsetshire County Council. I am standing myself now that the army has done with me. If I get in I shall beat my sword into a ploughshare. A figure of speech of course."

"And your golden locks time has to silver turned, Sir Robert," said Mrs. Morland, carried away by her literary leanings.

"Daresay it has," said Sir Robert, "but I'm damned—saving your presence—if I'll let anyone have my helmet for a beehive. I wanted to talk to Goble, but Emmy won't let me get a word in edgeways and makes me feel like King Lear. Those Pomfrets are a masterful lot. There's my wife. Looks like an angel—as she is—and ran the whole place all through the war while I was away and kept it on till I was retired. No one has a chance with those Pomfret women. Her mother, Lady Emily, was the same. She ran Rushwater and my father-in-law though everyone thought she was a half-wit," which was a very unfair description of Lady Emily but had some truth in it; for her ladyship had been a little like Mother Carey whom Tom met in the Water-Babies, apparently sitting and doing nothing most charmingly, yet causing all sorts of things to be arranged and carried out and all sorts of people to coalesce who seemed the most unlikely persons in the world to do so.

"And what's everyone doing?" said Sir Robert. "Emmy's down in the cow-sheds with Goble, trying to get a young heifer out of him—but she won't. Where are all the young people?"

Mrs. Morland said that as far as she knew they were mostly on the river, including Lord Mellings who had come over in his car.

"That's a nice boy of Pomfret's," said Sir Robert. "And his father did the right thing in sending him to Sandhurst. If you want your boy to be a soldier, get him into the Brigade. It's a pity Pomfret wasn't a soldier. His father was a poor piece of work and didn't bring the lad up properly, but he managed to bring himself up and that wife of his is a first-rate woman. And I know something about first-rate women. I must go and look at the hatches; those reeds want cutting again," and Sir Robert walked away with the erect and confident bearing of a man who not only knows his own job from end to end, but has also successfully commanded men, dealt as a military diplomat with politicians, and nearly always got his own way; which had meant on the whole the way that was best for England.

"Well, here we sit like a picture by Marcus Stone, R.A.," said

Lord Crosse, "only I can't think of a title, and his people are young and wear empire gowns and old-fashioned uniforms."

"'Does truth sound bitter,'" said Mrs. Morland. "How would that do?"

"Dear me, *how* my wife would have liked you," said Lord Crosse. "I know I have said it before, but I will say it again. She loved Browning and we used to read aloud to each other. Well, Mr. Browning shall say for me that I will hold your hand but as long as all may, or so very little longer."

"He certainly shall *not*," said Mrs. Morland firmly. "And I must go now because Lord Stoke is driving me back and I see him coming out of the farm gate. He has been doing cows or pigs with the bailiff," and she got up.

"Nay come, let's go together—at any rate as far as the drive," said Lord Crosse, which made them both laugh and the point of emotion was safely turned, leaving we think the foundation of a quiet and lasting friendship behind it.

Gradually the guests from outside were leaving. Lord Stoke, after a running fight with Goble in which both sides had lost and won ground, had asked for his dog-cart to be brought round.

"Oh, Lord Stoke, why didn't you come in your brougham?" said Edith, who ever since the day of her lunch at Rising Castle and the gift of the pearl necklace had felt slightly important.

"Not in this weather" said Lord Stoke. "The only trouble is my man doesn't like sitting with his back to the horse. Says it makes him feel sick. My old groom didn't feel sick, but these young fellers have no guts."

Edith looked for the young fellow, but only the elderly groom was visible.

"And how are your pearls, young woman?" said Lord Stoke to Edith.

"*Very* well, thank you," said Edith. "But I don't wear them when we go on the river, just in case. Cousin Sally is going to have a dance at the Towers in the autumn and I shall have a new dress and the pearls will be in all their glory. I *do* like them."

"That's a good girl," said Lord Stoke as he climbed to his seat. "Where's Mrs. Morland?"

Lady Graham then came out with Mrs. Morland. The groom, who had got down and was holding the horse's head saw her safely up, climbed up behind, and away went the equipage and cheers from the Graham and Leslie boys.

After a good deal of discussion the younger members then decided to drive into Barchester, dine at the White Hart, go to the Odeon where Glamora Tudor was co-starring (but in larger letters) with Buck Follanbee in Love in a Bath, described by its producers as the Great Erotic Drama of all Time, in which Charlotte Corday after starting the French Revolution has a suicide pact with a gentleman called Marat and they both cut their veins in a swimming tank about a hundred feet by twenty-five in Glorious Technicolour and the Wide Screen; so that everyone is happy, and apart from the blood being a kind of orange-pink and the water deep blue, the whole film is doubtless the super-factual representation which its makers claim. So they all went off in their own and other people's cars and peace descended on the house.

After dinner Sir Robert and Lady Graham sat outside, away from the breeze and watched the summer-time light dying.

"It *is* nice to have you at home Robert," said Lady Graham, as they sat looking across the water-meadows. "It makes me think of the night you proposed to me."

"I nearly didn't propose to you, my dear," said Sir Robert. "The stupid waiter had spilt some coffee down my shirt, and I had to go to my rooms and change first. I was in a perfect fright because you had been dancing with that young de Courcy and I thought he might get in first."

"George de Courcy?" said his wife. "The most *dreadful* lout like all those de Courcy boys. He smelt of wine and trod on my skirt and I nearly cried. In fact I did ask mother to take me

home, but she wouldn't and then most luckily George fell down
in the refreshment room and the caterers put him in their van to
sleep it off and delivered him at Ennismore Gardens next
day—that was where the de Courcys had taken a house for the
season. Now we shall have to see about a season for Edith."

"I don't know," said Sir Robert. "That girl of ours has a will of
her own. She wants to learn something about estate work. It's all
cut and dried. She wants to go to the Towers for a bit and do
some kind of course in Barchester and pick up hints from Roddy
Wicklow. What do you think?"

"Really nothing," said Lady Graham placidly. "Emmy went
off to Rushwater to do cows and got married and Clarissa went
off to college and she is married, so if Edith really wants to do an
estate agent course she will probably get married too. That poor
George Halliday rather cares for her, I think, so the Towers
mightn't be a bad plan for a few months."

"Young Crosse doesn't seem uninterested in her either, as far
as I have seen since I came down," said Sir Robert.

"And there is Ludo at the Towers," said Lady Graham.

"Good God!" said Sir Robert, more we think from surprise at
the number of possible pretendants to his daughter's hand than
from active disapproval of any one of them.

"Well, Robert, you know she will do exactly as she likes" said
Lady Graham, "and she is *your* daughter."

"I never thought she wasn't," said Sir Robert.

"Poor George," said Lady Graham, unmoved by her husband's insinuation. "He has enough to do with his father's death
and the place on his hands without thinking of Edith. I don't
know what arrangements his father might have made, but
death duties would be the end of Hatch House. Robert, ought
we—"

"Now don't worry," said Sir Robert. "If there's another war
the boys will be killed before I am. But I've done all I can and
Keith and Keith are pretty good at the job. Half the lawyers in
England must be doing nicely out of helping people to save their

places and their money. It's all a gamble. But I'm a good life, God willing, and in any case you are all right my dear."

"I was reading the Newcomes the other day" said her ladyship, "and the one really good, happy person in it is Lady Anne Newcome."

"Why, my dear?" said Sir Robert. "I haven't read it lately. Her old husband dies, doesn't he?"

"Yes, he does. But *you* are not old," said Lady Graham. "And when you are dead I shan't be able to retire to a large house in Wimbledon with my servants and a carriage and no bother about money. I shall have to live in Goble's cottage. And talking of houses, Robert, those Carters at the Old Manor House are extremely nice and quite the right sort and have done the house up beautifully."

Then they took a short walk along the river and watched the western sky turn from pink and gold to a lovely cold, clear green with one star shining, till the air became chill and they went indoors.

"Poor George Halliday," said Lady Graham, as her husband shut the inner door against the evening mists from the river. "Don't put the chain on the door, Robert. The children are out."

"I'm sorry he's lost his father," said Sir Robert, "but he's young."

"Young, but not so young," said Lady Graham. "And a widowed mother on his hands. I don't mean to be unkind because I might easily be a widow myself if things went wrong."

"Don't be so foolish, my dear," said Sir Robert. "Young Halliday has a good house and the farm should be paying quite well. He'll marry soon and then we'll find a cottage for Mrs. Halliday. Nice woman."

"I don't think he will marry, poor boy," said Lady Graham.

"A bit young to be a confirmed bachelor," said Sir Robert.

"Not so very young either," said Lady Graham. "None of

those soldiers are, Robert. But I think he is one of the people who deserve all the good luck they don't get."

"Now, stop talking like Old Moore, my dear, and go to bed," said Sir Robert. "I must write one or two letters and then I'm coming up. Good-night," and with a look of great affection at his wife he went into the little room which was known, according to what it was wanted for, as The Library, The Estate Room, Your Father's Room, The Study, and The Boot Hole because there Sir Robert had his boots and shoes, of which he had a large number, all kept in exquisite order by his own hands. He wrote one or two letters and then went to the outer door which was left open for the Barchester revellers' return.

"And now," he said to the stars, "we'll see who gets onto the County Council, Aberfordbury or myself," and there was no doubt at all in his voice, nor in his mind.

CHAPTER 9

After talking over the question of Edith, her parents agreed that much as they would miss her the plan of a long visit to the Towers would not be a bad plan. She could go daily to Barchester to her school or institute or whatever it was called. Roddy Wicklow—Lady Pomfret's brother and Lord Pomfret's estate agent—would take her riding about the place and let her see how things were done. There would be no one who would be likely to fall in love with her and she would be a good companion for her young cousin Lady Emily Foster who was an excellent horsewoman and quite uninhibited. At any rate Edith could go for a term to this estate agency school and perhaps her parents would join her at Christmas, for which joyful and depressing period Lady Pomfret had asked all the Grahams to come to the Towers for a week at least so that the family could have some really good talks and the young people have a dance and go to the Meet and there would be enough horses somehow for anyone who wanted to ride. Some of the Leslie cousins from Greshamsbury would be there too and as Edith Graham and Lady Emily Foster would be the only resident girls they ought to have the time of their lives.

"There is just one other thing, Agnes," said Lady Pomfret who had been having a long telephone talk with Lady Graham. "Merry has been very tired and run down. Dr. Ford says it's nothing that matters but she isn't as young as she was and she needs a change. Her only defect is that she *will* not go away. If you could quite angelically ask her to Holdings for a week or so fairly soon, I think she would go. She hasn't any particular home except a married sister where she is expected to make her bed and help with the grandchildren. Gillie's aunt used to take her to the villa in Florence every year, but Guido Strelsa doesn't offer it to us and I don't think Gillie would care to go if he did. There is that tiny place we have at Cap Ferrat and we would willingly pay for her to go there and a friend with her, but I don't even know if she has a friend and in any case she doesn't want to go. The Pomfret family, including dear Lady Emily, have eaten her up. She has been with it for something like twenty-five years now. We both feel rather guilty, but I think she would pine or go mad if she retired. And don't tell anyone this, but though we do love her and she has been invaluable, Gillie does really need someone younger. If she got a complete change now, I think she would feel better. Sorry to talk so much."

Lady Graham, whose first impulse—and indeed nearly every impulse—was to be kind, (except to people like Victoria, Lady Norton, or Lord Aberfordbury, where it would be sheer waste of time) at once said yes.

"Will you ask her for me?" she said, "or shall I write?" and Lady Pomfret said perhaps it would sound more as if it were Agnes's idea if she rang up. And after a little more family gossip that talk came to an end.

So Lady Graham rang up Miss Merriman and said not only was she going to feel rather lonely without Edith, but Sir Robert had a lot of papers to be sorted and if Lady Pomfret could spare her, would she come to Holdings for a fortnight or so. Miss Merriman's voice, as calm and self-contained as ever, said she would very much like to come but did not know if Lady Pomfret could spare her, with all the young people there.

"Well, do ask her," said Lady Graham. "Oh, and Merry, I quite forgot to tell you that I found a whole box of darling mamma's letters. It is extraordinary how things get put away in a house. There is an old uniform case of Robert's in the attic and it was stuffed with old letters that she must have brought from Rushwater. Some go as far back as darling Gay."

There was a silence and then Miss Merriman said, "I am so sorry, Lady Graham, but I don't know about Gay. Ought I to?"

"How stupid of me," said Lady Graham. "She was my brother John's first wife and such a darling. She died quite young and they had no children and then he married Mary Preston and they had those nice boys."

"Now I remember about her," said Miss Merriman. "I was at the Towers with Lady Pomfret then—my Lady Pomfret I mean—and everyone was grieved about Mrs. John Leslie. If I can be of any help I shall be delighted."

So an early date was arranged for her visit and Lady Graham told the news to Miss Merriman's friends in the village, who were many, for during the war years when she was at Holdings with Lady Emily she had been much liked by high and low, from the Hallidays to Geo. Panter at the Mellings Arms and both the local poachers.

Next day Mrs. Belton at Harefield, mother-in-law of Lady Graham's daughter Clarissa, and also a kind of cousin through a common connection with the very old Barsetshire family of Thornes of Ullathorne, rang up Lady Graham for a friendly talk and said did she know anyone who wanted a really useful secretary-help, because the elder daughter of Mr. Updike, the Harefield solicitor, was at a loose end. She had been a high-ranking WAAF during the war and had held various responsible administrative jobs since she was demobilized, and now wanted to be nearer home to keep an eye on her parents and was looking for a job and did Lady Graham happen to know of one. To which Lady Graham was able to say at once that she thought Lady Pomfret would be very glad to have a really competent woman as a kind of secretary-companion at any rate temporarily as Miss Merriman was going to have a much needed holiday at

Holdings. The job, she added, might be for longer as Miss Merriman badly needed a rest. She would be with the family, have her own private sitting-room and help Lady Pomfret with her many county activities. That, said Mrs. Belton, was exactly what Miss Updike wanted and how kind of Lady Graham, who said she would let Lady Pomfret know at once. Which she at once did.

"And I said more or less permanent to Mrs. Belton, Sally," said Lady Graham, "so that you could feel safe. I mean if Merry did need a long holiday she would be much happier if she knew you were all right. How handsome Ludo is looking. We loved having him."

"Yes, the ugly duckling is growing his feathers," said Lady Pomfret dispassionately, for there had been such difficulties with Lord Mellings when he was small and nervous and then when he was six feet high and trying not to show that he was nervous, that his parents had sometimes wished he and his young brother Giles could change places and Giles, who had not a nerve in his body and no fine feelings, would have banged and blustered about and been loved by all the people on the estate. Whereas poor Ludo had been nervous and shy from the days when as a little boy he went through agonies of anticipation and present fear and retrospective nightmares over riding. Then— owing to that nice Lady Merton at Northbridge—he had in the Coronation summer met Aubrey Clover the gifted actor-manager of the Cockspur Theatre and his almost equally gifted and very lovely wife Jessica Dean and had acted in a tiny play with them for the Coronation festivities, with a success which had suddenly given him confidence in himself. Since then he had at last stopped growing, put on weight, accepted with enthusiasm everything that Sandhurst and the prospect of the Brigade of Guards had to command or to offer, and showed every sign of ripening for every kind of county work as and when his profession, which he quietly loved, made it possible. So all his well-wishers—and they were many—hoped that Lord

Pomfret would go on living for a very long time, at least until Lord Mellings was a Major and covered with medals. And as none of his friends wanted another war, most of them having suffered from the last war in health, or pocket, or in losing relations and friends who were dear to them, let alone that glad confident morning had vanished for ever from their lives, we can only hope that all may be well, or at least that the hosts of Midian will confine themselves to prowling, which is quite bad enough.

Edith, having got permission to do what she wanted to do, was now not unnaturally suffering from anticipatory home-sickness, which however she managed to conceal pretty success-fully from her parents by dint of thinking of her interesting future. She had wanted to go to the school of estate manage-ment in Barchester and go she would, so the car that brought Miss Merriman over to Holdings was to take her and her luggage back to the Towers and there her home would be until Christmas and perhaps for longer. The news of her visit had of course gone round the village, via the Vicarage and the Old Manor House, and Lady Graham had rung up George Halliday and asked him to come to lunch on the day Edith was to go.

"It is a little sudden," she said, "but it all fitted in with Miss Merriman coming here and I think it will be quite a good thing for Edith. So do come, George."

George said he would love to come and would Lady Graham forgive him if he didn't stay long, as the vet was coming to look at a cow, and then he went back to whatever work he was engaged upon, feeling that one more trouble was more than he wanted or needed. But as no one knew of this trouble, nor did he wish them to, he might as well go. It would be fun for Edith to be at the Towers with her cousins, and Mellings was a nice lad and had the makings of a good soldier in him. And then he laughed at himself for being patronizing, because Mellings would be a real soldier and learn everything in its proper course, while he had only been an amateur, though a willing one. And then Panter, the carter, came in to ask about that new bit of harness he needed and George said he had better go into Barchester himself and see about it, knowing that a half-day off and a good time-wasting talk with the elderly saddler in Barley Street would do Panter as much good as a day at the sea. And when the saddler died, who would be able to do his work, to repair with love and pride a collar or a trace? Probably no one. One would have to buy and to throw away and then buy again. Soon there would not be a single good tradesman—in the older and better sense of that word—left in Barchester; perhaps not in the whole of West Barsetshire. Buy ready-made, use it till it rots or breaks, throw it away, buy again: that's what it would be now.

"And *that*," said George aloud to himself, angrily, "is that and grumbling won't help," so he did what he had got into the habit of calling "cleaning himself up," as Panter did once a week on Saturday night, and drove across the river to Holdings. Lady Graham, wishing to make a kind of general welcome to Miss Merriman, had also asked the Vicar and young Mr. Crosse. Miss Merriman in the Pomfrets' car was the first to arrive.

"Dear Merry, how glad we are to have you," said Lady Graham. "Edith is finishing her packing. Have you seen Miss Updike? Come into my room and tell me everything and your luggage will be taken up. If only darling mamma were here, how she would enjoy it all. She would have wanted to put flowers in your room herself. Do you remember at Rushwater when David was away somewhere and mamma painted some doves and green branches on the looking-glass in his room so that he couldn't see to shave? Oh, dear!" which was a kind of half-laugh, half a gentle tear over the lost past. "I have put you in your old room, so you will feel quite safe."

Miss Merriman, with her usual composure, thanked Lady Graham from a heart more full of memories than she liked to acknowledge and said Miss Updike seemed very pleasant, but excellent manners and would obviously master the work she had to do within a very short time.

"And Robert is looking forward so much to seeing you again,"
said Lady Graham. "He says you are the only person who could
ever manage darling mamma and he hopes you will manage me,
but I told him not to be foolish, because you are simply here to
rest and do nothing. We aren't a party. I just asked the Vicar and
that nice George Halliday because he works so hard at his farm
and never gets any treats, and Mr. Crosse because he gets on so
well with Robert and Edith and was in the war with George
Halliday. Of course the whole village is longing to see you and
the Mothers' Union and the Friends of Barchester Hospital
Sewing Society and the Women's Institute; and Goble hopes
the sow will farrow today or tomorrow—the White Porkminster—and that nice Mrs. Carter is longing to have you to
tea. BUT," her ladyship continued, "I am not going to allow
anyone to make any plans unless you want them. You will be
perfectly safe here," at which kind and very understanding
words Miss Merriman found herself quite gently crying. Not
with any noise, but a pricking behind the eyes and quiet tears
that would not cease their flow. Never before had anyone seen
Miss Merriman cry. Not even when Lady Emily so gently
departed. There was perhaps a night, many years ago now, after
old Lord Pomfret's heir, Gillie Foster as he was then, had
proposed to the agent's sister in the estate room and been
accepted; but what memories, what sighs that night may have
held were her own affair. Lady Graham's kind heart was much
moved and most sensibly she did not offer sympathy but took
Miss Merriman straight up to her room, told her that lunch
would be in about a quarter of an hour and left her to herself.

When a quiet, composed Miss Merriman came down, she
found the party assembling, the first being the Vicar. Then Sir
Robert came in from the farm and expressed his pleasure at
having her under his roof again. Edith came in with a rush
and hugged Miss Merriman violently. Mr. Choyce's kind face
beamed upon her. Mr. Crosse said his father wanted him to
bring her to Crosse Hall and would show her some old photo-

graphs of Lady Emily Leslie. Last, George Halliday came in with apologies for being late, but something had gone wrong with the tractor and he and Caxton had been underneath it and didn't notice how the time had gone. Sir Robert said those tractors could be the deuce and the differential sprocket in his was playing Old Harry and Goble couldn't get it right, and it meant sending for a man from Barchester and probably two or three days lost.

"We've had a bit of trouble with ours, sir," said George. "Could I have a look at it after lunch? If it's what it sounds like, I think we might patch it up," an offer which Sir Robert at once accepted, saying that it would be good for Goble to see someone who could deal with it, as he had been boasting a good deal of his own knowledge of machinery.

Then the party went in to lunch and talk was general, mostly about local affairs. Edith, excited by the thought of her new life at the Towers, was—as she had so often been—a little above herself, but not quite enough for her mother to have to give her a motherly look. Odeena did not commit any very appalling solecisms and in general it was a pleasant and civilized meal. And we may say,—though without the least wish to criticize Lady Graham—that Sir Robert's presence not only gave pleasure to his guests, but somehow produced a feeling of order and stability which were admirable foils to Lady Graham's peculiar divagations. Everyone drank Edith's health, as if she were going on a long voyage, not visiting cousins in the same county.

Presently the Pomfrets' chauffeur, who had been the life and soul of the kitchen and kissed the cook and got his face slapped for it to the incredulous joy of Odeena who suddenly saw The Pictures coming True, drove soberly up to the front door and there was almost as much good-byeing as if Edith were going to the end of the earth for ever. She hugged her father and mother—perhaps with a little anticipatory home-sickness— hugged Miss Merriman and then, in an access of general benevolence, hugged the Vicar.

"'Jenny kissed me'" said Mr. Choyce, surprised and flattered, but no one paid attention and we doubt if most of the party heard, or if they did hear, took the allusion.

"What about the Army?" said Mr. Crosse who was standing by George Halliday, upon which Edith with a further access of benevolence stood on tip-toe and hugged them both, which made everyone laugh and so they all went to the front of the house. Edith's luggage was already in the car. She got in, Mr. Crosse shut the door, and the car drove away.

"Well, that's that," said Mr. Crosse, "and I must get back to the bank or I'll be sacked, even if father is a governor. Good-bye Lady Graham. Good-bye, Sir Robert, and if you want an overdraft let me know and I'll put the heat on the board. Miss Merriman, I hope I may see you again before long," and he drove back to his desk: though we believe it was really a small room of his own rather comfortably furnished in which he did work about which we know nothing and received important customers with a grave manner that made him laugh at himself when he thought about it afterwards.

Sir Robert and George Halliday then went off to see the tractor and George, after listening with great patience to Goble's description of the machine's misdemeanours, asked if Goble could lend him some overalls and disappeared under it with a spanner and some other tools about which we know nothing. Presently he came out in a very undignified way on his back, feet foremost, got into the driver's seat, and pulled some handles. The great machine made an agreeable noise and began to move.

"That's all right, sir. You've done it," said Goble. "And if you're wanting a boar, sir, any time, our old Holdings Blunder-bore will oblige and proud to do it, as between friends. Just you let me know, sir," so of course George had to tip Goble for the work that he, George, had done on the tractor. But so do the wheels of life go round, and there is no oil like a pleasant word and some coin of the realm.

So with mutual esteem they parted and George went back to his lonely home. He hoped Edith would be very happy with her cousins at the Towers. Young Mellings had the makings of a good soldier in him and he wished him all good luck. He and Edith were cousins; cousins often married and after all they were cousins pretty far removed. Crosse was a good fellow too, with a property and title in the future to offer. Hatch House was no home to offer to anyone at present; nor was he himself much to offer—an ex-Serviceman, well into his thirties now. It wouldn't be fair, but one couldn't help thinking about it. In the day it was not so difficult because there was so much to do; and in the evening all those forms and papers and other county commitments. But when one was alone in the evening and had finished dealing with forms and papers, one could not help thinking and heaven knew where one's thoughts might go. Something Shakespeare had said somewhere about chewing the cud of sweet and bitter fancy. Well, chewing the cud—and seeing about the farm and the pigs and the fences and the hateful mass of unnecessary papers and forms one had to deal with. Time did pass. But one's thoughts remained. He put his car away and went indoors to see what the post had brought. Then he went out onto the farm and gave his mind to the land by which and on which his forbears had lived, and listened with justice and a good deal of patience to what various people had to say about the work and so the afternoon passed, and so, with more work at the endless papers, the evening passed and bed was there to lull one into a temporary peace and forgetfulness—if one could sleep. But he did sleep and even if he woke to a sense of loss the farm was there and the farmer must serve his land. So life goes on.

Mr. Choyce lingered a little at Holdings to tell Lady Graham and Miss Merriman about the very simple little memorial of Mr. Halliday which his widow and children were having put inside the church.

"It would be a privilege for me to show it to you" he said addressing Lady Graham and Miss Merriman. "I wonder if you would care to come back with me? I would drive you to the church and bring you back safely." Lady Graham was otherwise engaged, and urged Miss Merriman to go. So Mr. Choyce drove Miss Merriman to the church, where Mr. Halliday's grave was now smooth and all the wreaths gone.

"There will be a plain stone on the grave," said Mr. Choyce, "and the family have put the little memorial in the north wall, just above their pew. Come in," and he stood aside for Miss Merriman to enter the church. Above the Squire's pew, where rather ponderous stones on the wall described the virtues of past Hallidays, was a smaller stone bearing Mr. Halliday's name and the dates of his birth and death and below these the words "He dwelt among his own people."

"What a good epitaph," said Miss Merriman, speaking half to herself. "And what a good life. My epitaph should be, 'She dwelt in the houses of other people,'" and both were silent.

When they were outside the church Mr. Choyce asked her to come to the Vicarage and have some tea. "And then I will drive you home," he said. "I am indeed sorry to hear that you have not been well." So they drove to the Vicarage where Mr. Choyce put Miss Merriman into the most comfortable chair in his study while he went to the kitchen to put the kettle on. Miss Merriman sat and thought about nothing—or at any rate about so many things that they all made a kind of conglomeration that became a confusion and nothingness in her mind. So much so that when Mr. Choyce came back she was almost startled.

"I am afraid I came in rather abruptly," said Mr. Choyce. "I am so much alone that I rather forget my manners."

"No, indeed you didn't," said Miss Merriman. "I was just thinking and got rather lost."

Mr. Choyce said that people who were tired often got lost, but it meant nothing and they always came back. One had seen it again and again all through the war, he said, and once during the war he was having a week's holiday in Liverpool with a blitz every night and found he had completely forgotten where his old church was for several hours, but luckily his memory came back and he was just in time for the early service.

"I never met the war," said Miss Merriman. "I was with Lady Emily all the time. I haven't really met much in my life."

"But, my dear Miss Merriman," said Mr. Choyce, "a great many people never met the war and I am thankful that it was so. They were doing their duty in places which happened not to suffer. A bomb might just as well have fallen here as anywhere else, but it didn't. They were very near Barchester more than once, trying to get that camp at Sparrowhill, but no damage was done."

"I think I would have tried to do something real," said Miss Merriman, "but Lady Emily needed me."

"We all needed you," said Mr. Choyce. "Someone who keeps her head and can be relied on is exactly what one wants. If there had been a bomb I am sure you would have dealt with it most efficiently. No one could say for a moment that your work—and your life—aren't real."

"I am glad you think so," said Miss Merriman. "I can't. You see I have been That Useful Miss Merriman nearly all my life, and now I think I am soon going to be That Poor Old Miss Merriman," which she said without bitterness, as a mere matter of fact.

"My dear Miss Merriman," said Mr. Choyce, torn in two between the Friend and the Pastor, "you may be poor and you might—conceivably and not for a long time—be old; but *That* Miss Merriman never. Simply Miss Merriman, on whom so many people have relied for every kind of help. From what I have seen at Holdings, from what I have heard from people who knew the Towers in the late Lord Pomfret's time, you have been the quiet, the unceasingly watchful guardian of so many people—and of their homes."

Miss Merriman was silent. Then she said: "I am glad you

think so, Mr. Choyce. But—and I say it without any regrets or bitterness—service is no inheritance. No—I am ungrateful. To be able to help Lady Emily was an inheritance in itself. I think my real work was done when she died. When I say no inheritance I don't mean money. Lady Emily rewarded me generously for anything I did and so have Lord and Lady Pomfret. I have enough to live on, simply. But the life I have led for so long must soon come to an end and I must start again."

"With so many friends willing—wishing—to help you," said Mr. Choyce.

"I know I am ungrateful," said Miss Merriman. "I know I am stubborn—or pig-headed if you like—about my own—I can't think of the word I want—"

"I think I can," said Mr. Choyce. "It is Integrity. It has somehow got left out of the Christian virtues, but whether it is Christian, or Pagan, or as I think the best of both, it is your crowning virtue," to which words Miss Merriman did not reply.

"If it were not presumptuous," said Mr. Choyce, carefully choosing his words, "I would ask if I might be allowed to offer you any help I can give. We are such old friends now that you won't take this amiss?"

"I couldn't, I couldn't" said Miss Merriman, though she found speech extremely difficult.

"I do not wish to intrude in any way upon your private life," said Mr. Choyce. "But if now—or at any future time—though the sooner the better from my own selfish point of view—you could feel able to take on one more job of looking after someone, I would offer myself to be looked after. As a permanence. Don't speak. I know how difficult it is when one has been crying. I have a large clean handkerchief here which is at your service," and he pressed it into her hand.

"Do you mean—?" said Miss Merriman, but she was so sodden with tears that her speech was affected and she had to blow her nose violently.

"*That's* better," said Mr. Choyce in the voice that a nice Nanny might use to a be-blubbered child. "Yes, I do mean what I didn't say. Will you take me on as your next—and I hope your last—job of devoting yourself unselfishly to other people? Don't try to talk just yet. If you could perhaps nod your head?"

Miss Merriman, for the first time in her life no longer mistress of herself, nodded her head and blindly stretched out a hand which Mr. Choyce took and pressed.

"Now everything is all right," he said, adding, with a reminiscence of his war experiences in Liverpool, "All Clear. Don't try to talk. I expect you are ready for tea. My housekeeper is out so I have put the kettle on."

"Then I will come with you, Mr. Choyce," said Miss Merriman, and suddenly it occurred to both these middle-aged people that neither of them had ever heard the Christian name of the other.

"If you could call me Herbert, it would be delightful," said Mr. Choyce.

"Yes, Herbert," said Miss Merriman, her utterance still considerably impeded. "And my name is—"

"No, don't tell me just yet," said Mr. Choyce. "This is all rather overpowering and I can't stand much more. A thing like this has never happened to me before. May I call you Merry for the present?"

"Please do," said Miss Merriman. "It was Lady Emily who began calling me Merry and most of her friends have used it. I am really Dorothea."

"A *most* suitable name, my dear, and so much more pleasant than Theodora," said Mr. Choyce. "But Merry you have always been and shall be. And now if you will come into the kitchen we will get our tea."

Miss Merriman, her eyes dried and now mistress of herself, laid her head against his shoulder for a moment. Then they went together to the kitchen, to the hearth and the centre of the home.

COLOPHO*N*

This book is being reissued as part of Moyer
Bell's Angela Thirkell Series.

The text of this book was set in Caslon, a typeface
designed by William Caslon I (1692-1766). This
face designed in 1725 has gone through many
incarnations. It was the mainstay of British
printers for over one hundred years and
remains very popular today. The version used
here is Adobe Caslon. The display faces are
Adobe Caslon Outline, Calligraphic 421,
and Adobe Caslon.

Composed by Alabama Book Composition,
Deatsville, Alabama.

Never Too Late was printed by Data Reproductions,
Auburn Hills, Michigan on acid-free paper.

Moyer Bell
Kymbolde Way
Wakefield, RI 02879